SKIN DEEP

NBH

**A Simeon Grist
Suspense Novel**

SKIN DEEP

Timothy Hallinan

A DUTTON BOOK

DUTTON
Published by the Penguin Group
Penguin Books USA Inc., 375 Hudson Street,
New York, New York 10014, U.S.A.
Penguin Books Ltd, 27 Wrights Lane,
London W8 5TZ, England
Penguin Books Australia Ltd, Ringwood,
Victoria, Australia
Penguin Books Canada Ltd, 2801 John Street,
Markham, Ontario, Canada L3R 1B4
Penguin Books (N.Z.) Ltd, 182-190 Wairau Road,
Auckland 10, New Zealand

Penguin Books Ltd, Registered Offices:
Harmondsworth, Middlesex, England

First published by Dutton, an imprint of New American Library,
a division of Penguin Books USA Inc.
Distributed in Canada by McClelland & Stewart Inc.

First Printing, April, 1991
10 9 8 7 6 5 4 3 2 1

REGISTERED TRADEMARK—MARCA REGISTRADA

Lyric from "A Little Bit of Emotion" by Raymond Douglas Davies,
courtesy of Davray Music Ltd./Carlin Music Corp.

LIBRARY OF CONGRESS CATALOGING IN PUBLICATION DATA:

Hallinan, Timothy.
  Skin deep : a Simeon Grist suspense novel / by Timothy Hallinan.
    p. cm.
  I. Title.
PS3558.A3923S55 1991
813'.54—dc20   90-46801
                                                CIP

Printed in the United States of America
Set in Times Roman
Designed by Julian Hamer

To the memory of my father,
Kenneth Frank Hallinan
(January 1, 1914—January 7, 1991).
Pilot, pirate, and gentleman,
he vanquished the blue-nosed eagles.

Belated thanks to Matt Sartwell for the squeal;
And love, as always,
to Munyin Choy

. . . how frail they are,
the skin, the nerves, the blood and bone
that frame the soul's disguise.

—GEORGE HERBST,
1938

I

SKIN

▼

1

Fireworks

IN THAT CROWD, Mr. Beautiful and the Korean girl shimmered like millionaires in disguise, minor gods slumming incognito.

By seven-thirty, the crowd in question had jammed itself noisily into McGinty's of Malibu, which, all gussied up for the Fourth of July, was even more of a slag heap than usual. Red, white, and blue crepe paper sagged despondently from the rafters. Red, white, and blue beach balls had been tossed into the ropy fishnet that hung from the ceiling. They nestled among seashells, starfish, old floats, weights, and other nautical bric-a-brac to create a landscape that looked like the place where drowned children go to play.

The bunch jostling merrily beneath this doleful composition in primary colors was a cross section of virtually every objectionable white urban minority. There were guys who called each other "Dude." There were cowboys and cowgals wearing western hats with those infuriating feather sunbursts on them. There were people wearing both sunglasses and earphones. There were yuppies, puppies (yuppies who had tied their dogs outside), and suppies—garden-variety suckers, but with aspirations to urban chic. Members of the last-named club had thoughtfully identified themselves by ordering McGinty's "John Philip Sousa," a tall-glassed, red-white-and-blue error in judgment that, drunk on an empty stomach, was guaranteed to plant the happy patriot several feet beneath the Ould Sod. We had Topanga Canyon creek rats, out from their caves to blow a week's worth of recycled aluminum cans on a red, white, and blue drunk, and we had a patriotic trio of amphetamine burnouts, skeletal, wild-eyed, hoisting imaginary drinks and nattering together in a far corner. We had people who *still* hadn't run out of patchouli. And every moment more of them poured in from the Pacific Coast Highway outside, drawn to the beach to celebrate the freedom that, for better or for worse, made them possible.

Some seventies retro with lead ears had programmed the jukebox to play "Stairway to Heaven" nine times in a row. He'd also located the volume control. I was halfway into the basket, working simultaneously on drinking my fourth beer, ignoring the music, and flirting with the one of the female bartenders when a ripple of excited voices penetrated Led Zeppelin and drew my attention to the door.

The focus of the flutter seemed to be a man and a woman who had just pushed their way into the bar. The woman was convincing evidence for the Argument from Design: beautiful far beyond the demands of function, maybe Korean, maybe twenty, definitely sensational. She had long, tangled black hair, extravagant cheekbones, and a lower lip that seemed to have "Bite me" tattooed on it. Wrapped low around her hips was a short black skirt, and even her knees were perfect. The world is full of beautiful women who keep their knees under cover.

I was trying to rip my eyes off her and get back to my bartender when I noticed the guy. His sun-streaked hair was so perfect I was surprised he took it outdoors. The face framed by the artful tousles looked to be around thirty, deeply tanned and classically handsome, terminating in a chin with a cleft that could have been his fanny's little brother. The really blinding feature, though, was a set of teeth white enough and flawless enough to make me involuntarily close my mouth. The teeth were revealed in a grin that had probably sucked half the wattage from the urban grid. People in Santa Barbara were doing macramé in the dark. Below the neck he was trim and muscled, encased in tight black leather clothes that sported more fringe than all five members of the Buffalo Springfield in their prime. In all, he was just the kind of guy the rest of us hate.

But he seemed popular enough at the moment. People were slapping him on the back as he made his way through the crowd. The guys who call people Dude were giving him soul handshakes, pounding their open palms down into his with a smack that could be heard even over the music.

"Here's Godzilla," the bartender said sourly. It was the first sour thing she'd said, on an evening that was sour enough to parch peaches. She picked up a perfectly clean glass and polished it, turning her back pointedly toward the spot at the bar where room was being made for Mr. and Ms. Beautiful. "Simeon, it's seven-thirty," she said tightly, alerting me to the fact that I had apparently told her my name. I stared down at my glass, wondering whether she'd told me hers. "Why don't you finish up that beer and flee this den of contagion?" she asked, wiping the glass fiercely enough to break it. "Go up on the bluff, where all the nice people are waiting patiently for the fireworks. Watch parents hug their children. Look at young couples in love. Don't hang around here getting drunk with these mutants. What do you say?"

The other bartender, a large and aggressively shapeless female wearing a leather butcher's apron that looked like it had dried on her, gave my bartender a hard bump on the shoulder as she squeezed by to grab a bottle of tequila. "Thanks, Roxanne," she said nastily. "Remind me to do something for you sometime."

"I'll take him next drink, Felicia," Roxanne said. "Okay? We'll trade off." Felicia muttered something that would have made my mother sit up very straight indeed and toted the bottle back down the length of the bar as I refocused on

Roxanne. She reminded me of cream rising. There was something clean and dairy-maidish about her that made me expect her to have a milk mustache. She'd braided her long, loose brown hair for the occasion and had woven red, white, and blue gift-wrap ribbon into the braid. I suppose it was intended to make me feel patriotic. It just made me want to unwrap her.

"Are you listening?" she said a touch sharply.

"Of course," I said, sitting up and looking attentive. In fact, I'd been watching the shadowy little pulse in her throat, which was beating in time to Led Zeppelin, and wondering if she'd get upset if I leaned forward and licked it.

"Then are you going to do it?"

I went to mental replay. "Leave, you mean?"

"Sure."

"Uh," I said, looking at her pulse. "No."

Midway down the bar, Mr. Beautiful tasted his drink and spat it on the floor. He shoved the glass back at Felicia, and she missed it and it toppled off the inside edge of the bar. Standing behind him, the Korean girl looked apprehensive. Felicia looked like she'd enjoy taking Mr. Beautiful's hand off at the elbow with her teeth, but she got a new glass and began to mix. Mr. Beautiful yelled precise instructions over the music.

"Why not?" Roxanne said, taking no notice of the scene behind her even though she'd flinched when the glass shattered.

"Because I belong here," I said. "These are my people. Roxanne," I said, retrieving the name and committing it to whatever was passing itself off as my memory, "why should I deserve better? I got the blues so bad you could use me for a dye. Jesus, I haven't worked in weeks. Did I tell you I'm a private detective?"

She gave me an assessive squint, then picked up my glass and sloshed the fluid around. "How many of these have you had?"

"Tonight?" I said. "Or in my whole life?"

"Skip it," she said. "You've had four. And yes, you told me you were a private detective. Is that supposed to change my life? How many did you have before you got here?"

"Two," I lied. If you can't lie to a stranger, who can you lie to?

One corner of her mouth lifted, tickling a dimple into revealing itself. "You know," she said, "there's guys you can believe and guys you can't. And who cares, anyway? Half the trouble in this world is caused by believing. Give me more about your blues. Guys with the blues are so, I don't know, nostalgic."

"Hey," I said, warming to the subject, "blues. Did I tell you about my computer?"

"Yeah." She shrugged. "You can't work your computer. So who can work a computer? Dweebs, that's who."

"It cost two thousand bucks. It's the most expensive paperweight I ever owned."

"Paperweight?" she said. "Well, at least that's new." The other corner went up, and she was almost smiling.

"What time do you get off?" I asked.

"Slow down. You also said something about a girlfriend." Jimmy Page was launching into his guitar solo for what seemed like the fortieth time, and I leaned forward to hear. "A *girlfriend*," she shouted. The man on the stool next to me closed his book and stared accusingly.

"Ex," I said. "Ex-girlfriend." I glared at the guy to my right, and he reopened his book. Sartre, just what I should have expected. Eleanor Chan, my long-standing Significant Other, had wisely decided to take a walk, but if she'd been there, she would have sneered at him. "Ex," I said again, daring the guy to look back up at me.

"You told me about her, even if you don't exactly remember doing it," Roxanne said. "That's a point in your favor, that you told me. Maybe not a very big point, but there it is anyway. And besides, you're cute. So I'll break a rule and ask what's the problem."

"Somebody else," I said, skipping the fact that the breakup had been my fault.

"You don't mean someone she's just going out with."

"No. I mean a boyfriend."

Roxanne looked serious and patted my hand. "I'll bet he's a creep," she said. "I'll bet it lasts a week." She left her hand on mine in a sisterly fashion.

"So there I am," I said, cold-shouldering the attempt at comfort. "I'm in the attractive position of feeling hostile, aggressive, and sorry for myself, everything that fascinates women. So what time do you get off?"

"I'm thinking," she said. Then she took my little finger between her thumb and index finger and rubbed it all the way from the tip to the first knuckle in a manner that wasn't even remotely sisterly. She gave me a lazy smile with something very energetic behind it. "I'll give you a buck if you go away and come back for me at ten-thirty. You can buy me dinner."

"Is that a promise?" My little finger wanted more.

"I told you, I'm thinking." She looked around the room. "I don't see a better offer on the horizon. How about you finish your beer, if you must, and go watch the fireworks? I'll be here when you get back." She gave the hand another pat and turned her back to tend to three nervous underage guys at the other end of the bar. I lost myself in soulful appreciation of the twenty-four-year-old female form in retreat. Roxanne had a mountain climber's haunches and a foot plant that seemed to roll the earth away backward behind her. Then she disappeared behind the furious Felicia, and I twisted around on my stool to look at the Pacific, visible across the highway.

Compared to Roxanne, it wasn't much to look at. I'd seen better surf on the Great Salt Lake, and the sun had finally called it a day and rolled on to give skin cancer to people in Hawaii and Asia. Oh, I was in terrific shape.

If someone hadn't finally yanked the jukebox plug, I

wouldn't have heard it. There was a shout, and a chair hit the floor. I turned to see Mr. Buffalo Springfield shove the Korean girl away from him and then pour what was left of his drink over her head. Everything went into freeze frame. I saw Roxanne rigid behind the bar, watching. The Korean girl opened her mouth to say something, and the guy in the leather punched her in the face. It wasn't a slap, it was a punch. She went down as if she'd been sapped.

I think I remember throwing a few people out of my way to get to them. The next thing I'm *sure* I remember was the guy bending down over the girl, with one of his legs pulled back to kick her, and my hand grabbing his Simonized hair and yanking him upright. He came up faster than I'd figured, with the glass in his right hand, and he swung it in the general direction of my face. I pulled back and he missed, and the glass struck the edge of the bar and exploded in his hand. With the total disinterest of someone in another time zone, I saw blood spurt from his palm. Using my free hand, I did my level best to break one of the small bones in the side of his neck.

Necks are soft, but my knuckles popped as I hit him. He looked cross-eyed for a second and then started to go after me with the broken glass in his bleeding hand. I kissed the Marquis of Queensbury good-bye and kneed him in the nuts. When he folded forward, dropping the shards of glass onto the girl's stomach, I caught him under the chin with my other knee. His neck snapped back, and he let out an agonized little "whuff" and flopped backward into the sawdust on the floor. I put my foot on his throat and pressed down, hard.

"Finished?" I said happily. I was glad to see that he'd bitten his tongue when my knee hit his jaw. Blood flowed from his mouth and collected in the dimple on his chin. He didn't answer. Probably he couldn't.

"You stinkin' alkie cowboy," someone said behind me in an accent that was pure Panhandle. "Get off him, you dickhead." The voice belonged to the Korean girl, and she was crying. She'd pulled herself to a sitting position and she tugged her skirt down over her thighs in an oddly modest gesture, considering the fact that she'd just been decked in front of eighty or ninety people. She wiped a forearm across her eyes and looked at me fiercely. "Don't you dare hurt my baby," she said.

"Hurt him?" I said. I was confused. I was trying to play mix and match with the Korean face and the Texas voice and failing. "Um, lady," I said, giving up, "I don't want to hurt him. I want to kill him. Give me one good reason why I shouldn't."

" 'Cause," the Korean girl said, sitting back slightly. I must have looked pretty fierce myself. " 'Cause it's not his fault, dammit."

"Then whose fault is it?"

She passed a forefinger over her front teeth, checking to see that they were still there, and then cranked out a smile. A very small smile. "He's not usually like this. He's just drunk."

"So am I," I said. "And I've wanted to kill somebody all day." I ground my foot into his throat. "Yum, yum," I said.

A circle of people had gathered around us, watching as passively as if we were the film at eleven on the evening news. "Hey," the Korean girl called to the room at large, "isn't anybody gonna do anything?" Most everybody in the circle looked away, unwilling to get involved, but one zealous-looking jerk in a frontier-style plaid shirt shouldered through the folks around him and sprinted for the pay phone. "Do something," the Korean girl pleaded. "Jesus, something terrible could happen."

"If something terrible hasn't already happened, I'd like to read your datebook," I said. The bar had hushed except for the sound of the plaid shirt punching buttons on the telephone. I felt some of the adrenaline wane, and I looked down at Mr. Beautiful. His face was very red and the veins on both sides of his forehead were throbbing. With some reluctance, I lifted my foot. He rolled his head from side to side, gasping for breath and trying to spit out the blood in his mouth.

"Toby," the Korean girl was saying in thick Texan, "Toby, honey, I'm sorry." If I live until the third millennium, I'll never understand women.

I bent down. "I can either rearrange the rest of your facial furniture, or not," I said. "It's up to you."

"I'm through," he said.

"Toby," the girl said, bending over him. "Sweetie, you okay?"

He brought one hand up to his throat. "Do I look okay, you fucking idiot?" he said. I stepped on his throat again, hand and all, just to refresh his etiquette. He gagged, and the girl grabbed ineffectually at my ankle. As her fingers scraped at my skin I could hear the plaid shirt talking on the phone. I raised my shoe and inspected it. Mr. Beautiful hadn't bled on my laces.

He coughed. "Is he calling the cops?" he rasped, staring wildly at Mr. Zealous.

"I certainly hope so," I said.

"Jesus. Get me out of here. *Now*, get me out of here right now." He was talking to the circle, and he looked panicked. A buzz arose from the circle as its members began to discuss what they'd just seen as though it had happened on the other side of a television screen. "I can't have the cops," he said desperately. No one looked at him.

"Why?" I said. "The cops are a good deal compared to me. If it weren't for the sweetheart of the rodeo here, you'd be the Fourth of July dinner special. Asshole on the half shell."

"You don't understand," he said. *"You,"* he added vehemently. I was the only one making eye contact; all the others were melting away toward their tables, figuring out what they'd say tomorrow when they told the story. The music kicked in again, still Led Zeppelin, and he raised his voice. "You've got to get me out of here. If you don't, I'm finished." I looked over my shoulder, but there was no doubt about it. He was talking to me.

"Why in the world," I said, "would I help you?"

"Five hundred dollars," he said. "I'll pay you five hundred dollars to get me home."

Five hundred dollars sounded pretty good. It even made one or two of the chickens glance back. The plaid shirt had hung up the phone. In some corner of my subconscious my bankbook gave out a starved squeal. "Cash?" I said.

"Cash."

"Seven fifty," I said.

"Fine, fine, whatever. Just get me home."

"Why can't you get out of here yourself?"

"We got rid of the limo," he said, rubbing at his throat. "The asshole driver wanted to watch the fireworks."

"What about her?" I gestured toward the Korean girl.

His eyes rolled. "Who cares?"

I lifted my foot again. The muscles in my leg twitched rebelliously. "What about her?"

"Send her home in a cab," he said sullenly.

"*Toby,*" the girl said in an anguished squeal. "You got to be kidding."

"Just get her away from me," said the hero on the floor.

"That's the nicest thing you could do for her," I said, "but it costs."

"In my pocket."

"You can't," the Korean girl said. "I'm not old enough to drink, Toby. Cripes, you know about the ABC and the Spice Rack. I'll lose my job."

"Tough shit," he said.

Something dropped into place behind the beautiful face, a cold front that turned her dark eyes into holes I wouldn't have wanted to fall into. "Listen," she said in a tone of voice that could have sliced ripe tomatoes, "you can't shovel it at *anyone* forever. Sooner or later, you have to be nice."

"Hey," he said, glaring at her, "do you know how to spell 'fuck you'?"

I shoved my hand into the right front pocket of the hero's leather pants and came up with a wad of bills, mostly of the impressive denominations you see in ads for the California lottery. "Where do you live?" I asked her.

"Hollywood." She looked at Mr. Beautiful as though he were something that someone gravely ill had spit onto the floor. "You're going to be sorry, Toby," she said.

I gave her a fifty. "He's pretty sorry already," I said. "This is for the cab." I handed her a hundred. "And this is for your dry cleaning."

She looked from me down to him, the dregs of his drink dripping from her flowing hair. She still looked good. "Yeah? Who's going to clean me? Sooner or later he's going to come back and make smooches, and I'm going to brain him with a flower pot, and when I do he'll kill me. You don't know him."

"Honey, if he gives you any kind of trouble, even constructive criticism, I'll scramble him into an omelet and have him for breakfast." I leaned down to pick him up.

"Simeon," Roxanne said from behind the bar, "you're not going to help him?"

"It's better for everybody," I said, pulling Loverboy to his feet. "Otherwise, she's going to have to go to the police station, too."

"No way in the world," the Korean girl said. "Not as long as I can still run."

"But he's such *scum*," Roxanne said plaintively. "And he's got it coming."

I heard a siren in the distance. Loverboy tugged at me, looking trapped and terrified. I shrugged it off.

"When the cops get here, tell them he's already left. Tell them his horse showed up. I promise you, if he screws around with her again, I'll make sure he eats the whole deck, okay?" I turned to the Korean girl and fished a crumpled card from my pocket. "There's a phone number here. Use it if he gives you a problem. You can call it anytime, day or night." I looked up at Roxanne. "You going to help out or not?"

She shrugged. "I guess. I'll get her a cab."

"Get her two if she wants them, they're on Prince Valiant here. Are you going to be here when I get back?" The siren was louder now.

Roxanne gave me a dubious look and then a small shrug. "What the hell," she said.

"See you then," I said. I put my arm around the hero's shoulders. "Come on, beautiful," I told him, "this is your exit."

For the first twenty minutes or so after he told me to turn right—north, up toward the Malibu Colony—we shared your basic sullen silence. His fringe flapped in the breeze through the open window, and he sucked at his mangled tongue and fingered his jaw once in a while, but other than that he kept his conversational skills to himself.

That was fine with me.

Traffic on the Pacific Coast Highway was light in both directions. The fireworks were about to start, and most people were staying put. Sweet Alice, the low-rider's special I'd won at cards from a glue-sodden card player named Jaime on a night of which I had only fragmentary memories because of Jaime's generosity with his glue, was chugging along in an exemplary fashion. She was in temporary remission from the tubercular cough that had plagued her recently. Maybe it was the carburetor, whatever that was.

At any rate, that was the limit of my mechanical sophistication, a state I'd long considered remedying. My long-ago graduate adviser when I was taking my doctorate in English, a waspish and perfectly dressed Ph.D. named Miles

Brand, maintained that there were people who were put on earth solely to tend to the health of carburetors, and that any attempt by the rest of us to penetrate those mysteries was nothing more or less than irresponsible monkeying with God's master plan. Miles's comfortable faith in the secure future of the upper classes was much greater than mine, probably a result of his lifelong love for Victorian novelists. Trollope, Dickens, Gissing, and Thackeray in the nineteenth century—and, for that matter, Miles in the twentieth—didn't seem to worry as much about gravity as I did. What happens to the top of the social pyramid when you pull out the bottom three or four layers? In all, it seemed to me that the people who understood carburetors could get along much better without the people who understood Dickens and Thackeray than the people who understood Dickens and Thackeray could get along without the people who understood carburetors.

About twelve miles up the road, Mr. Beautiful stirred. He dabbed once or twice at his lip and then reached into his leather pocket and pulled out a small wad of tissue. "Don't hit any bumps," he said sulkily.

I aimed for something that could have been a large tortoise or a small land mine and hit it. Alice bounced. "Anything else?" I said. Roxanne had given us some paper towels as we left, and he'd wadded a couple around his cut palm. They got in his way as he tried to unwrap the tissues. He swore sharply and pulled the paper towels loose from his hand, tossed them to the floor, and peeled open the tissue. In it were six white pills, four small ones and two that were larger.

I've always had an active pharmaceutical curiosity, a vestige of several years of frequently terrifying experimentation. Against my will, I said, "What's that?"

"A load," he said. "Hey, don't make me talk, I've got to get some spit together." He worked his mouth for a moment, then threw his head back and tossed down all six at once. They went down as though he'd oiled his throat. "One perfect world coming up," he said.

"What's a load?" I'd never heard of it.

"Four codeine—four grams each—and two Doriden. I don't like you very much right now, but I could be crazy about you in a few minutes."

He swallowed hard a couple of times and leaned back. A mile glided by in the thickening dark. To our left, on the beach, one premature rocket slithered its lonely way into the heavens and then blew itself to smithereens, making a bright silver spider in the sky. "Have you got a mirror?" he asked.

I swiveled the rearview toward him without speaking.

He adjusted it and then looked at himself critically. First he extended the nipped tongue and regarded it. Then he took his nose, which I didn't remember having hit, between thumb and forefinger and bent it gently, once to the right and two or three times to the left. He touched a swollen lip and let out a *whoosh* of breath. "You messed me up pretty good," he said conversationally. "They'll have a shit fit tomorrow."

"What's tomorrow?"

"The usual, only earlier. I've got a six o'clock call."

"For what?"

He returned the mirror to something approximating its original position. "For what?" he repeated. "You're telling me you don't know who I am?"

"I haven't got the faintest idea who you are or who you're supposed to be. All I know is that you pick on people who can't pick back."

"Damsels in distress, is that the bit?" He whistled slowly and tunelessly between his teeth for a moment. "Damsel, that's a corruption of 'mademoiselle,' did you know that?" His voice was beginning to sound a little dreamy.

"Yes," I said.

"There are so many words," he said slowly. "Eskimos

are supposed to have a hundred words for snow because it's so important to them. Not because they like it, but because it's important. Do you know how many words we have for chicks?"

"Well, chicks," I said. "That's already a bad beginning."

"Oh, spare me. I am so *tired* of men who are sensitive to women. That little girl tonight, Nana, now that's a chick. You know what's her favorite art form? MTV. What does she read on a cold winter's night? The *Enquirer*. When she wants a challenge, *People* magazine. That's why she likes me. Oh, I forgot. You're not supposed to know who I am."

"I *don't* know who you are, and I'm losing interest rapidly."

"But *Nana's* interested. Nana's more than just interested. Nana's going to put up with anything I do because I'm supposed to be somebody special. *Anything* I want to do, that's okay with Nana. I mean, she's pretty enough to look at twice, but she's just another brainless chick. One out of a hundred and fifty million." He swallowed again and closed his eyes. "Oooh, here it comes," he said. Whatever was coming, it arrived quietly. He sat with his head thrown back. His eyelids twitched. There was a half smile on his face, slack and unmuscled, that robbed his features of the malicious intelligence that had animated them so far. Up close he looked older, and I revised my estimate of his age upward: thirty-four, maybe, holding for dear life on to twenty-nine. Getting a little pouchy here and there, but preserved from ruin by his matinee-idol bone structure. Not for long, though.

It was almost enough to make me feel sorry for him. Almost, but not quite. If there's anything I've learned in my work, it's this: You can always find reasons to feel sorry for shitheads. And when you're finished, they're still shitheads.

He moaned. It sounded like a moan of pleasure. Then, slowly, he pulled himself upright and squinted through the windshield as if he were trying to figure out how far we'd come.

"We keep starting conversations," he said. He was talking very slowly now, as if he had to fish the words out of oily water. "But we never finish them. Nobody ever finishes them. How many conversations have you ever really finished?"

"I'll finish this one. As soon as you get out of the car."

"Every time I try to talk to you, you give me a one-liner."

"This is talking? I thought we were just passing the time until we got to where you could put some ice on your lip. There. That's a two-liner."

"Hey," he said. "You're a person. I'm a person, too. You don't know what was going on. You don't know why I punched her. You came into the scene after the exposition was over. You were just changing channels."

"I didn't like the show."

"What, you put your fist through the screen every time you don't like a program?"

"This wasn't a program. And I don't watch TV. I shot my last one when I was a kid and Nixon was telling me he wasn't a crook."

"Well, hell. At least I didn't use a gun."

"Nixon didn't feel the bullet. Now he's walking around acting like an elder statesman. Even his hairline looks better. Anyway, shooting a television set is one thing. Hitting a woman is another."

"The impulse is the same."

"Impulses are what civilization was created to protect us from."

"Dead wrong." He swallowed thickly. "Civilization was set up to allow the largest number of people to gratify the largest number of impulses and get away with it." His head lolled forward for a moment, and then he snapped it upright. "Money, for example. Civilization's proudest product."

"I thought it was room service."

"Without civilization, Nana's family could kill me. *With* civilization, money can make it okay. Money is civilization's way of saying you're sorry. Do you really think she wouldn't let me hit her again if there was enough money involved?"

"I think you're full of shit," I said. "Why don't you just sit there and nurse your cuts? Why should you want a conversation with me?"

"It's just the dope," he said after a moment. "Loads make you want to talk to everybody. You want one?"

"No, thanks," I said. "I don't want to talk to everybody."

We rode in silence for a moment. Then he began to laugh. "You really *don't* like me, do you? I'm Toby Vane."

"Simeon Grist," I said grudgingly. Manners are manners.

"Look," he said. "I'm sorry, okay? I've had a crappy day, a crappy week, in fact, and I was loaded on the wrong stuff. My momma always told me not to drink."

"I'm not the one you should apologize to."

"I'll call her, with you right there, when we get home. I'll go down on my knees. I'll weep and wail. I'll send her a fur coat. I think I've got one around someplace." He laughed again. "It's been a long time since anyone told me I was full of shit."

"Maybe that's your problem. Where do I turn, anyway? We're halfway to Oxnard."

"It's past Zuma. Encinal Canyon, do you know it?"

"I'll find it."

"Ooohh, ooohh, ooohh. Heading into the zone."

"What zone?" I started looking for a speed trap.

"The load zone. Loading zone. I don't know, whatever rarefied zone a load puts me into." He twisted the mirror back toward him and looked into it. "I'm a mess. I'm going to have to wear more makeup tomorrow than Joan Crawford. What do you do for a living?"

"I'm an investigator."

"But you're not a cop." There was some alarm in his voice.

"If I were a cop, you'd have ink all over your fingers, wouldn't you?"

"I put my footprints into cement once." He made a snorting sound, halfway between a wheeze and a laugh. "That's supposed to be a big deal."

"Okay," I said. "You're an actor. You don't need to wear yourself out with oblique references. Here's Zuma."

"It's a few miles farther. Hey, you, ease up. I'm not entirely hopeless."

"You conceal it well."

"You're not still pissed off," he said, turning his head slowly from side to side. "You're just trying to make a point. You made it already, so why don't you lighten up?"

It was true. I wasn't still pissed off. My blues and my drunk were long gone. If anything, I was probably grateful. Toby Vane was not likely ever to become my favorite human being. Still, he was working hard to be liked, and he'd given me a chance to work off several weeks' worth of accumulated disgruntlement by slugging him, and to look like a hero in front of Roxanne while I was doing it.

"What's it like being a detective?" Toby Vane said.

"It's like permanently wondering where you left your car keys. What's it like being an actor?"

"You get up early. You drive or get driven to wherever you're working. You sit in a makeup chair while somebody makes you look like a Singapore transvestite. Then you stand around all day waiting to say something that doesn't sound like anything anyone's ever said in all the time since they invented verbs. Then, if you're very lucky, a man hands you a check for a ridiculous amount of money and you go back home. You get to say things like 'That's not where I'm coming from, Loretta.' Or 'I live for the highs, baby. That way the lows are just places to visit.' I had to say both of those sentences yesterday. In front of millions of people, eventually."

"Still," I said.

"Oh, sure. It pays a shitload. We're not really talking about relative values here. Take the right coming up. It gets a little steep going down." He swallowed again. "If the social value of what we do had anything to do with how much we get paid, I'd be standing in line for a bowl of soup. But think about disk jockeys. If the world were right, or anything like it, they'd get paid by having an inch sliced off their bodies for every hour they're on the air. Instead, they rake it in. Think about the members of the National Security Council."

"Court psychiatrists," I said.

"Network executives. The guys who market toys. Fashion designers." He was rolling. "Here it is, this driveway. Hang a right around that bush." I did, and we were there.

There was pretty impressive. The house was a free-form assemblage of timber and glass, framed by tall, undulating cypresses transplanted from a Van Gogh painting. When I cut Alice's engine I could hear the surf booming. "You live here alone?" I asked.

"Just me . . . and my shadow," he sang. "Actually, I have a lot of shadows," he added as he reached for the door handle. "It can get pretty crowded." He pushed the door open and then peered over at me, focusing through the drugs. "So come in," he said.

I looked at Alice's clock, the only thing about her that always worked. The drive had taken an hour. "I've got to get back," I said.

"The bartender? She's cute, but she'll wait. It's not even nine yet. Anyway, I don't have all your money on me. You've got to come in to get the rest of it." I must have hesitated for a moment, because he said, "Please. Please come in. I don't want to go in alone."

"Okay," I said. "But only for a minute."

"Good. I've never met a detective before."

He climbed out with some difficulty and closed the door. I followed. Midway to the house he stumbled, and I had to grab his arm to keep him from falling. "No photographers around, right?" he said. "That's what I need, a headline: BOY NEXT DOOR OVERDOSES." He used his hands to block out the words in the air. The effort made him tangle his feet again, and I had to hold him upright. "Heeere's Toby," he said to the night sky.

The front door was about twelve feet high. It was made of redwood, studded with massive iron nails that had rusted in the moist ocean air, trailing long dark lines of of oxidation into the grain of the wood below them. "That's on purpose, all that rust, can you believe it?" Toby Vane mumbled as he fished for a key. "Looks like shit and you pay extra for it. Typical." He turned the key, and the door creaked inward. "Come in and get paid," he said over his shoulder.

I followed him down an arched hallway and through a triple-size door. Lights came on. I found myself in a bright, spacious room with a cathedral ceiling, white walls, and a bleached oak floor. There was almost no furniture: one small couch with a glass table in front of it, pastel pillows scattered here and there, an eviscerated polar bear spread facedown on the floor, and a long, low bookcase along one wall. Most of the opposite wall was glass. Toby Vane stooped down and did something to a polished brass knob set into the floor, and lights blazed up on the other side of the glass. The Pacific surged and churned, hurling itself with patient, unwearying violence at two low, black, barnacle-covered rocks just a few yards from the glass.

"Very nice," I said.

"Want a toot?" He twisted another knob, and a spotlight struck the glass table in front of the small white couch. The light was focused on something that looked like a silver finger bowl, except that it was heaped to overflowing with a fine pinkish powder. The side of me that wishes I still got loaded all the time pricked up its ears and let its tongue loll in an unappealing fashion. The phone began to ring, but he ignored it.

"McDonald's makes the best straws," he said conversationally. "They're good sturdy plastic, and they're just the right diameter." He sat down on the couch and unrolled a brightly colored plastic straw from a sheet of tissue. The phone continued to ring. "All you've got to do to make them perfect is slice off the tip at a forty-five-degree angle with a razor blade." He scooped some of the powder from the bowl with a little spoon and made two tiny mountains on the table. "Want some?"

"No," I said without conviction.

"It's terrific. Pink, see? Very smooth, no jangles, no dental bills from uncontrollable teeth clenching. Excuse me." He leaned over and snorted the mountains. The phone stopped ringing. He ladled out two more little Mount Fujis and looked up at me, his eyes suddenly a lot clearer.

"What's the hardest part of being a detective?"

"Failure." The coke glistened malevolently at me.

"Does that happen?" He shoved a smidgen of coke into line.

"Once in a while." I sat on the floor on the other side of the table. I'd always wanted to climb Mount Fuji. "When the person you're after is a lot smarter than you are, or else so dumb that there's no way to figure out what he's done or why he's done it. Then you let somebody down and you feel terrible about it."

"You really do, don't you?" He started down toward the mountains but then stopped and lowered the straw. "I mean, you really care about the people you work for."

"Sure," I said, feeling uncomfortable. The phone began to ring again. "Oh, hell," I said. "Give me the straw."

He did, and I destroyed the tiny white landscape in front of me. He continued to regard me as if I were an exotic form of plant life as he scooped out some more cocaine. "And you hit me on the neck," he said admiringly, rubbing it with his free hand, "because you didn't want to mark me." The phone jangled on unheeded.

"No," I said. "I hit you on the neck so I wouldn't break my hand." He shook his head as though that were just what he'd expect someone as terrific as me to say. "What's the hard part about being an actor?" I said to change the subject.

"Acting, at least acting on television, is the art of failure." I felt the cocaine begin to buzz in my forebrain while Toby Vane vacuumed the tabletop with his nose. He looked up at me. "You fail as little as you can, that's all. And it has nothing to do with talent. It's electricity." The phone stopped ringing and instantly started in again. "TV is an electric medium. It's got a little tiny screen. Most of the sets are no good. In half the houses of America, I've got a green face. Reception is bad in some areas. You've got to find some electricity, some kind of juice, to cut through all that interference. If you don't, you're just another little pattern of dots in the corner of somebody's living room." He gave me an embarrassed grin. "It sounds immodest, but I suppose it's being able to turn on an electric personality."

The phone, thank God, had stopped. The only ringing now was the cocaine in my bloodstream. "So why do you hit women?" I said.

The grin disappeared. "Champ, I told you. That's not really me. I was drunk and down. She was bitching at me. Do you want me to phone her? I'll do it now." His tone was painfully earnest.

"That's up to you. It's your relationship."

"Relationship," he said. "My favorite word." His eyes went down to the table for a moment and then flicked back up to me. "I'll do it, but let me wash up first and get some ice. My tongue feels like a beanbag chair." He got up and headed for what I guessed was the kitchen. He stopped and turned back to me. "Want a beer or anything? More coke?"

"No, thanks. I passed my limit when I did the first one."

"Well, make yourself at home. I'll be a couple of minutes, and then we'll phone Nana." He disappeared.

Hearing its name, the phone began to ring again. I wondered how he stood it. Mine rang only once or twice a day. I wondered how *I* stood it. I looked at the coke for a moment and then got up quickly and walked to the other end of the room.

Above the bookcase the wall was hung with a series of bright, four-color magazine covers, maybe twenty in all. Toby's face was on every one of them.

He had a beaming, ingenuous, boyish smile. His expression was open, healthy, friendly. He looked about twenty-seven in most of the photographs.

TV Guide was the only one I recognized. The others all had names like *Fab* and *Rave* and *For Teens Only*. TOBY VANE OF *HIGH VELOCITY*—HIS SECRET SORROW, one shouted. WIN A DATE WITH *HIGH VELOCITY*'S TOBY VANE shrilled another. TOBY VANE TELLS ALL; TOBY VANE'S WEDDING WISH LIST; THE FAN TOBY VANE WILL NEVER FORGET; "WHY ME?" TOBY VANE CRIES.

Other magazines lay heaped on top of the bookcase. Toby's picture graced these, too, but he'd either gotten tired of cutting them out or he hadn't gotten around to it yet. I picked up one on which he looked particularly boyish and turned to page 28, which promised to tell me 100 THINGS TOBY DOESN'T WANT YOU TO KNOW ABOUT HIM.

Toby apparently didn't want much known about him. Among the riveting nuggets the magazine's crackerjack investigative team had unearthed were the facts that his favorite color was blue, that he cried at sad movies, that he'd had a German shepherd named Sam when he was a boy, and that his ideal girl was one with a lot of self-respect.

I was mulling that last one over when he called from the kitchen. "Simeon? Are you sure you don't want a beer?"

I dropped the magazine guiltily. "I'm fine," I said. "Just looking around." I partially straightened the stack of magazines, which was leaning forward alarmingly. "Is blue really your favorite color?" I shouted.

"What?"

I went to the kitchen door and leaned against it. He was leaning over a sink, holding a washcloth against his mouth. The washcloth was wrapped around something that might have been an ice cube. "Do you really cry at sad movies?"

He started to grin, and then he winced. "Don't," he said. "Don't make me laugh. They just make that stuff up. All I do is pose for the pictures."

"That's a fictitious character, the Toby Vane in those magazines?"

"All the Toby Vanes are fictitious characters. My real name is Jack Sprunk."

"What a peculiar way to live."

"I couldn't agree more. Now go away and let me work on my wounds."

I went back into the living room and straight to the magazines. They had a kind of horrid fascination. The one I picked up this time had a sincere-looking Toby on the cover and the headline TOBY VANE'S NEW YEAR WISHES FOR YOU. I decided I wasn't up to it and dropped the magazine onto the top of the tilting stack, and the whole slippery batch of them slid forward lazily and fell to the floor.

Beneath them was a cheap satin-covered photo album on which was written, in flowery script, "Precious Memories." Beneath that was another, inscribed "Loved Ones."

"Give me another minute," Toby shouted. "Then we can call Nana. Maybe we'll even go get her, if she's forgiven me." Even though I knew he was loaded to the gills on at least two kinds of dope, he sounded healthy and happy.

I opened the top album.

At first the shapes didn't make sense to me: they were just abstract patches of color and shadow. Then I realized what I was seeing. They were pictures, the kind of pictures you normally see only in magazines with names like *Pain and Punishment* or *Whipcrack*. But these hadn't been cut out of magazines.

They were Polaroids.

Many of them had been taken in the room I was in.

Women were tied into impossible positions. Women were gagged and handcuffed. A woman lay naked on her back with the photographer's shoe pressing into her chest. A very young girl, no more than sixteen, was covered with broken eggs. An even younger girl had mean-looking electrical clips dangling from her nipples. Then an entire page of close-ups of a woman with two closed, swollen eyes and a split lip.

It was Nana.

"Maybe we could all go out together," Toby was saying cheerfully in the kitchen. "Me and Nana and you and your bartender. Go to a movie or a late dinner or something. How does that sound?"

I closed the album and put the fan magazines back on top of it. I went to the door and through it, without slowing down, without trying to collect the rest of my seven hundred and fifty dollars. I didn't need it any more.

And I certainly didn't need Toby Vane. I didn't need anybody whose idea of an electric personality was an alternating current between Jack Armstrong and Vlad the Impaler. Smile or no smile, he was a sick boy.

I lost my way twice trying to get out of the canyon and up to the Pacific Coast Highway. By the time I finally reached it, it was ten o'clock. I drove south like Mario Andretti, but the holiday traffic was a series of Gordian knots and it was after eleven when I finally got to McGinty's of Malibu. Roxanne was gone.

I'd missed the fireworks, too.

2

Syndication

THE FIFTH OF July had a delayed case of the June glooms: dull and flat and gray, courtesy of low-hanging clouds that had slid in overnight to lower the ceiling and the spirits of everyone stuck under it. At eight-thirty in the morning the day looked as bright as it was likely to get. I was sitting with my chin on one hand, muffled and depressed from Toby Vane's cocaine, staring at a dark screen that had nothing on it but two characters that blinked in a bright, bilious green. This is what it said:

A>.

I'd been looking at A> for what seemed like months, wondering what was supposed to come next. So far, what had come next was frustration, surfing a wave of nostalgia for the user-chummy old Apple I'd given away.

A stack of fat books stood next to the computer. They were written in a language somewhere between beginning English and advanced Dada. The index to the one on top, the open one, said that the chapter called "Getting Started" began on page 92. I slapped it shut and hit one of the computer's keys at random, and the damn thing beeped at me. My blood pressure tripled. I found myself standing up with my fists clenched, took two breaths, and wandered over to say good morning to Hansel and Gretel, my parakeets. They ignored me. I ignored me too and climbed out onto the sundeck.

Topanga Canyon folded itself away toward the horizon.

In front of me, hidden by the hills to the northwest, was the Pacific; to the southeast was L.A. Below me was the thinnest of thin air. Someday, probably while I'm sleeping, the house I live in will fall into the canyon, where I fervently hope it will crush the heavy-metal drummer who pounds away, day and night, some six hundred feet below. Until then, the house just leans over the edge, a creaking testimonial to the resilience of seventy-year-old wood.

Mine is probably the oldest and certainly the worst-built house in the canyon. At one time, it was also the most remote. It was so remote that the death of its original owner, an unskilled hermit who'd slapped it together in the century's teens out of odds and ends and sheer hermetic rage, wasn't discovered until his mummified body was found hanging from the living room rafter almost a decade after he'd tied the knot in his final necktie. As far as anyone knew, he'd been driven to toss his good-bye kiss at the world by nothing more profound than the sight of Old Topanga Canyon Boulevard being paved beneath him.

Beneath the diluted daylight on the deck, I stretched. Joints popped. Kids' joints didn't pop. I guessed I wasn't a kid any more.

A hungry hawk sliced through the sky above me, and I realized I was lying down. It felt too early to lie down. It also felt too late to get up. Given the fact that I had a mild case of the post-coke heebie-jeebies, my first in years, I hadn't expected to be comfortable so soon. My eyes called for a vote. It came out two to one, with me on the losing side, and the eyes closed.

At the moment that my eyelashes converged, the phone rang. This was no tired, cranky, irritated ring like Toby Vane's phone had produced. It was a coloratura soprano trilling, full of hope and spring, the lighter-than-air notes of a diva who's finally been told she can sing after weeks of laryngitis. The phone had rung so rarely of late that I'd taken to waxing it.

On the seventh ring, I made my first big mistake of the day. I got up to answer it. First, though, I had to find it. I had a vague, watery memory of having tried to get Roxanne's number from information the night before, and of having dialed Eleanor when that attempt failed. I remembered turning off my own answering machine in petty revenge when Eleanor's machine had answered. What I didn't remember was where I'd put the phone.

It continued to trill merrily away while I began at the wall outlet and painstakingly traced the cord through many a loop and circumnavigation of my cluttered living room. Finally I lost patience, took the cord in both hands, and gave a sharp pull. The telephone emerged abruptly from one of the bookcases and clattered to the floor, taking Frederick B. Artz's *The Mind of the Middle Ages* with it. I slapped the book into place while the phone squawked at the floor, then picked up the receiver.

"So?" My voice sounded grumpy even to me.

"Hello?" someone said in a bright and friendly fashion. "Is Simeon Grist there?"

I weighed the pros and cons. "Depends."

"This is Norman Stillman's office calling."

"Mr. Stillman has a talking office?"

"Well, of course not." She sounded vaguely affronted. "I'm a secretary. Mr. Stillman would like to see you."

"About what?"

"I'm afraid I don't know."

"Mr. Stillman can talk, right? Even if his office can't."

"Well, of course."

"Then let him talk."

"He's very busy at the moment."

I gave half a weary eye to the computer screen. A> blinked at me. "So am I," I said. "I've got someone winking at me right now." She paused, and when she spoke again she'd given up on friendly. "I'll see if Mr. Stillman can come to the phone."

"Take the phone to him," I suggested. "It's not heavy."

I knew Norman Stillman, sort of. Everyone in Los Angeles did. A case I'd been working on had required my presence at the "launch" of one of the many television series let loose upon an unsuspecting world by Norman Stillman Productions. I remembered him as a slender, balding man in a nautical blazer who was fond of misquoting the classics. A very rich slender, balding man in a nautical blazer.

"Mr. Grist?" Norman Stillman's voice slithered bonelessly through the line. "We certainly owe you a world of thanks, don't we?"

"Do we?"

"Let's don't be modest, Mr. Grist. This is a delicate time, and you pulled the fat right out of the fire."

"Mr. Stillman." I closed my eyes and rubbed wearily at the bridge of my nose. The room reeled, and I quickly reopened my eyes. "I'm not being modest. I just don't know what you're talking about." Even as I said it, I realized that I knew exactly what he was talking about.

He chuckled lightly, something I've never been able to master. I can do a hearty chuckle when I've had a few strong ones, but a light chuckle is too Noel Coward for me. I was trying to imitate his when I realized he was talking.

". . . our boy," he said. "One more problem and we would all have been in very hot water."

"I don't know about you," I said, "but he passed simmer a long time ago."

"He speaks highly of you."

"With the chemical content of his blood, he can't speak any way but highly."

"Now, now," he said. "Let's not be judgmental."

It was too stupid to answer, so I examined the phone cord for knots. Phone cord knots, unlike anything else in the Universe, appear via spontaneous generation.

"I've practically watched him grow up," Stillman said

after a beat. "And you can take it from me, at heart Toby's a fine young man."

"I'll bet," I said, "that you called me for a reason."

Stillman cleared his throat of Toby. "Do you think you could be in my office around noon?"

"I don't know. Why?"

"I have a job for you."

I looked out the window, focusing through one of the holes in the screen on the mountains to the south. I had two hundred of Toby's dollars in my shirt pocket and owed $315 for rent. Then, also, there was the possibility of Roxanne. I couldn't very well ask her to pay for a date. At least, not a first date.

"Mr. Grist?"

"I'm here. I don't think I can make it at noon. What about one-thirty?"

"I have a screening at two. Oneish?"

"Okayish. Where are you?"

"Universal Studios. Just give your name at the Lankershim gate and the guard will direct you."

We muttered polite good-byes. If I was to meet him at one, my mental state needed emergency surgery, and the only way I knew how to do that was to run eight or nine hard, sweaty miles. Afterward I would need a long sauna and a good fifteen minutes under a shower before I could hope to regain that boyish glow. It was a full agenda. To my surprise, the day looked a little better.

Feeling righteous, I went over to the computer and snapped it off. It sputtered at me.

I completed my rise from the dead at UCLA in Westwood, where the sauna is hot and the coeds are the daughters of the California girls the Beach Boys warned us about. Iridescent from the sauna, I tossed my running shoes into Alice and pointed her north and east. Since I had a little time and I hadn't dipped into Hollywood in a few weeks, I tracked along Wilshire to Santa Monica and then east on Santa Monica to Highland. Winos dozed on bus benches. Little old ladies using walkers waited for the yellow light before beginning their long toddle across the street and then looked agitated as the horns blared. In the brown-paper-bag sunlight along Santa Monica Boulevard the hookers trolled the traffic for business with their thumbs extended. School was out, and the average age had dropped appreciably.

Highland Boulevard took me over the Cahuenga Pass and then turned mysteriously into Ventura Boulevard. A right onto Lankershim and a dip down the hill, and I was at Universal Studios. I parked Alice between a Rolls-Royce and a Maserati and left her, looking like a bright blue boil in a courtesan's box of beauty spots.

Stillman's office was a cute little million-dollar bungalow shaded by a couple of eucalyptus trees. I got my first surprise when he opened the door himself.

"You're Mr. Grist," he said enthusiastically. I agreed. He took my elbow to lead me, and I took it back. "I can see okay," I said.

Stillman laughed as if I'd said something funny. He was the sort of man who is always a little shorter than you remember him being, as though he'd shrunk while you weren't looking. I got an economical glimpse of immaculate white teeth that must have cost a fortune to straighten and cap, set off by a sunlamp tan and a pair of very small dark eyes huddling furtively beneath eyebrows that had, just possibly, known the sting of a tweezer. He'd traded his blazer for a hand-knitted sweater with a sailboat on the front. Still nautical, but not so formal. His balding head gleamed.

"Dierdre and Pauline are at lunch," he said, indicating a couple of empty desks with a careless wave. "You're certainly punctual. I appreciate that."

He continued to appreciate me as we passed through the secretarial area and into a short hallway. The closed door at the end of the hall said MR. STILLMAN on it in letters the size of the Hollywood sign. "Here we are," he said in case I'd missed them.

The room on the other side of the door looked bigger than the entire bungalow had looked from outside. I stepped onto Wedgwood blue carpeting that an iron-shod Percheron could have galloped across in silence. The window shades were drawn to keep the day at a tasteful distance, and the lighting was indirect. The mahogany-spoked wheel of a yacht hung on the opposite wall, behind a desk that looked like a bowling alley on legs. The only object on the desk's polished surface was a huge brass ship's compass.

"I don't know why," I said, "but I'd be willing to bet you've got a boat."

He laughed again and went to stand possessively behind his desk. "Half-right, Mr. Grist. In fact, I've got two of them. One's in the Marina, and one's on her way here from Hong Kong." He gestured at a large map of the Pacific that filled most of one wall. Two red pins were the only blemishes in its pale blue surface. "The *Cabuchon*. At this precise moment, she should be pulling into Honolulu."

"Lucky her."

"This is Mr. Cohen. Dixie, this is our hero, Mr. Grist."

I didn't see Dixie Cohen until he stood up; he had that kind of negative charisma. He'd been perching on a captain's chair near the door, and now he held his hand out to me, a thin, worried-looking, nearly completely bald little man on whose corduroy shoulders the angel of despair almost visibly perched. "Terrific work," he said mournfully. He wore professorial leather patches on the elbows of his jacket.

"Not on purpose," I said.

"The result is the same," Cohen said. Sitting down, Norman Stillman briskly rubbed his smooth, tapered hands together. They made a dry, powdery noise.

"Nothing in the press," Cohen murmured lugubriously to

the carpet, looking at it as though it were an old friend who had just died. "Good all around."

"Good for whom?" I fought off an urge to pat Dixie Cohen comfortingly on the shoulder and looked around for someplace to sit.

"For us, Mr. Grist." Stillman followed my glance. "Dixie," he commanded, "give Mr. Grist your chair." Cohen shuffled off across the carpet to grab one from a matched platoon lined up against the wall.

"What's so good?" I said, sitting. "Who cares if the little bedbug gets tossed in the can? It's better than he deserves."

"Let's not get sidetracked into a discussion of Toby's character," Stillman said. He looked down at the schooner sailing across the front of his sweater, spotted a wrinkle in the mainsail, tugged it straight, and then treated me to another million-dollar smile. The smile was as meaningless as Toby's, just something that staked claim to the lower half of Stillman's face whenever it felt like it. "Toby's approach to life is not the topic of the day."

"And what is the topic of the day?"

"Employment for you, Mr. Grist. I think I said that on the phone. Highly lucrative employment."

From behind me I heard Cohen lug a chair across the carpet. He sat down behind me and breathed resentfully once or twice.

"Would it be vulgar," I asked, "to mention an actual number?"

Stillman gave me his light chuckle. "That'll come. First, let's explain our little problem and see if it interests you. From what Toby's told me, I gather that's very much in your line. Quite the White Knight, Toby says." He cut off the chuckle and tapped the surface of his desk with a polished nail. "Dixie?"

Dixie stood up with a deep sigh that seemed to have its roots in his knees. He put his hands in his pockets and walked to the edge of Stillman's desk. Then he looked off into space until Stillman cleared his throat significantly.

"How much do you know about Toby Vane?" Cohen said to the room at large.

"He's an actor. He's on a lot of magazine covers. He's a certifiable sadist."

"That's succinct," Dixie Cohen acknowledged, staring at a spot above my head. "But you left one thing out. He's not just an actor, he's a star."

"I left out that he's an asshole, too," I said.

"Ah, yes," Dixie Cohen said sadly, "but he's *our* asshole." He eased his rear end onto the corner of Stillman's desk.

"Dixie," Stillman said sharply. Cohen straightened up as if he'd sat on a stove. Stillman reached over, way over, and brushed at the spot where Cohen had sat.

"*High Velocity* is in its sixth year," Cohen said with all the enthusiasm of a kid reciting the alphabet on command. "It's never been in the top five, but it's stayed out of the bottom thirty. This is, hip hooray, year last."

"Excuse me," I said, "but what's *High Velocity*?"

Stillman's mouth opened. Cohen couldn't have looked more surprised if I'd squatted on a lamp and started spitting maraschino cherries.

"It's Toby's series," he said. "You must have seen it."

"Nope."

"Even if you haven't, you must have heard of it. The publicity . . ." He spread his hands in sheer incomprehension.

"I've missed it," I said. Stillman looked at Cohen, and Cohen made a helpless gesture. Of course, I thought. He had to be the publicity man.

"Well," Cohen said, dredging up a mortician's smile, "most people who haven't spent the last six years at the bottom of a lead mine know about *High Velocity*. A hundred million or so of them have even watched it."

"Great show," Stillman said automatically. "Lots of action, but wholesome action. Nobody gets killed onscreen, or if they do, we cut away just before the plug gets pulled."

"Good role models," Cohen said. "Citation from the White House and everything."

"I get the point," I said. "It's a TV show."

"A very successful TV show, Mr. Grist," Norman Stillman said. "And it's all Toby Vane."

"A hundred percent," Cohen said. They sounded like Laurel and Hardy.

"And . . . ?"

"And we've got a problem." Dixie Cohen's face was even more furrowed and worried-looking than before.

"To hazard a wild surmise," I said, "Toby Vane."

"Exactly." Cohen looked hesitant. "Oh, well," he said. "Here goes. During the third season we were shooting on location in Northridge, you know Northridge?" He seemed to expect me to say no.

I said I knew Northridge.

"We were out near the college there, and the kids kept coming around to watch us work. Just regular Valley kids, you know? And, naturally, some of them were girls."

"Come on, Dixie," Stillman said, drumming his fingers on his desk. "Get on with it."

Cohen swallowed, and I suddenly recognized his discomfort for what it really was: he hated to be there. He would have given his life to be able to float straight up, through the ceiling, and into some pure, clear stratosphere where there was no Toby Vane to worry about. It made me like him better than I liked Stillman.

"There was this one little girl," Cohen was saying. "She hung around for a couple of days, and Toby began to talk to her. Real pretty little girl." He swallowed again. "About my daughter's age at the time. Anyway, Toby started talking to her, and then he got the director to let her have a walk-on. What Toby wants, goes."

"Right," I said. "I already had that feeling."

"So she finishes her bit, and she's all excited, and then Toby takes her to show her his dressing room, this big air-conditioned van. We all knew what was happening, or at least we thought we did. Then she started to scream. Everybody could hear her."

"No melodrama," Stillman said, looking at his fingernails. "Not *everybody* could hear her, there were *lots* of people who didn't hear anything at all. Just tell the story."

"Well, there were cops there. There always are when you're on location. We had to go into the trailer."

"Because of the cops," I said.

"Beg pardon?" Dixie's eyebrows rose.

"You mean you wouldn't have gone in if there hadn't been cops around?"

Cohen made his helpless gesture again. He'd had a lot of practice. "Sure we would have. I didn't mean that. We're not ghouls, you know. But cops being there made the whole thing more, well, urgent."

"More urgent than what?"

"Than it would have been otherwise," Stillman said smoothly. "Lord's sake, Mr. Grist, Toby wasn't killing her."

"Just a little fun," I said, thinking of the photo albums. I pulled my car keys from my pocket, and Stillman followed them anxiously with his eyes. "You know, this is a terrific office," I said, jingling the keys. "And I suppose that means that you guys aren't dumb. All things considered, though, I don't know why I shouldn't just get up and go to the beach. At least I'd know what I was doing there."

"Come *on*, Dixie," Stillman said. "Tell Mr. Grist why he's here."

Cohen looked like a man who'd just been given a choice between the rack and electric shock therapy. "Because of Toby," he finally said. "Because we need some help with Toby."

"Toby's the one who needs help," I said. "And I'm not

qualified to give it. I'm not sure anyone is who doesn't have twelve letters after his name and three or four degrees on the wall."

"You have a number of degrees," Cohen said. Someone had been doing homework.

"Sure," I said apologetically. "Dramatic literature, history, comparative religion, I forget what. But none in psychiatry."

Cohen grimaced. "Psychiatry takes time. We don't have any. We don't need a shrink, we need a keeper."

"*Dixie*," Stillman said. "Not a keeper, Mr. Grist." He extended a well-buffed hand and formed a word in the air. The word seemed to be shaped vaguely like a fish. "A *consultant*. Is that polite enough? A person who can help Toby, who can talk to him when he's about to do something self-destructive."

"*Self*-destructive? Toby's a human wrecking ball. I've seen enough buildings get knocked down to know that the wrecking ball usually comes out okay. It's everything else that gets leveled."

It was Stillman's turn to sigh, and he did it eloquently. "We're trying to tell you something," he said. "Don't interrupt, don't say anything for a minute, all right? There's a business opportunity here for you. At the moment, Toby's behavior is of very special importance. At this precise moment. We see you as a key, Mr. Grist. We'll pay a great deal to someone who can keep things on track."

"I still don't actually know what you're talking about. And even if I did, I haven't heard any money mentioned, except in the abstract."

"A thousand dollars a day," Stillman said. "Is that concrete enough for you?"

Now it was my turn to swallow. If Stillman and I kept gobbling up Cohen's mannerisms, there wouldn't be anything left of him but his sweater. I wondered if it would fit me. I looked at the two of them. Stillman returned my gaze, all frank and hearty and man to man. Cohen was still focused on the ceiling he wanted to float through. It seemed to be my line.

"Toby's been punching out women for at least three years, according to you. Why the sudden concern?"

They looked at each other again, but more confidently. "What do you know about syndication, Mr. Grist?" Stillman said.

"Nothing."

Stillman settled himself in his chair. "Syndication is the real bottom line of a series," he said in a loving voice. "It's why they get made in the first place. After a show has been on the air for a while, especially a hit show, it becomes valuable in a new way. Throughout its first run, it's produced for the network. The network pays what's known as a license fee. That means that the producer, say me, for example, gets paid a certain amount for every episode that airs. Say it's a million dollars." He drew an imaginary line on his desk with his index finger. "Are you following me so far?"

I nodded.

Stillman warmed to the task. "Fine. Let's say, just to pick another figure, that the series is supposed to cost nine hundred thou per hour." He drew another line. "That means a profit of a hundred thou for each show, right?"

"I can subtract."

"That's the problem," he said, making an imaginary X with his finger to cancel out the imaginary lines. "It's all subtraction. Half the episodes cost more than the license fee. Talent trouble, bad weather, weak scripts, the wrong director—any number of things can put a show over budget. In the long run, even with a hit series and a lot of creative bookkeeping, you wind up breaking even. Or, even worse, in the hole." He described a large circle on the desk's surface for my benefit. "The big eggola," he said.

I stayed put. The highly suspect smell of money filled the room.

"But," Stillman continued, smiling seraphically, "when the series is finally finished on the network, the producer can sell it to stations all over the country. One station at a time or ten stations at a time. Most of them aren't network affiliates, of course. They're independent stations, some little, some big, some rich and some poor. But they've all got money to spend. They need something to put on the air, and they're ready to pay for it."

"How much?"

He buffed his immaculate nails on his nautical sweater. "Well, that's the art of it," he said complacently, someone who had been fed all the answers. "Knowing how much a show is worth. The best guess I can make is that *High Velocity* is worth about three hundred thousand dollars an hour." He almost resisted the impulse to clear his throat.

I cleared my own throat. "How many hours?"

"Six seasons, Mr. Grist. One hundred and eighty hours."

Math was never my strong point. "That's, um . . ."

"Fifty-four million dollars."

All three of us were silent, I hoped for different reasons.

"Fifty-four million dollars," Stillman said dreamily. "That's essentially free money. The talent has gone home. No more dealing with actors, no more hassling with writers, directors, or network people. It's in the can. All you have to do is take it to the bank."

Stillman turned his hands palms up, the picture of calm reason. I envied his calm. Fifty-four million dollars would have kept the entire state of California in new shoes for a decade.

"And you sell all six seasons at once?" I said, just to make Stillman move his hands.

I won. He put his palms together. "If you've got the *cojones*," he said with subliminal pride. "You gamble that you've got a hit, and you hold off on the early seasons because you can get more money for the whole package. Also, maybe you don't want to spend the rest of your life hondling with some station in East Gonad, Arkansas. If you guessed right, you dump the whole package on a syndicator and let them do the work. And you get the whole"—he swallowed—"fifty-four million in one sweet lump."

"Fine," I said. "It's a lot of money. What's it got to do with me?"

"Dixie?" Norman Stillman prompted.

"Toby's the whole ball of wax," Cohen said. "He's the reason the show's a hit. He could be the reason the syndication rights go in the toilet. You're going to take care of Toby."

"Then you're not paying me enough," I said.

"All it would take," Cohen said as if I hadn't spoken, "is one more bad story, one more headline that the dream boy gets his rocks off by breaking girls' fingers. All we need is the *National Enquirer* headline reading TOBY PAID TO KICK ME and interviews with four abusees on *Geraldo*, and the show isn't worth the film it was shot on. We've had four headlines and three blind items already."

"I'm not interested in taking care of Toby Vane," I said. "I think he's the lowest form of life since Mr. Tooth Decay. And, as I said, you're not paying me enough."

"Let's take your points in reverse order," Stillman said, cutting off Cohen with an upraised palm. "Fifteen hundred a day. And you're not taking care of Toby, you're protecting the girls he might hurt."

"For how long? Assuming that I'll do it at all."

"Two weeks. At the outside. We'll be signed, sealed, and delivered by then."

"And after that?"

"Then it's Toby's problem," Stillman said with the air of one who'd anticipated the question.

"Not entirely."

"You mean the girls."

"Well, of course I do."

"Then it's their problem," Stillman said. "I can't worry about them after that. Are they more important than the people starving to death in Africa? I gave fifty thousand dollars to help them last year. They have less control over their destiny than the girls Toby Vane—or anybody, for that matter—beats up."

"I have to think," I said. "By the way, what happened to the girl in Toby's van?"

"Which girl?" Cohen said, sounding like someone whose dentist had just hit a nerve.

"The first one," I said. "You know, Northridge."

Cohen looked at Stillman, and Stillman nodded. "Her, um, her nose was broken." He looked embarrassed. Stillman just looked at me.

"How many have there been?"

Cohen shrugged. "Not that many. Eight or ten. After a while we caught on, started planting pros around."

"Pros don't bleed," I said.

"Pros don't talk to the press," Stillman said. "Let's get down to the bottom line. I have a screening to go to. Toby Vane is a big star, okay? Toby is a star because he's the boy every woman loves: he's a son to the middle-aged dames, a grandson to the old ones, the boy next door to preteens, and a fantasy lover to girls in their late teens and twenties. His show is worth fifty-four million dollars for exactly as long as that big friendly grin of his doesn't get shit all over it. If it does, *High Velocity* isn't worth carrots. I'm not going to let that happen. You're not going to let that happen. Dixie here isn't going to let that happen." He raised a hand, the man with the plan.

"We've all got our jobs cut out for us. You spend days and evenings with him, keeping him out of trouble. Dixie manages the press and keeps anything that's *already* happened from surfacing in some rag. And I negotiate the syndication deal as fast as I can, and pay both of you."

"Two weeks with Toby Vane," I said.

"Say ten days," Stillman said.

"Say two thousand a day," I said.

Stillman looked at Cohen. Cohen looked at Stillman. "Okay," Stillman said. "But you'd better keep his ass out of trouble."

"I'll wrap it in linen all the way up to the back of his neck," I said. "But I want to make one thing clear: if he gets out of hand, I'm going to deck him."

"Don't hit him in the face," Stillman said.

There was a moment of silence while we all listened to the echo. "I'll take the first five days on account," I said.

"Ten thousand dollars." Stillman pulled a checkbook from one desk drawer and a gold Mont Blanc fountain pen from another. The pen scratched expensively. He blew on the check for a moment and then held it out across the desk. He didn't get up.

I did.

"Dixie will take you to the set," he said. Now that he'd bought me, he wasn't quite so polite.

Ten thousand dollars richer, I followed Dixie to the door. I paused at the threshold.

"Tell me one thing," I said. "Why me?"

Stillman looked back up at me. "Don't you know, Mr. Grist? Toby likes you."

3

Panty Hose Oaks

"IT'S A SIMPLE MATTER of crisis control," Dixie Cohen said, maneuvering the big Mercedes through suicidal freeway traffic. The air conditioner roared away. "Problem is, there's no time between crises."

"Must be hard on the digestion." We were out of the Cahuenga Pass, heading for the Valley.

"I wouldn't know. Last thing I digested was my backbone. If I still had it, I'd have clobbered Toby long ago."

I looked over at him, figuring the odds on his decking Toby. His most conspicuous muscle was his Adam's apple. The hands on the leather-covered wheel were long, supple, yellowish, and fine-knuckled, a violinist's hands. It wasn't hard to imagine the sound of his fingers splintering on contact with Toby's jaw. He had a musician's profile, too. He looked like a guest conductor for a minor orchestra specializing in tragic opera.

"He's in his mid-thirties or something," I said, trying vainly to turn the air conditioner vent away from me. "It's a little late for corporal punishment. Why should you have clobbered him?" I settled for rolling down my sleeves.

"That's personal," Dixie said. It was as though he'd tugged a zipper closed between the front seats. He tightened his mouth like someone working up to a spit.

The Ventura Freeway hurtled by, bordered by laurels, oleanders, and other poisonous shrubbery. The Oracle at Delphi had chewed laurel, and look where it got her. I was

53

sighing, preparatory to changing subjects, when Dixie swerved the wheel sharply, dexterously cutting off a brown Japanese something in the lane to the left. We were awarded by an outraged beep.

"Crazy woman," Dixie said, although he'd been at fault. "If Toby were with us, he'd be screaming back to her with his head stuck out the window, even if he were driving. *Especially* if he were driving."

"Give me fifty words on Toby." It seemed like a safe subject.

"Which fifty?"

"Well, I already know his favorite color."

Dixie sucked in his cheeks, looking more than ever like a man on the verge of a satisfying spit. "Toby's tough," he said. "He likes being a star, and he might even hold on to it. He works. Knows his lines, shows up on time, gets the job done. How many words is that?"

"You've got a few left."

"He's smarter than you think—correction—smarter than *I* think. I found that out right away. He's got charm down cold. He's very, very good at being the little boy who can't figure out what he's done wrong. No matter what it is. He can look so sweet. And way down in the middle of it all, under the grin and the skin, he's so sick that Freud would have gotten a job as a bricklayer. Getting to know him is like opening a big, bright Christmas package and finding a box full of snakes."

"So," I said, "who was he before he was Toby?"

"Officially," Dixie said, "he was born in South Dakota, raised on a farm, and encouraged by a kindly, white-haired old drama teacher who loaned him the money to come to Hollywood. When he got here he took a job in a gas station and paid her back before he went on his first audition."

"*Her?* Hard to believe, Toby repaying a her."

"Yeah. That's one of the reasons I don't believe the story."

"What's the other reason?"

"I wrote it." The Laurel Canyon off ramp flashed by. The sun was out, and it was beginning to look like July again. "It's junk, all the way," Dixie volunteered, focused on the road. "I'd bet that Toby had a bad time as a kid. He's got a wincer's eyes. He may have grown up on a farm, but there weren't any sun-dappled fields."

"Where are we going, Dixie?" I didn't know the Valley very well.

"Location. West of Van Nuys and south of Ventura. High rent all the way. It's so genteel the trees wear panty hose."

"And you're setting Toby loose in it?"

He sucked in his cheeks again, punching the accelerator as though he had a grudge against it. "He's got something to look forward to today."

"Meaning?"

He went through the preliminaries for another spit and then swallowed. "You'll see."

The car was plusher than some of the rooms I'd slept in, and a lot colder. "So," I said, "Norman pays pretty good, does he?"

"What I go through," Dixie said, swinging the wheel to the right, "it better. What's the matter, you short a few zeros?"

"What do you go through, Dixie?"

"You should live to be a hundred," Dixie said, "and not find out."

We got off at Van Nuys Boulevard, a street that runs down the center of the Valley, as straight as the filling in a tamale. Dixie accelerated left through a red light and coasted across Ventura, heading south. The neighborhood did a quick-change act. Behind us were stucco storefronts and asphalt alleys, and in front of us were old oak trees, rolling lawns, dusty patches of ice plant, and ranch-style houses that rambled expensively through twelve to fourteen rooms.

I put my hand against the window, and it felt hot. We were surrounded by money, but the money hadn't been able to intimidate the heat.

"I hate locations," Dixie said, using up a little of the venom he'd been suppressing. "Hatteras, right?" He swung right, not waiting for an answer. "Wherever we are," he muttered, "here we are."

An oak tree ancient enough to command its own complement of Druids divided the road in front of us. Tacked to it like a G-string on a dowager was a cardboard sign reading HIGH VELOCITY. Beyond the tree was a scattering of equipment—trailers, moving vans, arc lights, and cameras—and a knot of people who seemed to be focused on one of the larger lawns. "People," Dixie said bitterly, braking. "Airplanes, weather. The light changes by two f-stops every thirty seconds. Noise. Crickets, for Christ's sake. Any of them can screw you up, force you to spend even more time with the actors. Give me a sound stage any day."

The wheels squealed against the curb, and we stopped. I threw open the door and climbed out, hot air slapping me in the chest. Dixie climbed out on his side, his face screwed up into a martyr's scowl. "The torture chamber," he said, indicating a van, larger than any of the others, that had MR. VANE painted on its side.

As we approached the set, the confusion began to resolve itself. Lights and big reflectors were angled to illuminate an area of brick walkway that led from the front door of a big wooden house down to the street. Bushes in tubs had been placed on either side of it to make the scene more lush. Two people I'd never seen before, a middle-aged woman and a gigantic male, came out of the open door, strolled down the walk, and paused there, doing nothing. Lights were focused on a black circle of paper hanging from the giant's neck. I saw Toby standing on the sidelines, arms crossed, looking sour and critical.

"Stand-ins," Dixie said. "They're lighting the shot."

"Who's Paul Bunyan standing in for?"

"Toby."

"That's the best you can do? He's twice Toby's height."

"That's John," Dixie said in a guarded voice. "That thing around his neck is where Toby's face will be. You want Toby, you get John. He's dumber than dirt, but Toby likes him."

"Hey, *Simeon*," someone called. A slim figure in blue jeans and a tank top came toward us, hugging a clipboard. As she neared she turned into Janie Gordon.

"What are you doing here?" she and I asked simultaneously.

Janie laughed, went onto tiptoe, and kissed me. "Working continuity," she said. "I've been on the show all year."

"How's your mom?"

It wasn't an idle question. Janie's mom was a seriously crazy lady who spent half her life driving away the people she loved and the other half trying to get them back. She'd hired me to bring Janie back, and I'd done it twice before we decided it wasn't doing anyone any good. We had more or less coerced her mother into therapy with an oily shrink who made his patients call him Howard, with the result that her mother had married and then divorced the therapist, and Janie had escaped into her own apartment. The last time I'd seen Janie, her mother was trying to get the therapist back.

"About a week away from Thorazine," Janie said. "Doctor Fine, that's the new one, and he's so ugly I don't worry about him, Dr. Fine is on vacation. She's at the stage where coffee gets her manic and she starts calling every fifteen minutes. That starts after the third cup, about ten-thirty. First thing I do when I get home every night is spend half an hour erasing everything on my answering machine. Jesus, you look great. When are you going to get old, anyway?"

"When I give up my bad habits. What's her complaint?"

"Guess. Nobody loves her. The world has forgotten her."

Janie rolled her eyes in an exact imitation of her mother. "She could have been a great actress if she hadn't given it all up for Daddy and me. Of course, she hadn't worked for years before she got married, but she doesn't remember that. And she sounds so alone."

"She's not alone," I said. "She's got Snuggie." Snuggie was a loathsome little fox terrier, the only dog I'd ever met who should have been born a cat.

"That's the problem. Snuggie ran away."

I tried not to laugh, but I couldn't help it. After a reproachful glance, Janie joined in. She put her hand on my arm and dropped her clipboard. "At least," she said between giggles, "she's forgotten about Howard." She bent down to pick up her clipboard, then snapped back up as someone gave her rear end a loud slap.

"Hey, champ," Toby said, letting his hand rest on the back of Janie's pants. He was grinning. "I see you've already met the beautiful Miss Somebody."

Janie dusted his hand off her rear and picked up the clipboard. She looked from Toby to me, and she wasn't laughing. "Don't catch anything," she said to me, "that you can't cure." Looking betrayed, she turned and walked quickly back toward the cameras.

"What a behind she's got on her," Toby said. "It's enough to make you believe in God. Almost. What happened to you last night?" The swelling on his lower lip had nearly subsided. His face was orange with makeup.

"I had to go someplace," I said.

"Hey," he said, throwing an arm around my shoulders and guiding me toward the set. "Don't wear yourself out apologizing. We could have had fun, you and your little bartender and Nana and me." He waved off a middle-aged woman who had materialized, autograph pad in hand. "Later, darling," he said. "Old Toby's working." He grinned at her sweetly and then turned to a beefy individual in a HIGH VELOCITY T-shirt who had apparently followed him. "Get that twat to the other side of the street." He was still grinning, but the steroid user jumped as though he'd been goosed with a cattle prod. The last I saw of the fan she was being hustled across the asphalt to the other side of the street.

"Did she want that autograph for herself?" he asked rhetorically. "No. It would have been for her cousin or her daughter or the milkman." His arm was heavy on my shoulders. "It's like asking for an autograph is admitting you're a retard, but tucked away somewhere in some low-rent dogshit house there's someone who's just dumb enough to want one. Still, they ask, and I suppose that's something."

We had reached the set, and people parted before us like the Red Sea in front of Moses. Toby plopped down into a canvas chair and stretched out his denim-clad legs. He was wearing lizard-skin boots. "A chair for my friend," he said, snapping his fingers in the direction of a nervous-looking girl wearing surplus-store military camouflage. Abashed that her cloak of invisibility hadn't worked, she scurried away and, seconds later, pressed a chair against the back of my legs. I sat, turning to smile thanks, but she was already in full retreat.

"So," Toby said, poking me with a finger. "You're mine now."

"Back off," I said. "Nobody bought me for you. I can go whenever I want."

"Okay," Toby said placidly. "You're on loan. Norman doesn't have a lot of good ideas, but this is one of them."

"You mean you like it? Why? I'd hate it."

"Nah. I can use a baby-sitter. Hell, I know that. I don't like to get into trouble, you know." He sounded as though trouble descended on him from the skies unexpectedly and at random. "And besides, I've got a piece of the syndication bucks. I sold my residuals to Norman for a couple million, but I've got a contingency if the loot tops forty."

A few yards away Janie Gordon glowered at us. I had

evidently gone over to the enemy's camp. I gave her a reassuring smile, but the effort involved muscles that seemed to have their roots in my hips, and she turned away. "You sold your residuals," I said to Toby. "What does that mean?"

"I keep forgetting you don't know anything," Toby said, fiddling with an expensive-looking watch. "Residuals are something that drudges like Norman pay us actors every time this crap gets boosted back onto the airwaves. My paycheck only covers the first two times. After that, some-one has to send me a little check, whether it's a network rerun or some dinky station in Crooked Elbow, Montana. It takes a lot of little checks to make two million, and it means I've always got to be looking at someone's books to make sure they're staying straight, which nobody does, least of all the Normans. That part you probably know about."

"For all that money," I said, "why don't you just put your hands in your pockets and keep them there? Why not buy big soft boxing gloves and punch out the swimsuit edition of *Sports Illustrated*?"

He shifted in his chair. "I've gotta work in a second."

"Fine," I said. "Duck it. Maybe, if you're lucky, the girls will duck, too."

"Don't be dumb," he said, sounding as comfortable as a man who was having his prostate probed. "It's not all that easy. Christ, if it was . . ."

The girl in camouflage cleared her throat behind him. "Ready, Mr. Vane," she said.

"And just in time," Toby said, getting up. "We were on the verge of a lovers' quarrel. Have I ever told you how pretty you are?" The girl laughed uneasily and led him up the walk and into the light. Toby's enormous stand-in came over and flopped into the chair Toby had vacated. I could feel him staring at me. The middle-aged woman stayed put as Toby joined her; I guessed she wasn't important enough to have a stand-in. With Toby in the shot, people all over the place snapped to attention, donning earphones, moving behind cameras, manipulating boom mikes. I started to get up, and a massive hand fell onto my forearm. I looked over into a pair of vacant blue eyes.

"Who are you," Toby's stand-in asked tonelessly. Up close, he looked even bigger.

"Well, hi," I said, trying to move my arm. No deal. He waited, the weight of his hand bearing down on me, giving me the patient gaze of someone for whom things have to be taken in order. "Um," I said, "I'm Simeon."

Right answer. He thought it over for a moment and then smiled. "I'm John," he said.

"Toby's friend," I said, probably more slowly than was necessary. His smile broadened, but that was it. "I'm Toby's friend, too," I heard myself saying as I eased my arm free. John nodded, smile frozen in place. It looked like it would be there for some time. That seemed to be the end of the conversation. I smiled back, got up, and strolled in the direction of Dixie's car. A little cold spot on the back of my neck told me that John's eyes were following me.

Lights snapped on all over the set. Across the street the crowd of onlookers surged forward expectantly. This was what they'd been waiting for. The middle-aged woman with the autograph book was right up front, staring at Toby and the actress as though the Second Coming, long overdue, had finally clambered down the steps and off the plane.

"So what the hell are you *doing* here, Simeon?" It was Janie, clipboard firmly in place against her slender waist.

"Experiencing the pangs of guilt," I said. "Are we allowed to talk now? Aren't they shooting or something?"

"No way. They'll rehearse it two or three times. For her, not for him. He always knows his lines."

"One-take Toby," I said.

"Well, well," she said acidly, "that proves it. There's something nice you can say about everyone. So you're his new buddy? What do you guys do for fun, tag-team matches against Girl Scouts?"

"Sure. In between rounds we go out and molest plants. Who's this?"

Janie turned to see a dusty Chevy station wagon pull in behind Dixie's Mercedes. A youngish woman got out. She could have been anywhere between her late twenties and her early forties, pretty in an exhausted way, her small face framed by a fluffy, outdated hairdo that fringed inward below her high cheekbones, below the dark circles that seemed to hold her eyes in place. Her clothes were determinedly young, a frilly blouse and a short skirt with a wide belt. Over her left breast was a large teddy bear pin that might have been made out of bread dough or hardened library paste, the kind of jewelry that got front-page placement in catalogs targeted to elementary-school teachers. A lanky man in a dark green shirt climbed out from the passenger side and opened the back. He began to pull out an array of photographic equipment.

"It's the fannies," Janie said, giving up on hostility for the moment.

"Fannies?"

"Come on, Simeon. Fannies as in fan magazines. Fan as in fantasy, fantasy pipelines for adolescent girls. Toby's constituency, right? The chenille downside of the American dream."

"Janie," I said, "what the hell are you doing here?"

"I asked you first." The hostility was back in full force, and she hugged the clipboard against her like a bulletproof shield.

"I'm Toby's watchdog," I said. "I'm supposed to protect the world from him. And it pays well."

"Yow," she said, avoiding my eyes, "you're messing with my ideals. Mommy was paying you, and you didn't have a nickel. You still helped me instead of her." She dug the toe of her boot into some inoffensive dirt and punted it past me.

"Sheesh," I said, replying to her yow, "there are the girls."

"Which girls?"

"The ones he'll beat up if I don't stop him."

"Yeah," Janie said. It was pretty halfhearted.

"Has he fooled with you?" Behind her the photographer in the green shirt was setting up a big wooden camera on a tripod and a complicated arrangement of iron pipes under the direction of the tired-looking young woman. He tugged a cord, and a roll of seamless blue paper dropped to the ground from the crossbar at the top of the pipes.

"Nothing I can't handle," Janie said. "The occasional hand on the fanny, like you saw today. He tried to feel me up once when we were on the sound stage."

"How many of his balls did you collect?"

She smiled for the first time in what seemed like days. "None. But I stomped his foot."

"And he did what?"

"Yanked my hair. I told him if he laid a finger on me, I'd take his eyes out. Meant it, too. He backed off and said something about chicks having no sense of humor."

"He didn't get you fired, obviously."

"No, Simeon, that's the funny thing. He's like a little kid. After he's bad to someone he gets really contrite. He brought me a Danish."

"Conscience?"

"*Toby?* His conscience must be smaller than Medusa's G-spot. Listen, he's twisted. It's just the way the man is."

"Well," I said, "he's my baby."

Back on the set the baby shouted something that sounded angry and impatient. The actress stepped back quickly, like someone expecting a raw fish across the face, and there was a general scurrying behind the cameras as people ducked into position. New banks of lights snapped on, and Toby and the actress came down the walk, the actress looking professionally apprehensive and Toby looking genuinely sympathetic. They paused in the hot spot of light and passed some dialogue back and forth, and then Toby patted the woman on the shoulder, gave her his most dazzling smile, and sprinted down the walkway to a long, low black vehicle I hadn't paid attention to before, something that was both high-tech and anthropomorphic, like a cross between a torpedo and My Mother, the Car. He opened the door, looked back over his shoulder, and then climbed back up the walkway while people frantically reangled lights and the camera was moved. Someone else closed the door of the vehicle, using a cloth so he wouldn't mar the shine. Toby reached out and almost touched the camera lens and then drew his hand back until his finger touched the tip of his nose. The cameraman nodded.

"His close-up," Janie said. "Here comes art."

There was a brief delay while the reflectors were brought around, and Toby snapped his fingers impatiently and said something unpleasant to the woman. "He's telling them to get their asses in gear," Janie said, watching. She glanced back over to the people behind the rope across the street. "He really hates standing out here with all these yokels staring at him."

"Then he should have been a plumber."

"He is," she said. "He's an emotional Roto-Rooter."

As they arranged things for Toby's close-up, Dixie Cohen joined the tired-looking woman and the photographer. The woman was smoking a very long cigarette, and Dixie looked worried. The photographer took refuge under a long black cloth that covered the top of his camera and motioned Dixie into camera range in front of the blue roll of paper. Dixie stood there dolefully, the world's least likely stand-in for Toby Vane. Meanwhile, up on the walkway, the real action had recommenced.

Toby and the actress came back down, found the light, and Toby traded in his sympathetic expression for a million-dollar grin. This time he squeezed the woman's arm reassuringly before jogging on down to the torpedo. Then, leaving the car door open again, he waved off the efforts of the director to bring him back and came toward us as the entire group around the cameras stared after him. One at a time, the lights went off. The actress stood there, looking lost.

"That's enough of that," Toby said as he joined us. "You'd think it was something worth watching. Stunt double's next, right, sweetheart?" he said to Janie.

Janie glanced at her clipboard, but by the time she looked up again, Toby was already gone. "Right," she said anyway. "You asshole." She looked up at me almost guiltily. "A girl's got to express herself," she said.

Toby reached the forlorn little band gathered in front of the roll of blue paper. He put his arm around Dixie's neck, clowning for the still camera. Dixie tried to pull away and then submitted in a resigned fashion. He even smiled. It was the complicated smile of a confirmed pessimist who's just been proven right by being sentenced to death. The big stand-in, John, had ambled over. He stood there, loose-jointed, watching.

"Hey, champ," Toby called to me. "Come over here and meet some people."

"His master's voice," Janie mumbled.

"Ease up, okay?" I said. "I'd like it if we could stay friends."

"Champ," Toby said. "We're being a little rude here."

"Go to it, champ," Janie said. Feeling like the Incredible Shrinking Man, I went over to Toby, who had slipped an arm around the youngish woman's waist.

"My man," Toby said, daring me to contradict him, "this is the extraordinary Betsi, with an *i*. Betsi with an *i* is the photo editor of one of America's favorite magazines, a magazine you probably read every day of your life. And this is, um, this is Betsi's photographer."

"Bert," said the lanky man behind the camera.

"Who said that?" Toby asked. "Do I need to be told the photographer's name? Bert here is my favorite photographer, champ. I asked for old Bert, didn't I, Betsi?"

"Sure, Toby," Betsi said mechanically. "You always ask for Bert."

"Always," Toby said, "unless I ask for someone else." He pinched the skin beneath Betsi's blouse. "Simeon here is supposed to keep me out of trouble. What the hell? *Somebody* has to do it."

"And good luck to both of us," I said.

"So what do we want here, Bets?" Toby turned his attention to her. "The usual head-and-hunk shots, or something special? And where's the mirror?"

"In the car," Betsi said. "Bert—"

"Not going to do anyone much good in the car, is it?" Toby said. "Are you busy or something, Bert?"

Bert scurried off to the station wagon and came back lugging a full-length mirror, which he set up behind the camera.

"*There* I am," Toby said, passing a hand over his hair. "Let's go. Forty minutes, no more. These clothes okay?"

"Fabulous," Betsi said a little nervously. "Couldn't be better."

"Does the film have to age or something?" Toby impatiently asked Bert. Bert ducked his head under the cloth draped over the back of the camera and went to work.

For the next fifteen minutes or so I got a crash course in star making. Toby worked the camera as though it were a long-distance telephone line over which he was talking to a wife he'd been deceiving for months. He teased it, flirted with it, arched his brows at it, gave it the smile of the century. Before every shot he checked the mirror. Bert's head never emerged from the black cloth. The people across the street edged closer, and Betsi lit one cigarette off another, stubbing out the old ones against her shoe with ravaged-cuticle fingers. Dixie stood uselessly on the sidelines, now and then asking Toby to check his hair in the mirror. Big John just watched silently, his mouth hanging open and his hands opening and closing on air.

Bert emerged from the black cloth like a Muslim woman renouncing the veil. He looked up at the sky, checking the light, and said, "That's enough heads." He pulled the camera back three or four feet.

"Toby," Betsi said, "we're going three-quarters now. Can you give us some profiles?"

"Which side?" Toby took a quick look at the mirror, giving a quick tug at the skin on either side of his eyes.

"Up to you," Betsi said.

Janie spoke from behind me. "At least twenty minutes," she said.

"I asked you which side," Toby said to Betsi as if Janie didn't exist.

"Really, Toby, it doesn't matter. You're the boss."

"But you're the genius, darling. Come on, just pick your favorite side of old Toby."

Betsi looked flustered. Then she took a vehement drag on her cigarette and said, "Left."

"*Left?*" Toby's eyes widened in surprise. "What's the matter with you today, Betsi? You want to shoot my left side?"

"Okay, okay, then, the right." Betsi was blushing deeply now and fiddling with the teddy bear pin. Bert had stepped away from the camera, staring down at the grass as if it hadn't been there a minute ago.

"Watch this," Janie whispered. "It may be educational."

"Just a fucking minute," Toby said to Betsi. "There's a principle here. I'm giving you this session because you need it, right? And I expect a little protection in return."

"Left," Betsi said desperately. "Wait, I mean right."

"Do you see this lip?" Toby demanded, tugging at the swelling. "Courtesy of my buddy Simeon, here, I might add. You donate your contact lenses to Greenpeace or something? Shit, if you can't see *that*, how do I know you can see the best shots? How do I know this isn't going to turn up in the *Enquirer*?" He framed a headline with his hands. "TOBY VANE GETS TRASHED AT LAST. I've got a little puffiness here, to put it charitably. What're you going to do, Bets, put it on the cover?"

"Toby," Betsi said desperately, "you know I'd never print a bad shot of you."

"Yeah, right. And I promise I'll pull out in time. The check is in the mail." The photographer had stepped back up to the camera and pulled the black cloth over his head to work on focus. "Just a minute, you—Bert—you, whoever you are. We shoot when I'm ready and not before."

"I'm sorry," Betsi said. "I'm double sorry. It's just that you look so *good* right now. . . ."

"I look like fucking Rocky Graziano," Toby said.

"No, no, we'll only get the right side. Only the right three-quarters, right, Bert? Only the right, okay, Toby?" She sounded as though she had something caught in her throat.

"Okay, okay, okay," Toby parroted. "You sound like a machine gun. You know what? You used to be prettier."

"Toby," Dixie said, "the public is here."

Toby looked at Betsi for a long moment and then turned toward the crowd of onlookers and made the thumbs-up sign. People clapped. Toby's grin broadened, and he still had it in place when he looked down at Betsi.

"Honey," he said, "I'm tired of these clothes."

Janie whispered something that sounded like "Shit."

Betsi swallowed. "You look great, Toby. You always look so nice."

"Not as nice as when you help. Come on, Betsi. You know how much I like your taste." He made it sound truly disgusting.

"I can't," Betsi said. "Please, Toby, not today."

"It's either that or no more watch the birdie. And with this puffiness, I may have to kill the whole session."

Betsi glanced around jerkily, as if she hoped no one was listening. She looked drawn and five years older. She picked up her cigarettes and pulled one out. Her hand was shaking.

"Now come on, Betsi," Toby said. "Even you can only suck on one thing at a time." He put his arm around her and led her to the trailer. The unlit cigarette dangled forgotten from her fingers. Bert managed to look very busy. At the door to the trailer, Toby waved at the crowd and said, "Be right back, folks." They went in, and Big John took up a stance in front of the door, his arms crossed like an Arabian genie who wanted to keep his hands near his scimitar.

"Congratulations, hero," Janie said.

My mouth tasted foul. "What happens now?"

"You want my best guess?"

"I suppose so."

"He makes her go down on him. He pulls her hair a few times to keep him interested. Then he makes her swallow it."

"There's nothing she can do?"

"Sure, she can get her pictures. No pictures, no job."

"This is what you meant when you said he had something to look forward to today?" I asked Dixie.

Dixie didn't look at me. "She's been around a while," he muttered.

"There are worse things than no job," I said to Janie.

"Simeon, she's been working for the fannies for seven years. Where do you go from there, CBS News? It's not like it was really journalism."

"Point taken," I said. "Screw it anyway."

I headed toward the door of the trailer. Big John shifted on the balls of his feet as I approached and uncrossed his arms. He looked vaguely alarmed.

"John," I said, "beat it."

"You," John said. A lot of people seemed to be calling me "you." "You beat it."

"In a minute." I moved to the left and then sidestepped around him to the right, hearing him grunt as he grabbed at where I'd been. My hand was on the doorknob when his arm went around my throat. He hoisted me like an empty nylon suitcase, bent my spine nearly double, and dumped me over his hip. I landed in the dirt at his feet.

"Get out of the way, John," I said, flat on my back. My words didn't seem as menacing as I'd meant them to be.

"Hnuh," he said. It could have been a laugh. He leaned down over me. I grabbed a bunch of pebbles and dirt and threw them at him and heard them ricochet against the trailer. John grabbed my belt buckle and tugged me up like a sack of rice, and Dixie's pale hand landed on his shoulder.

"Stop it," Dixie hissed at both of us. There wasn't much I could stop, but John dropped me back into the dirt and resumed his guardianship of the door. "Get up," Dixie said to me. "For Christ's sake, there are *people* over there. This isn't what Norman is paying you to do."

"It isn't?" I got up and dusted my trousers. My heart was drumming wildly in my throat. "Then what *am* I supposed to be doing, Dixie?"

"Not getting into the papers," Dixie said, looking wildly to right and left as though he expected the Associated Press to emerge from the bushes, cameras flashing. "There could be leaks here. She'll be okay, honest."

I looked at John, who was glaring at me, and then back at Dixie. "You want to change places with her?" I asked him. I started back toward John, who gave me a low-wattage grin.

"Do you want me to ask her?" Dixie demanded.

"Yeah, Dixie," I said, trying without much success to grin back at John. "Let's see you ask her."

Dixie gave me a schoolteacher's upraised index finger. "Stay here," he said. He advanced toward the door. "John," he said in an entirely different tone, "it's just me. I'm going to knock on the door. It'll be okay, John."

John looked from Dixie to me and then stepped aside as Dixie climbed the step and knocked. "Betsi," he said.

I used the moment to bend down and pick up some more pebbles and dirt, lobbing them at the trailer. If nothing else, I figured, the noise might scramble Toby's hormones. Dixie turned to glare at me, and the door opened from inside. Betsi peered out, her hair awry.

"Betsi," Dixie said as though he were talking to the mentally disadvantaged, "do you want to come out?"

She looked at him and then through him, and I took a step, and she looked at me and through me. She made a sound like a strangled garden hose and closed the door.

"Okay?" Dixie asked me.

"Dixie," I said, craning past John, "how do you sleep?" Three large men from the crew had materialized next to John.

Dixie's features got very pinched, squeezed from both sides by a vise I couldn't see. "Welcome to Hollywood," he said. He stepped around John and walked past me, and I glanced at John and his new allies and calculated my chances twice. Both times they came up nil.

I looked at Big John and at the closed door of the trailer that said TOBY VANE on it. "Jesus Christ," I said to Janie. "Has he always been like this?"

"Not exactly," Janie said. "Most stars start out nice and then get awful. But not our Toby. He started out awful and then got monstrous."

"But what's going to happen? He can't go on like this."

"Sure he can," she said. "He's a star, remember?" Someone called her, and she walked back to the set. I stood there watching the trailer. There didn't seem to be anything to say.

Janie was right about Toby. When, ten minutes later, he emerged from the trailer with a flushed and shaken-looking Betsi behind him, he was a different man. He didn't meet anyone's eyes, and he never glanced in my direction. After he finished giving Betsi her pictures, he went over to the crowd to sign autographs. He honored the middle-aged woman who had approached him earlier. He posed for a picture, kissing a little girl of three or four in her mother's arms. For the rest of the day, until the light faded and the shoot ended, he was a model of docility.

As they packed up the equipment, Toby went back into his trailer. I checked the set for Dixie but couldn't find him. His Mercedes was gone. I was walking back, looking for Janie, when Toby came out of the trailer.

"Champ," he said. He sounded tentative, like a kid trying to make friends.

"I quit, Toby."

He stood silent for a moment. "Please don't," he finally said.

"Betsi said please," I said. "Remember?"

He drew a hand across his eyes and then ran it through his hair. He looked forty. "Help me," he said.

"You don't need a detective, Toby. You need a doctor."

"I've had doctors. I've had doctors up the wazoo. Stay with me, Simeon, just for the next week or two. I promise, I'll be good. You can help me to be good. I'll even see another shrink if you want."

I thought about Betsi. I thought about Nana. I thought about Norman Stillman's check in my pocket. I thought about the rent, for about the sixth time that week, and I gave up.

"Oh, Christ, Toby," I said. "If I stick around, what are you going to do?"

"You mean tonight?"

"That'll do for a start."

He threw his arm around my shoulders, as though everything were settled at last. "Let's go to the Spice Rack," he said. "Let's go be nice to Nana."

4

The Spice Rack

MY KNEES WERE up somewhere around my chin, and my heart was competing with a hamburger for space in my throat. Toby drove even worse than Dixie said he did.

The roof of the Maserati was about four feet above road level. The console looked like a transplant from the space shuttle. Toby used both hands and both feet constantly just to keep us on the road, which, unfortunately for my peace of mind, was Laurel Canyon.

"Got your belt on?" he asked, taking a sharp downhill curve on two wheels. The burger, to which Toby had graciously treated me at a McDonald's, was refusing to obey the laws of gravity.

"Are you kidding? I'd have yours on, too, if I could get to it."

"Good. Because I can feel that load coming on."

This piece of news, added to the burger and my heart, was too much to swallow. "Toby," I said, "tell me that's a joke."

"In the trailer," he said. "Jesus, champ, I've been straight as a string all day."

"I wouldn't go that far," I said, looking for something to hold on to.

He popped the clutch and downshifted, keeping his eyes on the road. "That wasn't dope," he said finally, sounding uncomfortable. "That was just old Toby."

"You want to tell me why you did it?"

"I don't know. She just got me so damn mad. Whatever you think about my face, it's my only valid ticket. The wrong picture, even on the cover of *Baby-Kiss* or whatever it is—that's serious."

"Horsefeathers. You set it up."

The road straightened again, and he pressed down on the accelerator. "If I were you, champ," he said, "I'd let me concentrate on driving."

"You didn't answer my question."

"I don't know how to answer it. Listen, I like women, I really do. I always want them to be different, and they never are. They always say something stupid or fuck up in one way or another, and then it happens."

"What happens?"

"Yaaa, yaaa, yaaa," he said. "Something. Like pressure in my head, like, I don't know, like a headache, and my jaws get all stiff and tight, and then I want to break things. Why am I telling you this?"

"Because you like to talk about yourself."

"Boy, are you wrong there. I'd rather get a rabies shot."

"And when you hurt somebody, the feeling goes away."

He pulled up at a stoplight. Sunset Boulevard. He gunned the motor once, looking down at the tachometer. He examined his wristwatch as though it had just appeared on his wrist through spontaneous generation. He checked the fuel level and wiped a speck of dust off the glass on the gauge.

"Would you like to clean the ashtrays?" I asked. "Maybe get out and polish the car?"

"The sun comes out," he said brutally. "There are double fucking rainbows in the sky. For about two minutes. Then I start to feel like shit. But at least I'm not mad anymore. Haven't you ever hit a woman?"

"No. What was your life like at home?"

"I don't talk about home," he said.

"Why not?"

"What's to say? I was born, I grew up, I left. Same as everybody else."

"Go out and get dirty, go in and get clean."

"Say what?"

"According to a friend of mine, that's life in ten words."

We were speeding down Sunset now, and the sun was all the way down. Toby's face looked green in the glow from the Maserati's console.

"That's not bad," he said. "Except that sometimes you can get dirty when you're inside, too."

"Depends, doesn't it?"

"Don't moralize. You don't know me well enough. That's not what I need from you."

"So what do you think you need from me?"

"Protection."

"From whom, Toby?"

"Whom, whom," he said. "I'd have said, 'From who?'"
He changed lanes and sped up. "Whom, whom, whom," he said, pushing down on the accelerator each time.

"Increasing your word power?"

"I'm a car," he said. "I'm also getting pretty loaded."

"So why did you leave?" I asked, checking my seat belt for the fifth or sixth time.

"We're going to talk about this, huh?"

"Unless you want to say good-bye to me whenever we get where we're going."

"I wouldn't use that one too often, if I were you."

"I won't. That was the last time."

He navigated a couple of turns. "Who wouldn't leave? You ever been to South Dakota?"

"No."

"Keep it that way. It's a good place to leave."

"What's wrong with it?"

At first I thought he wasn't going to answer me. "To me, South Dakota just means cold," he said at last. "And clothesline."

"Clothesline? Why clothesline?"

"There are lots of reasons. The one I'll tell you about has to do with cold. Ever heard of a white-out?"

"Something to do with snow."

"Champ, it's *everything* to do with snow. In a white-out you can't see anything, not three feet in front of you. So I was supposed to string the clothesline from the house to the barn and to the garage and back again. Like a big ropy spiderweb."

We pulled up at the corner of Sunset and Doheny. A sudden squeal to our left caught my attention. A beat-up convertible with three teenage girls crowded into the front seat had pulled up next to us, and the girls were gawking and squealing and flapping their hands at Toby. They looked ecstatic. Toby smiled and gave them an extravagant wave and then made a sudden right-hand turn down Doheny to get away from them. "Dumb bitches," he said. "Did you see their faces?"

"That's your public," I said. "The clothesline."

"Wind-chill factor," he said, sounding grumpy. "It gets down to fifty or sixty below zero. Honest, champ, you can get killed in a white-out just going out to start your car. So you go hand over hand along the clothesline, like a blind person, feeling your way through the freeze and hoping your nose won't break off if you bump into the garage. Great way to start the morning."

A stoplight went yellow in front of us, and a car popped into the intersection from the right. Toby leaned on the horn and fishtailed the Maserati in front of the other car, heading left on Santa Monica. Brakes squealed behind us. "And one day Hollywood beckoned," Toby said with an air of finality. "Hollywood said, 'Come on out, Toby, and be a big star. Come on out and get warm.' "

"And that's the end of the story."

"Must be all that college," he said. "You don't get that smart on the street." He hummed something that sounded like "Camptown Races" and confirmed it by singing, " 'Doodah, doodah.' What's a bobtailed nag?"

"A horse with its tail bobbed."

"There's nothing like education. You keep talking about quitting. Is that on the level?"

"Yes."

"You really think you could give Norman his check back?"

"What do you know about Norman's check?"

"Are you kidding? Half of it comes out of my share of the syndication rights."

"To you it's small change," I said.

"Ho, ho, Simeon. Small change? Ten grand will get me through Bullock's in an afternoon. It'll pay for a lot of girls if the time ever comes when I need to pay for girls."

"Norman told you your half was ten grand?" I had a sudden insight into Hollywood bookkeeping.

"It's worth it to me," Toby said virtuously. "You still don't understand, do you? You still think I like to act the way I do."

"Toby," I said, "I'm tired. You don't want to talk to me about anything that matters, and I'm not going to waste my energy doing dime-store psychology on you."

"I don't need a psychologist," Toby said. "I need a friend."

I couldn't come up with anything to say, so I said the wrong thing. "That's the load talking."

"You think so?" He sounded stung.

"Toby, I don't know. I like part of you, too. Maybe it's just that I can't figure out whether it's the part that's named Toby Vane or the part that's named Jack Sprunk."

"They both suck," Toby said petulantly. "Here we are."

I couldn't see that we were much of anywhere. The block was an indiscriminate string of pizza parlors, furniture show-rooms, office equipment stores, and little "showcase" the-aters offering pay-for-play wish fulfillment to aspiring actors. And then, on the right, in hot pink neon I saw the words

SPICE RACK. Above that, printed in black on a yellow background was the legend LIVE NUDES. The letters were about six feet high.

"I love that," Toby said. "I always wonder what's the next hot ticket. Dead nudes?"

"This is where Nana works?"

"Sure. What did you think she was? A research chemist?"

We passed the Spice Rack and turned right into a little street and then right again into an alley. Toby pulled the Maserati into an empty parking space and leaned back, closing his eyes. "Made it," he said.

A minute loped by. I messed around with my door, looking for anything that resembled a handle. "Are we going to get out, or what?"

He opened his eyes and looked around. "Just hold on. Got to get a little riper." Reaching back into the pocket of his leather jeans, he produced a little jar with a black plastic top, unscrewed it, and poured a little of it onto the back of his left hand. "Want some?" His hands were shaking slightly.

"What is it?"

"Same old pink coke. Best there is, remember?"

"No, thanks," I said.

"More for me, then." He raised the back of his hand to his nose, sniffed sharply, and then repeated the ritual. "IQ on the rise," he said.

"Toby," I said, "you do the loads to slow down and the coke to speed up. Why don't you just stay in the middle?"

He regarded me gravely. "That's the first stupid thing I ever heard you say. This stuff is going to make me very popular tonight. Out we go, champ." He opened his door and climbed out. I was still fiddling with my seat belt when he opened my door from the outside and made a courtly bow. "After you, madame," he said.

"How the hell do you get out of this thing?"

"Professional secret," he said. "Comes in handy sometimes." I got out and closed the door behind me, and the car barked at me. I jumped.

"What was that?"

"The car. It's half Maserati and half Doberman." He'd almost reached the building's back door. "Remote alarm. I just push a button and the thing's on red alert. Jesus, this is *some* cocaine."

He went up a couple of steps and knocked heavily, first three times and then, after a beat, two more times. "Private entrance," he said over his shoulder. "Secret code. Real Hardy Boys stuff."

He waited, and I caught up with him. "Why the Spice Rack?"

"Used to be a restaurant, and neon's expensive. Tiny just gave all the girls spice names." As he was speaking the door opened about four inches, and a blast of music shredded the night. "Hey, Tiny," Toby said, producing the magazine-cover grin.

The door opened the rest of the way. The man called Tiny was sallow and coarse-featured, with oily black hair and thick, loose lips. His clothing, a white safari shirt and white pleated slacks, encased a body that must have weighed three hundred and fifty pounds. He ignored me, grimaced in welcome at Toby, and held the door wide. Toby went in. I followed, squeezing past Tiny's barrel of a belly, into a narrow hallway. "How's business?" Toby asked.

Tiny shrugged before I was completely by him. It was like surfing on an ocean of fat. "The recession," he said in a voice that sounded like several tons of gravel rolling downhill inside a steel drum. "Everybody's hurting."

"It'll pick up," Toby said. "Even poor people like girls."

"Go in and tip somebody," Tiny said, ignoring the offer of comfort. "These jack-offs have never heard of money, or if they have, they don't believe in it." He closed the door behind us, and even over the music I could hear the clatter of locks being forced into place.

Entering the Spice Rack through that hallway, I felt like Gepetto sliding down the whale's throat. The walls and ceiling were covered with a thick red paint with flecks of glitter mixed into it, something a serial killer might choose for his Christmas cards. Toby opened the door, and the music, already loud, exploded into the corridor.

Nothing remained to suggest the restaurant the Spice Rack had once been. The linen-clad tables and large bouquets of this month's fashionable flowers had been cleared away to make room for three stages, each raised about a yard off the floor. One of them was dark. Customers sat around the other two, working slowly on their drinks and staring at girls who were writhing around under pink and amber lights. One of the girls was wearing a ragged feather boa and cut-off jeans, and the other was completely naked. The naked one was lying on her back on the floor of the stage, doing gymnastic exercises that consisted mainly of lifting both knees to her chin. As if the girls on the stage weren't enough, nudes painted on black velvet hung in heavy museum frames on the walls.

Toby pulled out two chairs by the side of the other stage and plopped down. The blonde in the feather boa was cradling her breasts in her hand and paying special attention to customers who had put a buck or two onto the stage. She looked bored.

"Toby," I yelled over the music as I sat next to him, "are you sure we want to be here?"

"Of course," Toby said. "Don't you want to see Nana?"

"This is the kind of place I'm supposed to be keeping you out of."

"No prob," Toby said. "That's why the back door and the code. Tiny takes care of me."

A blond girl wearing a transparent, thigh-length negligee, a G-string, and about thirty-seven bracelets, gave Toby a peck on the cheek. "Hi, heartthrob," she said. "The usual?"

"Sure, Pepper. A Seven-Up from my private stock, and the same for my friend here." He winked at her, and she made little kiss lips and headed for the bar. The G-string disappeared completely between her buttocks. They were buttocks to remember.

"Pepper?" I said.

"Like I told you, all the girls are spices. This is Saffron on the stage here. The naked one is Clove." He put a ten on the counter, and Saffron shuffled over and did the breast-cupping act. By now they were tucked under her chin.

"How you doin', Tobe?" she said.

"Holding on. You're looking good."

"I'd better," Saffron said, "or I'll be sitting on the side-walk. Tiny's got the rag on."

Toby looked nervous. "Does he?"

"And how. Nobody's tipping, and they're making their drinks last until their birthdays. What a bunch of stiffs."

"You wish," Toby said. "Go make them rise to the occasion."

Saffron picked up the ten quickly, as though she were afraid it might disappear, and danced away in a leisurely fashion, focusing her charms on an embarrassed-looking Chicano with two crumpled dollar bills on the counter in front of him.

"This must be someone's idea of fun," I said.

"Loosen up, champ. You want to die before you even get tired? Here's the gorgeous Pepper."

Pepper put a tall glass in front of each of us, her brace-lets jangling. Toby gave her a tightly folded twenty and said, "Keep the change. Not much happening, is there?"

"I've had a bigger time in a library," Pepper said, slip-ping the twenty into the front of her G-string. "Who's your sweet little friend?"

"This is Simeon," Toby said. "He's my baby-sitter."

"He's a baby himself," Pepper said. "Jesus, what'd you do to Nana? Is she ever pissed off."

"Not for long. I've got some pink, Pepper."

"Darling," Pepper said, brightening visibly. "I think I have to go to the little girls' room."

"It's in the twenty," Toby said. "Don't hog it. I see a lot of hungry noses."

"My sisters will get theirs," Pepper said, "don't worry. Nice to meet you, Simeon." Her beautiful bottom twinkled at us as she headed for nostril heaven in the ladies' room. I picked up my 7-Up and took a big swallow. Then I began to cough, and it felt as though several pounds of steam were billowing out of my ears.

"Careful, champ," Toby said. "That's straight vodka."

"Thanks for the warning," I said, my eyes watering. "How come it's disguised as Seven-Up?"

"They can't serve liquor because the girls take their pants off. Go figure. Like I said, private stock for regular customers."

I blinked back tears and became aware that the music had ended. There was a scattering of applause. Saffron climbed down from the stage. The girl who had been dancing on the other stage blew a sarcastic kiss at the customers and then walked across the club, elegantly and carelessly naked, to disappear behind the same crimson curtain that Saffron had lifted only moments before.

"If they made twenty each, they're lucky," Toby said.

His voice sounded abnormally loud. We were the only ones in the place who were talking. All the other customers sat staring at their drinks or at the counter in front of them. I realized for the first time that there was an empty chair separating each customer from his neighbor. Chair, customer, chair, customer. Except for three Asian men, an obvious group, no two men were seated together. No one had looked at Toby for the simple reason that no one had looked at anyone.

"What do you care how much they make?" I took a careful swig of vodka. It tasted better this time.

"Who says I care?" he asked belligerently and altogether too loudly. "They dance, they should get paid. You think I'd do what I do for free? Where's Pepper, anyway?"

The music drowned out my reply, whatever it was. Then I forgot what I'd been going to say and leaned forward to watch.

It took me a few bars to recognize the song, even though the Kinks had been my favorite band for years. I was too preoccupied. Then Ray Davies began to sing, and I placed it.

Look at that lady dancing round with no clothes,
She'll show you all her body, that's if you got the dough.
She'll let you see most anything, but there's one thing that
she'll never show.
And that's a little bit of real emotion. . . .

Saffron came back onto the stage. She was wearing nothing at all, but I was watching the other stage. The girl on it was Nana.

"And on the small stage," said a fat Tiny clone seated next to the entrance, "is our bit of spice from the Far East. Let's bring both hands above the table and have a big round of soy sauce for the lovely Cinnamon." Three men clapped.

"A little bit of real emotion," Ray Davies sang. "In case a bit of real emotion should give her away."

"Nana's first song," Toby said. "She always uses it. She thinks no one gets it."

"Maybe nobody does," I said, looking at the customers. Most of them had their mouths open.

Nana was almost fatally beautiful. Her T-shirt, slashed strategically here and there, ended a good ten inches above a pair of crimson hot pants that stopped just this side of the melting point of platinum. Her hair had been teased into a lioness's mane. She had sprayed her body with droplets of water. She looked like a feral animal mistakenly rereleased into polite society.

Saffron did whatever she did, but it was wasted effort. Even the men around our stage—*her* stage—were watching Nana, or Cinnamon, or whatever her name was. If Nana had been wearing a tuxedo, an overcoat, a scarf, and a pair of hip-high wading boots, eighty men out of a hundred would have been watching her, no matter how naked Saffron was.

"Maybe there *is* a God," Toby said. He didn't sound like he was kidding. For a couple of minutes we sat there like everyone else, staring at Nana.

The song ended and Saffron picked up her tips, including another ten from Toby. Nana had already disappeared behind the crimson curtain that obviously led to the dressing room. Saffron worked her way clockwise, grabbing a dollar bill here and a five there. One customer, vaguely Middle Eastern-looking, tried to snatch back a few of the ones he had laid on the counter. Saffron kicked at the stage with her spike heels, and he gave up. She picked up the money and laughed.

"Golly," she said. "Thanks, Ahmed."

"Toby," said a gravelly voice. "Let's you and me talk."

It was Tiny, looming white and mountainous above us. Toby looked at me apologetically.

"Time to go," Toby said. "Have a good time, Simeon. Tip the girls with Norman's money." He got up and patted Tiny on the arm. "Lost some weight, Tiny? Six months from now you'll be wearing Yves St. Laurent."

"Eve who?" Tiny rumbled.

"New girl," Toby said. "Dancing at the Kama Sutra, up on Sunset."

"I don't need girls. I need customers." He hauled Toby toward the back of the club.

The music started again, anonymous heavy metal from a band whose idea of a good time was probably rusty iron spikes on the inside of their underwear. The intellectual theme of the song seemed to be "Get down and crawl."

Crawling was exactly what Nana was doing on the other stage. Wearing nothing now but the hot pants, she moved on her hands and knees, arching her back, tossing her mane, and hissing like a cat. The lurid pink light caught her high cheekbones and defined the fine, straight gully of her spine. I realized that I was definitely interested.

In fact, I was *so* interested that I didn't notice the new-comer on my stage until she lifted a foot and whacked the counter in front of me to get my attention. Snatched away from the vision of Nana, I looked up and then tried, without much success, to turn a cringe into a smile.

At about five two, she couldn't have weighed more than eighty pounds. Her face was tight and drawn, every muscle standing out in sharp, grieved relief. She was wearing more eyeliner than all the Egyptian queens in the Metropolitan Museum of Art put together, but it couldn't mask the infinite weariness in her eyes, the eyes of an ancient lizard glutted on spiders and flies. She wore a silk camisole over her bones, leopard-spotted panties, and elbow-length formal gloves. Her dancing consisted of shifting from foot to foot listlessly in front of me, her ravaged eyes focused on something in another galaxy a trillion light-years away.

Pepper touched my arm and pressed a little packet into my hand. "Tell Toby thanks," she said, sniffing. "Where'd he go?"

"He's with Fatso."

"Tiny," she said severely. "You want to be careful what you call Tiny, okay? He's touchy. Put out a little money, huh? She needs it."

I reached into my pocket, and my fingers encountered the serrated edge of Norman Stillman's check. Ten thousand dollars seemed excessive somehow, so I fumbled around until I produced a crumpled five. Pepper thumped the stage and hissed, *"Amber."* The girl named Amber tore herself away from whatever deep-space supernova she had been watching and contorted her mouth into a smile that missed me by a yard. Her teeth were stained and broken. "Shanksh," she said to the chair next to me.

"Ahmed," Pepper said to her, and I saw that the Middle Easterner had dropped a couple of ones on the counter in front of him. Amber trudged in his direction and then leaned over and swung her long, lifeless brown hair back and forth in a gesture that had probably been sexy ten years and a million dances earlier. Trying to straighten up, she lost her balance and fell on her tail. She didn't seem surprised, and Ahmed laughed. Nana looked over from the other stage.

"Wasted in excess," Pepper said. "She'll never make it until closing time."

"Wasted on what?"

"Name it, sweetie," Pepper said. "Don't give her any of Toby's coke, okay? Ambulances are bad for business."

I put the coke away and turned to watch Nana.

She was standing upright and toying with the top button of her hot pants, looking down at a hugely bearded customer who had put down a small mountain of money. With a smile that made me want to put on sunglasses, she undid the button and then swung her leg in a high arc over his head. He dropped a few more bills on the mountain and licked his lips, exaggerating the gesture to cartoon proportions. Nana gave him the classic "shame on you" signal, rubbing one forefinger over the other, and moved on to the next customer.

The music came to a merciful halt, and Nana left her stage quickly. She threw me an appraising glance, helped Amber climb down the stairs, and then put a protective arm around her waist. They disappeared together behind the red curtain. Amber kept getting her feet mixed up.

I took a long gulp of the vodka and, feeling its glow inside me, surveyed the room. In addition to Pepper, there were four women working as waitresses, all of them dressed for the first two pages of a *Penthouse* centerfold. Lingerie was conspicuously in evidence. Most of the girls seemed to be on the shy side, if that's the proper figure of speech, of twenty. Bellies were flat, buttocks were firm. Gravity was still lurking offstage, preening its villain's mustache. Cellulite and stretch marks were as absent as an intellectual at a Ku Klux Klan meeting. Despair was a decade away. At the same time, I felt as though I were watching balloons of bright hope passing through a sewing machine. On the other side of the needle was Amber.

During the long pause between songs, nobody said a word.

Then a cash register clanged to introduce Pink Floyd's "Money." The crimson curtain parted, and Amber's skeletal figure wobbled toward the stage with Nana's hand poised supportively in the middle of her back. Amber had taken off the camisole but retained the leopard-skin panties and the elbow-length gloves. Nana wore nothing but a slender gold chain that swaggered its way around her hips, about halfway between her navel and real trouble. She got Amber onto the stage and then, after a moment of concerned surveillance, went to her own. Her black hair, rippling and knotting as though it had a life of its own, cascaded down her back and brushed the dimpled cleft of her buttocks. Nana presented a new standard of nudity, like a third and, as yet, undiscovered sex. If all women looked like that, I thought, there would be no fashion industry.

Amber teetered precariously in front of me and then, more to keep her balance than for any other reason, abruptly turned her back. I was staring at the backs of her knees, and their delicate tangle of wrinkles and blue veins reminded me of the sturdy, inviolate legs of my first love, who had helped me through the demanding mathematics of third grade. I thought of her name for the first time in twenty years, and for a moment Amber was a child named Lynn Russell.

And then she turned back to face me, keeping her balance in defiance of all the laws of physics. Perspiration trickled down her face, taking vertical lines of mascara with it. Her elegant gloves had slipped down her arms, and I could see the tracks, red and angry-looking sores, that began on the insides of her elbows and reached almost to her wrists. Junkies often search for veins in the wrong direction. Down instead of up, farther from the heart instead of closer. I was watching a dead woman dance.

A shrill yell from the other stage cut through the music, and I turned to see the bearded man grabbing at Nana's legs. She was flat on her back on the stage floor, and he was trying to pull her toward him by the ankles. I was out of my chair and halfway there before I realized I was redundant. An avalanche of white descended on the bearded man, and Tiny literally picked him up by the collar of his shirt. The man struck out awkwardly, and Tiny shook him two or three times, like a terrier killing a rat. The man went slack. Tiny flipped him over, slipped an arm under his knees, and, looking like a parody of Rhett carrying Scarlett upstairs, toted him to the front door and through it. The Tiny clone opened the door and then got out of the way, fast. Nana, still flat on her back, had managed somehow to move to the next customer. She didn't look particularly disturbed.

Toby slid into the chair next to me. "Skip it," he said. "No one fools with the girls when Tiny's around. Anyway, Nana's used to it." His voice was controlled, but the muscles around his mouth and eyes were tight. "Having a good time?"

"I haven't had this much fun since I was circumcised."

Pink Floyd petered out, and Nana went around the stage collecting her tips. It looked like quite a wad. Amber had collected from no one but Ahmed and me, and now she sat on the edge of her stage and waited for Nana, her eyes closed. Nana took her arm, helped her to stand, and got her into the dressing room.

Toby drained his glass and signaled for another, holding up two fingers. A different girl, a brunette with spiky hair who looked all of fifteen, took our glasses.

"Toby," I said, "don't you think this is kind of sad?"

"Come off it," he said. "It's a job for the girls, and it's a place for the guys to go. Jesus, look at them. Do you think there's anyone here who could ever see a girl like Nana naked without coming to a place like this? Who's getting hurt?"

The spike haircut showed up with our drinks. Toby reached into his pocket, but the girl waved him off. "It's on Tiny," she said.

"Whoa, Nellie," Toby said. "This is a first. Wait, darling, this is for you." He gave her a ten and put a hand out to me. "The envelope, please."

I passed him the coke, and he palmed it and slipped it to the waitress. "Have a blast," he said. "It's pink. Just save some for the other members of the commune."

As she headed for the ladies' room, the Stones blared from the speakers. Pepper emerged from the dressing room and took the other stage, and Amber, anorexically naked, made the long climb onto ours. At the same time someone pulled out the chair next to me and sat down. I turned to look at Nana.

"Well, lookie who's here," she twanged. "The hero of Malibu." She was carrying a waitress's tray and wearing a sort of spangled bikini that featured her navel. She had a navel an orange would have written home about.

"And I thought you were mad at me," Toby said, grinning.

"Oh, hi, Toby," Nana said. "Are you here?" She turned away from him and looked down at the counter in front of me. "You're tipping Amber twenty bucks? Good for you."

"No one else looks very enthusiastic," I said. "It seemed like the thing to do."

"A romantic," Nana said. "The vanishing American."

"I'm not a romantic?" Toby asked. "Remember Santa Barbara?"

"Santa Barbara was two months and a couple of punches ago. Oh, I forgot. I'm not talking to you." She glanced up at Amber, who looked like someone who was trying to remember how to dance.

There was a silence, if you didn't count the music. Toby fooled around with his watch again and tossed back four ounces of vodka. His face was setting into sullen lines that made him look ten years older.

"Amber?" I said, just to say something. "Why Amber? Amber's not a spice."

Toby remained silent, taking another pull off his drink.

"Jeez," Nana said. "There are only so many spices. She didn't want to be called Garlic."

"What about chamomile?" Toby said, trying to rejoin the conversation. "Or tansy? I've always wondered what tansy was."

"Chamomile's an herb," I said since Nana showed no sign of replying.

"Herb, schmerb," Toby said impatiently. "Who cares? As long as you can eat it."

"Toby just drips class," Nana said to me. "Sometimes we have to mop the floor after he leaves."

"I came here to say I was sorry," Toby said. "But maybe you two would prefer to be alone."

"Honest to God, Toby," Nana said, "do you think you can just punch me out and leave me on the floor and then come back and make kissy-face? What do you think I am, a blow-up doll?"

The Stones faded out as Toby sulked, and Amber crawled around to pick up her tips before going very carefully down the steps and teetering toward the dressing room.

Nana shook her head, watching her. "Maybe six months," she said to herself. She caught me looking at her. "You can't junk like that and expect to collect an old-age pension."

"Nana," Toby said as though it cost him an effort. "I'm sorry." He was staring at his lap. "That's why Simeon and I came here. So I could say I was sorry."

"Sorry's a word, Toby. Like caring. Like love, if you'll pardon the expression. When I want words, I'll read a book."

The girl with the spike haircut put her hand on Toby's shoulder and tucked the coke into his shirt pocket. "Terrific, Toby," she said. "You've made my day. Maybe tomorrow, too."

"Great, baby," Toby said. He gave her the grin.

"So your name is Simeon," Nana said, lighting a cigarette and tilting her head up to blow smoke into the air. "I don't think I've ever met anyone named Simeon."

"Swell," Toby said truculently. "A new name. Maybe you want I should leave with a new girl."

"Why not two girls?" Nana said, turning on him. "Why not three? Why should you be a cheapskate your whole life?"

"Fine," Toby said, standing up and pushing his chair back. "See you lovebirds later."

"Where's he going?" I asked, watching him move toward the back of the club.

"He's going to pack his cute little nose," Nana said. "He's fine until about six, and then it's a long downhill slide until midnight. I don't know how his system stands it."

"What about your system?"

"Fooey. Half a load or so every night. Listen, you think I could dance like that straight?"

"What's the hardest thing to do?"

"Smiling," she said. "The hardest thing is smiling. Listen, I haven't said thank you."

"Nana," I said, "Toby really did come here to say he was sorry."

"Too late," she said. "You know, the dumb thing is that he really *is* sorry. It just doesn't last." She blew some more smoke and looked critically at the coal on her cigarette. "Sooner or later even someone as turkey-stupid as I am has to figure it out."

"Tell me something."

"Let's hear it first."

"How come you look like Madame Butterfly and sound like Tex Ritter?"

She laughed. It wasn't a ladylike laugh. There was no apology for not covering her mouth or for letting her teeth hang in the breeze. It was a laugh that came straight from the belly, without detours. She drummed her feet on the stage by way of emphasis.

"I mean, you're Korean, right?"

"Fifty-fifty," she said, fanning her face. "Whoo, pretty good. But Tex Ritter? God, honey, you must be older than snails."

"Half American," I ventured.

"You know what's an army brat?" she said. She waved the question away. "Aaah, skip it. Daddy's American, Mommy's Korean. Daddy took his gonads to Korea during the war. Hell, there wasn't anywhere he could park them. So he came home with Mommy and me."

"Home to Texas," I said.

"Home to Killeen. Home to wherever they stuck him. And her, and me, by the way. And now I'll ask you one, okay?"

"Shoot."

"What are you doing with Toby?"

"It's a job," I said for what felt like the fiftieth time. "I'm protecting the world from him."

She nodded, thinking it over, and the music kicked in again. A new girl climbed onto the stage, blond and pretty

except for a slight postacne moonscape that had been im-
printed on her cheeks a couple of years ago, when she was
maybe sixteen. Pepper followed, naked from the waist up,
and went onto the other stage.

"What kind of a job?" Nana finally said. "What do you
do, anyway?"

"I'm a private detective," I said, feeling as foolish as I
always did when I told anyone.

She sucked in her cheeks reflectively and nodded again,
then looked up as Tiny rippled whitely across the room and
disappeared into the dressing room. "Hope Amber's not
doping in there," she said. "Tiny will kill her."

"Of course she's doping," I said. "She has to stay up
there or she'll fall apart."

Nana patted my hand. "Honey, I know that. And he'd
kill himself before he'd kill her. She used to be his girlfriend,
and he hasn't got the faintest damn idea what to do about
her. He can't fire her because he's afraid she'll kill herself
all at once instead of slow, like she's doing now." She
glanced over my shoulder and stood up. "Excuse me," she
said. "Here comes the Dutch elm disease." She walked to
the bar without looking back.

"Somehow," Toby said, sitting, "I don't think a simple
apology will suffice." He waved for another drink. "Counting down," he said.

"To what?"

"The climax. Don't you know? Every scene should have
three stages, a beginning, middle, and end. You need a
climax—we're talking dramatically here—to punch up the
end of the scene. Otherwise, things get sloppy." He finished his drink and waved his hands around to demand the
refill. "An actor's work is never done."

Miss Spike put the drinks in front of us at the same time
that Amber and Saffron emerged from the dressing room in
street clothes and headed for the back of the club. Amber's

blue jeans were tightly belted, making vast ripples of excess denim gather around her waist.

"What gives?" I asked, watching them.

"Probably a private party," Toby said, inhaling part of his new drink. "You know, bachelor parties and shit. They dance around, take off their clothes, sit on a few laps, and come back to the club a hundred bucks richer. Tiny lets them go when things are slow, like tonight."

Tiny came out of the dressing room and looked angrily in the direction Amber had gone. Shaking his head, he went to the bar and talked to Nana, obviously asking her a question. Nana gave a negative, opening her hands to indicate her lack of information.

"Nana does that, too?" Somehow I didn't like the idea.

"Sure, champ. Who's Nana, anyway, the Virgin Mary? Believe it or not, I am going to make that girl happy with old Toby before we split tonight." He sounded full of cocaine confidence.

"Give it a couple of days," I said.

"It's a challenge. I'll do it if we have to stay here all night."

Tiny came over from the bar and tapped Toby on the shoulder. He still looked upset. "I need a minute," he rumbled.

"Tiny," Toby said, "I can't leave my friend alone in this environment. He might get corrupted."

"That's his problem," Tiny said. "*Now*, Toby."

"Watch my drink," Toby said to me, getting up to follow Tiny.

I hit my own drink lightly. I had a feeling it was going to be a long night. The record ended, the girls left the stage, and Nana sat down next to me. "Give me a gulp," she said. "Some nights are rougher than others." I watched the fine working of her throat as she swallowed several times. "I think Tiny caught her," she said, lowering the glass. "Whoo, is he mad."

"I don't think I'd get into a fight with Tiny," I said, "if I could borrow somebody else's body."

"Borrow Toby's," she said absently.

"So tell me about the parties."

"What parties?" She lit another cigarette, beating me to the lighter. "Skip it. I got two hands, same as you."

"The private parties, bachelor parties, whatever they are. Wherever Saffron and Amber went tonight."

"There aren't any parties tonight," she said. "They're scheduled days in advance, and it's my turn."

My stomach tightened. "Oh, Jesus," I said. "Oh, Jesus Christ. Hold on a minute, will you?"

I got up, feeling more of the vodka than I had anticipated, and lurched toward the hallway. I opened the door, careened down the hall, and threw the bolts between me and the parking lot. Toby's Maserati was gone.

I stood there like one of Faulkner's idiots, like Big John outside the dressing room, staring slackly at the empty space until I heard someone behind me. Nana put a hand on my arm.

"The son of a bitch," she said. "He's taken both of them."

Toby had engineered his climax.

5

Clothesline

"I OWE Y'ALL A RIDE HOME," Nana said, plunking herself down next to me again. Half an hour had passed, she'd danced another three-song set, on my stage this time, and the club was still three-quarters empty. I was more bored by the sight of female flesh than I ever thought would have been possible. I don't think I could have gotten interested if one of the girls had unzipped her skin and stepped out of it.

I felt like a counterfeit twenty. I'd been given the job of watchdogging Toby Vane, and I'd flunked out twice on the first day. I tried to blame the vodka and failed. Stillman's check sagged heavy in my pocket. It was probably the weight of all those zeros.

"What time is it, anyway?" I said. "You can't just walk out of here, can you?"

"I don't know why not," she said in her incongruous drawl. "If it were any slower, the place would start to decay. Anyway, Tiny better be nice to me. He knows Toby's my customer, and he set him up with Saffron and Amber." She tossed her head and ran a hand through the long tangles of her hair. "Besides," she said, "I'd like to see where you live. Never seen a detective's house before."

"You won't tonight, either. All I need is a ride back to my car, over at Universal."

"Well, that's just fine," she said. "I've never seen Universal, too."

"I hope you enjoy parking lots."

"I am a connoisseur of parking lots. I grew up next to a parking lot. My lifelong ambition is to have a small house by the side of a parking lot and be a friend to cars."

"You could plant Volkswagens in the garden."

"Chromeflowers and hubcap bouquets. Exhaust pipe trees."

"Maybe a bubbling stream of gasoline meandering through it all, with a few front seats placed strategically here and there for contemplation."

"I prefer backseats," she said. "Don't you?"

"Nana," I said, "or Cinnamon, or whatever I'm supposed to call you . . ."

She gave her lower lip an experimental tug. "Nana's okay."

"Is it your real name?"

"I've got more names than I've got fingers. Nana's the name they gave me at the last place I danced. Hell, it's better than Cinnamon. Somebody calls me Cinnamon, I feel like an apple pie. And loosen up, okay? Nothing going to happen tonight. Between Saffron and Amber, if anyone gets beat up, it'll be Toby. Wouldn't that be nice?"

"Terrific," I said. "I'm not supposed to let that happen, either."

"Oh, foop. He's got the weekend to get over it. That boy has the constitution of a Mack truck. Just set here a while and I'll go rub some fat on Tiny, and then we'll hit the road. By the time you get home you can call Toby and tell him what a dickhead he is. He'll be home, I promise. He's too cheap to take those two anywhere else."

"Cheap?" I said. "Gosh, he took you to McGinty's."

"And that's the nicest place he ever took me. I'll bet you ten bucks that if you had dinner with him before you came here, you ate at McDonald's."

"Drive-through," I said. "Do you want your ten now?"

"Keep it. We didn't shake on it. You want to know the

truth? I don't think Toby's got a nickel. He makes the earth, and he spends the solar system."

"But not on women."

"Oh, no. On Toby. You've seen his house."

"And so have you."

She looked me straight in the eye. "You already know that, and it's got nothing to do with you, so you don't have to say it. So far, I'm just somebody owes you a favor, right?"

I felt myself smile at her. "Right," I said.

"Then shut up and let me pay it back." She smiled back at me. "I'm sorry, I didn't mean to say 'shut up.' "

"No problem," I said.

"What I meant to say is stop acting like a drip."

"That's better."

"Well, you're not a drip, you're a nice guy, and Toby foxed you the first time out. Toby didn't fox people, he couldn't live, okay? Next time, he won't stand a chance."

"Fine," I said. "You go talk to Tiny."

Tiny was doing his Mount Everest imitation, looming whitely over the bar, his snow-capped peak rising in creased, pale-wrapped wrinkles of fat above his enormous waist, a lard avalanche waiting to happen. I wondered if his clothes were sewn from parachutes. Nana, whose entire outfit could have been cut from a single handkerchief with enough fabric left over to diaper a baby, went up to him languidly and put a slender hand on his arm. He glowered down at her and then, when he saw who she was, broke out into a paternal smile.

I knocked off the rest of the vodka. I'd no sooner put the glass down than Pepper plunked a full one in front of me. "Compliments of the house," she said, "again." She tossed a sympathetic glance at the girl on the stage and said, "She can work her ass off, for all anyone cares. This has to be the deadest Friday night in history. Jesus, you'd think it was Tuesday."

"Tuesday's usually bad?"

"It's so bad I don't work Tuesdays. You haven't been in here before."

"No." I handed her a five. "That's for you."

"I didn't think you had." She dropped the five on her tray. "You don't look like most of these sad sacks, sitting around sucking up their orange juice whenever they can yank their tongues out of the straw. You like Nana, huh?"

"How come all these free drinks? I gather that's not the usual policy."

"And then some. Don't worry, there's a tab being kept somewhere. Toby told Tiny to keep you happy."

"Happy?" I asked. "In here?"

"Some folks manage. I guess it's all in what you expect out of life."

Nana looked away from Tiny and toward us. She pursed her lips and then stuck out her tongue at Pepper.

"I think I just got a cue," Pepper said. "See you around, kid. Nana doesn't work on Thursdays. I do. It's like, you know, she's not here on Thursdays, but I am."

"Oh, no." I said. "I have my DAR meetings on Thursdays."

"DAR?"

"Daughters of the American Revolution. I'm one of the few male members."

"Yeah, well, the male member is what it's all about," she said. "Thanks for the five."

Over at the bar, Tiny reached down and benevolently patted Nana on her bare backside, and she headed toward us with a determined expression on her face. "Got to take care of all these customers," Pepper said hurriedly, edging away from me.

Four chairs down she picked up a full ashtray and replaced it with a clean one from her tray.

"So little Miss Jaws took a bite at you," Nana said. "One of these nights she's going to get a spike heel planted about four inches into her belly button."

"She told me Toby was paying for these drinks."

"Yeah, well, that's Toby. Do something shitty with one hand and make some lame apology with the other. Listen, no problem with Tiny. One of the girls who's supposed to be off tonight just had a fight with her boyfriend, and she called to ask if she could come in and work because she knows it ticks him off."

"You're sure this is no trouble."

She looked down at me with a perplexed expression. "Either you're very, *very* long on manners, or you're thick. I *want* to take you to your car. I will *enjoy* taking you to your car. Maybe I'll take you *farther* than your car. In fact, maybe I'll take you to dinner."

"Good idea," I said. "I'm finally finished with Toby's burger. But I'm buying."

"Bet your boots you are," Nana said. "What do you think I am, a feminist?"

"He's still not home." I pulled out my chair and sat down. Some of the food had arrived while I was gone, and Nana was in it up to her elbows.

"That's just good old Toby," she said happily around a mouthful of Thai noodles. "He never answers that phone. I counted fifty-one rings once, and he never even seemed to hear it. It would drive me crazy."

"Why doesn't he answer it?"

She helped herself to the pepper-and-garlic beef and spooned some white, sticky rice out of a carved wooden bowl. "Eat something," she said. "Don't worry your food cold, as my mama always used to say. Of course, she said it in Korean." She put a dollop of rice on my plate and pointed toward a sizzling iron platter of grilled prawns that I didn't remember ordering. "He doesn't answer it because it's always someone who wants something. They want to sell him dope or get dope from him. They want to invest his money or borrow some. They want him to do a part or help them get one." She worked on a prawn for a moment and then washed it down with some Singha beer. "He says that when you're a star, nobody ever just says Hello. They always say, Hello, listen, I've got this proposition."

"I just want to know he's home, that's all. I want to know he's not on some baseball field, using Amber as the bat and Saffron as the ball." I drank some beer, too. On top of the vodka, I felt it immediately.

"Maybe he's playing bird croquet," Nana said mushily. She swallowed. "Remember *Alice in Wonderland*? With the flamingos? I've always wanted to do that. I hate birds."

"Why in the world would anyone hate birds?"

"Because they're so stupid. Have you ever seen a flock of chickens? How they peck at each other? The one at the bottom of the pecking order is always bald from the wings back. Birds." She gave a mock shudder. "They give me the willies."

"I've got two birds."

"I'm sorry to hear that. Men should have big, fierce dogs, not teeny, stupid birds." She shrugged off the birds and wiped briefly at her mouth with her napkin. "I got to go to the toilet," she said. "I'll call him for you while I'm up. He might answer this time."

She sashayed across the room. There was a kind of liquid languor to her movement, as if she were walking underwater. All over the restaurant, Thai men looked up at her admiringly, and Thai women looked at Thai men sharply. The Thai men looked back down at their food. Thai women could be fierce.

An hour earlier she'd driven me back to Universal and smiled at the guard until he'd let us in so I could get Alice. Then I'd followed her home to a little circle of cottage apartments surrounding a courtyard on Vista, a narrow street lined by one-story stucco houses just north of Sunset in Hollywood. It was the kind of street, left over from the twenties, where the dominant foliage is birds of paradise

and decorative banana trees with their big, fringed, indo-
lent, rubbery leaves. Very California. We'd left her car
there and headed east on Sunset to Jitlada, my favorite
Thai restaurant, to start in on the beer and noodles.

The food was good, but I picked at it. I was worried, and
beer was more to the point. Mine was almost empty, so I
drained it and then grabbed Nana's, waving to the hurried
waitress for two more. They were on the table before Nana
got back.

"Eleven-thirty," she said, consulting a big yellow plastic
watch that encircled her right wrist. She was left-handed.
"Still no answer." She hoisted her beer. "This is interesting," she said. "It got full while I was getting empty."

"It's that kind of restaurant."

"It's pretty fine. Nothing like this in Texas." She downed
about six ounces of beer, directly from its brown bottle.
Nana wasn't a glass girl.

"How come you have this fund of information about
chickens? You don't look like the farmer's daughter."

"Toby told me. He grew up on a farm, you know."

I felt myself get interested. "Toby told you about his
childhood?"

"He was pretty wasted. He usually doesn't talk at all."

"I know. What did he say it was it like?"

She stopped chewing and parked her food in one cheek,
looking guarded. "Why do you want to know?"

"Nana," I said, "even if I'm a screw-up, I'm still supposed to be looking after the boy. Maybe it would be a
little easier if I knew something about him."

"Stop knocking yourself. It's too pitiful. How'd a fragile
soul like you get to be a detective, anyway?"

"I was in college and someone threw an inoffensive little
girl—a friend of the woman I was living with at the time—
off the top of a dormitory." I drank some beer. "She
splattered pretty good. The cops all seemed to be more

interested in writing parking tickets, so I decided to figure out who did it."

"And did you?"

"Yes."

"And then?"

"And then I broke a few of his bones and turned him in. It seemed like a good way to make a living. I thought we were talking about Toby."

"*You* were talking about Toby."

"Would you like another beer?"

"Does a chicken cross the road?"

"Then tell me what Toby said. About his home. About his family."

She finished her bottle before handing it to the waitress. "You're looking to get me killed, you know that?" She put both elbows on the table and rested her chin on her hands. Her wrists were smooth and slender. The brown skin on her arms was lined faintly by fine blue veins. I decided that the big vinyl wristwatch was definitely the yellowest thing I'd ever seen. I didn't say anything. She didn't, either. The beer arrived, and I took a slug at mine.

"Toby," she said at last. "Real nightmare time. He grew up on a farm, you know that?"

"South Dakota," I said.

"Right. Just lots of dirt and a little house in the middle of it. Snowed to beat the band."

"I already know about the climate in South Dakota."

"No, but he said it made the house seem smaller. Like there was nowhere else to go, you know? Inside was awful, but outside was worse. Are you sure I should tell you this?"

I shrugged. "Either you trust me or you don't."

She picked up her beer. "He cried the night he told me," she said.

"I promise I won't cry."

"I cried, too."

"Maybe you're an easier cry than I am."

"Don't be flip." She drank. "This isn't flip stuff."

"Nana," I said, "cut the shit and talk to me."

She drew a deep breath. "Well, it was mainly his daddy."

"What was mainly his daddy?"

"Toby was the only boy. He had two older sisters, but he was the only boy. He was his daddy's favorite." She paused and took another drink.

"And?"

"And Daddy just loved to beat up on the girls. He drank a lot, and the only thing that really made him happy when he was smashed was knocking the little woman around. It didn't make much difference which little woman, his wife or Toby's sisters, although I guess his wife got the worst of it. She definitely did after the girls left."

"When did they leave?"

"Soon as they could. They went off to Sioux Falls or Bismarck, or wherever you go in South Dakota, and got jobs or husbands or something. That left just Toby and his daddy and his mommy."

"His father never took it out on him?"

"Oh, no. He was always the favorite. Daddy's boy. He took Toby hunting and fishing, all those smelly macho things, but he was terrible to Toby's mother and the girls. Sometimes Toby said he used to be bad just to get his daddy to whop him once in a while instead of the girls."

"Bad like what?"

"Oh, I don't know. Killing chickens and stuff. Leaving the barn door open in the middle of winter. But it didn't seem to matter what he did, old Daddy would just pat him on the head and say what a great little dude he was. Then he'd go belt the women."

"And the women never fought back?"

"No. That was what drove Toby crazy. They'd just take it and take it, until they could run away. And then they ran away."

"But his mother couldn't run away."

"I guess not. I would have been out of there at the speed of light."

"But Toby's as bad as his father, and you kept going out with him."

She took a long swallow of beer. "Maybe we'll talk about that later," she said, "and maybe not. Like you said, we were talking about Toby."

"Okay, so his sisters left. How old was he then?"

"Nine or ten."

"And he remembers all of this?"

"He remembers everything. Like he had it on home movies."

"Or Polaroids," I said.

She put the bottle down and looked out through the window at nothing happening in the parking lot. "You know about that?"

"I've seen them."

"I'll tell you about that later, too." She picked at the wet label on the beer bottle with a long nail. "Maybe."

"Up to you. Toby's alone now with just his mother and his father."

"Yeah. Then it got worse. Toby says his dad used to chase her around the house with a belt, just cracking it down on her back while she yelled for help. She never turned and tried to take the belt away. She never ran outdoors. Maybe it was snowing."

"That upset Toby."

"Sure. He kept thinking that one day she'd just clobber him. The old man was always pretty drunk when it happened, Toby said. He figured she could have taken him if she'd really tried. He still doesn't understand why she didn't."

"So what happened?"

She drained her beer. "This is the bad part," she said.

"It's already pretty bad."

"I think I'd like another beer."

"Fine." I waved at the waitress, who took the order with an air of disbelief. We waited in silence until the bottles landed on the table, and then we hoisted them in unison. Nana wiped her lips on the back of her hand and put her bottle down.

"Now Toby's about ten," she said. "They're all in the kitchen, right? They always ate dinner in the kitchen. The old man was stewed, as usual, and there was something wrong with the dinner. Well, maybe there wasn't, but he said there was, you know?"

I nodded.

"So he popped her. But this time he did it with his fist. And then he hit her again. Toby says he remembers the blood coming down from her nose. He said he was screaming at his daddy and dancing around the kitchen, trying to get in between them, but his father just brushed him away and went on hitting his mother. His mother was on the floor, and his daddy kicked her. A couple of times, he thinks. And Toby kept screaming at her to get up and screaming at his daddy to stop, but it just went on and on."

"What did he do?" I asked.

"He got a knife, a bread knife, I think, and went after his daddy. Can you imagine? This grown woman on the floor, bleeding and crying, and this little kid waving a bread knife at his father. So, naturally, the old man took the knife away and smacked the kid around. I mean, he was only ten. And then he grabbed Toby by the neck and said to his wife, 'Go get the clothesline.' "

I felt a shiver run down my back. "The clothesline," I said.

"Yeah. And figure this. She *did* it. She hauled herself up from the floor, all covered in blood, and went and got the clothesline from the backyard and brought it back in. She gave it to him and then went back to the table and sat down. She didn't say anything, Toby said. She just sat there and cried, the damn sap."

"What happened with the clothesline?"

"Toby's daddy used it to tie Toby to the stove. First he tore off Toby's shirt, and then he tied him with his back to the side of the stove. Then he said something like 'You made a mistake, son,' and he turned on all the burners and both ovens. Then he grabbed his wife and made her stand up, and he said to Toby, 'We'll come back when the stove is red hot. We'll come back when we smell you cooking.' And then they both went away, into the living room or somewhere."

"Jesus," I said.

"Jesus was on shore leave. Toby said he waited. He could feel the stove warming up, but he still waited. He thought his mother would come in and get him, you see. He kept trying to pull the skin on his back away from the stove, but the ropes were too tight. His father could always tie a good knot, he said."

We both drank.

"After about a half hour, but who knows, it could have been less, he started to yell. He really thought he was going to get cooked, and Mommy wasn't going to help. Well, they let him yell. Then they let him scream. The stove kept getting hotter, he said. Finally, when he'd screamed his voice away, his daddy came into the kitchen and picked up the bread knife. Toby thought he was going to die right then, but the old man just leaned down and cut the clothesline. And then do you know what he said?"

"What?" I felt sick.

"He said, 'Stupid. Don't you know stoves don't get red hot?' Then he went away and left Toby sitting on the kitchen floor with his back to the stove, crying. Only he didn't have any voice left to cry with, so it was just air, you know? Just air."

"Let's get out of here." I gestured for the check.

"Poor little kid," she said. She looked down at the tablecloth, and when she looked up again, her eyes were wet. "Poor little idiot kid. Kids are so dumb."

"They're surrounded by monsters," I said. I put some money on the table.

"There really are monsters," she said. "They tell us that there aren't, but there really are. And they're all people."

"Come on. I'll take you home. There aren't any monsters at home."

She wiped her eyes on her napkin. "Promise?" she said.

"Promise. Let's go."

On the way to the parking lot she leaned against me, and I put my arm around her shoulders. At the car, she put her arms around me. "You asked me to tell you, and I told you," she said. "Did it help?"

"Maybe. Maybe Toby's just been waiting for some woman to fight back. I don't know, you don't know. Toby certainly doesn't know. I think Toby knows less about it than any of us."

She shivered. "Toby doesn't know anything," she said. I gave her a squeeze and opened the door.

"Simeon the southern gentleman." She tried a laugh, but it was a little shaky. I felt a little shaky myself.

On the way home, the chaos of Toby's childhood filled the car like soft cotton, muffling anything that might have been said. The night was clear above us, and Hollywood sparkled like a handful of rhinestones scattered over the hills. As usual at that hour, half the drivers were loaded on various misrepresented chemicals, and I drove carefully. Neither of us said anything, but as I turned left onto Vista, Nana slipped her hand into mine.

"Thanks, I guess," she said.

"You'll sleep."

"After a while."

"But eventually."

"Oh, sure. Everybody sleeps eventually."

"There's no way to come out of it alive," I said. "Nobody has yet."

"I wasn't being fancy. How about walking me to the door?"

Three-quarters of a moon clung tenaciously to its corner of the sky as we walked hand in hand through the courtyard. The all-night traffic of Hollywood was muted by the Spanish-style buildings that surrounded us. Poking out of dark green hedges, the needlessly extravagant flowers of copa de oro yawned eloquently around us, their rich russet orange washed to a muted beige, and big birds of paradise, planted close to the buildings, cawed silently in the moonlight. The air was luxurious with jasmine. Stretching high above our heads, palm trees cut hard black California silhouettes against the dimmed stars, and a birdbath in the center of the courtyard trickled an invitation to sleeping birds. We reached the door, and Nana looked up at me.

It felt like high school. "May I kiss you good night?" I asked.

"Boy," she said. "What a stupid question." She smiled up at me and raised herself onto tiptoe.

I kissed her, wondering what I was doing. It was a pretty good kiss, considering the circumstances. Then she stepped back abruptly and said, "Oh, shoot."

"Was it that bad?"

"No. It was sweet. It was the sweetest kiss I've had since I was twelve. But I forgot my damn cash caddy."

"Your what?"

"My cash caddy. The thing I put my tips into after I finish dancing. I was in such a hurry to get you to myself that I left it at the club."

"So?" I said. "It'll keep."

"Sure it will. It'll keep about as long as a hundred-dollar bill dropped in front of a Church of Scientology. That's my money, and I've got to go get it."

"But the club's closed, isn't it?"

"I've got a key. I can get it. Listen. Go home. Call me tomorrow, if you feel like it."

"For heaven's sake," I said, "I've got a car."

"For heaven's sake?" She smiled. "How dear. I'm not sure I ever heard anybody say that out loud before. You really want to take me?"

"Sure. Alice is warm. Even if she weren't, I'd carry you down to the club on my back. It's not that far."

"Obibah," she said.

"I beg your pardon?"

"Obibah. It's Korean for piggyback. Let's go, hero."

"Okay," I said. "But *obibah* to the car." I turned my back to her and bent down, waiting.

"You really *are* crazy, you know? Here goes." She saddled up, her legs straddling my middle and her warm arms around my neck. "Giddyup," she said.

"I'll go at my own pace, thanks." She hardly seemed to weigh anything at all. "You forget that I'm aged."

"You're drunk, too," she said, "but I want to see a good brisk trot here. Mush, senior citizen." She dug her heels meaningfully into my back. I carried her across the courtyard toward Alice, who stood gleaming at the curb.

"Hey?" she said into my ear. "I've always liked older men."

I deposited her on the sidewalk next to Alice. The traffic noise was louder here. She opened the door and got in, and I went around and joined her.

I flipped the ignition halfway and released the brake. We coasted down the hill in silence until I turned the key the rest of the way and popped the clutch to bring Alice into consciousness. She sputtered and then caught, and I swung left onto some nameless little street, heading south and downhill toward Santa Monica Boulevard. Several minutes passed in silence. Nana leaned against me and exhaled warmly on my arm. I made the last turn and cut the engine. "I'll come in with you," I said. The club was dark. Even the fleshy light of the neon in front had been shut off. The area looked like a slum that had gone out of business.

"Fine, hero. Come on in."

She yanked the car door open and got out, and I followed. The parking lot was empty, a black asphalt wasteland faintly striped by parking lines and littered with crumpled paper bags wrapped tightly around empty bottles. The late night lights of Hollywood glared and winked across the sky. I caught up with her and took her hand. She turned to me.

"One more kiss," she said. "I promise not to get possessive."

"That's what they all say." We kissed, and she chose a key and thrust it into the lock on the door.

"Dirty money, here I come," she said. She pulled the door open, and we faced the hallway I had come through earlier with Toby. It was completely dark, but as my eyes adjusted I could see a narrow horizontal strip of light low down at the other end. Nana fumbled for a second and then flipped a switch that brought a naked electric bulb above us to attention, flooding the hallway into a sparkling dark red. My sixth sense kicked in like a flood of cold air.

"Turn it off," I said.

"What?"

"Just turn it off. Now." I reached past her and pushed the switch down. Light gleamed below the door at the other end. "Why is that light on?" I said. Hairs bristled along my spine.

"How do I know?" She paused, then spoke more thoughtfully. "It shouldn't be. Tiny always turns everything off when he closes up. This is not a boy who wastes electricity."

"Well," I said, "it's on now."

"It sure is. So what?"

"So stay here. I want to go in first."

I groped my way down the corridor and found the handle

of the door. It turned easily in my hand, and I pulled it open.

The club was dark except for the pink lights above the smallest stage, the one that hadn't been used while I was there earlier in the evening. Something was spread out on it.

"Stand right where you are," I said over my shoulder. "Don't come in unless I call you. Just stay the hell out of here."

"What is it? What's wrong?"

"Keep your hand on the doorknob," I said. "Be ready to leave if I tell you to."

I went into the club. The velvet nudes gazed imperturbably down from the walls. The thing on the stage was Amber.

She lay flat on her back, stark naked, staring sightlessly up into the lights. Her eyes couldn't have been any deader if they'd been marbles.

"Simeon?" Nana called.

"Quiet," I said. "Be quiet and stay there."

Amber's face was battered and swollen, both lips split wide open. The blood hadn't caked yet, except where it was matted into her dry, broken-looking hair. She had bled from a wound hidden by the hair. Her arms were outflung. Normally my attention would have been drawn to the angry-looking tracks on the insides of her elbows, but now I could only look at her hands. Her hands were horrible.

The fingers splayed back grotesquely, angling every which way in a gesture that was both humanly imploring and humanly impossible. Every one of her fingers had been broken. They had been broken at all three joints.

A noise behind me told me that Nana had come into the room. I couldn't be bothered to turn around.

There was something totally wrong about Amber. Something about her posture. First I registered that her hands hadn't been tied, and then I realized that her feet *had* been. I slipped my hand under her body to check the temperature—the lights would have kept her front warm. She wasn't much colder than I was. Trying to keep my eyes from her hands, I checked her wrists for rope burns, imprints, anything. There weren't any. Then I turned my attention to her bound ankles.

They were wrapped in several turns of rope. The rope was thin and cottony. I took it between my fingers, feeling the unshaved roughness of Amber's shins beneath my knuckles.

The rope was clothesline.

"Dead nudes," I said.

6

Saffron Says

I BACKED AWAY, a thin, reedy singing shrilling cricketlike in my ears, a fine violin string being drawn back and forth through my brain. My heart was battering madly against my ribs. The dead woman on the stage gazed up blankly at the pink lights, her wide-open eyes as empty as those of a dog listening to music. Behind me, Nana shuffled nervously from foot to foot. The sound of her shoes seemed to scrape their way straight through my skin.

"Dead what?" she said. "Don't scare me." She moved closer. "Ducks in hell," she said. Her swallow carried all the way across the garish, empty room. "It isn't . . . she isn't . . ."

"Yeah, she is," I said. "Just hold it. Don't move, not a foot. Don't touch anything. Stay where you are. Goddamn it, Nana, where's the phone in this shithole?"

"Behind the bar. Over toward the left, under the bottles. Oh, Lordy," she said. "Oh, Simeon, I think I'm going to puke."

"Puke outside. Don't do it here. And don't touch *anything*. Not anything, got it?"

I found the phone on a shelf underneath the cash register. A dirty slip of paper pasted crookedly beneath the buttons said IS THIS CALL NECESSARY? I guessed it was. I grabbed a handful of paper napkins and used them to pick up the receiver. I was swearing at myself.

"What's Toby's number? At home."

"You mean you're not going to call the cops first?" Her voice was shaky, but she seemed to be getting herself under control. At any rate, she'd stopped sounding like she was going to hit the floor at any moment.

"In a minute. She's not going to get up and go home. What's Toby's number?" She gave me a couple of false starts and then the number, and I punched it up.

After what felt like five minutes the phone at the other end of the line rang tinnily, once, twice, three times. "This stinks," I said to no one in particular. Finally I heard the clatter of a receiver being lifted clumsily, and then Toby's voice crackled across the wire.

"This is Toby Vane's answering machine," he began. He sounded sleepy and irritable.

"Toby? This is Simeon. Where have you been?"

Nothing for a moment. Nana skittered behind me, letting out a small cough. "Toby," I said again, "I asked you a question."

"Hey, champ," Toby said. "Easy. Do you know what time it is?"

"Yes, I do, Toby, and I don't give a shit. Answer the question."

"Here, I've been here. For a couple of hours. What's it to you or anybody else? What am I, Information?"

"You haven't been answering your phone."

"I don't, you know? It's not in my contract that I have to jump every time the phone rings. At least, not yet." He paused while he located his personal switch for charm and hit it. "Listen," he said winningly, "I know you're pissed off. I'd be pissed off, too, but I just had to get out of there. Nana was just way out of line, you know? Hey, you got free drinks and the prettiest Korean lady in Hollywood. So okay, so I shouldn't have done it. I'm sorry."

"You don't have any idea how sorry you are," I said.

His voice changed. The charm evaporated as fast as the alcohol they rub on your arm before a shot. "What's that supposed to mean?" He grunted as he sat up.

I tightened my left hand around the receiver until my knuckles cracked. "Where's Amber?"

"Amber? Who cares? Home, I guess. That's where we left her. She was so skagged out she couldn't count her fingers." I visualized Amber's fingers and fought it down again. "No fun at *all*, you know what I mean? We ate a little something and then dropped her at her place."

"Who's we?"

"We? Saffron and me. Who do you think, Linda Evans?"

"Is Saffron there?"

"Sure. We've been playing mumblety-peg. Great game. You should try it sometime."

"Let me talk to her."

He paused. "You've already got Nana, haven't you? What're you after, a grand slam?"

"Toby. Put her on the phone. Right now."

"Right now? You mean, right this very minute? This instant, so to speak? What's that, an order or something? I must have gotten something wrong. I thought *you* were the hired help."

"Listen to me, Toby, if you know how. You want me to hang up the phone? Fine, I'll be glad to. You'll be in jail in about forty minutes. If you don't believe me, try it."

"Jail? What are you talking about?"

"Put Saffron on the phone. You've got five seconds."

There was some muttering on the other end and a whisper of movement behind me, and I became aware that Nana had somehow made it to the stage. She was staring down at Amber, her eyes glazed and her mouth wide open. She slowly reached out a delicate hand, as if to smooth the matted hair.

"No closer," I said to her. "You touch her and I'll leave you here."

"Huh?" Toby said. "Leave who?"

"You'll leave me here?" Nana said. "So what? I don't give a fuck. You think I need the big strong man's help?"

She met my eyes defiantly and then looked away, back at Amber. "She was my friend," she said in a muted voice.

"Well, she's not your friend anymore. And I'm getting enough crap from Toby without you pitching in. Get away from her. Now." She stepped back, staring at me as if she'd never seen me before.

"She's dead," she said.

"Honey, she's not just dead, she's murdered. Now be a good girl and put your hands behind your back, knot your fingers together, and keep them there." She shook her head helplessly, but she obeyed. From the sinewy movements of her arms, I could see that she was twisting her hands behind her back.

Toby said, "I hope you know what you're doing. Here she is." A woman's sleepy voice came on the line. "What is it?" she said. "What's happening?"

"Lots, and it's all bad. Saffron, I want you to tell me about your evening. Don't talk to Toby first. Tell me absolutely *everything* about your evening."

"Who can remember?" she said. "We ate at Johnny Rocket's, over on Melrose, you know?" Another hamburger. Toby was some sport. "Then we took Amber home because she was so wasted. The girl was way past the end zone. Then we came here and fooled around for a couple of hours. Then we went to sleep. Period. Why? What's so bad?"

"What time did you drop Amber off?"

"Ten, ten-thirty, eleven. Early, you know?"

"What time did you get to Toby's?"

"I don't know, about eleven, eleven-thirty. Maybe twelve."

"Any phone calls?"

"Oh, come on," she said. "It never stops."

"Did he answer any of them?"

"Not until now."

"You've been with Toby the whole evening?"

"Sure."

"You're willing to swear to that?"

"What do you mean, swear? Swear to who?"

"So you weren't together all the time?"

"Pretty much. He left me at the restaurant for about half an hour to score a couple of loads. That's all."

"Sure. They were super, the best I've had in a week, real pharmies, not street shit. We're still rolling."

"What time did he leave to get them?"

"Who knows? Nine-thirty, probably. Listen, Charlie, that's enough from me. I want to know what's going on."

"So nine-thirty to ten or so. That's the only time he wasn't with you. And Amber was with you then."

"I just said so."

"No," I said. "You said probably."

"What do you think?" she said. "You think I've got a digital watch tattooed on my arm? You think I'm Big Ben? What *is* this shit, anyway?"

"Let me talk to Toby."

"First tell me what's happening."

"Just give him the phone."

There was a pause. "You creep," she finally said. She dropped the phone deafeningly onto a hard surface. After a moment, I heard Toby's voice.

"I'm not really crazy about this, champ," he said. "I've just been sitting here at home, you know, lighting candles and burning incense and having a little private fun, and suddenly you're acting like Norman in one of his moods."

"Amber's dead," I said. "She's been beaten to death. Guess who suspect number one is."

Toby covered the mouthpiece with his hand and said something muffled. I could hear Saffron's voice, but I couldn't make out the words. Behind me, leaning against the far stage, Nana was crying.

"Where are you?" Toby asked.

"At the Spice Rack. She's laid out on one of the stages."

"I'm with Saffron," Toby said quickly. "You know I'm

with Saffron. We've been together the whole evening." He covered the phone again and said something else. "What do you mean, beaten to death?"

"I mean, for example, that her nose was broken. I mean that all her fingers have been snapped backward. In about thirty places. Toby, she looks like something junior sadists look at to earn their merit badges."

"You don't really think I could have done that."

"Compared to some of the things I think you could do, this is a Valentine's Day card."

"He did it," Nana said loudly. She had gotten as far away as possible by now, and her back was pressed against one of the glittering, blood-colored walls. Her slender back was mirrored behind her. "I know he did it."

"I heard that," Toby said. "That's my old buddy Nana. Nice to know what people really think of you."

"Great," I said. "You're agonizing over your self-image. Amber's been pounded into paste and you're worried about what people think of you."

"Don't get dramatic," Toby said. "I know it's terrible, but I've been here, old buddy. I've been with Saffron since we dropped Amber off. What do you want from me, blood?"

"No. We've got enough of that right here."

"She's really dead?" His voice finally sounded a little thinner. The fear was beginning to float to the surface, and he couldn't keep it down, not even with his actor's training. "She didn't just OD?"

"Sure she did," I said. "She OD'd on her own fists. Just before she broke all her own fingers." I realized I'd turned to stare at Amber again, and I tore my gaze away from her, swiveling my whole body to the left. I tried to focus on the wall in front of me. On it someone had written in pencil THE GOOD NEWS IS THAT THE GARDEN OF EDEN IS BETWEEN A WOMAN'S LEGS. THE BAD NEWS IS THAT YOU CAN'T GET IN.

Toby breathed heavily once or twice. "Jesus. So what do you want me to say?"

"Right now, nothing. Not to anyone."

"But you're not going to mention my name to the cops."

"Maybe you can explain to me how I'm supposed to do that. Especially since everyone working here saw you leave with Amber."

"Nobody saw me. Nobody except Tiny, and he won't say nothing," he insisted, his grammar slipping a notch. "Hell, Simeon, I'm more than an hour from there, even the way *I* drive. You want to talk to Saffron again? She'll tell you, we've been here all night."

"I'll talk to her later," I said. "Now I've got to call the cops." The prospect was not an exhilarating one, but part of me was still capable of doing mathematics, and the math came out more or less in Toby's favor. One hour, I thought. One to two hours ago, Amber had been alive, or whatever imitation of alive Amber had been doing.

"Toby," I said, "you'd better treat Saffron like a queen. She's the only thing between you and no more fan club, as far as I can see. Not to mention jail. You know how popular you'd be in jail, Toby? You know what a little delicacy you'd be in prison? You'd have to tie the soap to your wrist so you wouldn't drop it."

"I'm treating her fine," Toby said a little shakily. "Saffron." I heard him snap his fingers. "Saffron. Any complaints?"

An electronic version of a contented murmur insinuated itself into my ear. Saffron didn't sound too torn up about Amber.

"Okay," I said. "You're out of it, at least for the moment. I'm going to hang up and call the cops now. But Toby, this is important. If I'm not going to mention you tonight, you've got to promise me. You're not going anywhere tomorrow, you're not going to take Saffron home, you're not going to go to the bathroom alone, you're not going to do anything by yourself before you call me. Otherwise, you're on your own. You're under house arrest, understand?"

"I'm a suspect," he said dully.

"You're *the* suspect," I said. "Sleep on that." He was talking, but I hung up.

My arm ached as if the receiver had weighed fifty pounds. I put one hand on the sticky surface of the bar to steady myself and then turned around.

"Nana," I said, "do you trust your buddy Saffron?"

"It depends," she said in a low voice, "on whether I can see her or not."

"Well, great. That's just great."

The phone started to ring. "Toby knows this number?" She nodded. It rang again.

"Well, shit," I said, "let him sweat."

Nana's lower lip was trembling. "Poor baby," she said. "Poor little junked-out baby. She had so much bad luck."

"Whatever it's worth, that's over now." The phone kept ringing.

An enormous tear rolled down Nana's cheek. Another followed. She didn't bother to wipe them away. Her hands were still behind her. The tears dropped from her chin and left long dark tracks down the front of her blouse. She lowered her head. "That bastard," she said. "And you're going to protect him."

"Nana." She sniffled, childlike, but she didn't respond. "Come here. Come here, please."

She looked at me, but she still didn't move. The phone finally shut up, and I went to her, stepping wide around the stage with Amber on it. I put my arms around her. "I don't think he killed her," I said. "I could be wrong, but I don't think so. The cops will be here soon. They're going to ask a lot of questions. I'm not going to mention Toby, and I don't want you to, either."

She had nestled into my arms, her hot, moist forehead pressed hard against the front of my shirt. She was trembling uncontrollably. When I mentioned Toby's name, though, she pulled away quickly and gazed up at me with accusing eyes. Then she lowered her head and spat on the floor at my feet.

"Listen," I said again. She shook her head sharply. Then she made a convulsive movement, trying to shake my hands from her shoulders. She took a step sideways, edging along the wall to get away from me. I slapped her arms, and she looked up at me.

"I'll get him," I said, meaning it. "Whoever it is, I'll get him. Even if it's Toby. Especially if it's Toby. I promise you by whatever you swear by, I'll get him. And if I have to, I'll kill him."

My heart was pounding. I counted its beats for lack of anything else to do as she stood rigidly in front of me, her eyes fixed on the floor, her feelings a continent away. Then a long breath fled out of her, an impossibly long, serpentine kite of a breath. It seemed to empty her completely, leaving her small and frail in its passing. The trembling slowed and then stopped. My hands, wrapped around her thin shoulders, felt the fineness, the almost birdlike hollowness, of her bones.

She looked back up at me. "You really promise?" she asked in the smallest voice I'd ever heard from a human being. She swallowed again. "You'll kill him?"

"I swear."

She blinked twice, quickly, and two more tears tracked their shiny ways down her cheeks. "Then call the cops," she said. "Call them." She shook an arm free to wipe the wetness away in a rough gesture. "They won't do anything." She sounded fierce. "They won't give a shit. She was only a nude dancer, anyway."

She looked around the club and then back at me. "This place," she said between her teeth. "How I hate this place."

"Hate it all you want," I said. "Just watch what you say to the cops." I went to the phone and dialed 911.

II

NERVES

▼

7

Dead Old Dad

THREE O'CLOCK HAD SAID hello and good-bye by the time we were grudgingly allowed to leave. We'd forked over our names, addresses, driver's licenses, and telephone numbers, and we'd had an illuminating opportunity to watch L.A.'s finest at work, measuring, photographing, fingerprinting, and gossiping to their hearts' content. In the midst of all the abstract quantifying, Amber's death seemed like an incidental backdrop to the flurry of efficient, purposeful activity. Unless you looked at her face. I tried not to look at her face.

Once the responding officers had decided we weren't Public Enemies Numbers One and Two, they'd identified themselves as Officers Strick and Losey and started to treat us with a passable semblance of common courtesy. Nevertheless, when we were allowed to leave, Losey had followed us out and ostentatiously made a note of Alice's license plate number.

I'd wanted to avoid the kinds of questions they would have asked if they had known what my job was, so I'd put my license inside my sock before they arrived. Nevertheless, I'd screwed up early on, volunteering that the body had been warm when we found it and that Amber couldn't have been dead long.

"Yeah?" Strick had said suspiciously. "And what are your qualifications?"

Nana had jumped in before I could even work up a

stammer, saying that she'd touched Amber when we came in and that she knew all about loss of body heat. Then she'd told an appalling story about having come home one day when she was eleven and found the dangling body of her father, who had hanged himself in the kitchen. At first, she'd said, she thought he was just doing another one of his magic tricks. He always did magic tricks. She'd sat on the floor for a few minutes, waiting for the payoff. Finally she had cut him down and he'd still been warm. The Texas medical examiner, she'd said, bursting into tears, had told her all about body temperature. Strick and Losey had patted her ineffectually on the shoulder, big hulking men who had no idea what to say.

We got into Alice in silence. As we turned right onto Santa Monica Boulevard, Nana sagged against me and rested her head on my shoulder. "Yipes, cripes, Maria," she said. "I thought it would never end."

"It wouldn't have, if they'd learned what I do for a living." I blinked over scratchy eyeballs. "Thanks for yanking my foot out of my mouth."

"I had to," she said. "You had your shoe on." She stroked my arm.

I headed north up La Cienega, on the way to Sunset and her apartment. Nana stopped stroking my arm and said, "No."

"No, what?"

"I can't go home. You know I can't go home. Do you think I could go to sleep now?"

"I know I have to. Tomorrow's going to be a year long. And that's if everything goes okay."

She twisted to face me. "Maybe you don't understand this," she said. "That was Amber back there. She wasn't some fifth-rate whore, she was my friend. I talked to her tonight. I said hello, and she said hello back. I asked her how she was, and she didn't kick me in the teeth. She lied to me, like she did every night when I asked her how she was doing, because she wasn't looking for pity. So her life was a mess. Whose isn't?''

Sunset was coming up fast, and I decided to dodge the question. "Where do you want to go?"

"Where do you think? I want to go with you. Is that so unreasonable?"

"I don't know. I don't know what you think I can do for you. *I* don't know what I can do for you."

"You can hold me if I start to cry again. You can wake me up if I scream in my sleep. I'm not asking for community property, for Christ's sake. But that was Amber."

"And who was Amber?" I stopped at the red light at the top of the hill. It was either right or left from here on, either east toward Nana's or west toward Topanga and home. Amber's death hadn't slowed the planet's revolution any, and four A.M. was rolling toward us.

"Amber was Amber. She was fucked up, like the rest of us, and trying to get straight, like the rest of us. Don't *do* this to us now, okay?"

"Don't do what?" The DONT WALK sign had started blinking, its apostrophe a casualty of bureaucratic economy.

"Don't start acting like you're dense, even if you are a man. You're not that much a man, and I'm not that much a woman. We both know."

"Know what?"

"That it's hard either way. Maybe it's impossible either way. Maybe it's all luck, and you either have luck or you don't. If you don't, maybe you end up like Amber. Or like me. Maybe you decide to check out."

The light flickered and changed to green. Nana put her hand on my wrist and dug at the skin with her nails. I turned left and pointed Alice toward the ocean, toward home. Nana sighed. The pressure behind her fingers eased.

"Like your father," I said.

"What?" Sunset was empty. The moon had gone down long ago, taking with it most of the Hollywood lights.

"Your father."

She rubbed her head slowly against my shoulder, and then she laughed. "My father. Dear old dad." She laughed again. It wasn't the most pleasant laugh I'd ever heard. "Dead old dad."

I slowed the car. "It isn't true," I said. "He didn't hang himself."

"Sheer wish fulfillment." She stroked my arm again. "You were in trouble, remember?"

"So he's alive."

"Alive and kicking. Kicking everybody in sight."

"You made all that up, that whole story. Cutting him down and everything. The magic."

"Oh, no. He really did use to do magic, when he was drunk."

I didn't say anything.

"Come on, Simeon, I told that story because you were chewing on your shoe."

"I already said thanks. Is there anything else I'm not supposed to believe?"

"I don't care what you believe. No, that's wrong, I do care. If you have to decide right now what to believe, if you can't wait a day or two, then believe that my father makes Toby's dad look like Santa Claus. My fifth-grade teacher told me once that a bad lie always comes true. You can't imagine how many people I've told that my father is dead."

"What did he do to you?"

"That doesn't matter. Anyway, he's not dead, remember? He's still trying to do it."

"Do what?"

She looked out the window. "How about we let that wait?"

"We're letting a lot of things wait."

She attempted a laugh again. It was less real, but more pleasant, than her last try. "Please," she said. "Let a girl keep a little mystery."

Sunset curved sinuously to the left, and I willed Alice to follow the dotted line. She obeyed, with the usual groan of protest from the rear axle. Two or three miles piled up behind us in a tidy, linear fashion before either of us spoke. I turned on the radio, and some deluded disk jockey threw Led Zeppelin's "Stairway to Heaven" at us. It seemed like the only song I'd heard in months.

Nana beat me to the volume control, and silence reigned again. "Don't judge me," she said. "Don't pass any cheap judgments. Not yet, at least."

"I'm in the judgment business. I don't always like it, but that's what I do. I can't buy the feminine mystique. As far as I'm concerned, mystery is just sloppy business. It only means that someone hasn't asked the right questions."

She made an impatient gesture. "Questions. Can't you leave it alone for a while?"

"If you're satisfied to put Amber into the ground without talking about it, I can leave it alone."

"We weren't talking about Amber. We were talking about me."

"You're part of it. You and Amber had the same job. If I understand you a little better, maybe I'll understand Amber, too." I wasn't being entirely truthful. "She's not around to tell me about herself. I thought you wanted me to do something about Amber."

"I want somebody to burn at the stake," she said flatly.

"Then stop being Mata Hari. If you're not going to talk to me, tell me so. I don't want to hear about the feminine mystique. Like you said, it's hard either way, whether you're a man or a woman. So as one screwed-up human being to another, tell me the truth."

"I am telling you the truth."

"As far as it goes."

"If I tell you the truth," she said, "who *knows* how far it's going to go? Damn, Simeon. Maybe there are some things I don't want to tell you. If I want to hide something here and there, then let me. Maybe it hasn't got anything to do with Amber. What if there are things I'm ashamed to tell you?"

"Why?"

"Boy, you're simple sometimes. Maybe I care about something that doesn't have anything to do with Amber."

"Like what?"

"Like me. Like you, maybe."

"Nana, this is a job."

She straightened abruptly. "I am not a job."

"Okay," I said, "so you're not a job. So sit on your secrets. Keep them warm. Maybe they'll hatch into nightmares." Another mile passed, and she didn't say anything. I yawned. "Long night," I said conversationally.

"Don't make small talk."

"I'm not allowed to make any other kind."

She passed her fingernails lightly over the back of my hand.

"Think it'll rain tomorrow?" I said.

She settled herself resignedly into the seat. "I'm sure it will."

"Who do you think will win the Republican primary?"

"Somebody who dresses in feathers and gobbles."

"What's your favorite color?"

"Only men have favorite colors. Women choose colors that reflect their aura, and every fool knows that a woman's aura is always changing."

"What do you use to polish your aura?"

"Spit," she said. "Spit and saddle wax. What do you use on yours?"

"I have a no-polish aura. It's new from Du Pont."

She stretched like a cat and rolled her head back and forth. She had an extraordinarily long throat. "Do you really have to ask me questions?" she said.

"Only if I want answers."

"Okay," she said in a businesslike tone. "I started dancing because I had this girlfriend who was doing it and she kept asking me to. I was sixteen and a half, and my father had chased me out of the house a year before. He chased me all the way from Killeen to Hollywood. Killeen is a service town, lots of guys who used to be in Korea and lots of Korean women who were married to them. I got to Hollywood, got a fake ID, and started working at a bookstore, but I wasn't making any money. And then my girlfriend, who had become my roommate, started in on me. I knew the girls weren't whores or anything because I knew my roommate, and she was a nice girl. She still is a nice girl. I made a hundred and forty dollars a week at the bookstore, and they knocked off an hour if I went to lunch, so I didn't go to lunch. I was hungry all the time. The first night I danced, place down near the airport, I made three hundred and ninety, in cash. One guy tipped me a hundred bucks. I was the only Oriental girl in the club, and I guess I was a novelty."

"I didn't ask you how you started dancing."

"You were going to. Weren't you?"

"Sooner or later. Why did Amber start dancing?"

"She had a boyfriend who was supposed to be a writer. He was working on the great American haiku or something. Well, naturally, he couldn't do that, juggle all seventeen of those syllables and hold down a job, too. So he moved in with Amber and let her take care of him by dancing while he slaved every day over a hot typewriter."

"How was the haiku?"

"Who knows? He never finished it. Probably never started it. From what people tell me, he spent most of his time looking for something to stuff up his nose."

"Is he still around? You didn't mention him to the cops."

"Long gone. He picked the cutest way to move out. Amber went down to San Diego one afternoon to dance a party, and she stayed the night because they finished so late. When she got home the next day, she found some of her furniture in the front yard, and the door to the house was wide open. There was nothing inside, and I mean not a dish towel. He'd had a yard sale while she was gone. Sold all her stuff and split."

I negotiated a curve. "Sensitive guy."

"You know artists."

"When was this?"

"A couple years ago. Right about the time I came to the Spice Rack."

"I thought Amber was Tiny's."

"What a southern way of putting it."

"Maybe you could put your feminist umbrage on ice for a while so we could discuss the issues."

"She was pretty wiped out after el creepo split. I guess she thought she loved the jerk. Tiny came to the rescue, took care of her, let her move in with him, and picked up after her for six months or so. It could have been longer. I don't think he even fooled around with her. He just wanted to get her straight."

"It's hard to imagine Amber straight."

"She never really doped until Claude left. Claude, that was the creep's name. Jesus, I thought I'd forgotten it. Oh, you know, she coked once in a while to get her up so she could go on stage. Most of the girls do something. They have to."

"She had more tracks than the New York subway system."

"That was later. I don't think she ever shot up until she was living at Tiny's."

"Have you ever shot up?"

"We're not talking about Amber now," she said.

"No," I admitted.

"I tried it once. Somebody had to do it for me because I was afraid of the needle. I couldn't even look. I was sick for days."

"Lucky you."

"For once."

"So who hated Amber?"

"Nobody. Why would anyone hate her? Most days she couldn't put on her nail polish, much less hurt anyone. She danced to make money so she could do smack, and she did smack so she could dance. There wasn't much in between."

"No other men?"

"Not after Tiny. She got enough of men in the club."

"Do most of the girls have boyfriends?"

"Most of them have pimps," she said shortly.

"I thought they weren't whores."

"They have guys who pocket the money their girlfriends make dancing naked in front of other men. That's a pimp, as far as I'm concerned."

"Did Amber ever make a move on another girl's boyfriend?"

This was a new thought, and she looked out the window. "You think a woman could have done that to her? Broken her fingers like that?"

"It depends. If the woman was strong and Amber was wasted enough, why not? She was pretty thrashed earlier this evening."

"She was totaled. If she was a car, you would have had her hauled. But I don't think a woman could have done it."

"That's what they said about Lizzie Borden. An axe isn't a woman's weapon. Now who's stereotyping?"

"Naw. It's her fingers." She shuddered against me. "Whoever did that really hates women. Like Toby does."

We had come to the end of Sunset, and I turned north up the Pacific Coast Highway toward Topanga. The ocean was invisible to our left, suggested here and there by the mooring lights of a sailboat that bobbed up and down on the water's dark skin, the people in it asleep and dreaming of freedom.

"So did Amber ever fool around with anyone's boyfriend?"

"Simeon, I've told you. She never did anything except dance and try to find a vein. Honey, can we make a deal? You leave me alone now, and I'll talk to you tomorrow till your ears fall off. Right now, all I want is a soft bed and a warm shoulder. Give me about ten hours, okay?"

"I've got Toby tomorrow, too."

"You can handle us both."

"I'm not so sure. I haven't handled much so far."

She put her head on my shoulder and made a drowsy sound. "Stupid," it sounded like. The PCH was wide and dark and empty. After a few minutes I turned right up into the mountains, and we left the deep sleep of the sea behind us.

When we finally reached the top I shook her awake. With her hand in mine, I led her up the steep, unpaved driveway, steering her around the more cavernous ruts until we got to the house. The lights were on, courtesy of the electric timer, but darkness masked the grimmer dilapidation of the exterior. I opened the back door, and Nana stumbled in sleepily.

"Cozy," she said, her eyes half-open. "Where's the bedroom?"

"Well," I said, "there are only three rooms, and you can see the living room and the kitchen. So it must be the other one."

She focused. "Through that door," she said.

"You should give some thought to a career in private investigation."

"Tomorrow. You coming?"

"In a minute. Just go get comfortable."

She nodded drowsily and headed toward bed.

I gave some water to the birds, who didn't acknowledge it, and did a little fruitless tidying up. The red light on my answering machine blinked at me, heralding yet another thwarted attempt at human communication. I got a beer, pushed the playback button, and sat on the rug.

Calls one and two were from Toby. He wanted me to call when I got home, he said in the first one. He gave his number, as if I hadn't already called him once that evening.

In the second message he said he was going to sleep, but that I could call and wake him up if I wanted to make sure he hadn't gone anywhere. The third call wasn't from Toby.

"Hello, Simeon," Eleanor's voice said. "It's almost three in the morning. I couldn't sleep, and I wondered if you couldn't, too. Since you're not answering, I guess you can. . . . Um, I hate talking to this machine. Do you want to have dinner tomorrow night, or Sunday? If you do, call me in the morning. But not too early, please. I may get to sleep yet. I'm going to close my eyes and imagine myself enveloped in a bright white light. Or something. Bye-bye." There was a final-sounding click, and then a dial tone hummed across the wire.

I finished my beer. The narrow, safe life I'd led with Eleanor seemed as remote as an earlier incarnation. The curtains she had made for the house still hung on the windows, but nothing else tangible was left.

I gave the empty bottle a push, and it rolled under a table. I'd get it in the morning, I promised myself. Trying not to think about much of anything, I went into the bedroom.

Nana was lying on top of the blankets, fully clothed and fast asleep. I eased the blankets out from under her and covered her with them. She didn't even murmur. Then I closed the window next to the bed and looked down at her. She was breathing evenly, and she looked about fifteen.

There was a spare blanket folded at the foot of the bed. I grabbed it, turned off the lights, and went back out to the living room.

8

The Morning After

SATURDAY MAY HAVE dawned rosy-fingered, but I missed it.

When I finally swam reluctantly toward consciousness, it was already ten o'clock. Birds—not *my* birds, but their more energetic colleagues outdoors—were singing melodiously to warn each other to stay the hell out of their territory. I gave my lips an exploratory lick. My tongue felt like some supernatural prankster had sneaked in during the night and inserted it into one of those sheepskin seat covers that sports car drivers for some reason covet. A dull and monotonous brass bell clanged regularly in my forebrain. Samuel Johnson, who had something to say about everything, once said that when one woke up one should get up, and when one got up, one should do something. I weighed a very short list of the things I could possibly do and chose the bathroom. I figured I could lift my toothbrush.

Normally, I like waking up alone. I'm used to it. Of all the civilized skills, the power of speech is the last one to drop in on me each day. After I hung up the brush, wiped the rabid-looking foam from my chin, and turned off the water, I listened gratefully to the sound of Nana snoring daintily from the bedroom. I was happy that she wasn't up and around and bombarding me with snappy chatter, but those were pretty cloggy snores. I wondered whether someone had helped her to Toby's prized pink while Toby wasn't watching.

I spit out some Listerine and looked up. My face in the mirror looked like my face. I searched it for a moment and then turned the cold water back on and splashed myself to wash away the sleep. I keep waiting for some cataclysm to change my face. No dice. The only thing that seems to change the way I look is the patient accumulation of years. No matter what happens, nothing seems to surface away, any more than the dirt of Toby's life left any unscoured stains on the all-American billboard of his grin.

Feeling a little better, or at least a little cleaner, I went in and checked out the living room. It was a wreck. It looked like Grendel's lair, except that in place of the gnawed human bones Grendel and his mother scattered around after their nightly Viking shish kebab were more commonplace odds and ends: a woman's hairbrush I didn't recognize, an ashtray full of somebody else's cigarettes, and dust rats curled languidly under the furniture. I hid the hairbrush under a couch cushion, studied the lump it made, and resolved to see what was causing the other lumps at some time in the near future.

Eleanor, my ex-girlfriend, was born to tame furniture. She'd managed to keep the place presentable during our years together, but I'd given up the effort, waiting for the occasional girl to drop by with a sponge and a roll of paper towels. It had been weeks since that had happened. I was definitely not next in line for the cover of *Architectural Digest*.

Since I had time to putter, I puttered. Wrapping a towel around my middle, I gave some more water to the birds. Birds go through a lot of water. To my surprise, I was rewarded by a grateful cheep from Hansel. At least, I thought it was Hansel. With birds, who can tell? After last night, I wasn't even sure I could tell with people. Who, for example, was Toby? Or, hitting literally closer to home, who was Nana?

I realized I was gazing dully down into the birds' watering trough, roused myself, and headed for coffee. For what seemed like several hours I leaned against the kitchen counter, averting my eyes from the landscape of my life while I waited to hear water boiling. I managed to pour the water over the grounds without fatal consequences, found a relatively clean cup, and let the whole deal drip directly into it.

The first gulp took off on all cylinders, transversed the road map of my circulatory system on two wheels in the best Le Mans fashion, and screeched across the finish line into my brain, synapses snapping to attention behind it. The second swallow brought the sun out. Well, *well*, I thought, and went to call Toby.

I woke him up, the sluggard. "What time is it?" he mumbled.

"Rise and shine, both of you. I'll be down there in about an hour and a half, and we've got a lot to talk about."

"You didn't call me back." He sounded aggrieved.

"What do you think I'm doing now?"

"Last night," he said sulkily. "You were supposed to call me last night. Don't you know how upset we were?"

"Yeah. Sounds like you haven't closed your eyes all night."

"We didn't until about six. Finally we took a little something. What time did you say it was?"

"Almost eleven. I'll be there between one-thirty and two."

I could hear Saffron in the background. She sounded querulous and cranky. "No," Toby said. "I'll come to you. I've got to take Saffron home anyway." He lowered his voice. "Champ, if I don't get her out of here, I'm going to go crazy."

"Just don't hit her."

"What's a poor boy to do when he's not allowed to express himself? This girl is the ditz of the century."

"She's also your alibi."

"She's a dream walking. How do I get to your house?"

I told him and hung up. I was replacing the receiver when I suddenly felt very strongly that someone was looking at me. I turned slowly and stared into the dark, accusing screen of the computer.

What the hell, I thought. It's only a machine. How complicated can it be? I drained the cup, poured another, and, with an unsteady Toshiro Mifune swagger, pointed myself at the computer, reached it, and switched it on.

A whir as the fan came to life, a blink on the screen, a message: DISK ERROR OR NON-SYSTEM DISK. Balls. I'd forgotten to put anything in the drive. Well, be reasonable, it wasn't the machine's fault. I slipped the DOS diskette in and hit a key. The fan gave way to a buzzing, choking sound as the computer chewed some information off the surface of the disk, and my old nemesis shouldered its way onto the screen: A>

Okay. I'd been this far before. Unknown territory was only a keystroke away. There were twenty-six regular keys, ten numbers, a bunch of keys that said F1 and F2, up to F12, and an irregular cluster of others with labels like CTRL and SYSREQ. Surely one of them did something.

Talk to it, I thought. I typed HELLO. The word appeared on the screen. Terrific, but now what? I hit the Enter key.

BAD COMMAND OR FILE NAME, the screen said smugly. I growled a little in the back of my throat.

HOW YOU HANGING? I typed. The words hung there, glowing greener than electric chlorophyll. I hit Enter.

BAD COMMAND OR FILE NAME.

"It's not a command, you asshole," I said. "It's a polite greeting. You want a command, I'll give you a command." I typed ACHTUNG! and hit Enter. The machine, like a second-rate psychoanalyst, stuck with the tried and true: BAD COMMAND OR FILE NAME. It also beeped, by way of emphasis.

I was galvanized by a surge of adrenaline, my hangover

burned away by twelve million volts of emotional electricity. I leaned toward the computer screen, my throat tight. "Okay, you electronic illegal immigrant, wanna know what I did to my last turntable? I backed the car over it. Do you want to wind up in a burlap sack, in pieces small enough to inhale, being mailed back to the factory with FRAGILE written all over you so the post office will drop you as often as possible? *Do* you? Huh? *Huh?*" I slammed the keyboard once with my fist for emphasis.

The computer beeped and then laughed at me.

I sat back quickly and reached for my coffee, and the cup jangled nervously against the saucer. The computer laughed again. "Honey," it said, "you're out of your mind."

I almost jumped out of my chair as Nana's bare arms snaked around my neck and gave me a squeeze. "How come I slept alone?" she said. Her breath smelled good even in the morning.

I had to inhale twice before I could talk. "Don't startle me this early, okay? I'm a little bit jumpy. How are you feeling?"

"Great, better than I've felt in days."

I ran my tongue experimentally over my teeth. My mouth was as furry as an inside-out puppy. "What was so goddamn funny?" I asked a little sourly.

"You. Threatening that computer. How much RAM have you got?"

"As much as I need," I said defensively. What the hell was RAM?

"What, though? Three twenty K, six forty K, or thirty-eight thousand K?"

"Thirty-eight thousand. And change."

Nana gave my throat a vaguely threatening squeeze. "You simp," she said. "Where's the coffee?"

"Where do you think?"

"Aren't we sweet in the morning?" She slipped past me and ambled into the kitchen. Against my will, I turned to look. She'd changed. She was wearing a pair of underpants. My underpants. They hung lazily lopsided, high up on her right hip and so far down on her left that the cleft between her buttocks peeked demurely over the white elastic waistband. Tiny as she was, the elastic was doing its job. She had wonderful, teaspoon-size dimples on either side of the base of her spine. They were the kind of dimples I'd always wanted to fill with salt and dip celery into.

"You don't know squat," she said pleasantly as she poured. "Everybody knows that six forty is the maximum RAM for that machine. What in the world did you buy it for?"

"Work."

"Oh. Work." She slurped her coffee. "Whoo, hot," she said. "Where's the sugar?"

"In the cabinet. Behind you."

She pulled it down and poured half the box into her cup, then gave it a stir. Then she added some more. She sniffed it.

"Sugar doesn't smell," I said in spite of myself. "How do you know when you've got enough?"

"When the spoon stands up by itself," she said. She sipped it once and nodded, then dropped the spoon into the sink. "Coffee's finished," she said. "I'll make some more." She went through the motions, waited until the water was dripping, and turned back to me. "So, you're going to use a computer in your work. What's your software?"

"My what?"

"Software. You know, the stuff that teaches that thing how to think." The pot began to drip obediently behind her.

"I haven't gotten that far."

She came over to me and peered over my shoulder. I could feel her body heat on my arm. "Honey," she said, "you haven't got anywhere at all. What do you want to do first, write something?"

"Sure. I guess so."

"Okay, where are the disks?" She flipped up the neat little black file that I'd bought with the machine and pulled out a diskette. "WordPerfect," she said. "You're in luck. I know my way around this one." She yanked out the DOS diskette and slipped the new one in its place.

"Anything in B?" she asked rhetorically, snapping the drive open. "No, nothing in B. Well, we'll just use good old DOS, no need in wasting time formatting one. In we go."

"God, you're chatty."

"Get off the stool. I can't reach the keys. Scoot, scoot." I scooted. She typed WP and hit Enter, and the screen came to life. WELCOME TO WORDPERFECT 4.2 it said.

I leaned over her shoulder. "How'd you do that?"

"If you're sweet, I'll teach you. Get a piece of paper so you can write all this down."

Feeling like a third-grader, I got a piece of paper. Negligently naked at the keyboard, Nana initiated me into the mysteries of word processing. I took notes while she batted the machine around in an expert manner, and when she got up to check the coffeepot, I took over. "My God," I said while she clinked things around in the kitchen, "I'm writing."

"Now all you need is something to write about."

"Shush."

In fact, I did have something to write about. TOBY = JACK SPRUNK? I typed. CHECK. HOMETOWN? TOBY'S BUSINESS IN THE BACK ROOM WITH TINY. CHECK. WHO'S SAFFRON, REALLY? VERIFY THEIR STORY. NAMES OF OTHER GIRLS TOBY'S BELTED. DID AMBER HAVE A ROOMMATE?

"Sure, sweetie," Nana said, reading over my shoulder as she sipped a fresh cup of coffee. "That charmer, Pepper. You know, the one who was putting the arm on you while I was sweet-talking Tiny." The underpants had slipped a little lower, clinging for dear life to the sharp jut of her left hipbone. I put my thumb in her navel and gave it a soft twist. It returned immediately to its former shape. The muscles beneath were as smooth and firm as a trampoline.

"Jesus, you're elastic."

"Youth," she said. "You probably remember it."

"You know the answers to any of these other questions?"

"Not so's you'd notice. Saffron I know something about. Put your thumb back in my belly button. It's such an unusual approach."

"Later. What's with Toby and Tiny?"

"Toby likes him, I guess. Hell, I like him, too. But as for Toby, well, Tiny takes care of him, sees that nobody hassles him in the club, sets him up with a girl occasionally. Tiny knows a lot of girls."

"Girls for what?"

"What does that mean? You mean, does Toby pay for them, or what? He doesn't have to. Toby's a TV star, remember? They're thrilled just to be with him."

"I mean what does Toby do to the girls Tiny sets him up with?"

"The usual. He doesn't beat them up, I don't think. Tiny'd pasteurize him."

"He beat you up."

She colored slightly. "Tiny didn't know about that. I told him I'd had a car accident." She took my cup and filled it with the coffee she'd brewed.

"How thoughtful of you," I said as she placed the cup in my hand.

"Well, you feel ridiculous when you get slapped around, you know? I've had practice. Anyway, it was none of Tiny's business. I got myself into it, I got myself out of it. You know, you really shouldn't leave the screen on like that if you're not working. You can burn words into it. Have you got Screensave?"

"Have I got what?"

"*Eigo,*" she said. "That's Korean for 'you simp.' It's a utility. Got any utilities? Give me that stool."

She slid up onto it, swapped a couple of disks, and slapped some keys around. The screen went dark. "Now we've saved what you wrote onto the disk in the B drive. I'll show you how to get it back in a minute." Pulling the WordPerfect disk out of A, she put DOS into it, typed DIR, and hit Enter. A whole bunch of junk rolled past on the screen.

"Hoo-ha. There it is," she said. "Next time, before you put the word processing program in, type SCRNSAVE." She typed it as she said it.

"This is the worst coffee I ever drank," I said. "On the other hand, where'd you learn to do all this stuff?"

"Computer school. I went for a year daytimes, when I started dancing. I'm a real whiz kid. I even got Tiny to put the books at the Spice Rack on computer. Okay, here's WordPerfect back again, and here come your notes." Sure enough, they blinked back onto the screen. "Now watch." We watched. I slid my thumb up her spine to pass the time. After about a minute, the screen went blank.

"What happened?"

"That's Screensave. To get it back, just hit a key." I hit one, and there everything was again.

"It's a miracle," I said.

"This is totally excellent coffee," she said, sipping at hers. "The coffee of the gods. End of lesson number one. Do you want to ignore me, or what?" She gave the elastic on her underpants an exploratory snap. "How about or what?"

"I'd love to. But Toby's coming by, and I think we ought to get ready."

"Is he bringing Saffron?"

"I told him to. She's his alibi."

"How you going to get ready? Put on some insect repellent?"

"I thought a shower might be in order."

"Why? You'll just want another one after she leaves."

"You really don't like her, do you?"

"There's nothing wrong with her that demonic possession wouldn't improve. I mean, she's okay if you like people who lie and cheat and steal."

"Then I'd better shower now, before she steals the soap. Why don't you get dressed?"

"I'll bet you say that to all the girls. Am I doing something wrong?"

"Of course not." I gave her an appreciative pat on her round little rump. "But you see, I was injured in the war."

"No fooling," she said, concerned. "What war?"

"The War of 1812."

"Fine," she said, sounding grumpy. "Message noted."

"Nana. We hardly know each other."

"I know I like you."

"Well, I like you, too. Even if your coffee should be given serious consideration by the Pentagon. Let's see what happens." She looked at me doubtfully. "Okay?"

She chewed at her lip. "This doesn't happen to me often."

"Nothing's happened."

"That's what I mean." She sounded slighted.

"Hey. We don't have to fall into a frenzied clinch on our first morning together. Let's learn to talk to each other first."

"Fine," she said. "*Be* enlightened. Actually, I kind of like it. But it's not exactly the style I'm used to."

"That doesn't mean you have to put up with it."

"Sometimes I like that, too. Don't make me a victim, Simeon. It may be hard for you to understand, but I enjoy a lot of things about my life."

"For example."

"Freedom. I can do whatever I want, with whoever I want. I make cash every night, so I've always got money in my pocket. I don't want to work, I don't work. Little Korean girls don't get that much freedom."

I sipped at her truly awful coffee and then put it down. "So you kicked over the traces."

"I knocked down the whole damn house. It was that or be Daddy's girl."

"That doesn't mean what I think it means."

"It doesn't?" She didn't take her eyes off me.

"Well, I hope not." The screen on the computer went blank again. She leaned across me and hit a key to bring it back to life. She had a faint, sweet, yeasty smell, like fresh-baked bread. Her black hair brushed my arm. I put my hand on her warm, silky shoulder.

"Take a shower," she said. She smiled at me and shook her head. "You're a real innocent, you know? Listen, go get clean. Then you can face Toby and the lovely and talented Saffron with a pure heart. You'll need it."

I put my arms around her, and she tilted her head up and gave me a butterfly kiss on the throat. Wrapping my towel virtuously around me, I headed for the shower. When I came back out, wearing my Saturday jeans and a brightly colored, loose-fitting shirt that Eleanor had bought me from Bali a couple of years before, the living room looked as though the Angel of Good Housekeeping had paid a visit. The few things that could be polished actually looked polished. Nana had taken a dish towel and twisted it around her head like a turban and poured herself approximately into her clothes from the evening before. She was on her hands and knees, using a paper towel to roll up a particularly virulent looking dust rat underneath the table. I hadn't even known I had any paper towels.

"Honey," she said, "it's all well and good to be a bachelor, but this is ridiculous. You should send the whole house to the dry cleaner." She got up, went into the kitchen, and dumped the rolled-up towel into an overflowing wastebasket. "When do the trash men come, or do they?"

"They come," I said. "I just haven't figured out the schedule." A car door slammed down the hill. "And speaking of trash, here's Toby."

"Jesus. I look like Mother Hubbard." She yanked the dish towel off her head and gave her head a shake.

"I thought you didn't like Toby."

"I don't. I don't like Saffron, either. That's why I have to look good." She ran her fingers through her hair. "You know even less about women than you do about computers. It's kind of attractive."

"I'm full of negative virtues." I heard the scrunch of two people coming up the driveway, accompanied by an occasional ladylike gasp of displeasure from Saffron. I could imagine her teetering on her platform heels and clinging limply to Toby's arm as they negotiated the ruts. Nana vanished into the bedroom, tugging at obscure fastenings on her clothes. She was back before they knocked on the door, running her fingers through her hair. She looked beautiful.

Saffron came in first, out of breath and looking bad-tempered. "Well," she said, looking from Nana to me and back again. "Don't we work fast."

"Who's we, white girl?" Nana said. "And here's Toby."

Toby looked as if he really hadn't slept. His face was puffy and his eyes were red, and the patented hair was hanging limp. The mood of the moment was one of weary sincerity. "Nana," he said, "I'm sorry about Amber."

Nana's eyes flickered. If I'd been Toby, I would have stepped back. "Aren't we all?" she said shortly.

"You didn't really think I had anything to do with it."

"It's just a good thing you were with Cinderella here. Otherwise I'd have gone out there and cut your balls off."

"And a good morning to you, too," Saffron said.

"We can bicker in the living room," I said. "We've got some things to work out."

"Like what?" Saffron said icily. She hadn't moved a step. She was going to be the great lady.

"Like what you two are going to say to the cops when they finally get around to you. Now come the rest of the way in here and sit down. Nana's fixed some wonderful coffee."

Saffron and Nana maintained the greatest possible distance as we went into the living room. Saffron eyed the decor the way Margaret Dumont looked at Groucho's cigar. Toby cleared his throat but said nothing until he and Saffron were seated on the couch and Saffron had gathered her skirt around her as if she were afraid something might run up it. Then he said, "Jesus, champ, what're you, Davy Crockett? I didn't know anybody still had a wood-burning stove."

"Toby," I said, "just shut up for a couple of minutes. At this point I'm trying to figure out whether I want anything to do with you, and every time you open your mouth you just make it that much easier for me to decide."

"Right," he said. "I'll shut up." He patted Saffron's hand. "And you shut up, too, darling."

"Nana, get our guests some coffee."

"Yes, master," Nana said. "Six lumps or eight, dear?" she asked Saffron.

"I don't eat sugar," Saffron said haughtily.

Nana made a tiny gagging sound and went into the kitchen, banging things around a little more than was strictly required before reemerging with the worst mugs I owned. "Don't touch the red one," she said to Saffron as she set them down on the table. "It's mine. I wouldn't want to put any impurities into your system. They wouldn't last a moment, poor little things."

Saffron curled her fingers possessively around Toby's arm, ignoring his look of irritation, extended an elegant, red-tipped pinkie on the other hand, and picked up her mug. She swallowed, and her eyes widened. She put the cup down hastily. "Oh, my God," she said. "That's horrible."

None too gently, Toby disengaged his arm. "So why are the cops going to want to talk to us? We left her at home. She was okay then."

"Sooner or later they're going to find out I've got a private investigator's license, and they're going to ask what I was doing there."

"And you're going to tell them?"

"Maybe. It depends on you."

"On me? Why? What do you want me to do?"

"I want to know all there is to know about Amber, from you and from Saffron."

"What's your interest?"

"I've got two. First, if I'm going to keep working for you and Stillman, I want to be satisfied that you really didn't have anything to do with it." He made a gesture of protest, but I clapped my hands together to cut him off. "Second, I made a promise that I'd try to find out who *did* do it."

"A promise to who?"

"To me," Nana said fiercely. "He promised me."

"Damsels," Toby said. It didn't sound chivalrous.

"The girl was destroyed," I said. "Somebody broke her systematically, one little bone at a time. Somebody who took his time about it. Somebody who enjoyed it."

"Okay, okay," Toby said. "You don't have to be so goddamned vivid. I'll admit that I get a little out of hand from time to time, but I couldn't do anything like that." He put his hands out, palms up, his blue eyes wide and earnest. "Ask anyone."

Nana snorted.

"Damn it, Nana, you know it's true," Toby said.

"*Somebody* did it, Toby," she said.

"We all know it wasn't me," he said. He looked around the room. Nana looked out the window. Saffron was staring down into her coffee cup as if she expected to find a sugar cube floating on its surface.

"Don't we?" he demanded. "Does anybody here really think it was me?"

"You, you, you," Nana said, still facing the mountains. "That's all you ever talk about. If you'd delivered the Gettysburg address, it would have been about you."

"I know you didn't do it," Saffron said grandly. "You were with me."

"The whole time," I said.

"We've been over this," Toby said.

"The whole time," Saffron said.

"Maybe you did it together," Nana said.

The great lady went out the window fast. "You little gook *cunt*," Saffron said, getting up. I reached over and put my hand on her forehead and pushed. She sat back down, looking surprised. "Toby," she said imploringly.

"That's enough. If you ladies want to punch each other out, do it outdoors, and wait until we're finished. Now tell me about Amber. Everything you can think of. Where she lived, who she knew, who didn't like her, who she didn't like, where she got her dope, everything you can think of. Nana, you, too. Saffron, we'll start with you. Everybody else keep quiet unless you hear her tell a lie. If you do, speak up."

"I barely knew her," Saffron said sullenly.

"That's lie one," Nana said.

"Explain."

"Amber was always nice to her. She always shared coke with her. She even talked to her. She was the only one who could stand her." Nana sat back, daring Saffron to contradict her.

"Amber was nice to everybody," Toby said in a low voice. I looked at him, surprised.

"That's true," Nana said. Nobody spoke for a minute.

"She really was," Saffron said finally. "She was okay, Amber was." Her chin trembled, and she blinked twice. Nana made a sniffling sound. Even Toby was quiet. He stared down at the rug.

"Oh, hell," Nana said.

"Nana," Saffron said, "I'm sorry I said that. Amber was fine to me. She was the nicest junkie I ever met." A tear slid down her cheek, and she didn't brush it away.

"Poor little jerk," Nana said.

"Remember the garage sale?" Saffron was crying openly now.

"I told Simeon about it last night," Nana said. "That kid just couldn't pick a friend."

"I hated that bugger," Saffron said. "Oh, Jesus, remember Homer?"

"Who?" Nana asked.

"Who was Homer?" I asked Saffron.

"This dork Amber was supporting for a while. Before Claude."

"No," I said to Saffron. "We're going to have to be more specific than that. You're going to tell me everything you know about Amber, and we're going to start with Homer. Then we'll work backward. Then we'll work forward. Until we finish."

Nana looked at Saffron, and Saffron looked at Nana. Then the two of them looked at Toby.

"We're going to start now," I said.

Three hours later, I knew a lot more about Amber. I wasn't sure that any of it would help, but at least I had her address, a place to start looking, and someone who might have seen them drop her there. Toby had volunteered to give Nana a ride into town, and when they left she and Saffron were arm in arm. When women cry over someone they love, they forget who they hate.

I was on the way to the phone to call Eleanor when I heard a whirring sound. After a moment I identified it as the fan in the computer. The screen was dark. I touched a key, and words leapt onto the screen.

SIMEON IS OKAY WITH NANA, it said.

I looked at it for a long time and then went to call Eleanor.

9

Norman's Conquest

I'D HAD LAZIER WEEKENDS. After finishing with Toby, Nana, and Saffron, I'd made an arrangement to keep Toby under wraps for the duration of Saturday and, probably, Sunday as well. Then I'd fooled around with the computer, writing down practically everything the three of them had told me about Amber. Sooner or later, though, I was supposed to do something about it.

Well, the first thing to do was check the alibi.

Amber had apparently been shifting from place to place, and when they told her they were going to take her home—according to Saffron—she hadn't known where she wanted to go. That had the ring of truth to it; I didn't think she could have found her leg in the dark. After some futzing around, they'd taken her to Pepper's place and let her off. The last they'd seen of her she was stumbling toward the door.

The apartment house was on Fountain, on a block where paint was allowed to peel and most of the shrubbery had gotten a jump on the summer heat by dying months before. The building was two stories high, built in the shape of a V open to the street. Someone was frying bacon when I climbed out of Alice, several pounds of bacon by the smell of it. It was almost two. People get up late in Hollywood.

There was no answer when I thumped on the door of Pepper's apartment, which was to be expected. I'd been told she spent most of her nights abroad.

That left the Peeper, as Saffron had called him, an old man who lived on the second floor in the unit nearest the street. "I think he's got his finger caught in the window," she'd said. "I've seen him every time I swung by, and Pepper says he's always there. One of those, you know, voyers. One hand stuck in the window and the other one down his pants."

I knocked again, looked down at my watch, and glanced up at the Peeper's window. A white curtain dropped into place. There were stairs at the juncture of the V, and I climbed them two at a time, tiptoed to his window, and ran my nails down the screen.

The curtain flapped back, and I found myself inches away from a pair of very bright eyes set into an absolutely hairless head. "Well, hey," I said. "How you doing?"

"Who's askin'?" The voice sounded a lot like my fingers on the screen: scratchy and dry, as though it hadn't been used in years.

"It's about the girls downstairs," I said.

"There's a lot of girls downstairs." He sounded guilty, but he didn't drop the edge of the curtain.

"Those girls," I said, thumbing back toward Pepper's door.

"The hootchy-koo girls," he said. Then he laughed briefly, a sound like someone stepping on a glass in a paper sack. "What about 'em?"

"Oh, come on. Weren't the cops here today?"

"You with the cops?"

"How else would I know they were here?"

"You didn't get around to me the first time," he said. "Sloppy work. Well, you might as well come in. Lot of nosy folks here, don't want 'em to see me talking to you through the window." The curtain fell back into place. "Door's open," he rasped from behind it.

When I opened it, hundreds of girls smiled at me. Centerfolds gleamed down at me from the walls, all skin and teeth and amateurishly come-hither eyes. "Quite a collection," I said.

"They can't move very fast, either," he said, giving me the laugh again. He was sitting in a lawn chair, dressed in a white T-shirt and white boxer shorts. An aluminum walker straddled the carpet in front of him. His calves were thinner than his forearms.

"Stop looking," he said. "You'll be old, too, you know. Sooner than you think. What happened to the hootchy-koos?"

"One of them got into trouble last night."

"The one who came home or the other one?"

"Did one of them come home?"

"Cops," he said. "No manners atall." He pronounced it as one word. "Yeah, Mr. Question Man, one of 'em came home."

"Which one?"

"Slow down. You think I just sit herc and stare out the window?"

"Yes."

"He, he, he," he wheezed. "Well, I do. The one who dopes all the time. She can't walk no better than me."

"What time?"

He pursed his lips, making them disappear into a vortex of wrinkles. "Eleven," he said, "maybe eleven-ten."

"She went into the apartment?"

"Sure. Where else is she gonna go? Up here?"

"You know for sure it was the dopey one?"

"I was watching, wasn't I? Dropped her keys twice, kicked the door. Seen her do it before."

"Who was she with?"

"Nobody. Went in alone, for a change."

"Did someone drop her off?"

"That's a different question, ain't it? One of them little red cars."

"Who was in it?"

"Two people. One driving and one sitting, like usual. They drove off when she got to the door."

I took a deep breath. "Did she leave again?"

"Yup. Those girls don't stay home."

"When?"

"Pardon?" His eyes glittered maliciously.

"When did she leave?"

"Fifteen minutes. Walked out and turned left. That enough for you?"

"Was anybody waiting for her?"

"Nope. Staggering around on her own."

"And did she come back?"

"Dead, isn't she?" he asked.

"Why do you ask?"

"Well, she didn't. Come back. And then you cops turn up."

"We do indeed," I said.

"Finished?"

"Yes," I said, pulling the door open again, "I'm finished."

"Not exactly Academy Award time," Norman Stillman was saying in what was supposed to be an incisive tone. "Not exactly Bette Davis in *Dark Victory.*" Neither Dixie Cohen nor I pointed out that Davis had lost that year.

It was the next day. After I'd waved good-bye to the Peeper, who was watching me from his aerie, I'd called my answering machine from a pay phone at Fountain and Vista. Dixie had called and, in the tone of voice Dan Rather might use to announce that Europe had disappeared from the map, told me that Stillman wanted to see me Sunday at nine A.M. At his house.

We were in the den, an inevitably nautical room about the size of Colorado. If it had been any more shipshape, the floor would have rolled beneath our feet. I'd been kept waiting as a further hint that I was not the flavor of the month. After a precise fifteen minutes Stillman had swept in with Cohen in tow. He'd favored me with a well-practiced piercing glare and started right in by getting his Oscars wrong.

"You've only got one job," Stillman continued. "That's to stay with Toby. You've got ten thousand dollars of my money to stay with Toby. So what happens? On the first night out, you let him get away from you, and a girl gets killed."

Dixie clucked reprovingly and shook his head. The two of them were dressed right out of Western Costume: Stillman had come ashore in white slacks and a navy blue blazer with, honest to God, an anchor embroidered on the pocket in metallic thread, and Cohen was wearing yet another corduroy suit. *Cord du roy*, cloth of the king, come down a peg or two to hang on Dixie Cohen's despair-ridden, unregal figure.

"So?" Stillman said.

"I beg your pardon?" I'd stopped listening a minute ago, thinking about the "girl" who got killed. Stillman raised his eyes heavenward, a not-so-ancient mariner on the lookout for the albatross.

"So why shouldn't I can you right now?" he said.

"Can me. It's Toby's money anyway. He'll be interested to know that you're being so frugal with his residuals."

Stillman was too much of a pro to look surprised that I knew he'd paid me with Toby's money. "His *future* residuals," he said. "If he's not in prison where he can't collect them. And, by the way, are you threatening me?"

"Norman," Dixie Cohen said warningly.

"I'd like some coffee," I said. "It's early. And yes, I'm threatening you."

There was a moment of silence. Stillman discovered that his cuffs needed adjusting and adjusted them. Dixie thrust his hands deep into his trouser pockets and balled them into fists.

"You'll wreck your pleats," I told him. "It's hard to keep pleats in corduroy."

"Don't I know it," Cohen said wearily. He took his hands out of his pockets.

"Do we *have* coffee on this boat?" I asked. "Maybe I could have some hard tack or a ship's biscuit to go with it."

Stillman made a small impatient gesture, and Dixie scurried out the door. To avoid looking at me, Stillman went over to a map of the Pacific just like the one in his office and regarded it dramatically. A red pin informed me that the *Cabuchon* was still in Honolulu. I was wishing I were, too, when he yanked the pin and moved it an inch to the right. California bound.

"You should have a pin for Toby," I said.

He didn't turn to face me. "I thought you were my pin in Toby," he said acidly. "Apparently I was mistaken." I let it ride. Beverly Hills birds sang outside the window. They didn't sound any better than Topanga birds.

"I'm a successful man, Mr. Grist." Stillman finally passed on the Pacific and let his eyes wander around the den, taking in the results of all that success. "I'm not inclined to overlook failure."

"Stop talking like a KGB operative. Toby scammed me. He's good at it. You should know. Anyway, I kept the cops away from him, for now. Of course, that's an omission I can always correct."

"My God, you really *are* threatening me," Stillman said. He sounded relieved to be on familiar ground. "I'm not without influence, you know. I can have your license."

"What would you do with it?"

Dixie scuttled back in. In Stillman's presence, he seemed to walk sideways, like a crab eyeing a tourist. "Coffee's on the way," he said.

"That's not the point, and you know it," Stillman said to me. He still hadn't raised his voice. I didn't imagine he ever raised his voice. "The point is—"

"The point is that you're blowing smoke. It's only a matter of time before the cops get around to Toby. The boy's got bad habits, and the habits are on record, and the cops aren't stupid. What we should be talking about is where we go from here."

"You mean you don't know?" Dixie said. He sounded disappointed. Stillman went back to the Pacific.

"Sure, I know," I said. "We figure out who killed the young woman."

"A drug addict," Stillman said fastidiously, eyeing an area just north of Guam. I was liking him less by the minute. I hadn't liked him that much to begin with.

"Drug addicts can get killed just like the rest of us," I said. "They probably even object to it."

"That's not my problem," Stillman said.

"Yes, it is," Cohen and I said simultaneously. "Norman," Dixie added respectfully.

"Good for you, Dixie," I said. "You're beginning to figure it out."

"It doesn't make any difference whether he did it or not," Dixie explained to Stillman's back. "Once it gets out that the cops are talking to Toby, it's over. Six years of putting up with him down the toilet."

"Well, *I* know that," Stillman said nastily. "That's why you geniuses are here, to keep it from getting to Toby. Isn't that what we're talking about?"

"Of course, Norman," Dixie said.

"Well, excuse me," I said. "I thought we were talking about firing me."

"Oh, that," Stillman said, sounding impatient. "That was Dixie's idea." Now it was Dixie's turn to roll his eyes heavenward, but he did it behind Stillman's back.

A stout Hispanic maid came in carrying a silver coffee service, and Stillman tore himself away from the briny deep. Dixie stopped rolling his eyes. "Thank you, Vicenta," Stillman said. There was one cup on the tray. I took it without asking and poured.

Dixie cleared his throat. "I've already had a call, Norman," he said, "from Joanna Link."

Stillman paled beneath his sunlamp tan. "Oh, no," he said. "Anybody but Joanna Link."

"Sorry," Dixie said. "She wants to come to the set tomorrow."

"What have I done?" Stillman said. "I take care of my mother. I contribute to African famine. I give to the Urban League."

"Joanna who?" I said.

They looked at me as though I'd lapsed into Morse code. "Three hundred and fifty papers," Cohen said. "Joanna three hundred and fifty papers Link. Joanna Here's the Fucking News from Hollywood Link."

"Oh," I said. "Joanna *Link*." I'd never heard of her.

"Keep her away," Stillman said. "How does she know anything, anyway?"

"Keep Joanna Link away?" Cohen said. "I could keep the Huns from the gates of Rome if I had the time, I could keep Héloïse from Abelard, but keep Joanna Link away from a story? I'd have to kill her. Not that I haven't thought about it."

"How *does* she know anything?" I asked.

"The young lady's picture was in the paper this morning," Dixie said. "It's the kind of story they love. NUDE DANCER BATTERED." He sounded like Toby. "As luck would have it, one of Link's spies, some two-bit paparazzi, has a picture of Toby and this dame. Going into Nicky Blair's, can you imagine that?"

"Nicky Blair's?" Stillman parroted. "Toby took this junkie to Nicky *Blair's*?" He put both hands over his face. "He's got a death wish."

"Trouble is," I said, "she's the one who's dead. And she's not a junkie anymore."

"Spare me the self-righteous posturing. I've got enough on my mind. So you stay on the payroll, is that settled?"

"Not quite. I need an assistant."

"What time is Link supposed to be there?" Stillman asked Cohen nervously. "An assistant for what?" he asked me.

"Three o'clock," Cohen said. "We're on Stage Six tomorrow."

Stillman looked at his nautical watch, as if counting the hours between Sunday morning and Monday afternoon. Maybe the watch had Monday on it. It was big enough. "Does Toby know?"

"Not yet."

"Has he got much to do?"

"About twelve pages."

"Dialogue or action?"

"Dialogue. Including the scene with the little kid."

"Twelve pages, the little kid, and Link? He'll plotz."

"To watch Toby," I said.

Stillman looked at me blankly. "What?"

"To watch Toby. I need an assistant to watch Toby."

"I've missed something," Stillman said. "Something's got past me here. *You're* supposed to be watching Toby."

"Think, Mr. Stillman. How can I bird-dog Toby twenty-four hours a day and figure out who killed the girl? It's two different jobs, or at least you'd better hope it is. If it isn't, Joanna Link's going to have a very big story."

"Joanna Link," Dixie echoed, a kind of lugubrious verbal knee jerk.

"Dixie?" Stillman said doubtfully.

"I think you've gotta let him try it, Norman. It's not that much more money, considering."

"Exactly *how* much?" Stillman made a tent with his well-buffed fingers and regarded me through it. It was a gesture he'd put some work into.

"Three fifty a day." The woman's asking price was one fifty, but she'd have to put up with Toby, and I didn't feel like saving Stillman money.

"Jesus, I know agents I can get for that much."

"Good. Get an agent."

"Don't get huffy," Stillman said.

"Agents." Dixie made it sound like a profanity.

"Oh, damn it," I said, "don't nickel-and-dime me." I stood up. "We're lazing around here talking, and there are things I should be doing. Like it or not, the police are working their way toward Toby. Either you want to protect the goose who lays the golden eggs or you don't. Three fifty it is, and it's cheap at the price, considering the alternative."

Stillman gave me something that would have passed for a soothing smile if the room had been a lot dimmer. "We're just haggling," he said. "Nothing personal. Call your man in. I'll leave a pass so he can get on the lot."

"She'll come on the lot with Toby," I said. "She's been sitting on top of him since three yesterday afternoon."

The smile scattered to the four winds. "She?" Stillman said. "You're putting a woman with Toby?"

"She can handle him."

Stillman pursed his lips and then nodded. "Good," he said. "No more haggling." He worked up the smile again. "But think ahead, okay? I like a man who thinks ahead."

I smiled back. "And I like a man who likes a man who thinks ahead."

"Done, then," Stillman said. He walked briskly out of the room.

"Thank heaven," Dixie said. "That was getting disgusting." He picked up his oversize briefcase and gave it a tug to see if it had gained any weight during the conversation.

"Dixie," I said, "what in the world are you doing here?"

He looked surprised. "Earning my daily bread. Quite a lot of it, in fact."

"You're too mournful to be a press agent."

"I'm not a press agent." He drummed his fingers on the side of the case. "I'm a public relations consultant. Norman is my only client."

"You're a schoolteacher," I said. "Héloïse and Abelard indeed. I know a teacher when I see one. That chronic expression of impending disaster can only be acquired in a classroom. And then there's all that corduroy."

The closest thing I'd ever seen to a smile scudded briefly across Dixie's face. It was faster than the Roadrunner with the Coyote in full pursuit with his Acme rocket boosters on. "I'm an English teacher," he said. "*Was* an English teacher."

"Allow me to repeat my question. What are you doing here?"

He thought for a moment. "Othello," he said.

"As in the Moor of Venice?"

"That's the one. Good for you."

"Well, it's not a very common name."

"I don't think *I'd* like it," he said. "Othello Cohen."

"Not much of a ring to it. You'd probably have to change it."

"Othello Schwartz, maybe. That's a joke. Schwartz means black in German."

"I know. Would you like to fill in the blanks?"

"I was Norman's English teacher. He wasn't Norman then, which is to say that he was *Norman*, but he wasn't the Norman you've met."

"And whom we all know and love."

"Norman's all right. He really *likes* the shows he makes."

"He'd have a lot on his conscience if he didn't."

"Norman needed some polish back then. He's pretty slick now, don't you think?"

"Slicker than an Olympic rink."

"Well, twelve years ago, he was pure Jersey. That was before it was fashionable to be Jersey, if you're old enough to remember. If asked, he'd have requested a few of dese and a few of dose. He pronounced burger with an *o* and an *i*, heavy on the *i*. He'd just come out to L.A. and he was planning to be a big shot, and he was smart enough to know that he didn't sound smart. Plus you could have floated his frame of reference in a thimble."

"So he went to school."

"Cal State University out in Northridge. Far enough

from Hollywood that he wouldn't run into anybody he might know or eventually want to know, but closer than, say, Tucson. He walked into my Intro to Lit class and stayed. The next semester he was in all three of my classes. I've never had such an avid student. He listened so hard he made me forget what I was saying. You know, most of the kids are just sitting there letting the teacher provide the background music while they tune up their hormones. The estrogen level in the average undergrad classroom is higher than Alpha Centauri."

"I remember. I taught too, for about six weeks."

"Then you know. Well, Norman was different. He was older, of course, but that wasn't it. He sat there and sucked in everything I said. I never saw anybody make so many notes. Later he showed them to me; he'd made up his own form of speedwriting, and he had me practically verbatim. Well, that's flattering to someone who's used to feeling like Muzak. His papers were appalling, but there was so much evident effort that I couldn't flunk him, and so I asked him to come see me during office hours."

"Office hours," I said. "What a quaint concept."

"Yeah. I remember them fondly. It meant there were hours that weren't office hours. So he came, and we talked, and I asked him what he wanted out of school. He'd never said much in class, and I almost laughed out loud when he told me he was there for 'culchuh.' It took me a minute to realize that he meant culture. Pretty snotty reaction for a kid who grew up in Brooklyn, but I hadn't spent much time in the real world then. It was all college, first learning and then teaching.

"What he wanted was a sort of topographic map of the things a cultured person should know about. A Michelin guide to highbrow cocktail conversation, at least by Hollywood standards. I told him he was wasting his time shoveling through 'Piers Plowman' and the lyric poems of Leigh Hunt. L.A. cocktail glasses don't come that deep. Hell, they don't come that deep at Harvard."

We were walking toward the front door now, down a high, vaulted entrance hall. To our left a Spanish archway about fourteen feet wide opened into a sunken living room with the most beautifully buffed oak floor I'd ever seen. Everything in the room was seashell pink except for a chest-high vase of birds of paradise, an enormous ersatz Impressionist portrait of Stillman, a matching picture of a smashing blond lady I took to be Mrs. Stillman, and a wall lined from floor to ceiling with books. I had never been in such a silent house.

"Your legacy?" I said, meaning the books.

Dixie eyed them glumly. "He's read them all, too," he said. "He's like a terrier, just never lets go. We made out a list of about one hundred books and plays he had to read, and I loaned him a copy of H. G. Wells's *Outline of History* because it was short, so he could connect the dots. Norman went out and bought himself a roll of butcher paper, thirty feet long and five feet wide. He made a historical timeline on it as he read the Wells, and then he entered each of the hundred or so books and a few notes on its author. Damnedest thing you ever saw. In fact . . ."

He stopped and turned toward the kitchen. "Vicenta," he called. "Vicenta, *por favor?*"

After a moment the maid emerged. *"Señor Cohen?"* She gave him a warmer smile than she'd given Stillman.

"La sala por trabajo," he said in highly inventive Spanish. *"Es okay?"*

"Porqué no?" She shrugged and preceded us up the stairs.

Upstairs the front of the house was standard millionaire's Mediterranean, four doors leading off a central hallway into bedrooms and guest rooms, presumably with connecting bathrooms. Set into the left-hand hallway wall, the one facing the backyard, was a single door, only a few feet from the top of the stairs. Other than that, the wall was blank. Vicenta knocked once and then opened the door.

A single, enormous room ran the entire length of the house. The far wall was all window, looking out onto palm trees and a pale blue pool. Sprinklers spiraled sparkles across the grass.

The other three walls were books from the floor to waist high. Above the books, five feet wide and running the entire length and width of the room, was an unbroken sheet of paper more than sixty feet long. Three broad stripes ran its length, one blue, one red, one black. There was writing everywhere.

"This year's model," Cohen said. "He's never stopped. The red is history, the blue is science, and the black is the arts—you know, 'culchuh.' "

"Son of a bitch," I said.

"Norman's conquest of Western civilization. You've got to give it to him."

"There should be an award."

Dixie made a gesture that took in the room, house, yard, everything. "He hasn't exactly been stiffed."

"What's that?" I pointed toward a large box about two-thirds of the way down the timeline. The writing was black, and the entry branched off the black line, but the sides of the box were drawn in thick gold lines. It was the only place where a fourth color had been used.

"Take a look," Cohen said. I did.

OTHELLO, it said. "Tragedy (1603) in five acts by William Shakespeare (see entry). Themes: good, evil, trust, jealousy. Motorcycles."

"Motorcycles?" I said.

"That was the beginning of Norman Stillman," Dixie said. "*Othello* was the ninth or tenth thing I had him read. He turned it into a motorcycle movie. *Black Angel*, he called it. About the black leader of a motorcycle gang, his envious white second in command, and his white mama, if you'll excuse the expression. It was probably the last motorcycle movie to make any money, and it made a fortune.

Norman never looked back. Three years later he came and offered me four times my teaching salary to work for him."

"And you took it?"

Cohen looked out the window. "Teaching is for losers," he said. "For losers who don't have to pay alimony and child support." It sounded like something he'd rehearsed.

"It's a good job for the right person."

"I was the wrong person."

"So you've traded in the students for Joanna Link."

Dixie shuddered and glanced once more around the room. "At my present rate of pay, if the interview lasts an hour, Joanna Link comes in at about thirty-five dollars a pound. Even veal doesn't cost that much. I can always sneak looks at her and decide how I want the butcher to cut her up."

He closed the door on the world according to Norman Stillman and went back down the stairs. At the front door, he paused. "Where will you be tomorrow, if you're not going to be with us?"

"Out and around. I'll come back at three to hand-hold Toby through the Link interview if you think it's a good idea."

"All the help we can get," Cohen said. "And you're going to stay with him for the evening, or will your man do it?"

"Woman," I said. "I'll stay with him. We've got an appointment at seven."

"What kind of an appointment?"

"You don't want to know."

"Who says I don't?"

I wiggled my eyebrows at him. "It's a wake."

10

Fan Fare

NANA'S KEYS worked just fine.

I'd circled the block three times and strolled through the parking lot twice. Nana had told me that Tiny drove a big white dirty Lincoln Continental with dark windows and brass wire wheels. If it was anywhere within half a mile, I hadn't spotted it. Tiny didn't look like the kind of guy who walked more than a yard if he didn't have to.

So he probably wasn't around. Unless he'd had someone drive him. Unless someone had stolen his car. Unless he'd hidden the car because he knew I was coming and wanted to catch me by surprise and break every bone in my body. I gave my imagination an hour off, hefted the tire iron I was carrying in my gloved right hand, and pushed the door open.

A sour puff of air-conditioning and old cigarette smoke rolled out into the parking lot. It smelled like a year's worth of dry cleaning from a Holiday Inn. I leaned into the now familiar hallway, tapped the door politely with the tire iron, and called out cheerfully, "Hello? Anybody home?"

If anybody was, he kept it to himself.

The light switch did what it was supposed to do. The walls glistened at me like a giant throat. Going in, I felt like a tongue depressor.

"Open sesame," I said to the door at the end of the hall. It seemed like an appropriate password for the Spice Rack. All it took was that and the second of Nana's keys. I was back at the scene of the crime.

The lights for the main room were all the way across the room behind the bar, Nana had said, so I left the door open behind me until I found it. The first switch I hit turned on the overheads, rather than the dancers' spots. I went back and closed the door to the parking lot, locking it from inside.

Without the pink stage lights, the Spice Rack looked like the kind of place they show high school kids in the films that teach them how to avoid syphilis. The lurid red paint on the walls was patched and peeling, the chairs tattooed with cigarette burns. A couple of county-fair prize five-ounce cockroaches scurried across the stage where Amber had been laid out on Friday night.

I had no idea how long I might have. I gave only ten minutes to the main room; the cops had been over it pretty thoroughly. The bathrooms, which might have figured prominently in the same syphilis film, took about four minutes each. Except for a small packet of coke taped behind the toilet in the ladies' room—some blitzed-out dancer's forgotten stash—I found nothing of interest. I put the coke back; now that I'd seen the club in the daytime, I figured the poor girl would need it if she ever got her memory back.

None of Nana's keys fit the lock on Tiny's private office, but then I hadn't figured they would. That was one of the reasons I'd brought the tire iron.

It wasn't a particularly deft approach, but it didn't have to be. The locks were terrific, and Tiny had so much faith in them that he'd forgotten all about the doorjamb. The wood was old and rotten, and the nails that held the boards to the loose plaster of the wall might as well have been staples. A couple of good pulls on the iron, and the door frame kissed the wall good-bye. It was a pretty rough kiss. It carried the door with it, back out into the corridor.

I felt the odd thrill I always feel when I break into someone's inner sanctum. People have so many secrets, and they hide them so clumsily. I tried once to explain my reaction to Eleanor, and she said I should seek psychiatric help. Maybe someday I will. In the meantime I'll just grit my teeth and enjoy breaking and entering.

The office wasn't much. A computer sat on top of one of those old gray metal desks that people always think are secure, and the remainder of the decor consisted of a faded, greasy cloth couch that might once have been brown, a small rug, and a sliding door that I guessed led to Tiny's closet. The desk was locked and the closet wasn't, and I've always liked going through people's closets, so I started there.

Tiny had lots of white clothes. They hung neatly, with four pairs of surprisingly small white shoes lined up beneath them. I started with the shoes: all empty. Wondering whether Tiny kept so many changes of clothing in the club because he was likely to get bled on in the course of an evening, I sank my arms up to the elbows in their white folds and looked for pockets. There were a great many pockets, so many that you would have thought Tiny kept things in them. He didn't. The closet was a total bust. I didn't even learn the name of Tiny's tailor.

The part of the couch that wasn't dirt and grease was couch, pure and simple. It didn't do anything cute, like explode into a bed, and there was nothing underneath the cushions or in the folds beneath them. I pulled the whole thing out from the wall and winced. Tiny didn't have dust rats; he had dust giant sloths. The dust was just dust.

The desk popped open as if it had yearned for years to be searched. In it I found my first two surprises.

The first was a phone book. There were no names in it, only numbers, but I have a good memory for numbers. I found Nana's and Toby's. Then I got *very* interested because I was looking at mine. It was penciled in at the bottom of the last full page, obviously a recent addition. Just for the hell of it, I wrote down the other numbers in the book, using a pad on Tiny's desk that had a bright yellow butterfly at the top of it. I put the phone book back and tried the second drawer. It was double-locked, and it took me a good eight seconds to snap it open.

There was surprise number two, a trove of porno magazines thicker than the Manhattan Yellow Pages, hanging in Pendaflex folders. Someone in Tiny's position, I would have thought, would have been as fascinated by pornography as a man on a low-cholesterol diet is by a nice piece of steamed fish. There they were, though, a prurient testament to the art of the four-color printer. As porno went, these were pretty innocent. No hard-core action, just an undergraduate gynecologist's primer on immature female genitalia, except that the mature girls featured in *Teenage House Party* and *Young Whippersnappers* had clearly lied about their age.

No wonder Tiny was so sweet to the girls, I thought. What he really liked was pictures. A "voyer," Saffron would call him. And no wonder he'd fastened on Amber. Before the drugs raddled her body and fried her eyes, she could have made the cover of *Young Whippersnappers.*

And so what? I wasn't checking into Tiny's sexual predilections. Or, if I was, it was only a peripheral concern. And while I was certainly interested in Amber, I wasn't betting that any long-ago porno photographer had killed her. Nor did I think that sex had been involved in any way. The Saturday papers had said that the preliminary autopsy showed no evidence of sexual molestation, only extreme physical violence with massive trauma to the head. Amber's murder was hatred pure and simple. The only lust involved was bloodlust.

I sat on the couch and thought. I was missing something, and I knew it. Even given the porn, Tiny couldn't be this clean. I rifled the calendar on the wall and flipped through the papers on the desk. Nothing. I could barely work my own computer, so I certainly couldn't pry into Tiny's. Nevertheless, all my instincts told me I'd missed something. I listened to my watch tick.

"Well, stupid," I said out loud. "You haven't looked under the rug."

I peeled it back and found myself staring at the same dreary 1950s linoleum that covered the floor of the Spice Rack. Talk about wax buildup. It was thicker than Amber's mascara had been. Except for one perfect square, three tiles long on each side. The wax outlining that square was chipped and broken.

I got onto my hands and knees. To one side of the square, halfway down, was a tiny slit about a quarter of an inch long, wider at the bottom than at the top. It went right down through the linoleum. It looked a hell of a lot like a keyhole.

So, okay. The key, whatever it was, was either on Tiny or it was here. If Tiny had it, there was nothing I could do, so I chose to believe it was here. If it was here, it wasn't very big.

First I reopened the closet and went through the shoes again, shaking each one to check for a false heel. Nobody really has false heels, and Tiny was no exception. Then I ran my hands down the seams and linings of his clothes. No deal. Then I took the desk apart a second time. When I'd finished that, I spread the couch all over the office and put it back together again.

I looked down at it. For all its grease, it looked inviting. It was just the spot for a bout of concentration. I sank back into it and thought about hiding places. My watch told me I'd been in the club for forty-three minutes. I'd allowed myself forty-five.

The best hiding places are in plain sight. In a famous short story someone hides a diamond in a glass of water, where it would disappear. Trouble was, something long and thin could disappear almost anywhere. And I'd been almost everywhere in that office. Correction. I'd been everywhere.

Which meant it was someplace I'd already been.

Clothes hangers? No, too thick. Nails? Same problem.

Well, then, the next rule was to hide it where people were afraid to look. And then I remembered my friend Carl.

Carl made a living smuggling. Specifically, he smuggled religious pictures, and even more specifically, he smuggled them out of Asia and into the United States. He didn't make much money, but he liked Asia and the smuggling paid for his tickets. Getting his smuggled artworks into the United States was no problem because U.S. customs exempt art and antiques from duty. The problem was getting them out of Asia. Many Asian countries require a special duty charge to take antiques out, and others make it almost impossible to export a likeness of the Buddha. Asian art and Asian religions being what they were, antique likenesses of the Buddha are at the top of any small-time smuggler's shopping list. The solution, Carl discovered, lay in the intrinsic male-to-male sensitivity of the Asian customs inspector.

He'd buy a couple of copies of an inoffensive Asian skin magazine, say the heavily censored Singapore edition of *Playboy*, and he'd fold up his pictures and place them between the pages. Then he'd take a glue stick and run it around the edges of the pages and paste them together so the pictures were sealed from sight. When they dried he'd iron them to get rid of any telltale ripples and then hide them in his luggage as carefully as he would have if they'd been a kilo of heroin. When the inspectors found them, as they very frequently did, he'd blush scarlet and muster his most embarrassed smile. It worked every time except the last time; up until then, the customs inspector had always smiled back, one guy to another, and helped him hide the magazines so the women in line behind him didn't see them. The last time, unfortunately for Carl, the inspector was a woman.

The porno was in the double-locked drawer, hanging in Pendaflex folders. There was nothing in the magazines or at the bottom of the folders. Pendaflex folders hang in the file drawer courtesy of metal rods that run the width of the drawer and hook into steel runners on the upper inside walls of the drawers. Long thin metal rods.

The one I wanted was in the fifth folder back. At one end the rod was hooked, just like all the others, but the other end had been filed into an irregular serrated pattern. Despite the clumsiness of the gloves, I managed to pull it out of the folder and slip it into the crack in the linoleum. The square popped open. I was looking at surprise number three: six large brown glass jars.

Two of them held the smaller pills that Toby had identified as codeine, and the other four were full to the brim with Doriden. Good old paternal Tiny was dealing loads.

I'd been there more than an hour, and it was time to move. The linoleum square locked with Japanese precision, and the key slipped back into the folder. I didn't want Tiny to know that anyone had discovered his stash, even if his office and the desk had been broken into.

On the way out I used the tire iron to break open both doors, the one into the main room and the one leading from the parking lot into the hallway. Then I closed them as best I could. It wasn't perfect, but I didn't want it to be. At least no one would suspect that a key had been used.

Squinting in the sunlight of a bright, peaceful Sunday afternoon, I pointed Alice toward Fan Fare.

There isn't much of Hollywood left on Hollywood Boulevard, but Hollywood Boulevard was the only place Fan Fare could possibly have been. Fan Fare is the Smithsonian Institution of motion picture ephemera. Its proprietor, Wyl Will (born William Williams), is an aging, blue-haired gentleman who, had he had his druthers and been born a respectable middle-class lady, would have been the pride of any small-town library in America. Small towns in the fifties, however, were not a comfortable place for someone like Wyl, and he'd had the sense to head for California, where he became a librarian of a different kind. If anything's been written about Hollywood, Wyl knows where to find it.

Sunday is a big tourist day on Hollywood Boulevard. People from Ohio and Illinois rub sunburned shoulders with Japanese tourists, ogling the chewing gum that splatters the stars on the Walk of Fame and kicking the bags from McDonald's out of the way to force their big feet into Joan Crawford's tiny concrete footprints in the courtyard of what used to be Grauman's Chinese Theater.

Outside Fan Fare, a bunch of Hell's Angels from Central Casting straddled their bikes possessively and made derogatory remarks about the tourists. The dope of the day seemed to be downers mixed with French fries from Jack's Triple Burger. Jack's, long the BankAmerica of chemical ecstasy, had been taken over by Iranians. The Angels were still there, so I supposed the dope was, too.

When I opened the door to Fan Fare, an electronic doorbell played the first four bars of "Tara's Theme" from *Gone With the Wind.* The cotton fields that shimmered into my mind's eye were no match for the real vista of what seemed like miles of books and magazines, stacked neatly onto shelves and piled haphazardly onto tables, according to their worth. I knew Wyl made a tidy living from Fan Fare, but every time I went there I seemed to be the only customer in the world. With the exception of a pimpled youth in a long black cape who was transfixed by the section on Dracula, it was true that day as well.

"Wyl," I called out. "John Beresford Tipton has sent me to make you a millionaire."

"Again?" Wyl's voice floated from the back of the store. "I'll have to buy a king-size bed. My mattress is absolutely *stuffed.*"

I headed for the main counter, but Wyl intercepted me. He can do that: he's the only man I ever met who can actually materialize. "Dear Simeon," he said. "How's Eleanor?"

"I'll tell you tomorrow. I'm having dinner with her tonight."

"But things are still . . ." He hesitated. "Fait accompli?" He gave his hand a small loose-wristed shake, a gesture that means "no way" all over the world.

"As far as she's concerned. I'm still working on it."

He patted my arm. "Faint heart ne'er won fair lady," he said.

"Yo," I said to aggravate him. "No guts, no glory. If you want it, go for it."

"You make her sound like a strike in bowling. Altogether too blue-collar. Nothing against the huddled masses, of course. God knows my heart is with them." It was, too. Wyl was a socialist from way back.

"Wyl," I said, "what have you done to your eyes?"

He closed them halfway. "You tell me."

"They're, um, different. Not that they don't look nice."

"Please. We both know they look like Joan Collins at four A.M. Not that *that* doesn't have something to recommend it."

"To whom?"

"To Dr. Alfred Nesbit, for one. He's the one who did it. At my urging, of course, and at considerable cost."

"You have a doctor doing your eyes?"

"Well, only once, silly. Who could afford one every day? They're tattooed."

"Tattooed? But that means—"

"Exactly. That I can't take them off. But I forgot. Of course, you don't know, do you? Mother died."

"Oh, Wyl," I said. "I'm sorry."

He patted my hand. "That's sweet of you. But it was a mercy, really. She'd got to the point where she thought she was still in Shaker Heights. She didn't even know she was old anymore. Not a bad way to go, really."

"So you had your eyes tattooed?"

"Certainly. No more reason to take them off every night. God, it was such a bother to put them on again. When I was younger I enjoyed it, all those hours in front of the mirror to look simply killing in case fate decided to deal one an ace out of the clear blue sky. After one reaches a certain age, though, one becomes satisfied with kings, and, if one wishes to avoid queens, one learns to settle for jacks or even the occasional ten, and the tens don't usually care if one's eyes are perfect. But *I* know, don't I? This way, they're always fine."

"Like having your hair starched."

He mused for a moment. "I hadn't thought of that, actually. Might make sleeping difficult."

"Wyl," I said. "Toby Vane."

"Oooh," he said. "That terrible television show. Which I watch religiously every week, of course. What about him?"

"I want everything you've got."

Wyl narrowed his eyes in an attempt to look shrewd. "For reading or for buying?"

"For buying. And I'll make you a deal. After I've finished with it, I'll give it back to you and you can sell it all over again, assuming anyone is dumb enough to want it."

"Why would you do that?"

"Why not? I'm not out to create a permanent collection. You don't have to bind the stuff."

"I have some lovely vinyl."

"Bind it to death, then, if it'll make it easier for you to sell when I'm through with it."

"You must have *some* expense account. Do you know him?"

I thought about it. "In a manner of speaking."

"Is it true what they say about him?"

"That depends on what they say about him, doesn't it?"

"That he beats up a girl every morning just to work up an appetite for breakfast."

"Something like that."

"Honey," Wyl said, "the poor lad obviously hasn't admitted something to himself. Do you think it's ever occurred to him that he might prefer boys?"

"That's an interesting idea. But I'm sure it hasn't."

"Just as well," Wyl said thoughtfully. "He'd probably wind up punching them, too."

"Have you got much on him?"

"Scads, and all of it recent, naturally. Not difficult to find. Do you really want to give it back after you read it?"

"Sure, but there's a catch."

"Goes without saying. You're going to dog-ear it or something."

"No. Because you're going to do it for me. Every page that's got anything to do with Toby."

"Dog-earing is barbaric. Haven't you got any respect for the printed word?"

"But you'll do it."

"No, I won't. No dog-earing, no paper clips. Tell you what. I'll use those cute little yellow sticky things. You can just peel them off as you go."

"Buy some extras," I said, "and save the receipts."

"Honey, no need. My whole *life* is arranged around stick-its. One entire wall of my kitchen is literally papered with them. I use them for taxes, inventory, shopping lists, reminders, phone messages, calendars, everything. I even used one on a cut finger once. And, do you know, I'm so much a creature of habit that I wrote 'Cut' on it before I put it on my finger? That reminds me, did I ever tell you about the time I saw Lee J. Cobb?"

"Lee J. Cobb? No, I don't think you did."

Wyl took a long breath. "In the market, of all places, actually doing his shopping. Of course this was some time ago, almost before there was smog. He had such a mean mouth, you could tell he'd suffered. There I was in the checkout line, reading *TV Guide*, it was so little in those

days and Lucy was *always* on the cover, and I looked up
when someone bumped my derriere with a shopping cart,
and ohmygod it was Lee J. Cobb. I had this whole cart just
piled with stuff—Mother always saved coupons, and I did
my shopping for weeks at a time, more stuff than they put
with the pharaoh into the Great Pyramid—and he only had
some celery and a chicken breast, poor man must have
been trying to lose weight, and I know how that is, so
naturally I let him go first. He grunted at me."

"Grunted?"

"I knew it meant thanks. Well, I went home in an absolute daze and put everything away, labeling it first like I
always do, but this was before stick-its, so I just wrote on
the paper with a crayon, humming to myself and thinking
about *Death of a Salesman* and that adorable Kevin McCar-
thy. And you know, about a week later when I was having
some friends over for dinner, I went to the freezer to find
the leg of lamb I'd bought that day, and when I pulled it
out it had a great big LEE J. COBB written on it. Is it any
wonder I'm in this business?"

"Everything on Toby," I said. "Okay?"

"I thought we'd already settled that."

"The stick-its are fine."

"Don't you ever use them? They'd be perfect for you,
you could take notes on them. Come to think of it, I've
never seen you take any notes. Sometimes I don't actually
believe you're a detective."

"Let me use your phone, then. You can listen in, and
then you'll know."

"Of course. You know where it is by now. Just write
down the numbers of any toll calls on the stick-its next to
the phone and put them on the wall. Listen, I think Dracula
over there needs some help. Do you mind?"

"Not at all. But I thought you wanted to prove to yourself that I'm a private investigator."

"Honey, Draculas never take very long."

The phone was an old black number with a dial. It weighed about fifteen pounds. My first call was to Bernie Siegel, a professional graduate student who had abandoned his will to the siren call of UCLA and was there, apparently, for life. Bernie had more degrees than I did. He was the aging top gun of research, always waiting for some punk kid with thicker glasses to come along and prove he was faster with an index card.

He answered on the first ring; he was probably curled up next to the phone reading Heidegger or Swedenborg for a nice, relaxing afternoon.

"Bernie," I said, "fifteen dollars an hour."

"There are people I won't hurt, Simeon," he said. "Give me a minute and I'll think of some."

I gave him a minute. Then I gave him another one.

"Okay," he said. "Who is it?"

"Everybody in South Dakota named Sprunk. Only, you don't have to beat them up. You just have to get me their addresses and telephone numbers."

"That sounds more than fairly boring."

"That's why it's fifteen dollars an hour."

"How about North Dakota? They're the same except for a couple of letters."

Toby always said South Dakota. Would he have lied? After a moment, I realized that Toby probably couldn't spell a name for the Information operator without changing a few letters for fun. "Sure. Also the other states that border it."

"Canada borders it, too, if I have my geography right. No, I don't. But at least it borders North Dakota. Honest to Christ, why don't they just make it one big state and forget it?"

"This guy's not Canadian," I said with more assurance than I felt. "Just stick to that area of the USA, okay?"

"Sprunk? S-p-r-u-n-k?"

"How else would you spell Sprunk, Bernie?"

"Maybe he's French. Maybe it's with a q-u-e instead."

"Sprunque? That's not possible."

"Or German. Sprunch, with a hard *ch.*"

"Sprunk," I said, "the easy way. South Dakota and environs."

"Just making sure," he said. "How's Eleanor?"

"Why does everybody ask me how Eleanor is? Why don't you just ask Eleanor?"

"I don't have her phone number." Bernie had once been sweet on Eleanor in an appealingly sublimated way. He had taught her everything there was to know about the Chicago School of Architecture while working up the nerve to ask her out. By the time I met her she knew all about the infrastructure of skyscrapers, but she'd still never had a date with Bernie.

"And I'm not going to give it to you, either. Anyway, you've got all these Sprunks to keep you busy."

"When do you need it?"

"Tomorrow. I'll call you."

"I'll be waiting. Breathlessly," he added, "with my entire life held in precarious abeyance." He hung up.

Dolly Miles, the woman I'd hired as Toby's new watchdog, answered Toby's phone. "So how is he?" I asked.

"He's been good all day. He's just lying around in the sun with an aluminum reflector around his neck. Says that way he won't have to wear makeup tomorrow. But my God, Simeon, does he use a lot of dope."

"Stay away from it," I said.

"Stick it where the sun don't shine," Dolly said. "He'd just try to make a pass at me if he thought I was loaded." Dolly weighed almost two hundred pounds, but there was no telling about Toby.

"Keep your legs together," I said, "and let me talk to him."

Dolly muttered something resentful and dropped the phone. After a moment, Toby picked it up. Today he was featuring bluff but hearty.

"Champ," he said, "come on out and get some sun."

"Toby, listen to me. If you get that girl loaded and she loses you, I'll blame you and not her. And if I do, I'm going to break your nose, understand?"

"Hey, we're all in this together."

"Yeah, but I don't know how many of the Toby's are on my side."

"All of us," Toby said. "Toby, Toby, and Toby. Jack, too. Anyway, I'm sure Norman told you not to hit me in the face."

"Just behave," I said. "Think about your residuals, and don't lose Dolly."

"Meaty, isn't she? In fact, I wish she'd watch me from closer up."

This time I hung up. I was writing his phone number on a yellow stick-it when I became aware that Wyl was standing at my shoulder.

"God in heaven," he said. "Is that Toby Vane's home phone?"

I put it on the wall, and he leaned forward in a near-sighted fashion to read it. "How strange," he said. "All the numbers are odd, not an even one among them. How often do you see that? I wonder what a numerologist would make of it."

"Wyl. You show it to anyone or sell it to anyone, even a numerologist, and I'll have three Sicilians drop in on you and bleach out your eye makeup."

"Oh, *please*," Wyl said. "The Sicilians sound interesting, but don't you think I have any discretion? Don't you think I respect the stars? I know how they need their privacy."

I got up and headed for the door.

"My God," Wyl said behind me. "I didn't even ask Lee J. Cobb for his autograph."

11

Eleanor

"WHOA," Eleanor said, not quite sarcastically enough. "Hold on. Are you telling me you know Toby Vane? Gee. Holy moly. Radical." At the mention of Toby's name, several diners glanced over at us.

"Wyl says hello. He's had his eyes tattooed."

"What, like Queequeg?" Eleanor chose her reading by weight; she never opened anything that weighed less than a pound. "What color?"

"Kohl black. That's kohl, with an *h*."

"As in Egypt," she said patiently. "If you have to make puns, I guess they might as well be archaeological." She closed her eyes and held up a hand. "Wait, wait. Listen. Have you ever heard a joke with a punch line like 'So *that's* why they call it the Windy City'? Somebody told it to me a couple of days ago, but I can't remember how it began." She looked wonderful, one of nature's very best pieces of work. Her beautiful, straight black hair hung blunt cut at her collarbone, curving in slightly toward her pale, slender throat. Some tendrils were much longer than others. The bangs were feathered.

"No," I said. "And that's a new haircut."

"It's not so much a haircut as a landscape. You should have seen Dickie do it, all grim determination and serious snipping. I'm sure the people who splice genes do it with a lighter heart. I forgot, you don't know Dickie, do you. What's he like?"

182

"Who, Dickie?" I asked unpleasantly.

She ignored me, a skill she'd had considerable opportunity to cultivate. "Of course not. Toby."

"Jesus," I said. "The people I see all day ask me about you. Then I see you, and you ask me about Toby."

"How come nobody ever asks you about you?" she said.

"My point exactly. I used to be interesting."

She looked around the restaurant. "You're still interesting," she said in the tone she would have used to calm a querulous four-year-old. A well-dressed, upwardly mobile young couple seated themselves gracefully at the table next to us. Something on the woman's wrist sparkled discreetly. The man smiled. He looked like a commercial for a credit dentist.

"If I'm so interesting, how come you're looking at them?"

The man glanced over at her, and his smile broadened. I wouldn't have thought it was possible. Its corners were already crowding his ears. Eleanor gave him the merest ghost of a smile, a dimpling at the corners of her mouth that was a specialty of hers, in return. "Good to know I haven't lost it completely," she said complacently.

"I think you've got another fifty years."

Eleanor put her chin on her hand and glowed at me. "You *are* interesting," she said. "Interest me some more. For instance, tell me about Toby Vane."

"Oh, apes and monkeys. Don't tell me you watch the show, too."

"It takes a lot of people to make a rating point. I'm not too proud to be one of them. Anyway, he's a hunk."

"A hunk of what is the question."

She picked up a fork. "Is this the right one?"

"For what? There isn't any food yet."

"I thought I might stick it through your tongue."

"That one's not on the table. Waiter." I raised my hand.

"I hope it's dull," she said.

"I could arrange for you to meet him. He likes bouncing Oriental women around."

"Ah," she said, looking with great interest at her left forearm. "Is there one of those on the horizon?"

"Yes," I said, kicking myself under the table. "Half of one, anyway." The waiter appeared at my shoulder. "Do you want anything else to drink?" I asked Eleanor.

"Another 7-Up."

"And a white wine for me," I said. The waiter beamed at Eleanor as though she'd ordered a magnum of Dom Pérignon, ignored me completely, and left.

"Is she pretty?" Eleanor said. "And don't ask me who."

"I suppose she is."

"You forgot to ask for the fork."

"So I did."

"What's her name?"

"She's got a lot of names."

"Not the best character reference, is it?"

"Eleanor, I'm not checking her out for a security clearance. She's a girl, that's all."

"Ten years old? Twelve?"

"All right, a young woman."

"How young? And what do you mean, half of one?"

"How's what's-his-name?" I said.

"Don't start," Eleanor said. "You know perfectly well what his name is."

The salad arrived in the nick of time. We both chewed. It seemed safer than talking. While she was using her bread to mop up the plate, I said, "So. You watch the show."

"Sure. Who doesn't?"

"I don't, for one. What's it about?"

"The usual bang-bang. Screeching tires and breaking glass, ladies in distress, dope dealers, and Central American dictators. The same guest stars as every other show on the air. Stupid dialogue. Lots of commercials telling us what we're missing in life."

"And you give it an hour of your time every week."

"It's *my* time," she observed. "And that Toby's really something."

"The premise," I said. "Swallow once or twice so you don't drool on your blouse and tell me the premise."

She looked down. "You gave me this blouse."

"I know." I'd felt a pang in my heart when I saw that she was wearing it. "It goes with your skirt," I said. I hadn't given her the skirt.

She glanced at the skirt. "His name, as you know perfectly well, is Bart." She sipped her 7-Up. "You really haven't seen it? Not even one show?"

"Not even the credits."

She pushed her salad plate to one side. "Well," she said, "it's not easy if you haven't seen it. It's like Toby's not really human."

"You're telling me."

"No, listen. He's a machine, and so is this big black car he drives. It sounds terrible, and I'm sure it is, but Toby gets his strength from the car. Neither of them can do much of anything if the other isn't around."

"Who?" I was getting confused.

"Toby and the car. It's like Hercules and Antaeus. Remember Antaeus?"

"Sure. He had to keep his feet on the ground. Hercules totaled him by lifting him first. A little like sumo wrestling."

"Well, that's like Toby in the show. In the car or around it, he's invincible. But get him away from it and he's just normal. And if you keep him away from it long enough, he begins to get very weak."

"Weak barely describes it." The waiter delivered the entrées with a flourish: lamb for me and something that was all vegetables for Eleanor.

"A lot of people watch it." She used her salad fork experimentally to pick up something long and green.

"A lot of people eat zucchini, too," I said. "That doesn't make it any good."

She chewed a minuscule amount. Eleanor believed in tiny bites, spaced far apart. Something to do with the digestive juices that she'd attempted to explain to me over a number of meals. It had taken months to make her understand that thinking about my digestive juices actually slowed their work.

"If *High Velocity* were a vegetable," she said a trifle maliciously, "it would be a zucchini. A long, racy, highly phallic zucchini with metallic pinstripes."

"That's very enlightening." My lamb tasted like plywood. It had to be me. The Black Forest Inn's lamb is good enough to make you feel that sheep are superfluous.

"So," Eleanor said, "who's the girl?"

I put down my utensils. "Is this why we're here? So you can conduct a pop quiz on my personal life?"

"You're the one who brought her up," Eleanor said. She exhaled slowly and laid down her fork. "No," she said. "We're here because I wanted to see you."

"A girl got killed," I said. "No, not that girl, another girl. She got beaten to death. And she was a friend of Toby's."

"Friend. That sounds like a euphemism. And what about the other one?"

"She's a euphemism, too. It's the career of the nineties. Professional euphemism. You can get a degree in it now."

"Dispensing with my jealousy for the moment, you're saying that you think Toby might be involved."

"I guess. I don't know. Do I look like I know? Toby's complicated."

"He's an actor," she said as if that explained everything. Maybe it did.

"He's a white-knuckle sadist."

"Gosh," Eleanor said. She never swore. "And he looks so sweet."

"I wanted to see you, too," I said.

She waved it away. "Simeon, do you ever wonder whether this is a healthy profession?"

"You mean as in I could get killed?"

"As in you have to hang around with so much scum. You can't touch pitch without getting dirty, or something like that."

"It's not exactly like that."

"But you know what I mean, and anyway it's the Bible."

The waiter arrived. He laid a third 7-Up in front of Eleanor as if the glass containing it were the Holy Grail, plunked my white wine down with a blunt thud, and retired. Every table in the restaurant fell quiet, the way a room full of people will sometimes. Eleanor occupied the silence by lining up her silverware in more precisely parallel lines. They were already as parallel as a railroad track.

"I'll bet you were a champion at dodge ball in elementary school," she said. "Do you know how long we've known each other?"

"Eight years, seven months."

"And twelve days. And you still duck the issues."

"What's the issue?"

"See?"

"Swell. The issue of the moment is whether I can do my job without being corrupted. Maybe not. And then, maybe I'm corrupt already."

"We're all corrupt. That's the point we're supposed to work backward from."

"Eleanor, you sound like John Calvin."

"The average kid sees twelve thousand murders on TV by the time he's ten."

"He?"

"Or she." Eleanor shook her head impatiently. "If nits were a cash crop, you'd get rich picking them. Simeon, we're too old to waltz."

"And if that metaphor were any more mixed, it'd be an omelet. Cognac?"

"Oh, bull," she said, startling me. "I've never heard so much hot air."

"There we are," I said. "So *that's* why they call it the Windy City."

"Fine. Get some cognac. Get a whole bottle."

"What do you want from me, Eleanor? Somebody's dead."

"A lot of people are dead."

"Here," I said, holding out my bread plate. "Have a nit."

"Simeon." She put her hand on mine. "Why does it have to be you?"

"It doesn't. Somebody will do it, maybe. But I saw her." I gently bent Eleanor's index finger back. "All her fingers were broken. Three times."

"Maybe you think your fingers won't break," she said, giving mine a jerk upward. "Maybe you think you can't lose blood."

"We *are* talking about me getting killed?"

She knocked her precise silverware arrangement cock-eyed. "You idiot," she said. "Of course we are."

"I love you, too." I reached over and straightened the two remaining forks. The upwardly mobile woman at the next table laughed tinnily.

"How come men can laugh boom-boom-boom and women sound like goats?" Eleanor said. "How come men can chew gum and women look like cows when they do it? How come it's okay for men to get wasted and throw up, but a drunk woman embarrasses everybody?"

"I love you, too," I said again.

"Maybe people have a higher expectation for women," she said, looking everywhere in the restaurant except at me. "What a pain in the rear."

I didn't say anything.

Eleanor lifted an edge of her plate and let it drop onto the immaculate white tablecloth. The delicate muscles of her jaw worked, once and then again. "What a total, un-adulterated, one-hundred-percent pain in the *ass*," she said.

12

Saffron in the Morning

IT MAY HAVE BEEN one P.M. to the rest of the world, but to Saffron it was early morning.

She lived in the kind of neighborhood where they park on the lawn. The dry swimming pool was half-full of trash. I'd had to knock four times before a thick moan of protest announced that she was coming to the door. There was a prolonged fumbling with multiple chains and latches inside, a muttered expletive or two, and then the door swung open four inches, and Saffron peered out into the sunlight. Her chin rested on the taut chain.

"I paid the rent," she said. Then she focused. "Oh, shit. It's you." She pushed at the door, but it wouldn't close.

"The old foot in the door," I said. "It's amazing how many people still let you get a foot in the door."

"Listen, I just went to bed. How about you get out of here and come back next week? Or maybe Labor Day." She gave the door an exploratory shove.

The apartment behind her was dark, and I could hear the hum of a window air conditioner, part of a night person's standard insulation against the day. A door closed behind me, and a youngish man with vivid pimples decorating a pasty complexion beneath slicked-back black hair walked quickly across the courtyard and toward the street. He gave me a nervous glance. It seemed like a pretty furtive apartment house, all things considered.

"Saffron, I'm coming in, and you're going to talk to me."

189

"Fuck off," she said, shoving again at the door. It didn't budge. Her puffy face suddenly arranged itself into the expression of a four-year-old headed for a tantrum. It wasn't pretty.

"I could knock this door in with one hand," I said. "Then you'd have to talk to me, and you'd have to get your door fixed, too. Why don't you do it the easy way?"

"You push this door in and I'll call the cops."

"Oh, no, you won't."

She stamped her foot. She was wearing little white ankle socks and a short nightgown. Her chin trembled, and I thought for a moment she was going to cry. I wondered what wretched drugs she was on.

"Open the door," I said as gently as I could. "Please?"

She stared up at me through petulant eyes that looked like black-and-blue marks. "You'll have to move your foot," she said in an angry little-girl voice. "I can't undo the chain if you don't."

"Lock it and I'll come in through the window."

"I'm not going to lock it."

"Oh, good," I said. "My first opportunity to trust you."

I pulled my foot back, putting both palms against the door as a precaution. I needn't have bothered. She didn't close it all the way, just slid the lock off the catch and retreated back into the gloom. The door slowly swung open. It was cheap, hollow fiberboard. I probably could have walked through it.

"Let yourself in," she said.

I followed her into the darkness. The apartment was in total disorder. Saffron had more shoes than Imelda Marcos, but nowhere near the closet space. They were everywhere, on the floor, on the table and couch, even on the messy single bed that Saffron had just vacated. They fought for space with dresses, pants, blouses, slips, underwear. Saffron obviously belonged to the drop-it-where-you-take-it-off school of undressing. Blankets masked the light from the windows, so I left the door standing open.

Ashtrays overflowed with cigarettes. Most of them had half the filter torn out; white, fibrous little piles of whatever they make filters out of were everywhere. Saffron was smoking a lot of cocaine.

She sat on the bed, reached over to the table for one of her coco-puffs, and lit it. Sweet smoke curled toward me. Over the bed was a Day-Glo poster of Jimi Hendrix from the halcyon days of the Fillmore West. I revised my estimate of her age upward.

"Nice place," I said conversationally.

She took a deep hit. "Yours ain't exactly Camelot. What do you want?" One foot was curled beneath her, and it jiggled up and down nervously. Her shin needed shaving. Probably both of them did.

"Just a talk. Can you sleep after you smoke one of those?"

"I can sleep after a dozen. That what you want to talk about?"

"I want to talk about Amber."

"We've already done this scene. There was no payoff. Like I said before, go away."

"And Toby."

She inhaled again, held it for a second, and yawned out a plume of smoke. "Fuck Toby. Fuck you, too. I'm sorry I ever met him."

"Why?"

"Why not? Who needs the All-American boy when his idea of a sex toy is a Louisville Slugger?" She tried a laugh, but it didn't work. "It's enough to make you wish you liked girls." One strap of her nightgown fell loose over her shoulder. She left it there.

I leaned over and straightened it. She pulled away from me, regarded me darkly for a second, and then went back to work on the cigarette.

"Did he rough you up?"

She exhaled vehemently and coughed, doubling over on

the bed. "Toby can't say hello without sticking his elbow in your eye," she said when she'd caught her breath. "It's like a character flaw."

"It's a blemish the size of Van Nuys. You're an actress?"

She looked surprised. "Sure," she said. "I'm really Meryl Streep." She waved her cigarette around to indicate the apartment. "All this is just part of getting into character."

"But you came here—to Hollywood, I mean—to be an actress."

"Who says?" She sounded suspicious.

"You. You said we'd already done this scene. No payoff, you said. Real people don't talk like that. What do the folks back home think you're doing?"

Saffron started to stub out her cigarette and then thought better of it. She used it to light another and dropped the butt into an already overloaded ashtray. She sucked up the smoke from the new one. Wrinkles creased the area around her mouth.

Closing her eyes to get away from me, she exhaled. "They think I wait tables," she said after a moment.

"Well, you do, in a way."

"Yeah, and the pope's a Protestant. Stop sucking around and get to the point."

"Did Toby tell you he'd help you?"

Something that might have had a smile as a distant ancestor flitted across her tired face. "Well, he really did help, you know? That's the worst thing about Toby. We all know he's an asshole, but sometimes he comes through. He actually got me a part on *High Velocity*. Two parts, in fact, but they cut one of them out. Anyway, that was before."

"Before what?"

"Before he got what he wanted."

"And what was that?"

The smile was gone. "Never you fucking mind what he wanted. It's not anything I like to talk about. And don't play shrink with me."

"So he got you a couple of parts."

"The only ones in fourteen years. You know, after a while a girl begins to wonder whether she's got any talent, aside from what she can do with her feet pointed at the ceiling." She took another deep drag. "I wanted to be Julie Harris," she said, looking embarrassed. "You know, not a big star or anything, but someone who did good work. Trouble is, I've got the wrong equipment. All knockers and no brains. Why am I talking about this?"

"You're talking."

"It's the coke talking. And you're not my friend. You're just somebody who wants to keep Mr. Teen-cream from getting what's coming to him." She worried one of her long fingernails with her teeth, making a gritty little chewing noise.

It was time to let her think, so I got up and navigated the landscape of clothing until I reached a corner that I'd been glancing at since I first came in. It looked like a corner from another apartment entirely that had been grafted surgically onto Saffron's space. Stones from the seaside, rubbed smooth by the waves, had been piled carefully to create a kind of shrine. Plants grew from the center of the pile and cascaded down its sides. Above the plants, on the wall, was a vertical Zen garden: flat, vaguely rectangular stones with holes worn through them. Nails had been driven through the holes to hold the stones in place. They hung in an apparently random arrangement that nevertheless had a kind of finality about it. You couldn't have moved one without ruining the effect.

"Who did this?"

"Who do you think? Nobody here but us chickens."

"It's very nice."

"I don't look at it anymore. I don't remember the last time I turned on the lights."

"You water the plants."

"Sure. You have to water plants. If you don't, they die.

Even a detective should know that." Her voice was flatter than plane geometry.

"Why are you so upset at Toby? Because of something he did to you or something he did to Amber?"

"He started treating me like shit the minute we left your house," she said. Then she heard the rest of my question, and a current of alarm straightened her spine. She shook her head, bleached blond hair stiff over her shoulders. She had very nice shoulders. She must have been a beautiful girl once. "Toby didn't do anything to Amber. You know that."

"No, *you* know it. Or else you don't. You're his alibi, and he's yours. That's a tidy arrangement, but it's not very satisfying."

"We took her home." Her pitch had risen.

"I know you did, but the cops don't. They could be very unpleasant while they're figuring out that you're telling the truth."

She reached down under the mattress and came up with a small purse. "I'm not worried. And the cops don't have to know anything. Nothing happened, remember?" She pulled from the purse a small purple jar and twisted the lid off. It was full of a white cream. Taking the outside of the jar between her fingers she twisted again. The inside of the jar came loose, and she pulled it out. Beneath the shallow false bottom that held the cream, white powder glistened.

"We were straight with you," she said. "You can stiff the cops. We were straight with you." She dipped a fingernail into the powder and held it under a nostril, then sniffed sharply. She repeated the ritual for the other nostril. "Hey, what do you want from me? You bust in here before the birds get up, get me talking about stuff I never tell anybody, and then you try to screw me over." She did another couple of snorts.

"Amber was okay when you dropped her off?"

"I guess she was okay by Amber's standards. I hope to

God I never get like that," she said, wiping her nose. "But you know something? I thought she was totaled then. After you called, when Toby said she was dead, I figured it was an overdose."

"But nobody messed with her."

She'd dipped her nail into the jar again, but now she looked up at me. "Nobody messed with her," she said. "What do you think we are, sadists? I mean, what do you think I am? We both know about Toby." The nail came halfway to her nose.

"Where'd Toby get the loads?"

"Some street corner, Adams and Crenshaw, maybe. You can always get them there." The fingernail completed its trip, and she sniffed.

"He wasn't gone long enough."

"Hollywood and Highland, then. Who gives a shit?"

"Did he get them at the club? At the Spice Rack?"

Saffron looked at me for a long moment. Then, very deliberately, she screwed the top of the jar back on. "Goodbye," she said. "Close the door behind you."

"Is that where he got them?"

"Nobody scores at the Spice Rack. Now get out of here."

"The Spice Rack's clean, huh?"

"Cleaner than Betty Crocker. I thought you were leaving."

"If the Spice Rack is Girl Scout Central, how come you're so nervous?"

"Nervous? Who's nervous? I need to sleep. I'm dancing tonight. I've got a public to worry about. Now get out of here, or I really will call the cops."

"You can't. You'll be in detox before you can spell your name, whatever it really is."

"You're right," she said petulantly. "You're just so very clever. I can't call the cops. But I can call Tiny, and if I do, you'll wish I *had* called the cops. If you're not afraid of Tiny, you're not brave, just stupid."

An image of Tiny popped unbidden into my mind's eye. "I try not to be stupid," I said.

"Keep trying, you may make it yet. And remember, nobody scores at the Spice Rack."

I was going to have to face Tiny sooner or later, but later seemed to have a lot to recommend it. I went to the door and pulled it open. "Write down my phone number," I said.

"For what?" She sounded weary.

"Just in case. Get a pen and write it down." She fished something that could have been a pen out of a drawer, and I gave her the number. "Listen. If anything goes wrong or if things just get too crazy, call me. If you even just *think* things are getting crazy, call."

She flopped down on the bed and covered her eyes with her forearm. "Crazy?" she said. "In *my* life? Just close the door. I'll lock it later."

"Sleep well," I said. I closed the door. I was skirting the pool, looking down at the trash when I heard the locks being yanked into place.

On Sunset Boulevard I pulled Alice, gleaming her usual rabid horsefly iridescent blue, into a gas station. "Fill it up," I said to the Persian at the pump.

"This one, she takes gas, eh?" he said. He had a widow's peak that was about to exert territorial imperative over his eyebrows.

"No," I said. "She runs on Islamic fervor. I just give her gas once in a while to remind her of the good old days when all the oil came from Texas."

"You pay more here at this pumps. Self-serve are more cheaper."

"A receipt, okay? Do the pay phones work?"

"Sometimes. You know, punks." He pronounced it "ponks." "Sometimes they works."

I called Bernie first. No Sprunks in either of the Dakotas, he told me, sounding satisfied. Also no Sprunks in Idaho, Iowa, Nebraska, or Wyoming. One Sprunk, a widow in her seventies—I didn't ask how Bernie knew how old she was, but if he said so, it was right—in Montana. Minnesota had too many people to check. I told him to try it anyway. Then I called Wyl.

"Dear boy. It's all here and organized to a fare-thee-well, the total scope on Toby Vane. Such a terrible boy, really. It's enough to make you doubt appearances."

"Anything interesting?"

"Depends on the point of view, don't you know. A lot of the photos are absolutely riveting from my perspective, although I doubt you'd linger over them for very long."

"Jesus, how much is there?"

"More than you'd think. Most of it is fannies, of course. Since you're going to be kind enough to return it to me, I've broken it down into categories. The newspaper clips should be the most interesting. I don't think you really care what his favorite color is."

"Blue," I said.

"You almost never cease to surprise me. Are you going to pick it up?"

I looked at my watch. I had more than an hour before the dreaded Joanna Link was due at Universal. "Sure," I said. "Be there in ten minutes."

"I'll go in the back room and put my bells on," Wyl said before he hung up.

He was right. The newspaper clips were the most interesting. The second page I read told me something *very* interesting: it told me that both Stillman and Dixie had lied to me.

"May I use your phone?" I asked Wyl.

I had only one friend in the police department. Al Hammond was a sergeant, a prototypical middle-aged desk cop with a problem belly and creased skin on the back of his neck that was thicker than the average catcher's mitt. When I first decided that I had chosen a career that was going to put me into uneasy proximity to the police—uneasy for me, at any rate—I'd started drinking at a couple of police bars downtown. Hammond and I had gotten pulverized together four or five times before I told him what I did for a living. He wasn't thrilled, but he'd kept drinking with me.

"Records, Sergeant Hammond," he snarled. Then he remembered departmental public relations. "Oh, yeah, and how may I help you?"

"Your bedside manner is impeccable," I said. "This is Simeon."

"Would you spell that, sir?"

"Simeon," I said. "S-i-m—"

"Not that, shithead. Impeccable."

"With three different vowels."

"Are you still drinking?"

"Only when I'm thirsty."

"Thought maybe you'd gone to the Betty Ford Clinic or something. Seems to me it's been a few months since I saw you throw up."

"You've never seen me throw up. By the time I begin to get queasy, you're unconscious. Listen, I'm looking for a girl. Her name is Rebecca Hartsfield."

"Has she got a sheet?"

"I doubt it. She's more in the victim line. She got knocked silly about four years ago at Ontario Motor Speedway. A police report was filed."

"But not with us. You're talking to the LAPD, remember? You want the Ontario cops or the sheriffs, if Ontario's in L.A. County."

"I was hoping that you had some sort of relationship with the Ontario cops. You know, brotherhood of the blue or something like that."

"Yeah, well, they won't hang up on me if I call them. But four years ago? For battery? Jeez, Simeon, that's ancient history. If it was murder . . ."

"The weapon was fists. The fists belonged to an actor named Toby Vane."

"Oh," Hammond said. "My daughter likes him."

"On the other side of the TV screen, he's no problem. Just don't let her get any closer."

"Is this important?"

"Have I ever asked you to do anything stupid?"

He gave forth with a mirthless laugh. "How much time have we got?"

"I've got all day. I thought the police were busy."

"Are we involved?" "We" was the LAPD.

"No," I said. It was a lie I might have to answer for later.

"So what do you want?"

"A phone number, an address, whatever."

"Call me later. About four, okay?" He hung up.

"People are hanging up on me today," I said to Wyl.

"I can tell. Your left ear is getting callused."

I hefted the stack of stuff he'd given me. "Thanks for the archives," I said. "I'll get them back to you in a day or two." Yellow stick-it papers protruded from the pile of magazines and newspapers. Each was meticulously labeled with a date. "Must have been a lot of work," I said.

"It was fun, actually. I don't think he's got staying power, though. Steve McQueen he's not."

"Wyl," I said, "he's not even Butterfly McQueen."

"Oooh," Wyl said, *"Gone With the Wind.* She was terrific." "Tara's Theme" rang out behind me as I left.

Toby had caused hospital-scale injuries to a sixteen-year-old girl named Rebecca Hartsfield during a shoot at Ontario Motor Speedway four years ago—two years before the mayhem in Northridge that Dixie and Stillman had described as his first "problem" incident. As I pulled into the Universal lot I decided not to ask them about it until I'd talked to the girl, if I actually got to talk to the girl. People move in Southern California more often than they do anywhere else in the world, and a four-year-old address could be more outdated than the pillbox hat I remembered my mother buying because she liked Jackie Kennedy's.

When the guard pushed open the door to the closed set where *High Velocity* was filming, Norman Stillman himself greeted me. The requisite blue blazer and white slacks had been augmented by a captain's hat, but Stillman's expression was not that of a seasoned sea dog hardened by misadventure on the bounding main. He looked like the anxious, if overage, freshman who had sat down in Dixie's class all those years ago.

"*Here* you are," he said in a highly keyed stage whisper. "They're already in his dressing room. She came early, the bitch."

"How early?"

He steered me across the sound stage. "Half an hour."

"Good policy," I said. "She's no dope."

"Don't mention dope," Stillman hissed. "So far, no problem." The lights on the set were off, so his insistence on speaking sotto voce was an affectation, but it was an effective one. I found myself lowering my own voice in return.

"What are they talking about?"

"Before she kicked me out, she was asking about how he'd feel when *High Velocity* was finished."

"Not much news there," I said, wishing I'd been around when Joanna Link kicked Norman Stillman out of his own star's dressing room.

"That's what's worrying me. You don't talk to a star about his series when the ratings have dropped unless you plan to slip him a shiv."

"Shiv?" We were most of the way across the sound stage.

"You know, a knife. Unless you plan to stab him in the back," he explained with an air of exaggerated impatience. "Jesus, you don't know what a shiv is?"

"Sure. I was wondering how you knew." We were at Toby's door.

He looked blank. "Scripts," he said, thinking about something else. "Do you think she'll let you in?"

"Toby will let me in. Whether she'll let me stay in, that's the question."

"Well, *I* know that," he said for the second time in two days. I made a mental note to use it the next time I had nothing to say. "Good luck," Stillman said, pushing the door open.

"Do you think the young people of America have learned anything from *High Velocity*?" said a thickening blond lady with four-inch fingernails as the door closed behind me. She glanced up at me with irritation and gave the tiny tape recorder in front of her a businesslike shake as though she thought my intrusion might have caused its circuits to malfunction. Then she turned her attention back to Toby, who was seated in front of a mirror framed by globular white light bulbs. Dixie hovered behind him, looking fatally apprehensive.

"Joanna," Toby said, "this isn't Ibsen. Half the show is cars crashing into other cars." Dixie wilted visibly, and Toby caught it in the mirror. He gave Joanna Link a budgeted grin, sort of an amplified smirk. "We're doing entertainment here. But every episode has a moral: Crime doesn't pay; Drugs aren't good; Sooner or later, virtue triumphs."

"Usually later."

"Albert Schweitzer chatting with Pope John Paul for an hour isn't going to hold the people we're talking to. That's public television. People who watch public television don't get into trouble. Kids don't watch public television. Maybe it would be better if they did, but they don't. They watch us. And, week after week, we make a point that *Parents* magazine couldn't disagree with."

"So you think the departure of *High Velocity* will leave a moral void on television?" The tone was so snotty that I felt like giving her a handkerchief so she could blow her voice.

Toby ignored it. He reached out and took one of her

extravagantly clawed hands between his. "We'll be around in reruns," he said. "And even if we weren't, television is a responsible industry. As long as there are producers like Norman, the medium won't be a source of moral decay."

"This isn't quotable," she said, withdrawing her hand but giving his a coy little pat as she did it. "And who's he?" She indicated me, Chinese style, with her chin.

"Who, Simeon?" Toby said, his face as open as a freshly washed window. "He's a friend. We're going out together after we wrap today."

"He's not a PR man, is he? Dixie's more than enough PR for now." Dixie shrugged philosophically. He looked as if he were trying to get his suit high enough to hide him completely.

"Does he look like a PR man?" Toby asked in his most reasonable voice.

"No," she said. "He looks like something the hippies left behind." She had one of those decayed little-girl faces that always made me think of Shirley Temple on cortisone.

Dixie laughed despairingly. "Joanna," he said, "you're priceless."

"By which you mean unbuyable, I assume."

"How do you type with those fingernails?" I asked.

"Oh, we've heard from Toby's friend," she said, flexing her fingers. "These aren't nails, they're talons." Over her shoulder, Dixie waved frantically. She looked up at me and narrowed her puffy eyes. "At least that proves you aren't PR," she said. "No one in PR thinks I type my own stories."

"Simeon Grist, Joanna Link," Dixie said with more than a trace of desperation in his voice. "Joanna, Simeon."

Joanna Link turned her back on me. I might as well have been a heating vent. "So what about this girl, Toby?" she said.

Dixie's face slammed shut like the gates of heaven before Attila the Hun. Toby was better. "Girl?" he said. "What girl?"

"The stripper who was killed a few nights ago. This Amber something or other."

"Stackheimer," I said, volunteering the name Nana had given me. "Amber Stackheimer."

Now Dixie looked truly frantic. Even Toby's composure slipped a notch. Link turned slowly to face me.

"I'm talking to Toby," she said. She chewed her lower lip, leaving a scarlet smear of lipstick on her teeth. "You knew her?" she asked after a moment, scratching at the inside of her left arm with the claws on her right hand.

"We were dating," I said. "Terrible thing. She was just about to get her life in order. There are so many lost souls out there." I made a gesture in the general direction of East. "In L.A., you know."

Joanna Link looked from me to Toby and then back to me again. "Wait," she said. "We all know about Toby's little problem, even if we haven't written about it yet."

"And that's a good idea," Dixie put in, "unless we've got proof. And lots of very good insurance."

"Shut up," Joanna Link said absently. She chewed at the inside of her cheek. The woman was clearly orally fixated, probably an ex-smoker. "You were her date? You weren't in the pictures."

I shrugged. "I'm not a star."

"No," she said, "you're not. But how do I know you're not a liar?"

"That's an insulting question," I said. "Aren't journalists supposed to have manners?"

Her eyebrows rose until they almost disappeared into her hairline. "Dixie," she said, "am I supposed to have manners?"

Dixie managed a strangled consonant or two before I cut him off.

"We're all supposed to have manners," I said. "That's what they tell us differentiates us from the apes. Or maybe just from newspaper writers."

Joanna Link looked at me while Dixie made a suffocating sound. Then she tilted her head back a degree or two and laughed. It wasn't really a laugh, more a hog-tied chuckle. "Honey," she said, "just hope you're never a star. I'll barbecue you."

There was a moment of silence. Then Joanna Link leaned over and shut off her tape recorder. "You know I've got nothing," she said to Dixie. "It's a shame, really. I've got a great picture of Toby to go with my lead item, but I haven't got a lead item."

"Maybe next time," Dixie said.

"Next time," Joanna Link said, "if there is a next time, your boy could be in the jug. Nothing personal, Toby." She patted Toby's hand. His grin was as permanent as the smirk on the Apollo Belvedere. "And then I probably won't have an exclusive. Will I?"

Toby leaned in to her. "Joanna," he said, "if I commit murder, I promise I'll call you first." He kissed the air in her general direction.

After a beat or two, she blew a kiss back.

13

The Wake

AT SEVEN P.M. it was still hot; July had finally dug in its heels. Waning sunlight angled through a few scraggly eucalyptus trees and threw the trash in the parking lot into a sharp, melancholic relief. A crow coughed overhead. Out on Santa Monica Boulevard the rush-hour traffic was finally beginning to peter out.

The chain across the driveway to the Spice Rack dangled a bright yellow sign that said CLOSED. PRIVATE PARTY. Below that someone—Tiny, I guessed—had taped a piece of cardboard that said UNTIL 8:30. At eight-thirty, life, or what passed for life inside the Spice Rack, was scheduled to resume.

Toby and I had come in separate cars. He had driven his Maserati, with Dolly presumably clinging for dear life to the dashboard, and I had brought Alice. This way, at least, he couldn't leave us without wheels.

The parking lot, which we'd had to enter from the side street, was almost full. That was a surprise: Amber had some mourners. Nana's car wasn't there, and that caused me an involuntary twinge of worry. I did see Tiny's filthy white Continental, squatting in a double-size space that said RESERVED in big pink letters.

After I parked Alice I locked the doors against the unlikely eventuality of someone actually wanting her. I was straightening up and wondering what the hell I was doing there when Toby hailed me.

"*Banzai,*" he yelled, raising a clenched fist in the air. Dolly shambled along behind him, dressed for the occasion in an ancient rock and roll T-shirt that said SWEATHOGS on it and a pair of bulging aviator's pants. She'd twisted an industrial-strength rubber band around her short hair, creating a ponytail that stood straight up from the top of her head like a little eruption. Despite her tone on the phone, she wasn't completely indifferent to Toby's charm; she was wearing lipstick, the first I'd seen on her since the day her last divorce became final. Dolly got married the way some women went shopping.

"See this fist?" Toby called, brandishing his right in the air. "This fist is a power salute to the man who made Joanna Link eat her eyeliner."

Dolly tittered, a bad sign. Maybe a man would have been a better idea, even though I knew how Dolly hated woman beaters. Finding them was one of her specialties.

"Toby," I said, "I have several acres of rear end exposed on your account at the moment, not only with the police, but with the press as well. Play straight, or it'll be your rear end instead."

"Champ," Toby said, punching me lightly on the upper arm, "are those the proper sentiments for the occasion? Let's go in and pay our last respects."

This time we went in through the front door. Toby sent Dolly ahead to make sure there weren't any photographers lurking about. When she came back to report in the negative, the three of us hurried up the driveway from the parking lot and across the sidewalk. Toby went first, anxious to minimize his exposure. The entrance was masked by a heavy red velvet curtain, which Toby dropped in Dolly's face.

"He's nervous," Dolly explained apologetically.

"We're all nervous," I said, and, in fact, I was. Where the hell was Nana? "Dolly," I said, grabbing her arm, "don't let him bamboozle you."

She looked me straight in the eyes—she was as tall as I was—then dropped her gaze. A second later, she nodded. "Damn," she said, looking back at me, "but he sure is decorative."

Nana wasn't inside, either. The Spice Rack was more crowded than it had been the last time I was there. All the stageside chairs were full, and people who hadn't gotten seats were leaning against the walls. I saw Pepper, Clove, Saffron, a beautiful Hispanic called (naturally) Chili, and a couple of other girls I'd seen dancing but didn't know. Saffron glanced anxiously at Toby as we came in. Toby didn't even nod to her. He was supremely indifferent to the whole scene: in his mind, he was the star. Everyone else was an extra.

I went to work on the other men in attendance. Six or eight were customers, and Ahmed, the Middle Easterner with the disappearing dollar bills, was among them. The remaining regulars were resolutely invisible, slumped in their ugly chairs with their eyes downcast and their arms folded, presenting the smallest possible identifiable surface area to the world. The other men in the room, five that I could count for sure, were with the girls.

There was some quality that cut across all of them despite their superficial differences. Two were white, two were black, and one was Asian, possibly Chinese. They were the only males who looked unapologetic. Their eyes took in the club as if it were a golf course and they were tournament pros.

Toby saw me looking at them. "Scuzz," he said. "One step up from pimps. Is there anything worse?"

"You tell me. Where's Nana?"

"Who gives a shit? Champ, she's just the same as the rest of them."

"Shut the fuck up, Toby." It came out more vehemently than I had intended it to.

Toby squeezed my arm, and I pulled it away. "And cut,"

he said. "We're getting a little bit jumpy here. Anyway, time for the main attraction."

The speakers suddenly spouted music that the snob in me recognized and condemned as the love theme from Zeffirelli's *Romeo and Juliet*, and the garish stage lights slowly came on. Tiny had made his way into the club from his office—the door, I saw, was still broken—and now he moved toward the main stage. There, laid out in what I hoped was an unconscious parody of the dead Amber, were her dancing costumes: feather boas, wrinkled blouses, slit T-shirts, shorts, G-strings, boots. Only the girl inside was missing.

Tiny climbed ponderously onto the stage, dressed in his standard white. He held a tattered paperbound book to his chest. The girl called Pepper climbed up behind him. Tiny looked biblically grave.

He raised a fat hand, and the music faded away. He started to speak, failed, and cleared his throat. Pepper put a hand on his shoulder. He reached over and patted it once, looked at the faces of the people in the room, and began again.

"This is the worst day of my life," he said. "I'd be in bed now, but Amber asked me not to be. Amber asked—" He cleared his throat again and blinked quickly several times. "Amber asked me to be here."

"What's that supposed to mean?" Toby whispered. He sounded apprehensive.

"All of you, most of you, I mean, are here because she wanted you to be. You all had a place in her heart. Amber's heart was the biggest thing about her. There was room for a lot of people in it."

"Her heart was okay," Toby said in my ear. "It was her veins that were the problem."

Dolly tapped him on the shoulder and shook her head disapprovingly. Toby instantly arranged his features into a passable semblance of melancholy. It was like watching a Polaroid develop in a tenth of a second.

"Amber knew she was going to die," Tiny rumbled on. "She knew it a long time ago. I'm not being mystical. I don't mean she knew some bastard was going to beat her to death." He swallowed twice and then shook his head to clear it. He took a step back as though the stage had tilted suddenly beneath him.

"I'll tell them," Pepper said.

Tiny nodded and moved aside, staring at the wall opposite. Pepper, a seasoned performer, found the brightest light and then reached out a hand to Tiny. Slowly, he handed her the creased book. It had a unicorn on the cover.

"I guess a lot of you know that Amber stayed with me sometimes," Pepper said. Until that moment I'd only heard her shouting over the music in the club. Her voice now, in the silence, was unexpectedly musical. "When she didn't have any place to stay, or when one of her men treated her bad, she came to me. So she had a lot of stuff at my place, and one of the things she had there was her book."

She opened it and leafed through a couple of pages. "It's all here," she said. "Everything." Toby shifted from foot to foot, looking uneasy. "There are two pages here that are headed 'When I Die.' Not 'If I Die,' but 'When I Die.'

"She wanted you all to come here. 'I want my service to be at the club,' she wrote. 'My friends are at the club.' " Pepper's voice broke slightly. "Her friends. That's us. Her closest friends in the world." Tiny wiped at his nose with his sleeve. "Her wonderful friends," Pepper said.

She took a breath. "The things on the stage were hers. She's given them all to you. Every girl in the club gets something. It's all written down in the book. She even chose the music. It was her favorite song." She brushed her cheek with the back of her hand. "She was such a sap," she said. Her eyes were very bright. After a long moment she went on.

"Amber made four requests. The first was that you should

come here. She'd be happy to see you all here now. The second was that we should give her things away. We're going to do that in a little while. The third had to do with the money she'd saved, and Tiny will tell you about that. These aren't in any order," she said suddenly. "I've gotten them all mixed up."

"She wouldn't care," a girl said from somewhere in the room. "She loved you, Pepper." It was Nana's voice. I turned and saw her standing next to the door. She was dressed all in black, and her eyes were puffy and red.

Pepper nodded. "I guess the fourth thing comes first. She wanted Tiny to read a page to you. It was something she wrote a couple of months ago. Tiny read it for the first time today."

She turned to him and held out the book. "Can you?" she asked. At first I thought he couldn't. He hesitated for a long time and then grasped it. It took an act of will for him to force his eyes down to the open page.

"This is really for the girls," he said. "The rest of you can listen, but this is for the girls." He put a finger on the margin, squinted at the words, and breathed heavily before he began to read.

" 'Wednesday, May 8. I don't know how to write this, but why should I? I don't know how to do anything anymore. I think I used to know how to do things.' "

The thick index finger moved down the edge of the page. It was shaking. " 'I don't even know how to go home,' " he read. " 'Where is home now? Where is the place that makes me feel safe? Nobody took it away from me, I can't blame anybody else. I must have thrown it away. How do I get it back? Everywhere I go I take the dragons with me. When I close the door they're already inside.

" 'Tiny tried to help . . .' " His voice trembled. " 'But I wouldn't let him. Nana is good to me. Sarah—' " He looked up. "That's Pepper," he said. " 'Sarah is good to me. I have so many friends. But it's like they're on the other side of a window. I can see them, I can hear them, but I can't touch them. There's the window. And I'm outside looking in, and outside is nothing but me and the dark and the dragons.

" 'I know I should stop doing dope. I know the dope is killing me. I used to think life would come to a standstill without me. Now I don't. I lost my place in life a long time ago. I won't even be missed.' "

Someone snuffled. It sounded like Nana.

" 'I don't know where home is. I don't know how to get to my friends on the other side of the glass. My life is just someplace I lost the map to. And the one I lost was the only copy.' "

He looked up. There were tears streaming down his face. "She wanted you to hear that," he said. "She wanted you to hear that after she died. I guess maybe she thought some of us could learn something."

There was a long silence. The music had ended. Even Toby looked somber. I felt someone slip fingers under my arm and looked down at Nana. She pressed her forehead against my shoulder. She felt burning hot, even through my shirt and jacket.

In the silence, a few people began to whisper and then to talk. It was a kind of release, and it spread through the room. Someone even laughed.

"That's right," Pepper said, taking the book back. "She wanted you to hear it, she thought it might help you, but she didn't want to bum you out. Here are some presents. 'The boots are for Nana,' " she read, " 'who helped me buy them one day when I was too wasted to make up my mind. The T-shirts are for Saffron, who has more to fill them with.' " She turned a page. " 'Chili gets my belts because she's the only one they'll fit. Sarah,' " she stammered, " 'Sarah gets this book, with the love I tried to express on page forty-three.' " She looked up, on the verge of tears. "I'm not going to read that," she said.

One by one, the girls went up to the stage and took Amber's gifts. The litany went on until everything on the stage was gone. When it was over and the stage was empty, Tiny waved for silence.

"When Amber died, when she got killed, I mean, she had two hundred and eighty-four dollars in the bank. She left her bankbook inside her journal. Two hundred and eighty-four dollars isn't much after four years of stripping. But you know what happened. She gave money to some of you, and she spent the rest on dope. She spent too much on dope," the man who dealt loads said. There was no question that he meant it.

He seemed to regain his strength as he talked. "She didn't know how much she'd have when she died, but this is what she wrote: 'Please use fifty dollars to buy drinks for everyone. Real drinks, private stock, make sure Tiny knows that. No Cragmont Cola at my wake, Tiny.' " A couple of people laughed. Nana, with Amber's boots clenched in her hand, shook her head fiercely.

"That leaves two hundred and thirty-four dollars," Tiny said. "What Amber hoped is that the girls in the club would donate enough money to bring it up to the next hundred. That's three hundred bucks. She wanted that money given to an organization, and if anyone laughs, I'll kill you. She wanted it given to the Just Say No Foundation to keep little kids off drugs. Anybody think that's funny?"

Nobody even smiled. "I've got fifty bucks," Nana said.

"Me, too," said Pepper.

All around the room, the women dug into their purses and volunteered sums of money. Saffron put up a hundred. Women who probably hadn't had a straight day in months went to the stage and put their money down.

"That's six hundred and twenty-four dollars, counting Amber's," Tiny said after he counted it. "It'll be a bequest in her name. I'll put in a thousand for the club."

As he said it, he looked around. There must have been

something in my face, because he paused as he looked at me, and a tiny line of concentration creased the skin between his eyebrows. Our eyes locked for a moment.

"Me, too," Toby said suddenly. "A thousand and whatever it takes to bring it up to three thousand even." Tiny's eyes flicked to him, and Toby smiled apologetically. "I was never any good at math," he said.

"What it'll be," Tiny said, "is a thousand three hundred and seventy-six dollars." A murmur spread through the room as people recognized Toby. "And no checks," Tiny added.

"Coin of the realm," Toby said. He reached into his hip pocket and pulled out a folded wad of bills. Something square and white came out with them, but he shoved it back into his pocket. Only the corner showed. The edge was white, but the center area was black. It was a distinctive shape, and I had an uneasy feeling that I recognized it. "What do you think that is?" I said to Nana.

"What's what?" Her voice was muffled.

"Nothing. Are you okay?"

"Sure. I'm peachy. Best I've felt in weeks." She ground her head against my arm. "Simeon, can we go somewhere when this is over?"

Toby had put his money on the stage, and Tiny picked it up. "That's it, then," he said. "It doesn't seem like enough, but that's all she asked for."

"She never asked for enough," Pepper said.

"She wouldn't have known what to do with it anyway," Nana said to my arm. "Even if she'd gotten it, which she never did. Are we going to go someplace or not?"

"Depends," I said, "on what's in Toby's pocket."

She pulled away and gazed up at me. "I'm beginning to think the only thing in Toby's pocket is you."

"If it makes you happy," I said. Toby was coming toward us, and Tiny was talking again.

"Okay," he said. "Drinks on Amber for everybody. Knock it back. We've got half an hour before we open the doors."

"Half an hour," Toby said, giving Nana a token grin that wasn't returned. "As much as I'd like a drink, I think I'm going to just say no."

"Well, that's a twist," Nana said. All the animosity had returned. "No free booze for Toby?"

He leaned down toward her. "You're a beautiful girl, but you're a pain in the ass."

"I hope I am, Toby," she said. "As far as you're concerned, I hope I'm a hemorrhoid the size of a fist."

"Where are you going?" I asked him.

"Home. I've got a long day tomorrow."

"Fine. I'll walk you out."

"Don't bother, champ. I've got the lovely Dolly."

He headed for the door. Dolly started to follow, but I waved her off. Toby dropped the curtain after he passed through, and I had to pick it up again to get outside. Behind me I heard it drop again: Dolly, no doubt, and then again, and that could only be Nana.

"You know, champ," Toby said without looking back, "I have the distinct feeling that Tiny isn't crazy about me anymore."

The white corner was protruding from the hip pocket of his leather jeans. "He loved her," I said, squinting into the last rays of daylight and moving closer. "He probably doesn't like anybody very much right now."

"Yeah, but this felt personal. Jesus, I liked her, too."

"Did you?" I said. "You could have fooled me." I had my hand outstretched to snag the thing in Toby's pocket, but he turned to face me. We had reached the place where Alice was parked.

"What kind of thing is that to say? Hey, Simeon, don't push me all the time. Why am I here if I didn't like her?"

"Because you were invited," Nana said behind me. "Because you were on her list. Because you couldn't stay away without it looking weird."

He looked over my shoulder at her. "You don't believe

that. I mean, you and I have had some problems, but you don't believe I had anything to do with killing her."

"Don't I," she said.

"This sucks," Toby said. "Honest to Christ, what am I doing here in this crappy parking lot jeopardizing my whole career if I hurt that girl? What kind of sense does that make?"

"What's in your pocket, Toby?" I said.

He licked his lips. "My pocket? What are you talking about? I've got money, some ID, you know . . ."

"Your hip pocket," I said. "Dolly, you've got thirty seconds left on this job if you don't get behind your boyfriend Toby right now."

Dolly lunged as Toby reached for the pocket of his jeans. Their arms tangled, and then Dolly came up with what looked like a square of white paper with color at its center. She pushed Toby up against Alice and pinned him there, using all two hundred pounds.

"Simeon," Toby shouted, "I can *explain.*"

He twisted in Dolly's arms, and she let him go. Once released from constraint, Toby wilted. I actually thought he was going to slump to the pavement, but he caught himself. Without looking up, he said again, "I can explain."

"Give it to me," I said. Dolly put it into my hand.

I was looking at nothing: black surrounded by white. I turned it over, and it became a Polaroid photograph. Amber, caught by the flash on stage. But this was no publicity picture; her arms were twisted behind her, and her feet were bound by clothesline. She was exactly as I'd found her.

I heard a hiss behind me and saw a flash of red as Nana launched her nails at Toby's eyes.

14

Wastebaskets

SQUAWKING, Dolly damn near caught Nana on the fly. Toby, scrambling backward faster than I would have believed possible, bumped up against Alice hard and sat down on the pavement. Nana's momentum carried Dolly back a few steps, and she stumbled over Toby. The two of them went down on top of him, a pile of female elbows and feet. It looked like the closing moments of a tag team wrestling match.

I grabbed Nana by the belt loops on the back of her pants and yanked. She came up swearing and crying and turned to take a swipe at me. Behind her I saw Dolly's face. Her eyes were wide with betrayal, and three bright red lines ran down one cheek. Toby had rolled away from beneath her and was scrambling to get under Alice.

I started to laugh, but Nana slugged me in the chest. She pummeled me furiously with both fists, making terrible little "oof" noises. By the time I'd gotten my fingers untangled from her belt loops, a blow had caught me full on the throat. I choked. She kept on swinging at me, emitting a high, thin, shrilling sound, her eyes shut tight. I didn't think she had any idea who she was hitting.

Dolly got up, but instead of trying to help she backed away with a hand clamped flat over her bleeding face. She'd had enough of Nana. So had I. I hauled back and slapped her hard, twice, snapping her head left and then right. My nervous system was so hyped up that the slaps sounded like shots in my ears.

Nana just stopped. She let her arms go limp, and her hands fell to her sides. She didn't cry out or look at me or touch the burning red marks on her cheeks. She gazed down at the general area of my feet for a moment, her face closed and tight. Then, slowly and deliberately, she extended the middle finger of her right hand, stepped around me, and walked away, toward the entrance to the club.

"That girl's crazy," Dolly said from behind me.

"Did you look at this?" I still had the picture crumpled in my hand.

"No."

"Then shut up. Get your boyfriend out from under the car if you can."

She pulled her hand away from her cheek and looked at it, wincing when she saw the blood. "You won't scar," I said. "And if you do, you can say you got it in a duel. Toby, come out from under there."

No answer. I bent down and peered under the car. No Toby, either.

"Shit," I said as I heard the Maserati's engine catch.

I grabbed Dolly by the collar of her grungy T-shirt and hurled her in the general direction of the driveway, then sprinted toward the noise of Toby's car. "Don't let him get past you," I shouted.

Toby's tires smoked as the car shot in reverse out of its parking space. I was so close that his rearview mirror clipped my hip. It hurt. The car swerved wildly to reverse direction and came to a stop pointed at the driveway. I jumped in front of it.

Toby leaned on the horn, and I backed away, but the lot was too narrow: he couldn't get around me. If he was going to leave, he was going to leave over me. Dolly wailed something, but I couldn't make it out. All I heard was the car.

It revved once to a howling, red-lining rpm and then dropped, then revved again. Then Toby popped the clutch, and the thing pawed the ground and hurtled at me.

I backed up fast, and then it was my turn to trip. I went down hard on the seat of my pants, hearing the scream of the engine and the squeal of the tires. The next thing I knew, the Maserati was on top of me.

I threw myself flat on my back, cracking my head on the pavement. The front end of the car passed over my legs and suddenly stopped. I was most of the way under it, and the front bumper was at my chest.

Hands looped under my arms and pulled me free. I tried to get up, but my legs wouldn't hold me. Dolly tried to steady me, but she was shaking herself, and we both sat down directly in front of the Maserati.

"You fucking idiot," Dolly said. "How you going to pay me? Come *on*." The two of us managed an undignified, crablike scramble away from the car.

The next thing I knew, I was standing up and Dolly was brushing things off my back like a worried wife. "Never mind," I snapped. "The wheels didn't get me." I went over and pulled at the handle on the driver's door. It swung open, and I saw Toby with his head resting on the steering wheel. His hands were in his lap. "I can explain," he said again.

I hung on to the door for what seemed like a week. Toby didn't move. I took a deep breath. "So explain," I said.

"I got it today," he said. "It came in the mail." He still hadn't looked at me. "I had a late call for work, and I picked up the mail as I left. Dolly will tell you."

"He did get the mail," Dolly volunteered. "The mailbox is at the top of the hill, and he stopped there on the way out."

"So you got your mail today," I said. "So did I. So did most people. How do I know the picture was in it?"

Toby didn't say anything. Finally he looked up at me. "You don't," he said. "But it's true."

"Let's say it is. Just for the hell of it, let's say you're telling the truth. When did you open it?"

"At the studio."

"Where?"

"In my dressing room." He moved his hand.

I panted. "What time?"

"I don't know. I'd finished with makeup, but I hadn't worked yet."

"Say one, one-thirty," Dolly volunteered.

"Were you alone?"

"No." Toby glanced at Dolly. "She was with me."

"You said you hadn't seen it."

Dolly gave me a look of startled innocence. "I didn't. He opened a bunch of stuff. I didn't look at any of it. You didn't tell me to read his mail."

"No reaction?" I asked. "No raised eyebrows, no nothing?"

"Not that I noticed." She sounded ashamed of herself.

"I'm an actor," Toby said.

"Why didn't you show it to her?"

His face twisted. "Don't be dumb. I would have shown it to you when I got a chance." Dolly tried not to look hurt.

"Toby," I said, "the death penalty is alive and well in California. If it weren't for Saffron, you'd be talking to lawyers right now."

"I was going to show it to you," he said insistently. "It just didn't seem like something to do in a parking lot."

"So you tried to run over him," Dolly said. She was well past the stage of hero worship.

"He didn't," I said. "If he had, I'd be dead."

"Champ," Toby said earnestly, "the last thing I want is for anything to happen to you."

"No," I said. "The last thing you want is for anything to happen to Saffron."

"Well, sure," he said listlessly. "That goes without saying."

"What kind of an envelope did it come in?"

"An envelope, you know? Kind of brown, I think."

"What postmark?"

"Hollywood. I checked that."

"What does that tell us?" Dolly said. "Zilch."

"Right. But I want to see the envelope. Do you have it?"

Toby shook his head. "I threw it away."

"Well," I said, "that's really brilliant. Here's a piece of nice, tidy physical evidence that any half-wit cop would jug you for, and you throw away the envelope it came in. Amateurs," I said in disgust. "Just wait here. Dolly, you make sure he waits."

I hiked back up the driveway and went into the club. Rock music blared, and the heavyset Tiny clone stopped me as I lifted the curtain. "Seven dollars," he said.

"Don't be an idiot. I just left."

"No reentry without paying."

"I was here for Amber's funeral."

He shrugged. "I don't care if you were here for Washington's birthday. Seven bucks."

His jaw hung slack. I picked up a corner of the red curtain and jammed it in his mouth. "Eat this while I'm gone," I said. "I'll be back for dessert." He pushed it away with both hands and came up off his stool at me. A white arm billowed past me and shoved him back down, and I turned to look at Tiny.

"I don't need trouble," he said. "Not tonight."

"I want a minute with Nana."

"That'll be seven dollars for a minute, then."

I paid him. It didn't feel like a good idea to feed the curtain to Tiny.

Nana was at the bar, with her back to me. As I came up behind her, she said, "Go away."

"I am going away. Can I come back later?"

"If you can afford it."

"I'm sorry I hit you."

She shrugged. I was provoking a lot of shrugs. "I been hit before."

"He didn't take the picture. He got it in the mail."

"Yeah, and they find babies under cabbage leaves."

"Have it your way. I'll be back in a couple of hours."

"How will I stand the wait?" she said.

Tiny's hand landed on my shoulder. It was like standing under a falling redwood. "Minute's up," he said. The bartender glowered at me. Nana wouldn't give me a glance.

"Fine," I said. "Gee, everybody, have a good night."

It was getting dark when I reached Toby's car. The driver's door was still open, and Dolly was leaning against the front fender, looking like a hundred kilos of scorned woman. Toby hadn't moved.

"What time do they empty the wastebaskets in the dressing room?" I said.

"How do I know?"

I went around and got in on the passenger side. "Well," I said, "you're about to find out."

Twenty-five minutes later I was looking at a square, buff-colored envelope with a Hollywood postmark. The stamp had Susan B. Anthony on it. "Nice sense of irony," I said.

Toby was doing a line of cocaine. "Fingerprints," he said without much hope. "What about fingerprints?"

"It's rough paper. If I were the cops and I had a couple of billion dollars' worth of image-intensifying laser equipment, I might be able to lift a partial off the gummed strip. And you know what? It'd be yours."

"But the picture's smooth," Dolly said.

"Photographs are a great surface for prints, one of the best. But I'd bet my fee that Toby's are the only prints on it. And mine, of course, and yours. Nobody's a big enough schmuck to handle a photograph bare-handed after he's committed a murder.''

"Swell," Toby said. "I'm so glad we've got a specialist.''

"Toby,'' I said, "why would anyone send you that picture?''

For a second I thought I was going to get my third shrug of the evening. But then he shook his head. "To freak me out, maybe. To threaten me." He glanced up at Dolly and then back at me. "Maybe to tell me I'm next.''

"No," Dolly and I said simultaneously.

"This probably won't come as a complete surprise to you, Toby," I said, "but somebody hates your guts. I want a list. Everybody you've hurt, everybody who's related to somebody you've hurt." I glanced up at Dolly. "You might as well sit down," I said. "This could take a while.''

15

Things of the Spirit

THE SPIRIT, according to the people who believe in it, never sleeps. That was probably the reason the dreary little storefront with "Things of the Spirit" scrawled across the window had a large OPEN sign in its door at nine-fifteen on a Monday evening.

I'd checked my notes twice. This was the address that Hammond had grudgingly given me for Rebecca Hartsfield, the teenager whom Toby had matriculated in the school of hard knocks at the Ontario Motor Speedway. Things change fast in Hollywood, but things of the Spirit are eternal, and the shop certainly looked as though it had been sitting right where it was, on one of the scuzziest blocks of Hollywood Boulevard, for all eternity.

The window was crammed full of things of the Spirit. Crystals glittered from transparent nylon fishing lines that suspended them in space. Garish mandalas challenged my equilibrium with confusing permutations of concentric circles, looking like targets for spiritual archery. Reassuringly thick books offered answers to all the eternal questions between fake vellum covers embossed with confused combinations of crosses, pentacles, and symbols for infinity. Tiny glass vials filled with colored liquids glowed prismatically. In the whole window there wasn't anything I knew how to use.

I backed away to the curb and looked up. Like so many Hollywood storefronts, this one had once been the bottom floor of an apartment house. Two stories of apartments still squatted above it, lighted windows set in a plain brick wall. Maybe Rebecca Hartsfield lived in one of them.

A decidedly earthly buzzer announced my intrusion. Once it quit, I heard what I'd learned against my will to identify as new age music. Aimless and spacey, it meandered from unresolved keyboard chord to unresolved keyboard chord with some somnolent noodling in place of melody. Drooling pianos, music to sleepwalk by.

The music was almost immediately drowned out by the smell. Things of the Spirit stank like an old-fashioned whorehouse. The smell suggested that every bouquet ever picked had been reduced to its essence and crammed somehow into a single aerosol can, and that can had then been emptied into the store. It was enough to make a bee sneeze.

And I sneezed. "*God* bless you," someone said with more emphasis on the first word than on all the others put together. I heard a whisper of fabric, and I turned.

She was something to look at. Her age was impossible to guess. The skin on her face was as smooth and unlined as a girl of twenty, but her hair was snow white. At first glance it seemed as though there were yards of it, cascading over her shoulders and down her back. Framed by all that white, her face looked like an apple in the snow. The eyes were that pale, low-horizon sky blue that almost disappears in black-and-white photographs, giving the impression that, for once, the windows to the soul are two-way instead of mirrored from the outside. A seamless robe of blue, embroidered at the neck with what looked like amber snowflakes, hung straight from her shoulders to the floor.

She was smiling. I felt myself smiling back. "It's the concentration of aromas," she said as though we'd been talking for half an hour.

"What is?"

"Your sneeze. People used to believe that the soul could escape during a sneeze and be claimed by the Devil. That's

why we still say '*God* bless you.'" Again the emphasis on
the first word. "If the soul were to escape here, though, I
don't think the Devil could snare it. There's enough positive energy here to keep him or her miles away."

"Or at least across the street."

She looked puzzled for a second and then looked over
my shoulder and through the shop window. Then she
laughed. Her laugh was in the same key as the piano. "The
porno theater, and the massage parlor, you mean. Well,
yes. That's why we're here."

"It is?"

"Why carry coals to Newcastle? Why set up a fourth gas
station at an intersection where there are already three?"

"I've wondered why they did that. They always seem
to."

"The analogy isn't precise, I'm afraid. Credit cards is
why. Faced with a choice of gas stations, people will use
the card they carry. But the soul carries no credit cards."

"And it requires a different kind of fuel."

"Yes." She looked pleased. "That's exactly right. What
people buy here powers them upward as well as forward.
How may I help you?"

"What *are* the fragrances? I've never smelled anything
like them."

"Aromatherapy. We have the largest stock on the West
Coast. If you don't count San Francisco, that is."

Since San Francisco *is* on the West Coast, and will be
until it finally shakes loose and floats picturesquely into the
Pacific, the answer was less than ingenuous. On the other
hand, she'd popped the balloon herself, and I was willing to
give her credit for it.

"And aromatherapy does what?"

"Aromas are the cutting edge of holistic medicine. Given
a proper spiritual balance in the subject, aromas can
strengthen the body's defenses against any kind of infec-
tion. Would you like me to show you some?"

"Sure," I said, "if you think you can show someone an aroma."

The seraphic smile wilted slightly. "A literalist. Well, why don't you tell me what it is that ails you?"

"Insatiable curiosity."

She pursed her lips, sending the leftovers of the smile into some parallel universe, glanced down at my shoes, and then looked slowly up at the rest of me. It wasn't so much a look as a survey that mapped my clothes and placed them precisely in a low-rent district. I felt like I'd been denied admission to the new age.

"Curiosity," she said slowly. "I don't know that I've got a cure for that."

"Actually, I sort of hope not. Without curiosity, where would we be?"

"Happier, probably. What is it you're curious about?" We weren't having fun anymore.

I took the plunge. "Rebecca Hartsfield."

"Rebecca?"

"Hartsfield," I said.

"I heard you. I know the name. I'm Chantra Hartsfield. What do you want with Rebecca?"

"You're her sister," I said chivalrously.

"Ease up," she said. "Don't work quite so hard. Try mother."

"She's here, then."

"No. She's not."

"Where is she?"

"Not here."

"You already told me that." I tried a smile. No dice.

"*You* haven't told *me* anything," she said severely. "Not why you want to see Rebecca, not how you got this address. Nothing at all."

It was time to try frank. "I got the address from the police."

She put both hands into the pockets of her robe. "Police," she said. "Rebecca's not in trouble. I'd know. I always know."

She sounded so positive that I had to ask. "How do you always know?"

"Psychic linkage. Don't look skeptical, it's common between mother and daughter, if both women know how to tune in to it."

"You can read her mind?"

"Mind reading is a charlatan's stunt. No one can read anyone's mind. But people who have an affinity can feel strong emotions that the other person in the link experiences."

"Feel them how?"

"Why did the police give you this address?"

"Same answer as before. Because I asked."

"Why?"

We looked at each other for a moment.

"Well," I said, "we both want to know something, don't we?"

She tilted her head upward and studied me. "What exactly do you want to know?"

"How you feel the other person's emotions."

She gave a patient, well-bred sigh. "Hell, the same way I know that you don't mean any harm to Rebecca. If a person is open enough, the strong feelings of others resonate in her. Your emotions are part of the total electromagnetic field of your nervous system. Every thought, feeling, or dream you have is a scattering of electrical impulses, jumping across millions of synapses between the nerves. When you're extremely agitated or gripped by a powerful emotion, your electromagnetic field becomes stronger and more agitated. If a person is receptive, her nervous system will sense the other's static, producing a faint sensation of joy or fear or sorrow."

Since I couldn't think of anything to say, I nodded.

"It happens all the time between mothers and daughters, even at long distance. Does that explanation make sense to you?"

"Sure, I guess so. It's like magnetism. You can't see it, but you can see its effects."

She smiled again. "Amazing," she said. "Even the most skeptical person will accept an explanation if it's dressed up in enough electromagnetic mumbo-jumbo. There's no scientific explanation of gravity, either. Does that make you doubt its existence?"

"Not as long as the change in my pockets feels heavy."

"Money is heavy beyond its physical weight. Gram for gram, money is the heaviest thing in the world."

"Grams?" I said. "You're metric?"

"Ten is a powerful number."

"What about metric astrology? Which two signs of the zodiac would you eliminate to get it down to ten?"

For a moment I thought she was going to laugh. "Gemini and Cancer."

"Why?"

"My ex-husband was on the cusp." The laugh decided not to show up. "And now that we've finished playing, why did you ask the police how to find Rebecca?"

"I'm interested in something that happened four years ago. At Ontario Motor Speedway."

She closed her eyes for a long moment. When she reopened them they were fastened on mine. "We've let go of that," she said. "That's not part of our baggage anymore."

"I may have to ask Rebecca to reclaim it."

"Why would you do that?"

"Maybe to keep some other little girl from having to go through what Rebecca did."

She pulled her hands from her pockets and surprised me by cracking her knuckles. Large semiprecious stones sparkled on her fingers. "Well," she said, "you can't talk to Rebecca. She's at college, and I won't tell you where, so don't ask."

"Look. You've already figured out that I'm not dangerous. Is there someplace we can sit down?"

Her eyes burned into mine for a moment. Norman Still-man would have killed for that gaze. Then she walked briskly past me and reached into the window, turning around the OPEN sign. Before she did, I read the other side. It didn't say CLOSED. It said THE FLOW IS TEMPORARILY INTER-RUPTED. PLEASE COME BACK.

"The flow?" I said.

"Skip it," she said shortly, heading for the back of the shop. I followed her through a door behind the counter and into a back room. The smell, if anything, was more power-ful in there. The shelves were jammed with stock, and what seemed like millions of identical books were stacked every-where. She pulled out a chair, angled it around toward one of the stacks of books, and sat in it. "Take a load off," Chantra Hartsfield said.

"Where?"

"There." She pointed and let the smile bloom. "Don't worry, they'll hold you."

I sat on the books. They sank slightly beneath my weight and gave off a vaporous sigh of aroma that literally made my eyes water. "God in heaven," I said. "I feel like I've been sentenced to life imprisonment inside a flower."

"These are my catalogs. I'm going national."

I looked around at the stacks. "If you'll excuse my saying so, they don't seem to be moving very fast."

"It's a problem. I can't figure out how to market them."

"What do you mean? Buy a mailing list from the Scientologists or somebody and send them out."

"Yeah," she said, "that's just it. They're something brand new. They're the first scratch-and-sniff aromatherapy catalogs."

"Smells like a great idea."

"I think it is. But how do you control it? I mean, if an ounce of, let's say, chamomile will cure cancer of the colon in the right person, what effect would a scratch-and-sniff have on the common cold? I could put myself out of business."

"Ah," I said sympathetically.

She offered up a helpless smile. "I'm not really much good at business."

"Well," I said, "if you're selling chamomile to cure colon cancer, the profit margin must be pretty impressive."

"I'm not selling dink," she said without taking offense. "You're sitting on my catalogs."

I shrugged, a mistake in judgment that released several pounds of perfume directly into my nostrils. "I'm not much good at business, either," I said, fanning it away. "Hey, do you know anything about computers?"

"I can't work a calculator," she said. "It's a dilemma."

We commiserated silently for a moment, one failed businessperson to another. I shifted again, with the same result. "Listen," I said, "why not sew them into pillow slips and sell them as whoopie cushions?"

She thought about it, shook her head, and dusted her hands together in a workmanlike fashion. "So. Tell me why you're here."

"Our friend Toby Vane. I've been assigned to keep an eye on him."

"Assigned by whom? And for what reason?"

"By the company that produces his shows. To keep him from slamming any young women around for the time being."

"Since when do they care? What do you do for a living?"

"I'm supposed to be a detective."

"And you work for the production company?" There was an undertone in her voice I didn't understand.

"Yes."

"For Norman Stillman Productions?" The undertone was pure acid now. She said the words as though she had to get them out of her mouth before they dissolved and choked her.

"Right." I waited.

"Do you mind if I smoke?" she said. It was about the ninth time she'd surprised me.

"Not if you give me one, too."

I got arched eyebrows. "You don't look like a smoker."

"Neither do you. But I'd smoke a highway flare to muffle these damned aromas."

She gave me a staccato laugh, crinkling appealingly around the eyes, and opened a drawer in a little wooden desk to withdraw a package of the same long cigarettes Nana smoked. She handed me one and lit them both with practiced precision. "I can't smoke in the shop," she said. "Bad for the image. I learned about image the hard way. Image is the reason the geniuses at Norman Stillman Productions would want to keep me quiet."

I parked that one for the meantime. "What happened?"

"Very bad energies. Rebecca was just a kid. She had a crush on Toby Vane. Her stepfather told her about the thing at Ontario, and she wanted to go. I figured what the hell, and we went."

"And Toby got his hands on her."

"Well, that was easy under the circumstances. He was all charm. She was right in the front row, naturally."

"Why naturally?"

She gave me her level gaze. It made me want to ask her out to dinner. "That'll keep," she said, waving a dismissive hand and fanning some lavender toward me. "So he asked her if she wanted to see the car up close, and she did. Then he asked if she'd like to see his dressing room. I wasn't near her at the time. It was a big trailer that was parked right near the track."

"I've seen it."

"And the next thing I knew I felt something terrible sweep over me and found myself running toward the trailer. I was about a hundred feet away when the door opened and Rebecca fell out of it, down the stairs, and onto the ground. Her face was covered with blood."

"He'd hit her."

"He'd hit her many times. Her nose was fractured and

her lip was split, and two of her teeth were broken. When I took her in my arms she coughed the teeth into my lap."

She gave me an apologetic smile. "I don't mean to be dramatic, but that's what happened. She was hysterical. This was her hero. She had his pictures all over her room. They were signed. They said 'To Rebecca with love, Toby.' When I got home I tore them all down. She'd been taken to the hospital by then."

"Where was her stepfather?"

"Oh, he was busy. He was busy for hours. He had to clean up after Toby. When he got home I told him I was leaving. By the time I got Rebecca out of the hospital I was already gone. I'd taken the apartment over this shop."

"Who is he?"

"You really don't know?" I shook my head.

"Hartsfield is my first husband's name," she said. "In addition to being a widow, I'm deliriously happy to be the ex-Mrs. Dixie Cohen."

I sat back, and the books creaked and let out an aromatic gust. The two of us smoked in self-defense. The silence stretched around us. In the street someone laughed drunkenly.

"So," she said. "Is there anything else?"

"Yeah," I said. "Charge for the catalogs. Three bucks each. That way you're ahead either way."

She gave me a full-bore smile. "I knew I liked you," she said.

16

La Maison

MY THIRD STOP of the evening was in the Valley, so I had plenty of time to think as I drove. I needed it.

The main hope, of course, given the source of my almost fictitiously large paycheck, was that someone was trying to frame Toby. Unless, that was, Toby really had killed Amber, a notion that even an eyewitness couldn't altogether drive from my mind, given what I knew about the lad.

Even if he'd had nothing to do with Amber, there were plenty of people who might have wanted to put a big black period at the end of his life. When you live like Toby lived, there are always going to be people who want to pop your cork for good.

Heading west on Ventura Boulevard, a cherried-out old Buick, vintage 1953 or thereabouts, blew a fishtail kiss at Alice and began playing tag with me. First it tailgated me, and then it passed me, got in front, and slowed down. What looked like four very large kids kept glancing back, waiting for me to hit the horn or give them a bump in the rear. In Los Angeles that's a good way to get shot, so I just pulled into a service station and earned a disappointed finger from the kid in the front passenger seat. Hell, maybe *they* killed Amber. Three days on the case and I hadn't ruled anybody out, not even the golden boy himself, and new possibilities were blooming like wildflowers.

At two thousand a day I felt overpaid.

And I was curiously fuzzy about things. My mental state

wasn't helped any by the fact that everybody who was involved seemed to have made up a name just for me. Toby, Nana, Dixie, Tiny, Saffron, certainly Chantra—almost everybody had an AKA; nobody had the Christian name he or she was born with. And the few who did, Norman Stillman, for example, had invented personalities instead.

It didn't delight me that I was now on my way to an encounter with the most improbable name of all.

Dixie, back in the good old days when I thought he was leveling with me, had given me the names and numbers of four of the pros he and Stillman had hired for Toby to knock around as a safe outlet for his boyish energies. One of the numbers had also popped up on the yellow pad I'd used to copy the contents of Tiny's phone book. Hookers move even more frequently than the average Angeleno, and that was the only number out of the four that was still good. My call had reached a machine that informed me that business hours were ten in the morning until twelve midnight and that she'd be at something called La Maison. I was headed for La Maison, and the woman I was going to see called herself Mistress Kareema.

Ventura Boulevard is a sad street. Back in the days of the third or fourth real estate boom, when Bob Hope and Bing Crosby owned everything the Chandler family didn't, the Valley had been positioned as paradise: no smog, an orange tree or six in every yard, the grime and crime of the city at a safe remove across the mountains. Ventura Boulevard was the artery of optimism, the pioneering east-west street, the first to be developed, with stucco storefronts and palatial motion picture houses. After fifty years, Ventura was a dotted line of prosperity and decline. No building material in history has ever decayed with quite the speed of stucco.

Mistress Kareema, whoever she might be, practiced her trade on a street named Sunnyvista, which, as I might have expected from the way things were going, was one of the few shady spots in the Valley. It was a narrow ribbon of asphalt that gnarled and knotted its way south of the boulevard, overhung with oaks and eucalyptus that had grown to an antebellum, Edward Gorey thickness. Even the moon couldn't peek through. The storefronts extended south a couple of blocks, and La Maison was the last commercial establishment before the houses took over.

La Maison had all the discretion of accomplished vice: whatever happened there, it happened inside a pale, anonymous stucco box with two windows in front that could have been installed to display anything from guitars to tires. The windows were masked with brown paper, new territory for Stillman's timeline. The sign was about the size of a piece of legal paper, and the building was as anonymous as the French Foreign Legion. The front door looked solid and locked. Junk newspapers littered the doorway. As I pulled through the driveway to park Alice in the rear, I wondered if it were even open.

I had started on foot toward the front of the building when I saw the back door. The sign, larger than the one in front, said LA MAISON. La Maison looked like the kind of place one entered through the back door, and I gave it a try.

It wasn't locked. A bell rang as I opened it, nothing electronic, just a regular old bell that got slammed by a piece of metal every time the door opened. I was in a dark corridor, not that much different from the Spice Rack. A single naked light bulb in a bare porcelain socket flung its forty watts valiantly into the gloom. The gloom won. I stood there in it, waiting for someone to answer the bell's summons.

After about twenty seconds, I heard somebody moan. Then she cried out. Then she cried out again, a choked, panicked, whimpering sound that made the hair on my arms stand straight up. Wishing I had the gun I'd left in Alice's glove compartment, I started down the hallway.

Ten feet down, the corridor turned left. There were doors on either side now. In each door there was a small window, about four inches by six. All but one were dark.

The cry turned into a scream. The scream died away into a kind of hopeless sobbing. Then I heard a *smack* that sounded like something hard against bare flesh, and I headed for the lighted window.

"No," a woman's voice cried out. "No, please, no. No more, no more, no more." She coughed, or choked, and I was at the window.

I was looking at a living room. There was a lot of ordinary furniture, most of it red: a red couch, a coffee table, red pictures on the walls. There was also one piece of extraordinary furniture, a kind of aluminum frame that looked like a cross between a sawhorse and a torture rack. On it was a small blond girl. She was strapped to it, bent over it brutally, spread-eagle and as naked as a saint's forehead. Between us stood Toby Vane, stripped to the waist with his back to me. In his hand was a whip. I surveyed the room as best I could through the little window. No Big John. Then Toby lifted the whip and brought it whistling down across the girl's spine. She cried out again and arched her slim back.

I kicked the door in on the first try. My right foot caught Toby behind the knee before he had a chance to turn around, and he crumpled headlong toward the floor. I managed to catch his chin with my foot as he fell. The sound of his neck snapping up was deeply satisfying. He twisted and landed on his face, and I slammed his left kidney with my heel for the sheer pleasure of it. He moaned and rolled over, curling into an embryonically protective ball.

That was when things started to go wrong.

The first thing I registered was that it wasn't Toby. It was someone I'd never seen before, a young man with so little chin that he must have knotted his tie directly below his overbite. The second thing I registered was the voice of the girl. She didn't say, "Thank God," or, "My hero." What she said was, "What the *fuck.*"

Whoever was on the floor moaned. Whoever was on the rack muttered nastily. Whoever had come into the room behind me said, "Alma, language, please," and then she said, "Who the hell are you?"

Until that moment I don't think I'd ever known what the word *nonplussed* meant, but now it shouldered its way through the orderly ranks of my vocabulary and leapt unfettered out of my mouth. "I'm nonplussed," I said.

"What you just did usually costs three hundred bucks," said the woman in the doorway. She was wearing a black outfit that looked like the kind of lingerie the Spanish Inquisition might have designed—a whalebone black corset, fishnet stockings, and high-heeled boots that reached her knees. Her hair was an impossible bottle black, and her eyebrows arched higher than Lucille Ball's. "Maybe if you give it to poor William here, he won't call the cops on you."

"*He's* going to call the cops? What about her?"

"Holy Mary, mother of God," said the girl on the rack in a resigned tone. William, still on the floor, used his elbows to put a couple of yards between him and me and looked up at me with the kind of rolling eyes that up till then I'd only seen on hooked fish. I looked again at his nonexistent chin and wondered how I'd managed to catch it with my foot.

"I thought I was helping," I said. "Is William really in a position to call the cops?" William tried to shake his head and then grabbed his throat. Obviously I hadn't hit his chin at all. The whip curled limply from his left hand.

"In a perfect world, maybe," the lady with the lingerie

said. The barest hint of a smile curled the corners of her mouth. "Since the world is manifestly imperfect, a simple apology will probably suffice."

Etiquette classes had not prepared me for this, so I did the only thing I could think of. I reached down to William. He cringed. "Jesus, William," I said. "I'm sorry. I thought you were somebody else."

"I'm not," he croaked. "I'm me. I'm only me."

"*Only* you? You're a strong man, William," said the lady in the lingerie. "He caught you from behind. You'd have killed him if he hadn't." William attempted a nod and then rubbed his throat again. "We all know who you are, William, and we're all afraid of you. But," she said to me in a tone like a shredded tire, "who did *you* think he was?"

What the hell, I figured. "Toby Vane."

The girl on the rack turned quickly to look at me, and Miss Lingerie of 1564 gave me a sharp glance. "See, William," she said, looking at me in a speculative fashion. "He thought you were Toby Vane. It must have taken a lot of courage for him to attack you like that."

"Not really," I said without thinking. Both women looked at me imploringly. "I mean, I was behind you," I improvised. "It wasn't fair."

"No," the one in the lingerie said as though she were talking to a child. "It wasn't fair at all. It was dirty fighting." I managed a nod. "Now come on," she said to me, "let's leave William and Alma alone. Alma, are you sure it's all right if we leave you alone with William?"

"I don't know, Mistress Kareema," the girl on the rack said plaintively. She had a fourth-grader's lisp. "Maybe he's mad now."

"Of course he's mad," Mistress Kareema said, "but not at you. That's right, isn't it, William?"

William had lifted himself cautiously to a sitting position. "No," he squeaked. "It's not her I'm mad at." Then he shifted his fish-eyes toward Mistress Kareema. "Is it?"

"It's him," she said, indicating me. "But I don't want trouble, so I'm going to get him out of here before you take vengeance. Now, I want you to promise that you won't take it out on Alma."

"Oh, *pleeeease*," Alma squealed. "Not on me, William." She twitched her bare bottom.

"I like Alma," William said in a voice as soft as rainwater. "But keep *him* away from me, or I won't answer for the consequences." He gave the whip a sad little shake.

"He's going. Now, Alma, you give William a good time, you hear? But call me if he gets too rough."

"Oh, I will," Alma said. "Stay close, please?" She rolled her eyes at William in an approximation of terror that wouldn't have fooled a blind man. Mistress Kareema put three solid steel fingers around my wrist and tugged me toward the door. "Be sweet, William," she said, pushing me past her. "Remember, Alma's at your mercy."

William gave a brusque macho nod, and Kareema shoved me the rest of the way through the door and closed it behind us.

"Jesus Christ," she said. "That's a good customer, twice a week, at least. You can't fuck with their libidos like that. These are very fragile guys."

"What about Alma? What's she made of, magnesium?"

"Alma can take care of herself. One word from her and William will be on his knees begging for forgiveness and thankful for the opportunity. Come with me."

She led me into one of the dark rooms and flicked on the light. It was decked out as a medieval torture chamber. False stone walls dripped real water. "Have a seat." I sat on something that passed as a ledge. She tapped her foot. "What's this shit about Toby Vane?"

"But she's tied to that thing."

"Relax. Alma's been at this gig for three years. She's only gotten hurt once."

"By whom?"

"If you hadn't said his name, I'd have brained you on the spot." She dropped something heavy onto the stone sacrificial slab in front of me. It wasn't anything fancy, just a good old-fashioned sap. "You'd have been hearing birds for weeks," she said. She was still standing.

I was at a loss, and I attempted to compensate by getting comfortable.

"Get your feet off the slab," Mistress Kareema said in a voice that could have sliced through a diamond. "Where do you think you are, at home? Alma's the submissive here. I like to be in charge. What are you up to, anyway?"

"I got your number from Dixie Cohen."

She looked like she was going to spit. "Some reference. You've got two minutes to tell me what's going on, and then out."

I gave it to her in ninety seconds. She nodded a couple of times and then reached into her cleavage and pulled out a pack of cigarettes. She lit up without offering me one. "So you're supposed to keep him out of trouble. So what? What's that got to do with Alma and me? Don't answer that." She turned away. "Wait'll I turn off the drip. Jesus, have you looked at your water bill lately?" A moment after she left the room, the water stopped trickling down the walls.

She came back, and I described what had happened to Amber. Her eyes narrowed, and she knocked the cigarettes over to me, pulling up a wooden stool.

"Could be," she said, sitting. "He broke Alma's thumb. That cost him five thousand bucks. It wasn't enough. Alma almost quit, and that would have cost him a lot more. It's hard to find a real submissive these days."

She could have been discussing housekeepers. I held up a hand, and she tossed me her lighter, hard and fast. I stalled by lighting one of her cigarettes, hoping I wasn't going to start again.

The door opened and Alma came in wearing a violet robe with little white flowers on it. She was about twenty-four, with tousled wheat-colored hair and big blue eyes. "He's going home," she said to Mistress Kareema. "He couldn't get it going again."

"You saw him scared," Kareema said. "Took the wind out of his sails." She gave me something halfway between a smile and a grimace and said, "You better hope he comes back."

"He said tomorrow night," Alma said. "He tipped me two hundred."

"Then he'll be back. By the time he gets home he'll feel like a big man again."

"He had a nosebleed. He was worried about what his wife would say."

"He's *married*?" I asked. "Does he knock his wife around, too?"

Mistress Kareema snorted. "She turns him to tapioca. That's why he rents little Alma here, isn't it, kitten?" Alma nodded assent and sat on the edge of Kareema's stool. Kareema gave Alma's flax-colored thigh an affectionate catlike scratch with her long salmon nails.

"They're all scared of women," Alma said. "All of them except Toby. Toby really hates us." She looked down at her right hand. Its thumb was unnaturally crooked. "You're not a friend of his, are you?"

"If I were, I wouldn't have cold-cocked William, would I? I thought he was Toby."

"That's right," she said gravely. "You did. I wish he *had* been. I would have liked to see that. The sonofabitch." Wrapped in her little-girl voice, the words were startling.

"You still haven't really said why you're here," Mistress Kareema cut in.

"Well, I'm not a hundred percent sure. I really don't think Toby murdered that girl. He's got a good alibi."

"Murdered?" Alma said. Her eyes were huge.

"Later, sugar," Kareema said. "What sort?"

"Someone was with him. She swears he never got out of her sight. And someone else saw the dead girl get out of their car."

"Shit," Kareema said. "That's what I'd really like. Murder one is what he deserves." Unconsciously she reached over and caressed Alma's right thumb.

"I just want to know everything I can about him. I feel like I'm driving blind, and I don't like it."

"He's a gold-plated dipstick," Mistress Kareema said. "He'll never find his own level because nobody can go that low. What happens here, someone like William, it's mostly theater. The whip is just silk. But Toby likes the blood to be real, and he likes lots of it. Alma's his type. She looks like a baby, talks like a baby. When she really gets hurt she cries. We get a lot of guys in here, they ought to be seeing a shrink. Hell, we even get shrinks. . . ."

"Doctors are the kinkiest of all," Alma put in. "There's one doctor, a dentist, really—"

"But Toby's the sickest," Kareema said, waving away the digression. "He's running on pure hate, and what he hates is girls."

"He hates us something awful," Alma said. "After he broke my thumb, you know what he said? He said, 'It's okay, honey, you can pick your nose with the other hand.' And then he tried to do my other hand."

"What did you do?" I was fascinated in a horrid sort of way.

"I kicked him in the balls," Alma said in her ten-year-old's voice. "He didn't even feel it at first because he was having so much fun. He kept coming after me. Then he felt it, and he fell down. He was screaming that he was going to kill me. Since he was lying down I kicked him again."

"Too bad he's only got two," I said.

"His face got all red, and he was spitting at me. I was trying to get the door to his trailer open, but I couldn't figure out how to work it, it's not a regular doorknob, you know? And he got up and he was coming toward me, and I finally got it open. I fell down the steps into the dirt. Some man, the man who had hired me, grabbed me and pulled me away and into his car."

"That's your reference," Kareema said. "Dixie."

"Whoever he was, he didn't care dirt about me," Alma said. "I kept telling him about my thumb because I couldn't move it and it looked like it was on all backward, but he just told me to shut up, everything was okay now, and to stay in the car and not make trouble. Then he went into the trailer. After about ten minutes he came out and said not to worry, Toby was sorry. Then he had somebody else take me to the hospital."

"Toby was sorry," I said.

"Yeah, like that was supposed to make everything all right. Jeez, what a weirdo." Kareema gave Alma a pat on the wrist. "That's who you're protecting," she said.

"Did he call here afterward? Did he seem ashamed of himself?"

She looked surprised. "Five or six times. He kept asking for Alma, saying he wanted her to forgive him. Finally I let him talk to her. Tell the man what happened, kitten."

"He cried," Alma said. "He really cried."

"He always does," I put in.

"Then, the next day I got an envelope. It had five thousand dollars in it, all in twenties and fifties. And this card, like a Valentine's card, with all these sticky things written on it."

"And that was it?"

"Not really," Kareema said. "He still calls once in a while. Says he'd like to take Alma out, show her he's really a nice guy. Talk about sick."

"Does he?" I said, thinking. "That's very interesting." It

was so interesting that I lighted another of Kareema's cigarettes before I realized what I was doing.

"Two or three times he said he was going to come by," Kareema continued. "I told him I'd call the cops the minute he set foot in the place. Women don't frighten him, maybe, but cops he's afraid of."

She beckoned for her cigarettes, and I threw them to her. She lit up. We all looked at each other for a minute.

"When was the last time he called?"

"Last week sometime. Maybe Wednesday or Thursday."

"Well, well, well," I said. "Isn't that nice?"

"What's nice about it?" Kareema demanded. The bell rang in the hallway.

"I'll get it," Alma said. "You two just sit tight." She went to the door, looking like a teenager at a slumber party.

"That's it?" Kareema said.

"I guess so." I got up. "Make me a promise."

"Depends on what it is."

"Let me know the next time he calls." I gave her a card.

"What for?"

"Why not? It can't hurt, it may help. It may help put Toby on ice."

"I don't see how. I'm not going to let him get near her. I don't care what he wants to pay. I've got a business to think about. You know, this isn't a job where you can get workers comp."

The door opened and Alma came back in. "It's the dentist," she said.

"Hell," Mistress Kareema said. "It's going to be a long night. Good-bye, detective. That *is* all, isn't it?"

"Except for one thing."

"What's that?" She sounded weary.

"I'm tired of phony names. What's your real one?"

She regarded me. "Shirley," she finally said.

"How'd you choose Kareema?"

"None of your business." She sounded defensive, but Alma laughed.

"Basketball," Alma said. "She's crazy for basketball." Kareema gave her a shove, but she sidestepped. "Her idea of a great time would be Kareem Abdul-Jabbar." Alma dissolved into giggles. Kareema actually blushed.

"You can call me Shirley," she said to me. "Now get out of here. Alma and I have to get into our nurses' uniforms."

On the way to Alice I passed the dentist's Ferrari. The wages of sin, I thought. I hoped they were high.

17

The Tornado

NANA WAS GLASSY-EYED, but she was still at the bar. When I took her arm she twisted in slow-mo to see who I was, and her eyes almost crossed. Then she turned back to the bar, reeling slightly with the effort. As an afterthought, she shrugged my hand away.

"Oh, boy," she mumbled. "The hero's hero is here. Quick, everybody, put on your tights and cape." A glass stood on the bar in front of her, next to her cigarettes. On top of the cigarettes was a pack of matches that advised the world to EAT OUT MORE OFTEN.

I sniffed the glass. "What have you been drinking?"

"Seven-Up. Toby's private stock. Who wants to know?" The words were slurred and sullen.

"I think it's more like Tiny's private stock," I said. "Out of the little jars in the office."

Pinpoints of alarm kindled in her eyes. "For chrissakes, shut up. Somebody might hear you."

"I'll say it over the PA system if you like. How many?"

She wiped her nose inelegantly. "How many what?"

"Loads, stupid. How many loads?"

"Two," she said. "Or three." She made a careless gesture with her hand. "So what? I was among friends until you came in."

I took her arm again, harder this time. "Say good-bye to your friends. We're leaving."

"And now," said the clown at the door, speaking into a

hand mike and trying for a swinger's drawl, "here's our hot little treat from south of the border. Five feet two of pure salsa and *cucarachas.*" He obviously didn't speak Spanish. "Let's hear it for Chili." The Hispanic girl I'd seen before climbed up onto the big stage wearing nothing but a T-shirt and a spangled red G-string that looked like leftover yardage from Dorothy's ruby slippers. Business was slow, but the girls weren't. A few customers applauded laconically.

Nana yanked her arm away and cranked her eyes around to look at me again, but I was too close and she couldn't focus. The tub of lard at the front door, the one who'd demanded seven dollars earlier in the evening, had put the mike down and was staring at us. It wasn't a sweet stare.

"I'm not going anywhere. Not with you, anyway. Someone reminded me of a word for you about an hour ago. You're a louse. 'He's a louse,' he said, and I said, 'You're right.' " Her voice was thicker than maple syrup.

"And you're loaded. In fact, you're loaded beyond any kind of civilized belief."

"Get off my back," she said. "In *fact,* as you might say, college boy, get out of my sight. You're on that toadstool's side. Lips that touch toadstools shall never touch mine." She giggled halfheartedly and then hiccupped.

"Honey," I said, "I don't mean to go all masculine on you, but if you don't get your ass in gear, I'm going to go up to that cretin over there and take his microphone away, and then I'm going to tell the crowd exactly where they can find Tiny's stash of loads. I might even tell them who gave me the key to this shithole."

"You wouldn't," she said. She was having no trouble focusing now.

"Watch," I said. I put down her drink and started around her. She made a feeble grab at my arm and missed. I was up the steps toward the door in two long strides, and Mr. Adipose was looking up in a dimly alarmed fashion when Nana finally caught up with me.

"Okay," she hissed with a slight stagger as she tried to stop moving. "Let's go." The lump of animal fat on the stool looked at us suspiciously, and she added, "Darling." She rubbed her forehead on my arm, teetered precariously, and said to him, "Some men. You never know when they're going to show up."

Fatso started to say something, but I shoved the curtain open and hauled Nana outside.

Nana shuddered, and I started to laugh. Now that we were outside she was subdued. "You're crazy, you know that?" she said. "Tiny could take your head off."

"It's time to be crazy. Nothing else will work now. Our whole problem is that we've been acting like we were dealing with sane people. If anybody on this case were sane, it wouldn't have happened in the first place. Get in." I held Alice's passenger door open.

She did, a little more cautiously than usual, and then slumped onto the seat. She was silent until we were a couple of blocks up Santa Monica. Then she snickered. "Boy," she said, "I've been kidnapped. Right out from under Tiny's nose." The snicker turned into a laugh, and she leaned back and shook her head.

"I'm glad you're amused. It may have cost you a job."

"Who cares? There's other nude bars. I can always go back to the airport." She waved a loose hand in front of her face as though she were too warm. "Swept away," she said.

"Or go back to computer school."

"Oh, sure," she said. "DOS eight-point-oh or whatever it's up to now. It could be DOS thirty-six for all I know. Or care."

"DOS thirty-eight sounds like your IQ this evening. In your case, DOS stands for Downers Over Sense."

"You're not my mother. You're not even dead old dad." She stopped talking abruptly and swallowed. Eventually she said, "He was there tonight, by the way."

SKIN DEEP **249**

"Who was?"

"Dead old dad. Aren't you listening?"

"What'd he want?"

She squinted fuzzily through the windshield. "Where are we going?"

"We're going home."

"Whose home?"

"What did your father want?"

She tangled her fingers together and twisted her hands. "If I answer you, will you answer me?" It sounded like a kids' game.

"Sure."

"Promise?"

I kept driving.

"He had this great idea," she said. Her voice was very tight. "He thought maybe we should move to Hawaii. Just the two of us, just Daddy and Nana. He wants to buy a club there."

"Club? What kind of club?"

She made a strangled sound that was somewhere between laughing and crying. "Sherlock Holmes," she said. "What kind of club do you think? Honest to fucking Christ, what kind of club do you think? Oh, Jesus," she said, and then everything fell apart and she was crying full out, nothing cosmetic or dainty, the kind of crying that puffs up people's eyes and makes stuff dangle from their nose.

I pulled Alice over to the curb and tried to get an arm around her. "No," I said. "He didn't mean that."

She yanked herself away from me. "Don't you tell me what he meant, you middle-class white asshole. He meant a nude club. He meant a place where girls dance naked and be real sweet to the customers." She leaned against the door opposite me.

"And what were you supposed to be?"

"Me?" she said. "I'm supposed to be Miss Oriental Universe. That way he gets to make money and watch me at the same time."

Traffic, L.A. traffic, whizzed by us as if it knew where it was going. The spotlight in front of us turned from green to red and then back again before I had any idea what to say.

"Honey," I said at last, "you're an orphan. Shine him on, say good-bye. Give Daddy a good punt into the far, far end of the end zone where Toby lives and start over."

She looked up at me, and her face, reflecting the bluish glow of the streetlights, was streaked with tears. "Right," she said. "Sure. Except you're talking about my father. When I was a little girl, you know? I mean, a *real* little girl, before . . . Oh, shit. Forget it."

"Nana." I put my hand on her arm. "I'm not going to forget it. For God's sake, trust me. I deserve that much."

"Why should I trust you all of a sudden? I haven't trusted anybody since I was twelve."

"Then don't trust me. You're on your own anyway. You've known that for years."

"I used to pray, you know? When I was eleven, twelve years old and he started coming into my room, I used to pray. I prayed real loud. I hoped Mom would hear me even if You Know Who didn't. Nobody heard me."

"I hear you."

"And who knows what you want? Why should you want anything different? I'm shit. I've always been shit." She lifted her knees and dropped her chin onto them, crumpling into a smaller space than I would have believed possible. "If I hadn't been shit, he'd have treated me like a good little girl. He wouldn't have wanted me."

"*He's* shit," I said. "Toby's shit. Listen, everybody's shit sometimes. Everybody's crazy, and nobody wants to be. You never had a chance."

She threw both arms over her face and wailed. I sat as far from her as I could get in the enclosed space of the car and concentrated on counting to twenty. There was nothing else to do. She had her face cradled in her arms.

"Nana," I said into her sobs, "I can't fix anything. I can't make your life right, only you can do that. But you *can* do that. I'm not trying to sound like the *Hour of Power* or Ann Landers, but you can. And you already know it."

No answer, but she was crying more softly. Maybe she was listening. Great. Now I had to say something.

"I can't tell you anything you don't already know. Most of the time I don't even believe anybody can help anybody. But I do believe you've got to try."

Nana was sitting up now, gazing out the windshield through swollen eyes. Tears dripped from her chin. "So what should I do?" she asked.

I thought. "Eat out more often," I said.

Her look was an eloquent reproach. "If that's supposed to be funny, it isn't."

"I'm not a guru. I don't know what I'm talking about. But since you're acting as if I did, it seems to me that you're trapped inside your life, same as Amber was. She said she'd lost the map. What I think she meant was that she'd lost the map that would get her out."

"Out of what?"

"The track she knew. The track she'd worn down chasing herself around and around until it felt familiar because she was following her own footsteps. Go from home to the club. Go from the club to home. Stop on the way to score. She could have quit any time, but she didn't. It caused her pain, but the pain was familiar. She was like everybody else. She was used to the familiar pain and afraid of the pain that might be new. Maybe what she should have done was throw some cold water on her face and stop. Get up the next morning and do something new."

"Amber was a junkie."

"You're not."

"Not yet, anyway."

"You're not going to be a junkie. You won't let it happen. I won't let it happen."

"You," she said. "You can't sit on my shoulder forever, telling me what's right and what's wrong. Life doesn't work that way."

"I don't have to. You already know."

"Tell me what I know."

"You know you don't have to go back to the club, for one thing. Sex is what went wrong first in your life, and you're selling sex for a living. I mean, Jesus, if Daddy wants into your life-style, it's the wrong life-style."

"I should learn from Daddy?" She shook her head again, and I could feel her withdraw.

"Daddy's nothing, Daddy's less than nothing. Daddy's just litmus paper to tell you when you're wrong. When the people we should hate cheer up, we're doing something wrong. We should deprive them of that, if only for the simple pleasure of watching their faces fall."

"That's all what I'm not supposed to do. What *should* I do?"

"How the hell do I know? Go to the zoo. Grow a mustache. Go back to computer school. Become Florence Nightingale, work with lepers. Run for Congress. You speak Korean and English; become a simultaneous translator for the U.N. Eat out more often."

"I can't do those things."

"When your girlfriend, may her flesh rot from her bones, first suggested you should dance nude, did you think you could do it?"

She lifted her knees and crossed her beautiful arms over them. Then she rested her chin on her arms. "No," she said. "I thought it would kill me."

"Of course you did. It was unthinkable. But now it's the pain you're familiar with."

After a full minute, she nodded. "Learn from it," she said.

I leaned back. I felt like I'd run twenty miles.

She looked over at me. "I'm not stupid," she said.

"Nana. You're probably smarter than I am."

Her eyes engaged mine and held them. "Probably," she said, "but you're sweet." She reached out and tried to circle my wrist with her fingers. Her hand was too small. "I'm through at the club anyway," she said. "They'll never take me back now. Let's go home."

"Home it is." We eased out into traffic, and she busied herself with her face. When I turned onto Vista she sat back and said, "Thanks."

"You're welcome," I said. "We're here." I pulled Alice into the curb.

"Okay," Nana said with a final sniffle. "I'm welcome. Well, I've got a hidden agenda. I promise I won't hang around, I won't be embarrassing."

"Nana," I reminded her, "we're home."

"And you're not going to walk me to the door?" She cupped my chin in her hands and raised her face to kiss me. It was almost a chaste little kiss—not quite, but almost. Minus the tip of her tongue it would have qualified. When it was finished she sighed. "You're going to let me walk across the courtyard alone?"

Miss Courtney's etiquette class surfaced. "No," I said, "of course not."

I joined her on the sidewalk, and she slipped her hand into mine. When I took it she gave me a squeeze. "I'm afraid of the birds of paradise," she said. "I really hate birds of paradise. They look like they eat meat."

I stopped without knowing why. An unseasonal breeze stirred the foliage, the birds of paradise cawed silently, and I felt the skin on the back of my neck prickle. Then I saw the strip of light. "Nana," I said, "did you leave your door open?"

"In your hat. In Hollywood? That's what locks are for, right? Why?"

"Because it's open now."

She looked, and her grip on my hand tightened. "No," she said in a whisper. "I locked it this morning, same as ever."

"Stay here. I'll be back in a minute."

"No way, no way in the world. I'm not standing here alone. Come on, Simeon, let's just leave."

"Go to the car," I said, lowering my voice to a whisper. "Lock the doors and stay there."

"What are you going to do?"

"I'm going in."

She swallowed noisily, and I fought the urge to hush her. "Then I'm going with you."

It didn't seem like either the time or place for an argument. "Suit yourself," I said. "But stay a few steps back and keep quiet."

I could feel her behind me as I moved toward the open door. My running shoes made no sound, and neither, surprisingly, did her high heels. At the door I paused for a moment and listened. Either no one was inside or whoever it was was listening too. I lifted my foot, kicked the door open, and jumped to one side, yanking Nana with me.

"Lordy," she said on an indrawn breath.

The place was a ruin.

Keeping her hand in my left, I reached around with my right and pushed the door all the way open. It slammed against the wall and groaned back toward us a foot or so. At least nobody was standing behind it. I counted my blessings and got as high as one.

"I'm going in." I squeezed her hand hard enough to make the joints pop. "You stay right here. If I say come in, come in. If I say anything else at all, run like hell. Get to a phone and call the cops. Got it?"

She nodded, looking past me into the room. I patted her cheek and went inside, hoping that I looked braver than I felt.

The living room was a clutter of junk, trashed objects that had once been possessions. The overhead lights were on, or there wouldn't have been any light at all; both lamps were strewn in fragments across the floor. Pictures had been ripped from the walls and their frames snapped over somebody's knee, probably the same knee that had shattered Amber's arms. Bright shards of light glittered from sharp pieces of glass and mirror. There wasn't a square foot of the floor visible.

The door leading to the hallway was closed. Stepping over the wreckage on the floor as if the crown jewels of England were scattered there, I moved toward it. I put a hand on the knob, counted ten to slow the beating of my heart, and shoved it open.

Blackness. I felt for a light switch. There wasn't one. Either the hallway was unlighted, which seemed unlikely, or the switch was at the other end, a typically dysfunctional example of Hollywood architecture. I was going to have to go in. The small amount of light that filtered in from the living room would be just enough to allow me to see my own blood. Closing my mind's eye tight, I went in.

More junk littered the floor, but otherwise the hallway was empty. The bathroom door yawned open at its far end, and I snapped on the light inside. Nobody behind me, nobody in the bathroom. The destroyer hadn't missed much: even the mirror on the medicine cabinet had been broken. Aspirin, hairpins, and tampons were scattered across the tiles.

That left the bedroom. The door was ajar, and I shoved it, hard. Lights were on, throwing the devastation into sharp, ugly relief.

The bed had been eviscerated. A sharp knife had slit the mattress from top to bottom, and the stuffings had been thrown around the room. The contents of the open closet were strewn around like the random refuse of a tornado.

Across one wall, written on a crooked diagonal in Nana's lipstick, were the words WHORES DIE.

"I don't believe it," I said.

I heard a sudden sound behind me and whirled, my hands drawn back and open to blind or kill. I was halfway into the air when I saw Nana. I grabbed the edge of the table to stop myself, and my feet tangled in a blanket and I fell. It was a heavy fall.

"That wasn't your cue," I said from the floor. "If you heard that, you should be running by now."

"And leave you here alone?" She reached down to help me up. All her attention was concentrated on me. She wasn't even looking at the room. If I hadn't been flat on my face and feeling like an idiot, I would have been flattered.

"You're okay?" she asked.

I waved away her offer of help and stood up. "Yeah, sure. I'm fine."

"Jeez," she said, finally looking around. The words on the wall caught her eye. "Oh. That's really sick."

I waited until my pulse had slowed to double speed. "What do you need?"

"For what?"

"To leave, to be gone for a few days while we arrange to get this cleaned up. Find what you need and let's get out of here."

"Why? Why should I go? Some dickhead trashed my place and probably took everything I own, but why should I leave?" Her jaw was as knobby as Lincoln's before he grew his beard. "Let's just straighten up a little, and I'll stay here."

"You're leaving," I said. "I don't think anybody took anything. I think something's on the move and you're in its way. I don't know why, but you are. Get what you need. We're going."

She took a steely look around. "I don't need anything.

You got a toothbrush and shampoo, right? You got aspirin? We *are* going to your place, aren't we?"

"Of course we are."

"Oh, darling," she said. "I thought you'd never ask."

The birds chirped at her when we let ourselves in. It had to be for her; they never did it for me. Nana moved to the birds' cage and made little kissing sounds at them. They both looked at her. Hansel, I think, cocked his head appealingly.

She pushed a finger into the cage.

"Careful," I said. "The little peckers peck."

"Not me they don't," she said smugly. Hansel jumped up onto her finger and perched there, looking more proud of himself than anything with the brains God grudgingly doled out to a bird had any right to look. "He's sweet," Nana said.

"I thought you hated birds."

"Well, hell, I'd rather you had a Weimaraner trained to attack, especially after tonight. But women learn early to be satisfied."

"Explain tonight."

She coaxed her finger back through the bars, and Hansel leapt up onto the perch and let loose a volley of song. "Who knows?" she said, watching him. "Maybe it didn't have anything to do with anything. Maybe it was a bunch of skaggers who ran out of skag or some Jesus freaks who ran out of Jesus. Maybe they didn't even know who lived there."

"Do you believe that?"

"No." She turned to face me.

"Me neither. Where murder is concerned, I don't believe in coincidence. I'm just glad you weren't there."

She looked away and then back to me. "Me, too," she said.

"Nana, do you have any idea what's going on? Any idea at all?"

"Somebody hates somebody," she said. "More than I've ever hated anybody, more than I hate snakes. It's somebody who hates even better than me. Somebody like Toby."

"Toby didn't kill Amber."

"Because Saffron says so? Little Miss Saffron?" She almost laughed. "Saffron could lie to a Senate subcommittee with her left hand while her right was dealing blackjack. And winning. She lies for the sheer fun of it."

"It's not just Saffron," I said. "Let's go to sleep."

"No." She crossed the room and took both my hands in hers. "Let's go to *bed.* I don't want to sleep alone. Come on, Texas Ranger, even your heart can't be that pure."

It wasn't. After her shower and my shower and some meaningless small talk, I smelled the warm yeasty fragrance of her skin and passed my tongue over its impossible smoothness. She laughed when it tickled and reached down to caress me, and I said, "No, don't. This is a one-man show."

"Don't be silly," she said, grasping me, and our arms and legs tangled into the ancient knot, and after a while we achieved the ancient release. As I dropped into sleep I heard her voice, lazy and contented.

"I promise," she said. "I won't be a bother."

III

BLOOD AND BONE

▼

18

Polaroids

SO SAFFRON WAS A LIAR. It wasn't the first time I'd heard it, and it didn't mean as much as it would have if I hadn't talked to the Peeper, but it put her ahead of Pepper on my list of people to bother. The best time to catch all the ladies with their guards down was in the morning, so I woke Nana with a hot cup of coffee and a boatload of good intentions at six-thirty. The coffee went down quickly, and the good intentions hoisted anchor and set sail when she shrugged the sheet from her shoulders, placed the hot cup between her breasts for a moment, and then removed it and invited me to warm my unacceptable nose. "No gentleman has a cold nose," she said.

Following the dictates of etiquette, I warmed my nose.

It was nine-twenty, and we were both sporting satisfied Toby-class grins by the time we coasted down Topanga Canyon Boulevard toward the sea. As we hit the Pacific Coast Highway an offshore breeze kicked up, right on cue, fracturing the sunlit ocean skin into a tangled riot of scattered light. Two surfers slid gracefully down the smooth slope of a single wave.

The PCH was clogged with the usual rush-hour glut, a ten-mile-long line of cars two abreast, their drivers staring straight ahead at the rear end of the car in front, ignoring the hypnotic blue expanse of the Pacific, minds full of columns of figures, morning meetings, and the possibility of a pink slip at the end of the day.

"Where are they all going?" Nana said, surveying the traffic. "Why don't they just stay here? Why don't *we* just stay here?"

"They've got things to do," I said as the light changed and I eased Alice out into the left-hand lane heading south. "Money to make, promises to keep. Miles to go before they sleep."

"I know that one," she said. "That poet with all the white hair."

"Kris Kringle?"

"Something like that, something about winter." She was wearing white shorts that had miraculously materialized from her purse and one of my shirts, so big on her that its shoulders hung to her elbows. Her hipbones jutted beneath the belt loops of the shorts. A wisp of black hair, still damp from her, or our, shower, was plastered to her cheek, nestled into the curved shadow below her cheekbone. I reached over and gently lifted it loose. It promptly fell back into precisely the same place. It knew where it belonged.

She turned her head and leaned over to nuzzle my neck as I tried to concentrate on not rear-ending the convertible Mercedes in front of me. The retro at the wheel was putting his top down so everybody could see him talking on his car phone. "What I need now," Nana was saying, "is a complex carbohydrate."

"For instance?"

"For instance, pizza."

"At this hour?"

"At any hour you might care to name. With pepperoni and lots of extra garlic."

"Not until I get a convertible."

She pulled a long strand of hair down and gnawed at it. We'd crept maybe half a mile. "Koreans eat garlic for breakfast," she said. "Do you like me?"

"When you're straight."

"I'm always straight. Even when I'm loaded out of my mind, I'm straight."

"Compared to what?"

"Well, Toby. Or Saffron. I'm straighter at four-thirty Saturday morning than Saffron ever was in Sunday school, if she went to Sunday school, which I doubt. The crucifix would have jumped from the wall."

"Speaking of Saffron," I said.

"Do we have to?"

"You're the one who wanted to come along. You could have spent the day sunbathing, brushing up your computer skills, seducing my birds."

"I wanted to be with you," she said. I shut up. A minute later she giggled. "Boy," she said, "are *your* buttons up front."

On Chatauqua I turned left and headed up to Sunset, hoping for a stretch of open road. We were lucky. For fifteen minutes or so we stayed within hailing distance of the speed limit, winding between eucalyptus trees, their tall crowns browsing the sky. Normally I like eucalyptus, but now all I could think was that they, too, were operating under false pretenses: the most Californian of all California trees, they'd been imported from Australia. Well, at least they hadn't changed their name.

"What's Saffron's real name?" I said as Nana twisted the dial of Alice's radio in search of heavy metal. She settled for something that sounded like an alcoholic's trash being emptied at four A.M. and sat back. "Jackie, I think," she said. "We're not what you'd call close. I think it's something dykey like Jackie."

"Jackie," I said. "Jack."

"Jack who?"

"Jack Sprunk. Toby, in other words."

"Look out for that stupid cat," she said, pointing through the windshield at a battered tabby scampering suicidally across the road. "Who's Jack Sprunk?"

"Toby Vane. Wake up, Nana. That's his real name."

She turned up the radio as an electric guitarist did a remarkable realistic imitation of a corpse's fingernails being dragged down a drainpipe. "I don't think so," she said.

I turned the radio down and slapped her hand as she reached for the volume knob. "You don't think what?"

"That Toby was ever a Jack. I think he was a Bob."

"Bob?" I said stupidly.

"Or Bobby. Maybe Bobby. Since he's Toby now, maybe he was Bobby then."

"Why Bobby?"

"Well, you know, Toby's such a dumb name. If he'd been a Bob, maybe now he'd be a Tobe."

"But why not Jack?"

"Because he used to be Bobby. When he told me that shitarooni story, you know, the one about the stove, I told it to you in the restaurant, he said Bobby. He said his father called him Bobby when he tied him up. He said, 'We'll come back when we smell Bobby burning,' or something like that." She sat back. "Am I going to get a pizza or not?"

"Not. Not until lunch, anyway. You're certain he said Bobby and not Jack?"

"They don't sound very much alike, you know. Even if I think in Korean sometimes, I can tell Bobby from Jack. Just like I can tell Kris Kringle from Robert Frost."

"How loaded was he?"

"Loaded enough to tell me something personal for a change, but not loaded enough to get his own name wrong. I mean, *nobody* gets that loaded."

She turned the volume up again, and I turned it back down. Her left hand landed lightly on my thigh, and her nails toyed with my inseam. "Ever do it in a car?" she said.

"More times than I can count." She yanked her hand away. "Let me think for a minute." I did.

"Okay," she said. "I'll bite. I always told myself I'd never ask a man this question, no matter how much he looked like he was thinking, but I'll make an exception in your case." She furrowed her brow and looked intense. "Simeon," she said, "what are you thinking about?"

"Why Toby lied to me about his name."

"Yaah," she said. "Toby couldn't tell the truth to the bathroom mirror. He said his name was Jack?"

"Jack Sprunk."

She shrugged. "Who could make up Jack Sprunk? Maybe he was lying to *me*."

"Bobby what?"

"Who knows? He was a little kid in that story. Little kids don't have last names. Is this important?"

"I don't know. Yes, I do. Anything that has to do with Toby is important now."

"So why are we going to see Saffron?"

"To learn something about Toby." I reached over and turned up the volume. Cats fought in stereo.

Saffron's neighborhood looked parched and curled at the edges in the morning light. The same cars were parked on the same brown lawns. Tools, engine blocks, and more esoteric components of the process of internal combustion glinted in the sun. A group of brown-skinned guys hunkered down in front of one of the cars, looking justifiably bewildered.

I stopped Alice illegally in front of a fire hydrant. A four-alarm fire was just what the block needed. Saffron's apartment house, a three-story affair made out of aquamarine Gunite with something sparkly mixed into it, reared rectangular in front of us. It looked like a swimming pool yanked inside out. Nana shut the passenger door behind her and took my hand.

"Now what?"

"Now we look around a little. Then we wake up Sleeping Beauty."

"There's nothing to look at. I mean, Drab with a capital D. Imagine living here?"

"People do."

"Well, that's a piercing insight. All these years, my life has been on hold while I waited for a man who could say something like that to me."

"Maybe you'd prefer to wait in the car," I said. "Or under it."

"Sorry. It's just that it's hard to keep a lid on all this irony. Lead the way and I'll be good."

The apartment house had seen its best days in the first forty-eight hours or so after it was built, sometime in the late fifties. It formed a garish U around a paved central courtyard with a minuscule pool in its center. Dying palms sprouted despairingly here and there. The concrete surrounding the pool was cracked and broken. Weeds shouldered their spiky way up through the openings, heading single-mindedly for the sunlight. You don't fool around with photosynthesis.

Once blue water might have sparkled in the pool, but now it was a sun-baked parody of coolness and wet. The same old trash lay jumbled in its bottom: cardboard cartons, paper cups and napkins, plastic utensils from fast-food outlets. What was new was a humming of flies, bluebottles, hundreds of them, crawling all over the cartons at the deep end beneath the diving board.

"God, that's grungy," Nana said. "Simeon? I have a request. Get me out of here. As soon as possible."

"As soon as we finish with Jackie. Or whatever her name is."

"One E," she said.

"You've been here before."

"Loads party. Lots of vodka and head banging. But at least there was pizza and music you wouldn't like. And it was nighttime, so it didn't look so bad. There's a lot to be said for the dark."

I followed her to the door I already knew, and she stepped aside so I could knock. I had knocked three or four times before I saw that the screen over the sliding aluminum window was missing and that the window was open. A white curtain made of some indestructible synthetic was drawn inside. It billowed faintly in the breeze.

"Girl knows how to sleep," Nana said.

"Hold on. I'll show you a private detective's trick. Would you like to close your eyes so I don't give away any secrets of the trade?"

"Oh, sure," she said, putting a hand over her face. "I can hardly see through my fingers at all."

"If you peek, you'll ruin Christmas forever."

"I'm a Buddhist. Trust me anyway."

I leaned through the window and pushed the curtain aside. The first thing I saw was the screen, lying on the floor just inside the window. The second thing I saw was the devastation.

"Nana," I said, "get out of here."

"Oh, look," she said at the same time. "We don't need any tricks. The door's not locked." She gave it a shove, and then she said, "Oh. Oh, no."

She stepped back, and I put a hand on her shoulder. "I don't think you should be here."

Inside I could hear still more flies buzzing, cousins to the ones in the pool.

"Well, I am," she said. "Let's get it over with." She pushed me forward and followed a single step behind. I closed the door behind us and locked it.

Saffron was in the bedroom, facedown and still, the center of a humming vortex of bluebottles. She had been cut, and she had been broken. From the extent of the stains—still damp—on the mattress, she had probably been dead before her joints had been snapped backward and her bones had been methodically fractured. It was a small mercy, but it was the only mercy she'd been shown.

Her ankles were tied with clothesline.

"This can't be happening," Nana said from the doorway. Her voice was faint.

"If you'd been home last night," I said, "it would have happened to you. Help me turn her over."

"Why? I mean, I can't. Simeon, I can't touch her."

"Well, you're going to touch her. Goddammit, this isn't a movie. You can't head for the lobby every time things get sticky. Get over here and grab her feet. Or else go to the car and wait there, and stay out of my hair from now on."

She looked down at what was left of Saffron and then back at me. She licked her lips. "Why should we turn her over? I mean, what's under her?"

"If I'd killed her," I said, "it's where I'd leave the picture. Right where the cops would find it."

Her eyes widened. "The picture. You mean, like in Toby's pocket."

"Come on. We can theorize later."

She extended her hands far in front of her even before she started to cross the room. I went to the other end of the bed and reached under Saffron's shoulders. Her blood was thick and sticky on my hands. "On three," I said, feeling like someone about to try to lift a piano. Nana touched Saffron's bound ankles and recoiled involuntarily. Running on sheer will, she reached back down and got a grip. Her eyes were closed.

"To your right, now. One, two, *three.*" We both pulled, and Saffron rolled heavily onto her side and then, slowly, onto her back.

I was wrong.

There wasn't one Polaroid there. There were two.

Both of them were coated in blood.

Nana swayed as I started to wipe them with my sleeve. "Knock it off," I said, and then the pounding on the front door began. It echoed through the empty apartment.

A moment's silence. Then it began again.

"Simeon," Nana said, "What about let's go."

"Great," I said, "a sound idea. But go where?"

From the front of the apartment, a bass voice bellowed, "Open up. Police."

"Out the back," she said. "There's a back door. Simeon, let's *go*."

We went. We doubled over as we passed through the living room, looking like a couple of guerrilla fighters trapped in short grass and hoping that no one was looking through the window. A boot cracked against the door as Nana led me through an abbreviated kitchen. God was in his heaven for once, and there was a door there.

It was standing open. I closed it behind me.

We tripped over one another, rolling like Chinese acrobats end over end down one of the few remaining Hollywood slopes. Foxtails pierced my clothes, and the spikes of puncherweeds made holes in my skin. Nana wound up on top of me, grass projecting at odd angles from her hair. We were in a dusty cluster of brush and eucalyptus. The apartment house was out of sight.

"Now what?" she said.

I gave her a quick kiss. "Now we dust each other off and take the longest possible way back to the street like a couple with nothing on their minds more important than when the post office opens. Then we get into Alice and drive very slowly away." I tugged the legs of her shorts down to a respectable level. Cops are men, too.

"But Saffron."

"There's nothing we can do for Saffron."

We spent a few seconds doing some perfunctory tidying. Sirens wailed in the distance.

"Who called the police?" she asked.

"The same person who killed Saffron. He wanted them to find these."

"What are they?"

"They're pictures." I wiped the first one off. "Of Saffron." I wiped the other one. "Oh," I said. "Sure."

Nana didn't look. "What is it?"

"The other one's Amber." Nana and I started down toward the boulevard. I put the pictures in my hip pocket and took her hand in mine. Just a couple of Hollywood lovers out for an early stroll.

"There goes half of Toby's alibi," I said.

19

The Widow Sprunk

"SHE'S SEVENTY-FOUR," Bernie said, "but she's sharp." His intelligent, slightly startled looking blue eyes peered across the desk at me. Outside the grimy narrow window of his research assistant's office, UCLA went on being UCLA, sane and healthy and full of libraries and beautiful girls. Bernie's impossibly curly hair clustered around his head in tight coils like a convention of Slinky toys, and his sleeveless sweatshirt read K.535. MOZART WROTE IT FOR ME. Intellectual jock chic.

"Who's sharp?" I had a headache.

"The Widow Sprunk."

"Bernie," I said, wincing against the pain, "didn't you used to have a mustache?"

He looked at me with a certain amount of concern. "I don't know how to tell you this, Simeon," he said, "but I still have a mustache." Then he reached up to finger it as if he were making sure.

I rubbed my eyes, trying to ease the hammering in my skull and feeling very tired. "Well, something's different."

"I'll give you a hint. They perched on my nose, and I used to look at you through them."

"Ah," I said. "How in the world are you functioning without them?"

"You may have heard of contacts. Joyce likes me better with them."

"I'm surprised you can blink," I said, remembering the

sheer heft of Bernie's almost opaque glasses. "Christ, they must be thicker than potato chips. And who's Joyce?"

"Someone new," he said shortly. "Would you like my ophthalmologist's phone number, or are you interested in the Widow Sprunk?"

He sounded mildly miffed, so I tried a little balm. "How did you get her to talk to you?"

"She's seventy-four, Simeon. Our society being what it is, no one's asked her opinion about anything in years. The natural resource we're wasting, not turning to later-life citizens for wisdom. Joyce is a gerontologist."

"Later-life citizens?"

He made an impatient gesture. "Old people to you," he said. "The reserve of experience they have."

"The living encyclopedia of our times," I suggested.

He looked as though he wished he had a book to slam shut. "Fine," he said, "be snide. Skip the Widow Sprunk. You still owe me almost three hundred dollars." Like most academics, Bernie was very interested in money.

"I'm listening," I said. "I'm just tired."

"Sure. The detective's life. Fast cars and fast women." He'd thrown a series of speculative and seriously envious glances at Nana while she'd used his phone to call a cab to take her back to Topanga. She'd protested, but I'd won. It had taken some doing, and I'd had to do some of the doing in front of Bernie. "It must be especially difficult at your age," he added nastily.

"Tell me about the Widow Sprunk."

He sat back, looking satisfied. "The Widow Sprunk has a great-nephew named, as I'm sure you've guessed, Jack Sprunk. The great-nephew—Jack, in other words—is in this case the son of her husband's mother's son. Her husband's mother's third son. Out of four."

I sighed. Genealogy was not my strong point, but it was one of Bernie's Great Themes. His mother, who had fed me regularly when Bernie and I were undergraduates, could regale a snoring dinner table for hours with tales about seventh cousins twice removed who had married into obscure offshoots of the Rothschild clan and had gone on to invent the piano or the oboe or something. The stories were equal in complexity to Chinese interlocking rhymes because just when you thought they were finally over and you could stop pretending to chew and say something, the couple had children, and the children went on to invent harmony. In classical China, some interlocking rhymes had gone on for years.

"And Jack was the husband's brother's son's third son. Did you get that?"

"Good thing we're not into exponentials," I said. "We'd be at the sixth power by now."

Bernie raised an admonitory hand. "We've gotten to Jack Sprunk, in case you hadn't noticed."

"I'm all ears, except for a few remaining shreds of intellect."

"Save what you've got left," Bernie said. "You'll need it. And do you know why? Of course you don't. Jack Sprunk was deeply defective in the intellect department."

"Hell, Bernie," I said. "I already know Toby. Speaking mentally, he could stand on the shoulders of giants, to paraphrase Newton, and he'd still be shorter than Billy Barty."

"You're not listening. Jack Sprunk was seriously shortchanged. This was a Centigrade IQ. If you asked him how many fingers he had on his right hand, you would have had to give him an error factor of plus or minus two. We're talking about a permanent fourth-grader here."

I sat up. "Oh," I said.

"He got to high school by an act of collective charity," Bernie said. He looked pleased with himself, an expression that allowed his gold right front tooth to glint rakishly. "No one had the heart to flunk him. Small town and all that, you can't make the kid study harder unless you're a heartless sonofabitch, which there aren't any of in small towns, because he wasn't capable of studying harder. The best he could do with his books was carry them home and bring them back again. Which was good practice, because whether he ever graduated or not, he was going to wind up moving heavy objects aimlessly from room to room in his father's hardware store, so why not pass him?"

He paused dramatically.

"So he passed," I said a little impatiently.

"In a manner of speaking. He passed out of sight." He looked smug enough to choke.

"Bernie, if you don't stop being cryptic, I'm going to steal your notes and leave."

"He only had one friend in school," Bernie said. "The bad boy, naturally, the kid who could tell old Jack what to do for his own evil ends." He raised his eyebrows Groucho style. "This was the absolutely worst kid in the whole school. One morning the town woke up—rurally early, no doubt—and poor, dumb Jack Sprunk and the other kid were gone."

"And the other kid's name?"

"Pepper."

That made two Peppers and one Peeper. "That was his first name?"

"Last."

"Bobby Pepper," I said.

"Well, shit," Bernie said. "If you already knew that, why'd you let me keep talking?"

"I didn't know it. I guessed. You've done great. You've earned every nickel."

"Hey, allow me a point once in a while. Do you want me to go on?" He squinted elaborately through his new contacts at a black plastic runner's watch. The watch he usually wore was made of four pounds of steel. I had a feeling Joyce was into fitness.

"You mean there's more?" I asked submissively.

"Sure there is, the best part as far as the Widow Sprunk is concerned."

"Do we have to keep calling her the Widow Sprunk? Isn't that sexist or something?"

"Clara," he said sulkily. "Clara Sprunk."

"So what was the best part for Ms. Sprunk?"

"If I'd called her Ms., she would have hung up on me."

"So you called her Clara. You devil, you."

"I called her Mrs. Sprunk. Simeon, even money goes just so far."

"Sorry, Bern. You mean that Bobby Pepper showed up on TV one night, but his name was Toby Vane."

"That's one-third of it. And since you're being so insufferable, I'll tell you the other two-thirds out of order. First, or actually second, chronologically speaking, some little twit from Hollywood who said he was Toby Vane's personal press agent—"

"Dixie Cohen?" I said, wondering whether Dixie had known that Toby wasn't really Jack Sprunk.

"No, some guy named Chubb. Bertram Chubb," he added, consulting his notes. "Mrs. Sprunk said he sounded like he was wearing a bow tie. You'd like Mrs. Sprunk."

"And what did Bertram Chubb do?"

"He called the town's mayor. Did I mention that the town is called Crooked Elbow?"

"Crooked Elbow?"

"Crooked Elbow, Montana. There's a story behind it."

"I'm sure there is. Maybe later."

"The mayor is also the barber. Barbers talk, as I'm sure you know."

"I didn't even know there were still barbers. I thought they were all stylists now."

"In Montana, they're still barbers. Anybody calling himself a stylist would be quarantined."

"Probably a good idea."

"Well, Bertram Chubb asked Mr. Ingstad—that's the

barber's name, lot of Norwegians up in Montana, apparently —whether the town wouldn't like to host a big homecoming parade for Toby Vane."

"And what did the barber say to Bertram Chubb?"

"He said thanks, but no, thanks. He said, to paraphrase, that Crooked Elbow would receive the return of Toby Vane with mixed emotions, and that the mixture would be one part fear and two parts loathing. He said that he couldn't guarantee Toby's personal bodily safety, much less a ticker-tape parade."

"And Mrs. Sprunk knows all this."

"As I believe I've already said, barbers talk."

"I'm surprised it didn't make the papers."

"It'll never make the papers. As far as the good people of Crooked Elbow, Montana, are concerned, Bobby Pepper, AKA Toby Vane, doesn't exist. They'd like to keep it that way."

"But he must have had some family. Even bad boys have family."

Bernie put a defensive hand, palm down, over the four-by-five cards containing his notes. "Can you read upside down?" he asked in a suspicious tone of voice.

"Bernie, I couldn't read your handwriting right-side up."

"Well, Bobby's family is the first part of the story, chronologically speaking. There are no longer any Peppers in Crooked Elbow."

"Is that so?" I was beginning to feel uncomfortable.

"There were five little Peppers to begin with. Bobby, two sisters, Mommy, and Daddy. Daddy Pepper was apparently someone who, in a larger town, would have been confined to a small white room relatively early in his career, minus his belt and shoelaces. He just loved to knock the shit out of women."

"I know some of this already," I said.

"In L.A. or New York, he would have been classified as a psychotic, probably irreversible. In Crooked Elbow, people just thought he was mean." Bernie looked across the desk at me. "This is pretty sordid stuff."

"I'll survive," I said. "Just tell me about the Peppers."

"Daddy clubbed the two girls until they ran away," Bernie said distastefully. "Nobody in town knows where they went, apparently they were pretty careful about that. They covered their tracks and went, about a year apart. That left Bobby and Mommy to take whatever Daddy wanted to dish out."

"Poor Mommy," I said. "So what happened?"

"Bobby finally ran away. Nobody would have looked very hard for him, Mrs. Sprunk said. But Jack was gone, too, and him they were worried about. It was winter, and there'd just been a blizzard. They were afraid he might have lost his way and frozen to death. They went around checking snowdrifts and looking down wells. About three days later, they found out that the Pepper farmhouse had burned down."

"No," I said.

"Because they lived so far from anything or anyone, and because of the storm, no one went out there until someone suggested that's where Jack might be. Even then it took them a day to get there. Roads were bad, cars wouldn't start, the wind chill factor was around absolute zero. Real frontier days, you know?"

I nodded. I was even more tired than I had realized, but I'd forgotten about my headache. Now that I thought about it, it came back.

"Well, the house was gone. Just two walls standing and part of one room. The room that was left was the whole original house. It had been built out of sod about a hundred years before. The rest of the place was wood, and it caught like cellophane."

"Who was in the room that was standing?" I said, knowing the answer.

"Mrs. Pepper. Simeon, she'd been tied up. She was

partially burned, but they could see that she'd been tied hand and foot. Like a heifer, Mrs. Sprunk said." He swallowed.

"With clothesline," I said.

Bernie flipped through his notes. "Gee," he said. "I didn't ask what kind of rope it was."

"It was clothesline," I said. "Take my word."

"Does that mean something? Obviously it does."

"Is there more? Are we finished, or is there more?"

"Sure there's more. If there weren't, your boy would be in jail. The house had been doused with gasoline. Halfway between the house and the garage, up to his shoulders in snow, they found Daddy Pepper. He was as frozen as most fresh fish. They had to break his fingers to get the gasoline can out of his hands. Mrs. Sprunk said he got lost in the snow in his own backyard. Whiteout or something. Case closed."

"The clothesline had been taken down," I said. "He needed it."

"What's all this about clothesline?"

"Skip it," I said. "After I leave, shut the door and forget about it." I stood up and reached into my pocket. Trying to keep my hands from shaking, I peeled off three hundred dollars of Stillman's and Toby's money. Then I added another hundred.

"What's that for?" Bernie asked. "It was only three hundred, actually two eighty-five. I had my watch running the whole time."

"Use it to clean your clothes. Clean your desk. Send the phone to the cleaner's, if you like. Clean everything you used or touched while you were working for me. I'm sorry, Bernie. I shouldn't have gotten you involved. Apologize to Joyce for me. Next time, we'll all go to Anna Maria's for Italian."

"Great," he said. "And what about you? What are you going to do?"

"Me?" I said. "I'm going for a run."

I ran six miles, maybe the fastest six miles of my life. The Sunset Boulevard uphill, about six-tenths of a mile at a grade of about roughly forty percent, was the hardest. I skipped the sauna but made up for it with an extra-long shower. Then, with a towel wrapped around my middle, I called the *High Velocity* set at Universal and talked to Dolly. Toby was there, she said. They'd been there since eight-thirty.

"Has he been out of your sight?"

"Not since last night."

"What about the big guy, the stand-in? John," I added, since Dolly's silence indicated a certain level of confusion.

"He's here. He's across the stage from me now. They're setting up a shot."

"Has he been there all day?"

"Gosh, Simeon, I don't know. You didn't say anything about watching him."

"Forget it. Try to talk Toby into keeping John with him for the rest of the day. Maybe even after work."

"Sure, but why? Has he got something to do with it?"

"Yes," I said. Dolly was asking another question when I hung up.

I dialed my house and got my answering machine. After my idiotic message was over, I said, "Nana, it's me. Pick up the phone, would you?"

"H'lo, Simeon," she said. She sounded drowsy. "What time is it?"

"A little after two. How are you doing?"

"I fell asleep in the sun. It's nice up here. Somebody named Eleanor called."

"Shit," I said. "Did you pick up the phone?"

She laughed. "You peckerhead. Of course not. I just listened after the machine picked up."

"Good. Keep doing that. I don't want you to talk to anybody but me, not even if somebody asks for you. Especially not if somebody asks for you."

"Nobody knows I'm here," she said a trifle anxiously.

"Don't be silly," I said to reassure her. "We're just being extra careful."

"Okay. What if there's a call for you that sounds important?"

"Listen to the machine and write down the name and number. I'll call in from time to time to check. Pick up the phone when you hear me."

"What are you going to do while I work on my tan lines?"

"I'll tell you after I do it."

"You're not going to be silly, are you? I mean, you're not going to stick out your big thick neck or anything."

"My neck is not thick."

"I'd like it even if it weren't. Take care of it for me."

"At last," I said. "A reason to live."

"What time will you be home? I could make something to eat."

"Don't plan on it. I'll be there when I get there, but I'll keep in touch. Go back into the sunshine."

"Maybe I'll work on getting rid of my tan lines instead. Nobody can see me."

"I like tan lines," I said, visualizing hers.

"Your kind always does. When you get back I'll model them for you. Front and back."

"Good-bye, Nana."

She kissed the mouthpiece and hung up. I readjusted my towel in front and strolled back through the locker room, hoping that no one would get the wrong idea. At any rate, no one whistled at me.

20

Out Of Order

"WHAT DO YOU MEAN, another one?" Dixie said. "You mean dead?" He looked terrified. We were on the set, between shots. Toby was in his dressing room with Dolly and Big John. "Is Toby . . ." He looked around and lowered his voice. "Is it possible Toby's involved?"

"He is and he isn't."

"That's very informative. That's what I need, right now, the Riddle of the Sphinx. Cryptic, that's what I need. You want to give me a straight answer, or do you want to go on being interesting?"

"Where were you late last night, early this morning?"

"What kind of question is that? What about Toby?"

"We'll get to Toby. What about Rebecca?"

Dixie leaned against a prop wall, and it teetered. He straightened up and rubbed his face with both hands. "You know about Rebecca?" he asked in a spiritless voice. "How do you know?"

"No thanks to you," I said. "Northridge, my ass."

"I was ashamed of myself. I know I should have told you, but I was ashamed of myself. I acted like a putz after it happened. I've never acted worse in my life. So you talked to Charlene?"

"You mean Chantra."

"Chantra." He made the name sound like he was spitting. "Imagine, Chantra. A grown woman. Did she sell you any perfume? A crystal for your rearview mirror, keep you

281

from getting rear-ended? Maybe a map to the lines on your palm? A lifetime subscription to the *Harmonic Times*?"

"Where were you late last night?"

"So now I'm a suspect? I don't tell you something, and that makes me a suspect? Oh, no, it doesn't. Don't give me that. We hired you, remember?" His voice had risen, and he waved his hands in front of him as if he were trying to shush himself. "Remember that?" he said in a half whisper. "We were the ones who hired you. Why would we have hired you if I were going around killing people? You think I could kill somebody? You haven't even told me who it was."

"You haven't asked."

He put a hand up and rubbed the back of his neck. "This is the kind of day they invented aspirin for. Who was she?"

"The girl who was with Toby when Amber got killed."

He transferred the hand from the back of his neck to the bridge of his nose and rubbed that for a while. "Swell," he said with his eyes closed. "Another naked dancer. This gets more Hearst papers every day. If Joanna Link ever figures it out, we'll all be on *Sixty Minutes*."

"That's what I meant when I said Toby was involved. What I meant when I said that he wasn't involved was that he didn't do it."

"You know that for sure?" He looked hopeful for the first time.

"Dolly was with him. She hasn't been more than ten feet from him since seven last night, and the lady was alive at seven last night because I saw her. So Dolly was with him. Who was with you, Dixie?"

"I'm a divorced man," he said testily. "I sleep alone."

"Do you own a camera?"

"Look," he said, "I own lots of cameras. So what, you know? So does Norman. So does Toby. So does everybody in the movie or TV business. We *like* cameras. We don't get enough of them grinding away during our ten-, twelve-hour workdays, so we run out and buy them before the stores close. Where do you think the pictures come from for all those *Mommie Dearest* books? This whole town is camera happy. Shake down the average film crew, you'll find more cameras than a busload of Japanese tourists. Betacams, too. Home movie cameras. Christ, Norman's got a thing that makes daguerreotypes like in the Civil War, ought to be in a museum. So what has this got to do with anything?"

I reached into my hip pocket. "Look at these," I said.

He did, for maybe half a second. Then he slammed his eyes shut, and the color left his face. His forehead was suddenly damp.

"Thanks anyway," he said, "but you can't make me." He sounded like a little boy. "Put them away or I won't open my eyes."

I put them away. His eyes were still closed. "What do you know about clothesline?"

He opened half an eye to make sure the pictures were gone. "Clothesline? It's what they used before dryers. Where did those come from?"

"They were under the girl's body. Where the cops would find them. What did you do with the Polaroids of Rebecca, Dixie?"

I could actually hear him grind his teeth. "Burned them," he said. "What would you have done, willed them to the Louvre? She's my stepdaughter."

"Toby let you have them?"

"Toby was in his apologetic mode, his shit-eating, 'omigod, I didn't mean to hurt her' mode. I should have pushed his face in."

"But you didn't," I said unkindly.

"I didn't do jack shit. That cost me everything, everything I cared about."

"You've still got your job."

He glared up at me. "Fuck you." He looked around at

the sound stage as though he'd never seen it before. "Fuck all of this, too." He started to walk away.

I put a hand on his arm, and he jerked away from me. "Don't touch me, you schmuck."

"Dixie," I said, "people are staring."

It was true. Grips, stagehands, makeup women, they were all looking at us. Janie Gordon sat in a canvas chair, an open script cradled in her lap and a pencil between her teeth. When I caught her eyes she looked away.

Dixie stopped walking. *"Damn,"* he said. "Damn, damn, damn, damn." He stood slack and empty, looking at nothing, like a man suspended from a string.

The door of Toby's dressing room opened, and Dolly came out. She searched the set with her eyes and then came over to us.

"I'll be in my office," Dixie said flatly. "You know where it is."

By the time Dolly reached me he was halfway across the set, a little man in a creased corduroy suit that sagged from the shoulders. A stagehand carrying a small table stepped in front of him, and Dixie trudged into him, stumbled, and kept on walking. The stagehand looked after him, shook his head, and then put the table down on top of a cross of masking tape stuck to the floor.

"What's with him?" Dolly said.

"His life's too big for him. How's Toby?"

"Okay. Putting the usual amount up his nose. He's been asking for you."

"Don't tell him I was here."

"You're going? You just got here."

"Exactly, Dolly. Bull's-eye. I'm going. What time are you going to shut down?"

"About another hour. Six, six-thirty, I guess. There's only one scene left, and it's mainly Toby, so it should go pretty fast."

"My," I said nastily, "aren't we learning a lot?"

Dolly's face, as always, was guileless. "Isn't that what I'm supposed to be doing? You got to give the guy credit, if I did as much junk as he does, I couldn't find my pockets. But he's always where he's supposed to be, always has the words right and everything."

Dolly started to say something else, but I cut her off. "Just keep them together, Toby and John, got it? Don't let them split up. Take them to dinner somewhere, you've got an expense account. Don't be stingy. As J. P. Morgan said, you've got to spend money to make money."

"Well," Dolly said, "it's your money."

At eight-twenty that evening I got the first busy signal.

I'd been active, staying in motion to fight the feeling that I was chasing my tail. Tomorrow's edition of the *Daily News* had hit the streets with Saffron's death on page one, in the lower right-hand corner to be sure, but page one nevertheless. The lead mentioned Amber, and there were pictures of both women. Amber's looked like a snapshot taken on one of her bad nights, but Saffron's was a studio still from the seventies, the kind actresses pay too much for, all hopeful eyes and carefully disarranged hair. I was right: she had been beautiful.

Things of the Spirit was unaccountably closed at seven o'clock. Chantra's message about the flow being interrupted hung in the door. The shop was dark, and an iron grid inside the window protected the crystals and aromas from the fingers of unevolved beings who might have wanted to snatch them without paying the proper karmic price. Five minutes of hammering on the door had brought no response, and I didn't see a light in the apartment windows above the store.

I'd spent twenty or thirty minutes circling the block outside the Spice Rack, watching a large number of cops come and go. Customers had turned away at the sight of the squad cars. It was getting so I recognized some of them,

among them Ahmed, the Middle Easterner with the yo-yo
dollar bills, and a couple of sad sacks from my first night
there. I couldn't very well go in, so after my tenth or
eleventh pass I gave it up and choked down a hamburger
up at the Sunset Grill. I'd phoned Nana from there, and
she'd answered, sounding a little high.

"Don't go all Puritan on me," she'd said. "It's just red
wine."

"Did you find anything to eat?"

"Sure. Tunut and penis butter." She'd laughed "Whoo.
Is that a Freudian slip, or what? I mean tuna and peanut
butter."

"Not together, I hope."

"Why not? All goes to the same place eventually."

My burger threatened a reappearance. "Any calls?"

"Not so's you'd notice. Couple of wrong numbers, but
they hung up when they heard the machine."

"Well, don't answer."

"You're the only one I want to talk to. Hurry home
before I get crazy."

Eventually I fetched up at Fan Fare to flip through Wyl's
stack of clips again in the hope of finding something I
hadn't found before. Wyl hovered anxiously over me as
though he were to blame.

I'd finished my first pass through the material when I got
the busy signal on my own number. Oh, well, I thought, I
hadn't told her not to call anybody, just not to answer the
phone. All the same, I didn't like it. I flipped back through
the stack of clips and started again at page one.

"Honey," Wyl said, "you'll ruin your eyes in this light.
It's not like TV, you know. It's not different every time you
turn it on . . . well, neither is TV, for that matter, except
for the evangelists, but you know what I mean. You can
read it from here to Valentine's Day and it'll always be the
same."

I pushed the paper away. "Wyl, do you ever feel like you don't know what you're doing?"

"Literally all the time. The last time I really knew what I was doing was back when Mother was still alive. Taking care of her, right? Trying to pay back a little of what she'd given me. She was so old and helpless, it made me feel terrible, but at the same time I remembered when I was young and helpless, and she was always there, even when I was just awful to her, even later when she realized I was, well, you know, different, as people used to say." He sat down opposite me. His tattooed eyes were shining wetly.

"She knew?"

"Of course she did. I was her son. She knew all the time, I guess. And she never said anything, not a word to make me feel bad. I just took off the makeup every night so I wouldn't make her any more uncomfortable about things than she was anyway." He gestured improvisationally with both hands, trying to make a snowball out of air. "They always know, mothers," he said. "Maybe it's a good thing that there are some people you can't keep secrets from."

"Maybe it is," I said. "Depends on the secrets. May I use your phone again?"

"Need you ask? But then, you were always polite. So few people are polite these days. Far be it from me to discourage it."

I dialed my number again. Still busy. Then I called Universal and got a security man with no public relations skills whatsoever. First he stonewalled me with a rigidity the Watergate crew would have envied. When I said I worked for Norman Stillman and that he could be back patroling parking lots in Reseda tomorrow morning if he didn't tell me what I wanted to know, he paused and recalibrated his attitude. *High Velocity* had shut down, he told me grudgingly. Everybody was gone. Did I want to leave a message?

"No," I said, "I don't want to leave a fucking message."
I hung up.

"*That* wasn't polite," Wyl said. "That wasn't polite at all."

I apologized and climbed into Alice. It was finally dark enough to take another look at the other half of Toby's alibi. For some reason there wasn't much traffic as I headed south toward Fountain, and it gave me too much time to think. *Something's moving*, I'd said to Nana, and it felt like it was moving too fast, like it was gaining on me from behind. I kept checking the rearview mirror, I didn't know for what, and almost rear-ended a car turning left off of Highland onto Fountain. Chastened, I followed it to 1424.

A streetlight, the only one on the block that worked, glared down at me as I sat at the curb. There had been plenty of light for the Peeper to see Toby and Saffron in the car when they let Amber out. I looked up at the window and didn't see him at his usual post. So he didn't watch all the time. So maybe he'd gone to the bathroom. Or, on the other hand, maybe he watched the centerfolds on his walls until he heard something.

The only thing to do with a theory is to test it. I got out and slammed the door. Still no one at the Peeper's window. Counting seconds in the classic "one thousand, two thousand" style, I headed up the walk, and when I got to five I looked up, and there he was. I waved up at him, but he was still watching my car.

And no wonder. The streetlight was about fifteen yards up the street. I was standing in almost complete darkness, cut off from its rays by the edge of the building. I shuffled my feet and cleared my throat, and he finally looked down toward me. I could see his face clearly. His window, the one nearest the street, was illuminated. The hard, dark edge of shadow made by the other wing of the V climbed the wall just to the left of his window.

He was looking into the light. I was in the dark. I had to

wave again before he saw me. When he did, he let the curtain fall back into place. He hadn't lifted it again when I fired up Alice and pulled back into traffic.

At the first phone booth I saw, I called home again. Still busy. Ants were walking up and down my spine. I tried again, with the same result, and then started to try again. I dropped in my quarter and stood there, listening to the buzz of the dial tone. It reminded me of something, but I shouldered it away. Who could Nana be talking to? The dial tone buzzed in my ear again, steady and sure, and I barked my knuckles hanging up the phone. I knew what it reminded me of, and I ran toward Alice.

Hollywood isn't very big. I pulled up to the curb of Saffron's apartment house six minutes later and pulled a little flashlight from the glove compartment. No one was around, no peepers were at the windows, and the only things I heard were the hum of traffic and the thump of my heart, which seemed to have taken up permanent residence in my ears. I marched in time to the heartbeat all the way to the pool.

Nana had wanted to leave, wanted to see Saffron right away and get out of there. If she hadn't, maybe I'd have checked the pool. And maybe not. It seemed like weeks since I'd done anything right. I hoisted myself down the ladder at the shallow end and waded through the trash until I was beneath the diving board.

The flies were gone, until morning, and they'd taken their buzz with them. The beam of the flashlight played over the junk at the deep end. I could only use one hand to toss things aside because of the flashlight, but most of the stuff down there was large, cardboard cartons and pieces of what might once have been pool furniture. Within a minute I was looking at the bottom of the pool.

Except that I wasn't looking at the bottom. I was looking at a large, rust-colored stain that tapered off on the down-hill slope toward the drain. The irrelevant fact that the drain still worked flashed across my mind. There must have been quite a lot of blood. How much did the human body hold? Six quarts? Eight? How much difference did it make if the body was a small one?

The math calmed me as I climbed back up the ladder. In the car, I made myself breathe slowly for two minutes and then headed up Highland toward the Ventura Freeway. Toby was with Dolly, I told myself. So was John. Why hadn't I told her where to take them for dinner? At least I'd know. Just before I got to the freeway I saw a coin phone in a minimall, one of the thousands that now scar Los Angeles, and shoved the same old quarter into the slot.

My number was busy. It *couldn't* be busy that long.

I got the operator on the line. After we'd negotiated the price for an emergency break-in and I'd fed the last of my remaining change into the phone, she left the line. When she came back she said triumphantly, "That phone is out of order."

"No way," I said.

"Then it's off the hook. You've overdeposited," she said. "I told you fifty cents. If you'll give me your full name and number, I'll see that it's credited to your account."

I left the receiver dangling and sprinted to Alice.

There wasn't much traffic at that hour, but there was too much. More than thirty minutes had passed before I turned off Topanga Canyon onto Old Topanga, swearing at Alice for not being a Porsche. Her springs creaked on the curves, and I nearly burned out the clutch going uphill on Topanga Skyline. I jumped out at the bottom of the driveway, left the door open, and went up as quietly as I could.

All the lights were on.

I circled the house before I went in, but the windows were too high for me to see anything. They'd always been too high. Why should tonight be different? I grabbed a shovel and headed up the little corridor that led to the front door.

It had been kicked in. It sagged from its hinges dispiritedly like a shot sentry. It had been broken in two places, both above and below the latch.

My foot hit something as I went in. It was an empty bottle of red wine. I watched it roll reproachfully away from me before I lifted my eyes.

Devastation.

The coffee table was overturned. The throw rug was crumpled against the far wall. The couch was halfway into the middle of the room, as if someone had tried to take cover behind it. The door to the sun deck hung open. It creaked as a breeze stirred it.

Hefting the shovel in both hands, blade forward, I went into the bedroom. Nobody. Nobody in the bathroom, just a tap dripping water. I shut it off and went out onto the sun deck.

The lights of Topanga stretched below me, each light representing a little room where people sat together, safe from the night. To my right and far away, a coyote howled at the moon. I knew there was no one in the room beneath my feet, but I went outside and down the hill to check anyway. I was right.

Back in the living room, I sat down on the floor and tossed the shovel halfway across the room. It landed with a thump and a clatter. A flash of bright blue near the overturned table caught my attention, and I crawled over on my hands and knees to look.

It was Hansel. His head had been torn off. There was more blood on the floor than Hansel's body could possibly have held. I put an exploratory finger into the nearest pool. It was thick and tacky.

Something chirped, and I looked up. Gretel sat on top of a curtain rod, looking down at me. She cocked her head for a better look and then chirped again.

"Good for you," I said thickly. I looked over at the birds' cage. It was battered and broken. The door was gone. Suddenly the hair on my arms stood straight up, my heart slammed against my throat, and I was bathed in sweat—and I realized that I was angrier than I'd ever been in my life.

The anger focused me. I got up and picked up the phone, putting the receiver back on the hook. The red light on the answering machine blinked at me steadily, and I hit the button for playback.

First I got Eleanor. For the first time since I'd known her, I fast-forwarded the machine past her message. Then I was listening to Nana and me. "Tunut," Nana said. I hit fast forward again and then pushed the play button.

"Nana," a male voice whispered coarsely. "Nana, pick up the phone. I know you're there, Nana." Then nothing, just the hum of the line. Whoever it was had disconnected with a sharp click.

I waited. "Wednesday, eight-oh-three P.M.," the machine said tonelessly. The tape continued to roll.

Then the whisper was back. "Nana," it said, "pick up the phone. Something has happened to Simeon. Pick up the phone."

"Hello?" Nana's voice said. "Hello? Who is this? What's happened? Is he all right?"

No answer. Just the wind howling through the phone lines again. "Is he all right?" Nana said insistently. There was a click.

"Wednesday, eight-oh-five P.M.," the machine said.

Then there was nothing. Nothing at all.

I sat there, feeling my blood pressure subside and listening to the silence. Crickets made cricket noises. The house creaked. There was one other sound, one I couldn't identify at first. A kind of whirring. The refrigerator? No, not the refrigerator.

It came from the computer.

I went over to it, stood over it. The screen was dark, but

the machine was on. I touched a key. Screensave, Nana had called it.

The message leapt into life before me on the screen.

IT'S ABOUT EIGHT, it said. SIMEON, SOMEONE CALLED HERE. SAID SOMETHING WAS WRONG WITH YOU. WHEN I ANSWERED HE HUNG UP. SIMEON, SOMEONE JUST CALLED AGAIN. IT'S A LITTLE AFTER EIGHT NOW. SIMEON, I'M SCARED.

There was a blank space on the screen, then some more words.

SOMEBODY'S HERE. I HEAR THEM OUTSIDE. I HEAR

That was the end of it.

I paced the length of the living room. The pool of blood caught my eye. Then I had an idea and went back to the computer. I pushed the key that said Page Down.

A single word appeared neatly centered in the middle of the screen. It was all in capital letters. It said:

TOBY

21

Murder

FIRST I CALLED THE POLICE and reported Toby's Maserati stolen. The license plate was easy, since the last time I'd seen it I'd been flat on my back and it had been two feet from my chin: TOBY 1.

I could think of only one place he might have taken her, but if I was wrong, they could still be on the road. They couldn't have been gone much more than forty minutes. Red Maseratis aren't that common, even in Los Angeles; some alert cop might get lucky and spot the car. And I might win the state lottery next month, too.

Then I ran back down the driveway, leaving the broken door sagging open behind me, to check out the only remotely likely guess I had.

I coaxed extra speed out of Alice down the winding roads of the canyon, keeping my mind blank and my breathing even. Halfway to the coast I got stuck behind a necking couple with more eyes for the moon and each other than for the road. I hit the horn twice and got an aggressive slowdown from the lovesick creep at the wheel, a display of automotive macho for the little lady. I waited for a right-hand curve, gunned Alice, and slammed into the driver's side of the creep's rear bumper. He fishtailed off to the right, and I passed him on a blind curve and left him stalled out most of the way onto the shoulder.

By the time I ran the red light on the PCH and headed north at seventy miles per hour, fourteen minutes had elapsed since I left the house.

Try as I might, I couldn't keep my mind from working. I was doing the only thing I could think to do, but there was a tickle in the back of my head that I couldn't ignore.

I knew Toby hadn't killed Saffron.

I had bet Nana's safety on the assumption that he hadn't killed, or at least intended to kill, Amber, that he wasn't a cold-blooded murderer. And, except for Nana, Toby was the only person involved who knew where I lived. Even Dixie only had my phone number.

And then, as Malibu Canyon receded behind me, that particular security blanket ripped right down the middle.

Saffron had known. She'd been there.

Whoever killed Saffron had played with her for a long time.

I tried to accelerate, but my foot was already pushed to the floor. To the left the Pacific rolled in as black as blood. Something like drowsiness kept slipping over my consciousness, and it took too long for me to identify it as defeat. The minute I'd found Saffron dead I should have known I couldn't take Nana home.

You've killed her, a voice said in my ear.

I shook my head and shoved vainly at the accelerator.

There was so much blood, the voice said. Hansel's headless body popped into my mind's eye. *She's dead*, the voice said.

"Fuck you," I said to the voice, and turned left into Encinal Canyon. The turn had caught me unaware, and Alice almost spun out. It had been more than thirty minutes.

I parked partway down and ran the rest of the way to the house. From the driveway the house looked dark, but there was enough moonlight to show me that Toby's car wasn't there. There *was* a car there, though, pulled crookedly into the drive with both its front doors open.

I knew whose car it was.

The tide was out, so I went around to the beach side of the house, climbing over slippery, still wet rocks, falling once before I got to the picture windows. The curtains were drawn, but lights burned inside. Then there was a flash, like small-scale lightning. But from inside. Then another.

He was taking pictures.

A surge of pure adrenaline joined forces with another flashbulb to carry me through knee-deep water and up onto the beach to the front door. It was open.

It would be. She couldn't walk, not after all that blood. He'd had to carry her inside. He didn't plan to stay long.

I listened: not a sound. No more flashes. Then I heard footsteps across a hardwood floor, and a door opened somewhere in the house.

Now.

My wet running shoes made squelching rubbery sounds as I moved across the dark entrance hall toward the pale rectangle of light that fell from the archway leading into the living room. The room was empty and not empty.

No one was standing there, but what looked like a heap of clothing was crumpled in the corner between the bookcases. Multiple images of Toby's face grinned down from the wall at what was left of Nana. Black hair and red blood. One slender arm was outthrown. It was broken midway between the elbow and the wrist.

The next thing I remember, I had gathered her in my arms and was picking her up. I had carried her before, but now she was horribly light. I wondered how much all that blood weighed. Her head lolled back, and a savaged face caught the light. It was impossible to tell if she was alive or dead. Her eyes were swollen and open and empty. She looked like she could see through walls. I took two steps toward the front door.

"Put her down," said a voice from behind me.

A tremor ran through me, and I turned with her dangling from my arms. The door to the beach was open, and Tiny stood in it. He bloomed there, gigantic in white, framed by the darkness. A little nickel-plated gun gleamed in his hand.

"I got your clue," I said in the most level voice I could manage. "Nice touch." The front of his white shirt was stained brown. Butcher brown.

"Give her the credit. She'd already written my name on the screen when I knocked the door down. All I had to do was change two letters. But I never figured you'd get home so early, much less turn up here before I was gone. Now what am I going to do with you?"

"Is she dead?" Nana hadn't stirred.

"She wasn't supposed to be. She was supposed to call the cops and tell them to come here and then be dead." He gave me a grimace that he thought was a smile. "Downers," he said, giving his head a ponderous shake. "Bad dope. Get you out of control sometimes."

His pupils were enormous, and his fat face was sheened over with sweat.

"Like at her apartment?" I said.

"She was supposed to be there," he said in a reasonable tone. "I guess I just got pissed off. Put her down now." He wiggled the little gun. "I don't want to confuse things," he said. "No prints but Toby's, nobody but Toby. That was the idea."

"Tiny. The idea's already gone wrong."

"Why? Because of you? Just stay where you are, I'll figure you out. You'll be as dead as she is as soon as I work out where to put you."

"That doesn't give me much incentive to cooperate."

"You will, though. As long as you figure you've got a chance to stay alive, like maybe you can outsmart me, get the gun or something, you'll do anything I tell you. I would, in your shoes. And now you're going to put her down, right where you found her."

I looked into his flat black eyes for a long moment. There was nobody inside. I knelt slowly.

"You can drop her," he said in the same calm, toneless voice. "She won't feel it. Drop her on her head if you like."

I laid her down as gently as I could. Her limbs splayed out gracelessly, angular and lifeless. Matted hair masked her face.

"Why her?" I said, standing up again. "I know why you killed Saffron, but why her? What the fuck did she ever do to you? She liked you."

"It wasn't me she did it to," he said. "I wouldn't kill anyone who hurt me. I don't matter that much. I never really mattered." A furrow appeared between his brows as he replayed what I'd said. "Hold on. Stop. You know why I killed Saffron?"

"Sure. Because she and Toby killed Amber."

His face twisted and hardened. "You knew that? You knew that, and you were still on their side?" His mouth worked convulsively for a second, and then he spat on the floor. "That makes it easier," he said. "It wasn't going to be hard anyway, but that makes it even easier."

"I didn't know it until tonight," I said. "They didn't mean to."

"You think that makes any difference to Amber?"

"Tell me what happened."

His eyes filled with laborious cunning. "I thought you knew," he said slowly.

"The swimming pool, Saffron's swimming pool. It happened in the swimming pool."

The fat little eyes became alarming—still empty, but alarming. All force, no intellect: he looked like a one-man holy war. "Who told you? Toby?"

"Nobody told me. I guessed part of it from the way Saffron behaved, but I didn't figure it out until tonight, when I went to Saffron's apartment house and saw the bottom of the pool."

"They played a game with her," he said dreamily. The gun sagged in his hand. "Toby bought a bunch of loads at the Rack, and they had a make-believe contest, you know? Who could take the most loads. Except they only pretended to take theirs, they pretended to take the same loads over and over. It must have been real funny. Amber, she took four or five. And she was already pretty fucked up."

"From junk," I said, measuring the distance between us. The gun was pointed at the floor. Tiny swayed.

"Junk," he said. "I hate junk. Oh, you don't know. You don't know how many times I tried to get her to quit. I even cried." He closed his eyes, but before I could move he pulled them open again. "That's not easy for a Lebanese, crying in front of a woman, but I cried. I begged her to quit. I even hit her a few times, but that just made it worse. She started using it as an anesthetic."

"You tried," I said.

"I never tried anything harder in my life." He shrugged his massive shoulders. "I loved her."

"But you set her up with Toby that night."

"That was different. That was business. She understood the business. Toby was an important customer. Customers were customers. I was, I was supposed to be, something else. Something different." He swayed again. The gun hung limp from his hand.

"And they killed her," he said conversationally. "After they got her so stoned she couldn't walk, they played a game. You know Simon says? Little kids' game. They played Simon says. First she had to close her eyes and touch her nose. Then she had to stand on one leg. Well, she fell, of course. She fell on that whore's floor, and they both laughed."

"Then they went outside," I said.

"First the sidewalk, then the gate to the apartment house. She fell again, off the gate. Then the diving board."

"And she fell off the diving board."

"Sure. Who do you think she was, some Olympic gold medalist? She was a little girl fucked up on twelve kinds of dope. You know how much she weighed?"

"About the same as she does now." I indicated Nana.

He shook his head. "Even less. Even less."

"And she fell."

"Nine feet, I think. She fell on her head."

"But she wasn't dead."

"They didn't know that. Not any more than you know whether that one is dead." He pointed the gun at Nana, and I took a step toward him. His hand tightened on the gun. He closed his left eye to sight. I moved between them, trying to think of something to say.

"So they took her to the Spice Rack, right? I haven't figured that out. Why the Spice Rack? Why not home? Why not someplace else?"

He opened the eye and looked at me. "Oh, they took her home," he said in a sulfurous voice. "Saffron sat on her lap, you hear me? Saffron sat on her lap in that little shit car and then got out and walked like a drunk to the door so that old pervert upstairs would see her. You're telling me they didn't mean to kill her?" He spat on the floor. "She sat on Amber's lap so the guy upstairs would see a girl in the passenger seat when Toby drove away. She acted loaded, imitating Amber. Then she used Amber's keys to get in and waited, and then she left and Toby picked her up around the block, and she sat in Amber's lap again until they got to the Spice Rack. Then they dumped her, just shoved her out of the car. They made the mistake of taking her where I was. They didn't know I was there. They didn't know I was inside, counting the receipts. Usually I don't. Usually I do that at home." His eyelids clamped closed, and he gulped a gallon of air.

"And they didn't know she was alive," I said, just to say something.

He arched a four-pound eyebrow. It looked like it cost him a lot of effort. "I already said that. I already told you that. They thought they could just dump her in the parking lot like garbage and then go home and finish their party.

Like garbage. They figured the cops would think someone got her between home and the club."

"But you came out and found her."

He made the grimace again. "She found me. Somehow she crawled to the back door and made some noise." His eyes strayed to a point over my shoulder and focused there. They seemed to move independently of each other. "She had a lot of guts," he said.

A wave broke outside, thundering onto the sand. I had a prickly feeling that if I turned my head, I'd see Amber standing behind me, looking into Tiny's eyes.

"She wouldn't have wanted this," I said.

"She was too soft. Toby has to pay."

"And that was why you broke her arms and legs?"

He forced his eyes back down to me. "One arm was already broken. That's why I started with an arm on this one and Saffron. I carried her to the stage and put her on it, and her arm was all wrong. I tried to put it back, but I couldn't make it look right again. Then." He stopped for a moment, looking suddenly smaller somehow. "Then she died," he said. "She caught a big breath like she was going to say something, and when she let it out something rattled, and then she went away."

"Wait. Wait a minute. She didn't tell you anything?"

"I knew where she'd been. I knew who she was with. I knew about Toby, what Toby was, what Toby likes to do to women. I'd seen *her*"—he jerked the gun toward Nana—"when Toby was finished with her. She gave me some bullshit story, but I knew Toby. I told him then if he ever touched another one of my girls in the wrong way, I'd hurt him. But for Amber, for hurting Amber, I'd kill him."

"You brutalized her. And you didn't even know for sure what had happened."

"She was dead. I stood over her, crying like a big baby, and broke whatever I could break. I did it one bone at a time, thinking about Toby. You see, he's not just going to die. The whole world is going to know what he is before the law kills him. They're going to know what filth he is. They're going to hate him as much as I hate him. That means he'll die twice. I wish I could figure a way to make him die three times."

"Why didn't you just turn him in?" I was hoping he'd let the gun droop again.

"And let Saffron go? She had to die, too."

"Saffron told you what happened that night," I said.

"Saffron told me a lot of things. Saffron told me everything I could possibly want to know. She was dying to tell me." He made a choking sort of sound that eventually turned into a laugh. "That's a joke," he said. "She was dying to tell me. It only took one arm and a couple of cuts, little cuts, and she was dying to tell me."

"What about the clothesline? How'd you know about the clothesline?"

"That one," he said, gesturing toward Nana. "That tramp on the floor there. She told Amber all about poor little Toby. You're the big detective, you should have figured that out. There was clothesline strung in the girls' dressing room. They use it to dry their costumes between sets. I just put up a new rope the next morning."

"Congratulations, Tiny," I said. "You figured it all out. It's a shame it's not going to work."

He gave me a loose-lipped smile. "It's gonna work," he said. "There's no reason, not a reason on the world, I'd kill these girls. But everybody who matters knows about Toby, even the cops. And they're going to find her here, and there's gonna be three Polaroids in Toby's little album over there."

"That's the problem," I improvised. "The Polaroids."

The little gun came up and pointed directly at my chin. "Explain," he said.

"The cops have the picture of Amber. Someone was with Toby when he got it in the mail. She made him take it to the cops. I was the one who found Saffron, and I gave them both of the pictures you left there. Toby's got an alibi for Saffron." I licked my lips. They felt like sandpaper. "Toby's with the cops now," I said.

"You asshole," Tiny said in a tight little voice. "That's why I killed Nana, because she was working with you." He blinked, the heaviest blinks since Charles Laughton, two or three times. "Okay," he said. "First we kill you, and then we wait for Toby. I'll worry about me after I kill Toby."

He extended his arm and cocked the gun.

I'd run out of things to say.

Toby's front door slammed shut.

The hand with the gun in it wavered. "Sit down," he whispered, "or I'll blow your brains out right now."

I remained standing, watching the little pig eyes shift toward the hallway as boots sounded on the wooden floor. The hall light came on. Tiny kept the gun on me but swiveled his eyes to the archway between the hall and the living room.

Big John, AKA Jack Sprunk, stood in the doorway. Tiny looked bewildered and shifted the gun to a point halfway between us. "Stay where you are," he said to John.

John looked at me and smiled. "Hello," he said. Then he started to walk toward Tiny. Even compared with Tiny, he looked big. The smile stayed on his face. He looked from one of us to the other, as calm as a postulant taking communion. I gathered myself for a leap.

A door somewhere on the other side of the kitchen opened and closed.

Tiny looked at me and then toward the kitchen. John kept walking. Tiny swallowed and pivoted toward the kitchen door.

But he shot John first.

The gun made a bright, hard *spang* sound: small caliber. Tiny was already facing the kitchen when he realized that John was still coming at him and turned to fire again. The second shot caught John in the collarbone and threw him to the floor. Dolly appeared in the kitchen door, and Tiny aimed the gun at her.

At the same moment, Toby flew through the door leading to the beach and jumped onto Tiny's back, grabbing Tiny's gun hand. Dolly let out a yell I didn't know she had in her and leapt toward Tiny and Toby, now tangled together into a furious, whirling knot. A shot reverberated through the room. Three. Tiny looked like a boar attacked by dogs, trying to toss them off through sheer force of weight.

Acting on automatic pilot, I bent down and picked up Nana. I carried her through the kitchen door and put her on the floor, protected by the wall from stray bullets.

As I put her down she moaned.

I touched her throat. The echoes of another shot slammed back and forth between floor and walls. Four. A pulse was beating there, slow and erratic, but a pulse, goddammit, a pulse.

It was no time for sentiment. I headed for the living room.

And got there just in time to see Dolly land on the floor near the door to the beach, next to Toby. Tiny stood a few feet away, heaving with the effort, pointing the gun at them.

"Stay where you are, on the floor," he said. He turned his head toward me. "You. Get over there. Move wrong and I'll kill you. I'll kill all of you."

"You can't," I said, getting as close to them as I could. "You're a bullet short, fatso."

The word registered. "Then you're first," he said, pointing the gun at me.

Behind him John Ames pulled himself slowly to a sitting position.

"Well, that's a problem, isn't it?" I said. "Who's first? It really ought to be old Toby here. He's the one you're after. He's the one who killed Amber."

Tiny's eyes zigzagged sluggishly between me and Toby. He was dripping perspiration, and his face was green. Then the gun started to move. Toby crawled backward frantically.

John was on all fours now. He shook his head to clear it.

"On the other hand," I said, "maybe you ought to kill the one who's most likely to go for you after you shoot Toby. That's got to be me, you disgusting, porno-eating, obese piece of shit, you fat, ridiculous dope. Why'd you think that Amber or anybody could love you? She laughed at you, lard-ass. Who wouldn't? You tub, you perverted gob of spit masquerading as a human being, you . . ."

The gun was aimed directly between my eyes.

My voice failed.

"She loved me," Tiny said in a hoarse whisper. Then John's arm encircled his neck, just as it had encircled mine, and all hell broke loose.

Tiny's head snapped back, and the gun went off. The bullet sang past my right ear and thunked into the wall behind me. Toby and Dolly were trying to scramble to their feet, and Tiny was hunching his back, heaving his body to throw John off.

John was just too big. Tiny's face turned red and then purple. His gun hand sagged. Toby was already up. He reached out and took the gun from Tiny's dangling hand.

He pointed it at Tiny. "Simeon," he said, every inch the television hero, "is Nana okay?"

"She's alive," I said. "Give me the gun, Toby."

He pointed it at me. Tiny was emitting small wet gasps as John's arm tightened. His eyes had disappeared completely.

"In a minute," Toby said. "Let go of him, John."

John did as he was told. Moving like a zombie, he took two or three steps back and then sat down. He was covered in blood from shoulders to waist.

Tiny raised both hands to his throat and sank to his knees. He managed somehow to get his eyes open and looked up at Toby.

"You're right," Toby said with his biggest, broadest grin. "She did love you." Then he pulled the trigger.

A red hibiscus blossomed in the dead-white center of Tiny's chest. He looked down at it as though astonished, lifted his gaze to Toby, and fell.

Toby looked at him, fascinated. The grin had frozen on his face, and his nostrils flared as if he were sniffing the moment. He exhaled slowly, closing his eyes, like a man who had just put down something heavy. Then he turned to me. He held out the gun. "Now you can have it," he said.

"No, Toby," I said. "It's your trophy. You keep it. You've earned it. Hasn't he, Dolly?"

Toby glanced over at Dolly, and I took one step and blindsided him backhand with both fists, fingers laced together. The shock of the impact traveled all the way up my arms to my shoulders. Toby went down, and I put a foot on his throat. He made a strangled sound and tried to bring the pistol up at me.

"This is where we began," I said. "The gun's empty, by the way." Then I stepped back and kicked him in the stomach, twice.

"That's for Amber and Saffron," I said. He curled into a ball, arms clutched over his midsection. I lifted my right leg and kicked his face. If his skull hadn't been attached to his neck, it would have been a field goal in any football stadium on earth. His head snapped back, an ear squeaking on the hardwood floor.

"That's for Nana," I said. "You want to take one, Dolly?"

Looking bewildered, Dolly extended her hands, palm up, and shook her head.

"Well," I said, "duty is duty. Someone's got to do it." I kicked Toby in the face again. "That's probably for Tiny. And this one"—I kicked him one more time—"this one is for Jack, you asshole. For sending him in first." I started to walk away, toward the telephone, but something red and hot came over me. "One more for me," I said in a voice I didn't even recognize, turning back.

"No, Simeon," Dolly squealed. "You'll kill him!"

I looked down at him. Red bubbled in the corners of his mouth, but he was still conscious. "How I wish," I said. "Oh, how I wish. This protozoan, this virus. How I wish it were that easy to kill him."

Dolly was looking at me as if I were the Loch Ness monster come ashore. "Right," I said, fighting for control. "The telephone." I picked it up and started to dial.

"If you want to finish him while I'm busy, I won't tell," I said. Dolly knelt down beside Toby and put her hand under his head to cradle it. Hero worship dies hard.

"Too bad we're out of bullets," I said.

My first call was for an ambulance for Nana and John. Tiny didn't need an ambulance. The second call was to the police.

"I'm calling from Toby Vane's house in Encinal Canyon," I said, hating every syllable. "I want to report a shooting. Please come quickly."

After we'd finished with the details, I called Dixie. His voice was thick with sleep. "Get up," I said. "You know where Toby lives?"

"Sure," Dixie said. "What's going on?"

"Toby just shot the guy who's been killing these women," I said. "We've got at least one dead body. Get your ass over here and make your boy into a hero."

I dropped the phone onto the floor and went into the kitchen to hold Nana until they came.

22

The Last Session

"THAT'S AN EXTRA FIVE THOUSAND," Norman Stillman said with a generous smile, dropping a check onto his immaculate desk and looking as jaunty as ever. His blazer looked like the winning entry in the national dry cleaner's playoffs.

"What's it for?" I asked. Dixie hovered in the background, looking vaguely embarrassed.

"A little bonus. Value given for value received. Toby's price, I mean *High Velocity*'s price, went up yesterday, thanks largely to you. And they bought it without a murmur, didn't they, Dixie?"

"Everybody wants the hero's show," Dixie said, sounding as though he were choking on his heart.

I picked up the check and looked at it. Then I dropped it back onto the desk.

"I'll need more," I said. "Eight thousand more."

Stillman's smile got a lot more muscular. "What does that mean?"

"It means the girl's hospital bills are almost eight thousand. And that's just for emergency care."

Stillman gave me an elaborate shrug. "Oh, well," he said, "you can't expect me . . ."

I looked at Dixie. "I can't?" I said.

Dixie met Stillman's gaze. "Under the circumstances," he said. He still had an obstruction in his throat.

Stillman pursed his lips. It made him look like a little old lady. "Seems pretty stiff," he said.

Neither Dixie nor I said anything, although Dixie swallowed twice.

"Still," Stillman said unconvincingly, "if it's the right thing to do." Then, slowly enough to preserve his dignity, he slid open the drawer in front of him and pulled out his gold Mont Blanc pen and a checkbook. He filled in a check and tore it loose. "I do this out of the goodness of my heart, not because of any threat," he said. Placing a hand protectively over the check, he pulled a sheet of typewritten paper out of the drawer and slid it over the polished wood toward me. "Just sign this," he said. "It's only a formality."

"What kind of formality?"

"Nothing," he and Dixie said at the same time. Stillman gave Dixie a glare, and Dixie subsided. Whatever resentment had flared inside him seemed to have burned itself out, probably smothered by the damp mass of his paycheck. Stillman provided an unnecessary coup de grace in the form of a barely audible sniff.

"As I was saying," he continued. "It's nothing. It's like a contract, I suppose. Nothing you wouldn't do anyway. You're a man of honor, we all know that. You wouldn't violate it even if you didn't sign it." He gave me the smile again.

I gave it back. "Then why sign it?" I said.

"For peace of mind."

"Whose?"

"Everyone's. It's just a promise that you won't tell anyone what really happened." He spread his polished hands in a gesture of pure reason.

"For how long?"

"Forever," he said in a firmer tone. "For always."

"Or what?" I'd stopped smiling.

Stillman leaned forward and crossed his hands. "Or it gets sent to the cops," he said. "It's . . ." He leaned back ruminatively. "It's an account of the facts in the case. What really happened in the last week or so. Nothing that isn't true. I'm sure you won't object to signing it."

"If it became public," I said, "I'd lose my license."

"Faster than instant coffee dissolves," Stillman agreed. "Still . . ." He picked up the check and gave it a little wave.

I pulled the document closer to me and looked at it. "It's all true?" I said.

He nodded.

"And all I have to do is sign it and I get the thirteen thousand?"

Stillman put the check down again and said, "Yes."

"Dixie," I said, "have you read this?"

"Sure," he said. "Sure I have. I wrote it, with some help from the lawyers."

"Everything in it is true? I mean, man to man, it's all accurate?"

"Truer than the history books," Stillman said.

I looked at the piece of paper again. The language was direct enough. The facts seemed straight. I put out a hand.

After a momentary hesitation, Stillman handed me the Mont Blanc.

"I'm just a country boy," I said. "I sure hope I'm doing the right thing."

I snapped the Mont Blanc in two. Stillman gasped, and ink flooded over my hands and the desk.

"Gosh, I'm sorry," I said. I picked up the contract and wiped my hands with it. Then I used it to wipe up the pool of ink on the desk, crumpled the blackened paper into a ball, and flipped it at Stillman. It caught him right on his embroidered anchor and bounced into his lap. He looked at me, his face dark and still.

"I *will* take the checks," I said, reaching over and picking them up. "And don't bother telling me I'll never work in this town again. I might have to laugh, and I'm not sure I've got the energy."

I went to the door. "Don't worry," I said. "You won't hear anything about this unless you do something truly stupid, like stopping payment. You poor dumb soul, do you really think I'd talk about this? Don't you know I'm ashamed of myself for having had anything to do with it? Or with you, for that matter?"

He just glared at me. Dixie had his fists in his pockets again.

"Jesus," I said. "Producers."

I had to let more than a week go by before I could finish. Wounds take time to heal, and at least some of them had to heal by the time I could wrap things up.

The eight thousand went to the hospital. It was short, so that took care of another thousand of the bonus. I paid Kareema and Alma a thousand for their part in what I had planned, although they offered to do it for free.

A hundred and fifty went to rent a van with a ramp. It had to have a ramp. Twenty-five hundred took the form of a donation, in Toby's name, to a West Hollywood institution. Toby would get the tax break, not I, but he was welcome to it.

That left me with three hundred and fifty bucks from my bonus on Sunday morning when I stepped into ABC Discount Premiums on Beverly Boulevard. When I came out I had less than two hundred left, but I also had a paper bag in my hand.

It was a beautiful day.

I took the freeway through the Valley to avoid the beach traffic and then drove through Malibu Canyon to the coast. It was still early, but the PCH was full of cars carrying surfers and sun-crazy high school kids to the sea. Here and there was a family in a station wagon packed to the roof with coolers, towels, inflatable rafts, meals big enough for Henry the Eighth and all six of his wives. In the twentieth century families take as much to go from the Valley to the beach as their great-great-grandparents carried on the long trek across the plains toward paradise.

Toby's red Maserati was in the driveway, parked next to

a car I'd never seen before. Next to that was the van. As I
climbed out of Alice and trekked toward the house, the
van's occupants waved at me. I lifted the bag above my
head and waved it back at them. Tinny applause sounded
from inside.

Heading for the house, I heard the van's ramp drop into
position.

The front door was open, as it was supposed to be. I
took everything out of the bag and went into the living
room.

Toby had acquired a new piece of furniture. It was made
of bright and shiny aluminum, and it still looked like a
cross between a sawhorse and a medieval torture rack.
Toby was strapped to it, as naked as the day he was born.

"Simeon!" he shouted, trying to twist free. Then he saw
the expression on my face, and he stopped shouting.

"He can't get loose," Alma lisped. She was wearing a
red corset with black stockings and a Victorian garter belt.
Above the neck she looked like a Sunday-school teacher.
"Look. His wrists and ankles are cuffed, and there's this
cute little loop around his neck that tightens if he tries to
turn his head. Not to mention the silk cord around his
teensie little wienie. Here, watch."

She reached down and tickled Toby's ribs. Toby arched
and twisted his neck, and then his face went red and he had
to stop.

"Kootchy kootchy koo," Alma said sweetly.

"That's enough, Alma," Kareema said, coming out of
the kitchen, a glass of water in her hand. "Don't wear him
out." She was wearing an outfit that could be best described as Nazi nightmare nurse: low and strapless, cut high
above the thighs, all in black leather with a cute little black
leather nurse's cap to match. "You're late," she said in her
usual commanding voice. She handed the water to Alma.

"Sunday drivers," I said. I was exactly four minutes late.
I got down on my knees and studied Toby. He avoided my
eyes. "How's the face, Bobby?"

He started at the name and looked up at me briefly and then down at the floor. Most of the swelling had gone down. His lower lip was puffy—again—and one eye was partly closed, but the girls had put makeup over the worst of the bruises, and there was no question that it was Toby's face.

"I'll get you," he said in a low voice.

"No, Bobby, old boy. We'll get you. And then you'll never get anybody again."

His eyes dropped to the thing I had put on the floor, and his skin went ashen. "No," he said. "You can't."

"Can't I? Do something to him, ladies. But turn your faces away."

Alma and Kareema did something to him. I suppose to some people it would have looked like fun. I waited until the girls' faces were averted and Toby's tongue was sticking out, and then I took a Polaroid. I waited for it to develop.

"Honest to God, Bobby," I said to pass the minute. "Boy, it's hard for me to get used to calling you Bobby. Well, whatever your name is, how gullible can you be? Why would Alma run away from you for months and then call you up all hot and bothered? Didn't you suspect *anything*? Who said, 'Vanity, thy name is Woman'? How wrong can you be?"

I looked at the picture. "Very good, for a beginner. Look, Alma. There's old Toby, and there are all the little Tobys on the magazines. The big Toby looks okay, doesn't he? Good enough for the National Enquirer, at any rate."

"Good enough for the cover of *Time*, if you ask me," Alma said in her little-girl voice.

"You flatter me," I said. I heard a sound from the hallway. "Ah," I said. "The rest of our guests. Say hello, Toby."

He couldn't help but look. Then he closed his eyes and let his head droop.

Janie Gordon came in first. Her first glance was an equal

mixture of surprise and concern, but then she looked at me and started to laugh. She was still laughing when Betsi, the woman from the fan magazines, came in. She was followed by Chantra Hartsfield. She hadn't let me invite Rebecca.

Toby opened his eyes just in time to see Dixie. He started to brighten, and then he saw what Dixie was pushing, a wheelchair. Nana was in it.

"Don't just mill around," I said. "That's the trouble with parties, that moment of awkwardness at the beginning. This is Alma in the red corset and Kareema in the whatever it is . . ."

"It's a dress," Kareema said. "Hi, how are you all?"

"And you already know our host. You'll understand if he doesn't get up to greet you."

"He's all tied up at the moment," Alma said, "ho, ho, ho."

I went to Nana and kissed her on the largest piece of available skin. "You're beautiful," I said.

Most of her face was bandaged, and her right arm and leg were in casts.

"I look like the Invisible Man," she said. "But I look better than Toby."

"And that's the point," I said, raising my voice. "Toby. This is a working party. We're going to shoot Toby Vane's new publicity pictures. Alma and Kareema, who have their own reasons to want to be here, have volunteered to help out. This is our set, and we've already taken care of makeup. Costume, as you can see, is going to be no problem."

Betsi came and stood behind me. "You're going to shoot from here?" she said critically.

"I thought so."

"Well, you want to catch the pictures on the wall, but you ought to move him toward the corner. No reason to get the kitchen door."

"Can we move him?" I asked.

"No sweat," Kareema said, glancing at Betsi. "Nice to

know we've got a pro here." She popped four little levers at the bottom of the rack, and wheels snapped out.

"Hi-tech torture," Alma said, giggling. The two of them wheeled Toby into the corner. Toby's eyes had remained shut since he'd seen Dixie. They were still shut.

"Here." I handed the camera to Betsi. "No reason to trust to beginner's luck any farther than we have to. Just don't catch Alma's and Kareema's faces."

"You'll never see them." Chewing her lower lip, she looked down at Toby. "What about his face? I mean, he has to look up or you'll never recognize him."

"Honey," Kareema said, "believe me, we can make him look up. We can make him sing the 'Marseillaise,' even if he doesn't know the French."

"Trust them," I said. I clapped my hands twice for attention.

"Okay, this shouldn't take more than fifteen minutes, and then we'll all go to lunch at Gladstone's. As I've said, this is a photo shoot, and first I want to explain to our star just how important it is."

I knelt down again. "Are you listening to me, Bobby?"

No reaction. Alma leaned over and did something tiny and mean, and Toby yelped and opened his eyes. He looked like a man ready to die of fury.

"Calm down," I said. "This won't take long. And if you behave yourself, no one will ever see any of these pictures. Do you understand?" He tried to nod, forgetting the restraint on his neck, and made a small choking sound. It didn't look like it improved his mood.

"Here's what's happening. Don't nod, just raise an eyebrow. First, you're never going to lift your hand against another woman. If you do, and if I hear about it, these pictures are going to everybody from UPI to *TV Guide*. Got it?"

He gave an infinitesimal nod. Maybe he didn't know how to raise one eyebrow.

I took a piece of paper from my pocket. "This is a tax-deductible receipt. Earlier this week, acting at your request, of course, I donated twenty-five hundred dollars to the West Hollywood Woman's Hospice. WH squared, as they call themselves, maintain a home for battered women. Your donation, which will be repeated monthly for the next two years, will be used to rent five additional apartments for women who are trying to avoid husbands or boyfriends who enjoy breaking their faces. I rejected their suggestion that they issue a press release naming it the Toby Vane Wing. You agree that you'll keep the contribution coming on a monthly basis?" Someone behind me clapped.

Toby nodded again.

"Finally," I said, unfolding the receipt and taking a smaller piece of paper from its center, "this is the name and phone number of a Dr. Elena Gutierrez. Dr. Gutierrez was recommended by the people at WH squared as the best psychiatrist in Los Angeles for the treatment of men who batter women. You have an appointment with Dr. Gutierrez for Tuesday evening at seven, after filming finishes. That's your regular appointment from now on. I've told her nothing, only that you have a problem and that you want help. The rest is up to you. Are you going to see her?"

This time he looked at me. Then he nodded again.

"Great. Fine. Well, that's it, then." I stood up and turned to Betsi. "Take your pictures," I said. "I'll want them when you're finished."

Betsi maneuvered into position, and Alma and Kareema went to work. A flashbulb popped. "Oh, golly," Janie Gordon whispered. It sounded like she'd learned something interesting. I didn't turn around to see what. Instead I went to Nana.

"I'll take her, Dixie," I said.

Dixie stepped aside, taking him closer to Chantra. She didn't move away. She looked over at him and then put her arm around his shoulders in a maternal gesture.

Another bulb popped as I took the handles of Nana's chair. I started to turn her, and she said, "Wait. I want to see." Another flash. "Okay," she said. "Now we can go."

I wheeled her out into the sunlight and up the driveway toward the van. I trundled her up the ramp and sat beside her.

"You're going to be okay," I said.

"Of course I am. I'm young." She sounded faintly impatient.

"You may not be able to dance for a while."

"I'll never dance again. Except with you, I mean. Whoops, I said I wouldn't do that. Except on a dance floor, with some nice man. And all my clothes on." She sobered. "Poor Tiny," she said. "He didn't mean to do it."

I didn't say anything.

"But didn't Toby look fantastic?" she asked.

"I guess, all things considered. A little black and blue, but the boy really knows how to take a close-up."

"You simp," she said. She leaned forward to kiss me, and said, "Ow." She fingered the livid yellow flesh around her mouth.

"You don't understand, you simp," she said. "You didn't look."

"I didn't want to look. He just looked like Toby."

"That's what I mean," she said triumphantly. "After all this time, after all those big smiles. He finally looked exactly like Toby."

Postscript

SOME OF THE CHARACTERS in this book are based more directly than is usual, or legally advisable, on human beings. Others are based on carnivorous bipeds who pass, or passed, as humans.

The girl who was the model for Nana quit dancing a few months before the book was finished and went back to computer school. Four months after that she died in Hollywood of an overdose of cocaine. Her heart just stopped beating.

Janie Gordon is now an assistant director. Her credits feature a middle initial I didn't know she had.

Alma married the dentist.

The actor who inspired Toby still lives on the beach. Aside from an occasional appearance on *Bowling for Dollars*, he's not working, and he stays out of the papers.

Los Angeles is still there. Bigger and more fun than ever.